THE MAURIZIUS CASE

THE MAURIZIUS CASE

JACOB WASSERMANN

Translated by Caroline Newton

CARROLL & GRAF PUBLISHERS, INC.
New York

First Carroll & Graf Edition 1985

Carroll & Graf Publishers, Inc.
260 Fifth Avenue
New York, N.Y. 10001

ISBN: 0-88184-164-1

Manufactured in the United States of America

CONTENTS

CHAPTER I

I.

THE boy Etzel had a presentiment of evil even before the man wearing a captain's cap turned up. Perhaps the letter with the Swiss postmark was the cause. Coming home from school he had seen the letter on the table under the mirror in the front hall. He took it in his hand and scrutinized it closely with his short-sighted eyes. The character of the handwriting moved him with the force of a forgotten object which cannot immediately be located in memory's annals. A mysterious thing—a sealed letter! "To Baron Wolf von Andergast, Attorney-General," was the address, written in a round swift hand, which seemed to run upon wheels. "What kind of a letter is that, Rie?" he said, turning to the housekeeper as she emerged from the kitchen. Since his childhood he had been calling Frau Rie just Rie, for short. She had been with them for nine years and was as familiar to him as a woman can be who is called upon to assume the place of a mother and who actually fills the place in all external respects. Upon this occasion it may at once be stated that Herr von Andergast had already been divorced nine and a half years; the rigorous conditions of the divorce constrained his wife to keep away from her child; she could neither see him, nor write to him; he too was of course forbidden to write to her and no one was permitted to speak of her in his presence. So the boy, now sixteen years old, knew nothing of his mother; the spirit which ruled the house had even stifled the impulse to inquire about her. He had only been told casually, a long time ago, as if it were a question of some indifferent stranger, that she lived in Geneva and could not come to him for reasons which he would find out when he was grown up. He had accepted this explanation because he could not do otherwise. Whether he was secretly interested in the matter or not could not be ascertained because of the reserve he showed in all matters touching his personal life. He had learned to keep silent, for he knew the insuperable barriers that were erected to oppose his curiosity in such a case as this. The greater the demands made on his sympathy, the more self-control he felt obliged to show. Thus, the question addressed to Frau Rie had sounded as if it were a trap, and this was always the case when he wanted to find out something. He stood in ambush and his short-sighted eyes watched events and persons with tense concentration.

Rie had not yet seen the letter. She took it from the boy's hand, looked at it intently and, forcing herself to look unconcerned, said: "That concerns your father; don't bother about it. Your bread and butter is inside on the table. One does not concern oneself with letters addressed to others."

"Heavens! How tiresome you are, Rie!" replied the boy. "You don't really think that I do not know whom the letter is from? Do they come often? Does she write often?"

Rie hesitated and looked with surprise at the determined countenance which the boy raised towards her. "Not to my knowledge," she murmured with embarrassment; "so far as I know this is the first time." And again she looked at the small white intelligent face and her daunted glance dropped so that it no longer surveyed more than the delicate boyish form, from the shoulders down.

"Is that really so, Rie?" asked Etzel with a knavish smile from out of his ambush.

"What has given you this notion?" asked Rie with irritation. "You're a perfect detective. Are you laying a trap for me? I am as sly as you by a long shot."

"No, Rie, I swear you're not as sly as all that," replied

Etzel, as he looked at her pityingly. "Tell me honestly, do such letters often come? Have you ever seen one?" he asked with wide-open eyes from the grey-green depths of which shot bronze sparks. His pity was directed towards the awkward manner in which the good lady sought to deceive him. Whenever he had occasion to compare the sharpness of his senses with those of other people he wondered pityingly, or even became frightened like someone who becomes conscious of a weakness of his own of which he has been hitherto unaware.

"No, I tell you, it is the first time," replied Rie.

"I'd like to be there when he opens the letter and reads it," murmured Etzel, biting the knuckle of his middle finger, which he thoughtfully kept between his teeth. *He;* the sound of his voice contained respect, fear, belief and aversion. The boy turned upon his heel, and twirling his strapped school-books in his right hand, still keeping the knuckle of the middle finger of his left hand in his mouth, he strode towards his room.

Rie looked after him with dissatisfaction. She did not like conversations which left one uncertain, when they were over, whether one's companion was displeased or not. Etzel was the only person in the house in whom she felt a response to her own thoughts. In this house, feelings were neither required nor revered. It was an austere home. The master could not bear intimacy, nor did he ask it. Silent fulfilment of duty was what he expected; he would tolerate sympathetic feelings only when they were sufficiently taciturn. Even self-sacrificing endeavours would have encountered the unfeeling observation, from his lips, that he paid his servants for their work, in fact, even for their sacrifices.

Rie heard Etzel walking up and down in his room. His steps were ridiculously short. The recollection of his up-raised face with the bronze sparks in the depths of his eyes filled her with anxiety. She thought: there is a human being, all of a sudden; up to now there was only a silly little boy; where does the human being suddenly come from?

She had known him so long. A quiet child, rather meditative than lively, easily managed because he was not avid or covetous, and principally because he did not suffer from the spells of boredom—inadequate word—which weigh like an enigmatic torture upon many a childhood. There was constantly an air of merriness about him. His acumen had something of the comic; his grandmother, the old Baroness von Andergast, who chattered to her acquaintances about his amusing speeches, called him the philosopher, the "tiny doctor." Rie regarded herself entirely as his mother, duly appointed, for the mother constituted by God, about whom she had nothing but hearsay, if not outright lies, had withdrawn herself from her duty. She regarded matters thus, for she had been influenced by the atmosphere of the house; fulfilment of duty, neglect of duty, these were the positive and negative poles between which the Andergast world—and that was the *whole* world—revolved. In her eyes Etzel was a child, a deserted child, and since she could mother him she had shut him up in her heart and believed—above everything else—that she understood him. A mistake in which she was happy according to her fashion.

2.

Probably Herr von Andergast too was of the opinion that the silly little boy had become a human being overnight, as it were, for Etzel's activities, the division of his day, his work and his reading were now even more strictly controlled than formerly. A hint from Rie about the incident with the letter had sufficed to make Herr von Andergast sense danger from that quarter, and he took his measures accordingly. That he was informed of such occurrences resulted from the inner compulsion which he exerted upon the people in his surroundings; when such a report was incomplete he filled it in with that perfect constructive talent which was one of his most redoubtable and ingratiating qualities. It kept him constantly assured of the possession of hidden reserves, which as a rule he was no longer obliged to call upon, once he had assigned persons and events where he needed them and where they were useful to him, without their noticing the wires by which he pulled them. It was like a model electrical plant, a reliable operation of contacts, secret wires and time-saving circuits.

Etzel had grown up under the operation of these faultless arrangements and his nerves had adjusted themselves to them, although they rebelled at times. He lived between glass walls. Offences of which he was guilty were not discussed; he was not threatened; the infractions were merely noted. It was a silent system. In a critical situation all the inhabitants of the house seemed voluntarily to assume the duty of spies. Tradespeople, errand boys, letter carriers, court messengers were everywhere subordinate to this superior will, which ruled without proclaiming its sovereignty, or stressing it particularly in each case. They were brought to obedience and trained to espionage merely by the fact that the sovereign will was present, magnificent and heavy as a mountain.

These were the impressions of Etzel's childhood, all of which had been placed under a lynx-eyed, but unobtrusive surveillance. There was nothing that escaped supervision. Calendar, hours of work, clock, notebook, school report, everything went according to schedule and tended to a cold, business-like standardization. And yet, no instructions were issued in so many words, nor was observance openly enforced; it was only silently communicated, and the icy matter-of-course progress with which the thing proceeded did not permit even a thought of contradiction to arise. The daily routine, the course of time—all was branded with the spirit of regulation: lunch, one-fifteen; supper, seven-thirty; bath,

Wednesday and Saturday at nine o'clock; pocket money, one mark per week; acquaintance with X. Y., not advisable, therefore to cease. In case of looking surprised: is there anything to say? In case of embarrassed hesitation: well? Very friendly, but very cold. Very measured. Perfect *savoir-faire,* perfect *savoir-vivre.*

When a real personality leaves the room the atmosphere is not quit of him for a long time. His energy is communicated to lifeless objects. How must he then be felt in the rooms in which he lives and breathes, the bed in which he sleeps, the chair in which he sits, the mirror into which he looks, the desk at which he works, the cigar holder and ash tray which he uses! All these bear his stamp, something of his appearance and his gestures, yes, even his bodily temperature, as if he daily yielded up to them an imperceptible fraction of his blood.

Ever since he could think and remember Etzel had heard a certain door open and shut in one and the same way, the orifice slowly and spaciously broadened as if the powerful figure must first measure the space with his eye, control it visually; the closing was irrevocable, as one seals a letter fraught with destiny. Out of this the imagination welded a chain of unchanging conceptions, withdrawal from a world in which life was ghastly; a ceremonious affixing of one's name to portentous pieces of writing; an intimidating loneliness. As a child he had often slipped to the door and looked at it for a long time with big eyes, as if trying to decipher the invisible runic letters with which it was inscribed. When he heard his father clearing his throat, the tread of his feet on the floor, or his heavy striding up and down the room, which had the rhythm of a man attacking an army of evil thoughts, he withdrew quietly and sought in the silence of his room to guess some of these thoughts, some of the ratified decisions—in fact, all of his father's sombre and dangerous universe.

It was the same with the sound of the bell which sounded

so peremptorily curt only when the signal was given from his father's room, punctually at half-past seven in the morning from the bedroom; at two-thirty sharp, after the afternoon nap, from the study, except on days when the court sat until afternoon. Etzel jumped at each stroke, twice a day he was overcome by the same tense nervousness, the same beating of his heart. It still happened not infrequently, and to the child it had been a veritable nightmare, that he would start out of his sleep because the bell had sounded in his dreams. He would listen and see before him, plastically clear in the darkness, his father's hand with the index finger imperiously extended. He knew this hand better than his own; it even appeared in a number of apparitions recurring in his dreams; it was a narrow and distinguished hand with fingers tapering to a point, nails verging on yellow, and a film of brown silky hair on the back. Sometimes, in his dream, the hand moved like a curious reptile over the blue folder of a document. Its silent loquaciousness, or its telling silence, made one at times think of the hand of an actor—of a particularly experienced and superior actor, however, who accepts only serious and thoughtful rôles and "plays" them with much poise, not one who acts them, but who plays in order to emphasize that he retains his aloofness. With this conception of distance Etzel had become familiar fairly early, although his own nature, in contrast to that of his father, was dependent upon proximity. This was outwardly emphasized by his short-sightedness.

3.

This system of silent control scarcely fulfilled its purpose any longer, even in appearance, since Etzel had already found successful methods of freeing himself from its inconvenient trammels. This was, of course, more difficult for him than for other boys in the same situation, since he felt bound by his loyalty to agreements, and his mental independence prevented him from confiding in those of his own age. Nor was it possible for him to attach himself to one of the groups, or parties, which his comrades had formed and were constantly forming anew. He took no pleasure in their debates and attended their meetings but seldom and unwillingly. He could hardly be induced to express himself either for or against a question, and their categorical decisions merely aroused his doubts. There was more courage in his reticence than in the noisy vehemence of his companions; this was recognized. Curiously enough he was respected for it. The only friend whom he had—for himself he restricted the term "friend" carefully, although for the outer world he permitted it to pass out of courtesy—was a radical and restless fellow. In the end, however, it was not because of Robert Thielemann's views that he had chosen him as a companion, but for a certain largeness and candour which pleased him; and thus there resulted a relationship based upon an adjustment of temperaments, in which large and small, clumsy and alert, rough and delicate were supplemented by their opposites. Thielemann loved to play the part of Etzel's protector, while recognizing his mental superiority as well as his superiority in personal form. He did not understand Etzel's originality of thought, which sometimes verged on the bizarre, but the boy's lack of physical development (together with a certain subtle quality)—underneath which there was a force which he did not perceive—led him to mother the younger and weaker boy. And not Thielemann only, all of Etzel's companions were indulgent in their attitude towards him.

Etzel, as we have said, did not idealize his friendship with Thielemann. He recognized clearly the temporariness as well as the insufficiency of it and behaved like a person who, perhaps through modesty, because he does not want to be conspicuous, or because he has not found anything better, gladly agrees to occupy a house which is too small for him, though his means would permit him to take a better one. In general a feeling of their temporary nature dominated all his relationships, without his knowing whence it came, and without his being able to struggle against it. It was difficult enough to conceal this from the world at times when he could not prevent himself from perceiving it. That was just it; he had the gift of concealing something from himself, a difficult process requiring cunning and some degree of fantasy. He did not, however, place any value upon fantasy; he did not want to know anything about it; and this was a further peculiarity of his character.

He would gladly have talked to Robert Thielemann about the man with the captain's cap, but he refrained from doing so because he feared to reveal to himself too clearly the uneasiness which it caused him. The thrice repeated appearance of the old man occupied—and darkened—his thoughts constantly. On the day when he had learned that the mysterious man followed his father's footsteps too, that he dared even to confront him, and when he realized that this, in spite of his father's pride and cold inaccessibility, was not an indifferent matter to him, not a mere trivial episode—of this Etzel believed himself certain—on this day his uneasiness changed into a continuous irritated distrust directed towards everyone and everything in his surroundings. It was as if the walls could no longer be depended upon to support the roof, as if the closets were filled with a pervading venom, as if a fuse were burning in the cellar which must soon cause a chest of dynamite to explode. This condition of painful expectation lasted, with greater or lesser intervals, until he found in one of his father's folders the paper which decisively influenced all his future life.

4.

The manner and appearance of the man with the captain's cap, although at first quite inconspicuous and ordinary, nevertheless had something ghostlike about it. This impression came in part from the tense and penetrating scrutiny with which he observed the boy at their first meeting; then he followed his every step for a time, seeking to catch up with him, in order, when he had succeeded, to stare at him again, and finally disappearing as unexpectedly as he had appeared. He was a small, lean old man, not a gentleman nor a workingman; rather he belonged, to judge from his appearance, to some petty bourgeois calling. He seemed to be about seventy, but looked fairly robust; his movements were not lacking in agility. He wore a shabby brown fur coat, his hands cased in woollen gloves, with so-called pulse-warmers, red-edged, around his wrists; his left arm hung stiffly by his side. The first two times he had smoked a short English pipe, or perhaps had only held it unlighted between his teeth; in any case between the thin line of his cleanly shaven lips one could see his poor teeth, almost black. Etzel could have reproduced every line of the bony, tense, malicious face, the little spying, glistening eyes, which had an astigmatic look, as if one eye were of glass, the funny ears protruding over the grey-green side-whiskers, reminding one of two birds plucked to their skins standing in a parched copse. The first time, Etzel had seen him on the lower bridge over the river Main. Etzel was accompanied by Robert Thielemann, the stutterer Schlehlein, long-necked Max Schuster, who played a rôle in the Youth Movement; fat Klaus Mohl—the Greedy, as they called him, because of his constant voracious appetite—and Müller I and Müller II. A political quarrel had arisen. The cause was a bitter remark by Thielemann about Schuster's treacherous machinations. The group which he led had spread nasty rumours about the republican group, and Thielemann had reproached them for their contemptible tricks, for allowing themselves, without ever declaring their position, to be manipulated like manikins by people about whom they did not even know whether they were paid agents of the reactionaries or not. "You're fine fellows," he exclaimed constantly, and his broad dialect was in peculiar contrast to his anger. He waved his arms about in the air, and his screeching aroused the displeasure of the passers-by. His appearance was not particularly calculated to arouse confidence, his face covered with coffee-coloured freckles, his cloak waving over his shoulders. When finally he hurled the reproach at them that they and their supporters had already terrorized those among the teachers whom one had reason, thus far, to consider honest—even a man like Camill Raff no longer openly avowed his stand, but crept away shyly to a position of aloofness—he was green with rage and seemed not disinclined to attack Schuster and the two Müllers. The former grinned half embarrassedly, half challengingly; the stutterer Schlehlein, knowing he was backed by superior numbers, planted himself in front of Thielemann, and said impudently: "That is t-t-true, your Raff is—is—is one of those who l-l-look to their b-b-bread and b-b-butter; is afraid of lo-losing his j-j-job." Thielemann cast him a look of contempt and exclaimed, "Shut up! you fool." He looked around for support, but there was no one there, for Etzel, to whom such scenes were unpleasant, had separated himself from his squabbling companions and gone on ahead. They had gotten from the Schweizerplatz to the bridge, and while Thielemann was looking about in search of help, his face assumed an expression of fright; he saw Etzel in the middle of the street, lost in thought, walking towards an automobile truck which was bearing rapidly down upon him, and which the next second would have knocked him down. He screamed loudly, "Take care, Andergast, the devil, take care," and with a jump was beside the endangered boy, snatching him back just in time, so that the mud-guard of the vehicle only grazed his hip.

Hearing the name Andergast, a man who was standing at the railing of the bridge with a pipe between his lips, looking down into the river, as if he neither saw nor heard what was going on about him, turned around with a sudden jerk and looked at the group of boys. He fastened his glance sharply upon Etzel, and when Thielemann pushed his arm through Etzel's and said, half-commandingly, half-irritably, "Come along, Andergast, let's leave those scamps," he followed the two to the Neue Mainzerstrasse, keeping about twenty steps behind them. He did not catch up with them until they reached the square in front of the Opera House, where they looked into the show-window of a bookshop; then he waited until they continued on their way, and looked at Etzel again as he had done on the bridge with a penetrating, glistening glance which was both quiet and thoughtful. "Do you know him?" asked Thielemann with surprise, as they walked along. Etzel said no, and an uncomfortable feeling ran down his spine.

Two days later the man stood before the entrance to the Gymnasium. It was twelve o'clock noon; the classes streamed out of the entrance-hall, scattering in every direction with a deafening noise. Etzel was among the stragglers; his first glance when he stepped outside fell upon the man with the captain's cap; his eyes grew big and round; he was puzzled. The man looked at him without smiling, and without any change of expression, and then walked along behind him. Since the unpleasant sensation in Etzel's spine recurred more strongly than the day before, he pushed his pile of books tight into the hollow of his arm and set out at a trot which left his unknown pursuer half a mile behind in a few minutes.

5.

The third time, he was standing before the Andergast house, at the corner of the Lindenstrasse, when Etzel came home from his physical training, together with Heinz Ellmers. This Ellmers, the son of a builder, an excellent mathematician, had offered to help Etzel with a problem in algebra which he was to have done at home and before which he had sat helpless the whole evening before. As a matter of fact he could not bear Ellmers, who was loud-mouthed and pushing, and had almost been boycotted by the whole class a few months before, on account of some incident of tale-bearing which had never been quite cleared up. Ellmers had offered Etzel his help with such straight-forward insistence—he probably wanted to be able to say that he had been to Baron Andergast's—that Etzel saw no reason for not yielding. This time Etzel was scared when he saw the man with the captain's cap. It was the repetition which had something threatening about it, something productive of a feeling of coercion. It was the closeness of the man, it was the lonely stillness of the street; all this combined to evoke terror. His short-sightedness had prevented him up to now from seeing the features of the stranger and the details of his appearance. Now the man stood so close to him that he could see the yellow-grey of his eyes and even the shabby cloth buttons of his fur coat. When he entered the front garden from the street, Ellmers following at his heels, the caretaker stood talking to a guard in the gateway. The caretaker greeted Etzel, and the guard saluted, knowing him to be the son of the solicitor-general. Etzel felt giddy when he noticed the man with the captain's cap also preparing to enter the house. Probably he counted on passing the caretaker without being approached, and upon avoiding troublesome questions, by following upon the heels of the two boys; one could read this thought upon his face. And he succeeded; the caretaker threw him a suspicious glance, but let him pass. In the hall he remained standing and looked after the boys. Etzel dropped his pile of strapped books. Ellmers picked it up. "Thanks," said Etzel. He listened with strained attention; the higher they went towards the second story the more tensely he listened. A few steps beyond the first story he turned and listened. Ellmers looked anxiously into Etzel's face and asked: "Is something wrong with you, Andergast? You look so white." Etzel listened and whispered, "Is he coming?" The other replied with astonishment, "Who; whom do you mean?" Etzel clung tightly to the banister. Etzel heard steps groping up clumsily. What kind of a person is he, that he clings to one so obstinately? thought Etzel, the obstinate persecution of the unknown man filling him with more and more fear. Heinz Ellmers, however, senses at just this moment as never before that Etzel thoroughly dislikes him and he looks up gloomily and with some hostility at the boy standing two steps above him, who looks up in turn, with a new tenseness in his face, for he hears steps coming down too, steps with which he is familiar. After a time Herr von Andergast's neat figure appears against the corner of the window. He is just turning around the corner of the stairs; below, the man with the captain's cap is turning the corner of the stairs. It seems to Etzel as if this movement were full of meaning, although his common sense can only regard it as a chance meeting. Herr von Andergast nods to the boys and asks some indifferent question—are you already through for the day? or something of the sort—without pausing in his descent, then his glance falls upon the man with the captain's cap. The latter at once stands still and with his back towards the wall places two fingers against the brim of his cap in military attention and says, in a funny croaking voice, with military brevity, which also produces a comical effect: "My name is Maurizius." At the same time he puts his left hand, awkwardly on account of the evident stiffness of his arm, into the pocket of his fur coat and wants to get something out of it. Herr von Andergast turns his head and looks at him, one second, two seconds, assuming his haughty expression; the dull glance through his half-closed lids rests on the man. Then he goes on. He turns his head once more, his brow is slightly wrinkled, he makes an impatient gesture with his hand and hastens his steps. All this does not take more than a minute and a half, but Etzel now knows with certainty that his father too knows the man with the captain's cap. He has realized, from the expression of his father's face, from his angry gesture, also from the motion of his back, and the way in which he goes down the staircase step by step, that he has not seen the man for the first time on these steps, while the Maurizius fellow still stands against the wall at military attention, his left hand inside his fur coat, and his eyes, with their astigmatic look, facing downward into the twilight of the staircase.

6.

And so it was indeed. Herr von Andergast had often seen the old man with his indolent repose, his persistent watchfulness, prowling about and repeatedly bobbing up before him. There were many who crossed his path, none without timidity, few without nervousness. This man seemed to feel neither timidity nor nervousness. He did not appear to be a tramp or one who had lost caste, not in the least; he reminded one rather of a provincial, someone in poor circumstances who did not quite know how to behave in the capital. Nevertheless there was in his manners a lack of respect, an impertinence even, which grated on Herr von Andergast's nerves. He did not know who the man was. He had never, as he supposed, seen him before. One day the man stood before him like one who obstinately wishes to be noticed at any price. It was the noon hour. With the same shiver which always came over him when he left the court house, and which the warmth of the March sun did not alter today, Herr von Andergast buttoned his coat, replied without a glance to the porter's respectful greeting, and set out towards home. He walked this distance daily. On the animated streets he was forced to lift his hat countless times, and although he executed this ceremony also without a glance, nevertheless his bearing and gesture had in each case the shade which corresponded to the social rank of the person greeted, from a brief touch of the brim to the lifting of the hat in a measured short half-circle described in the air before deliberately restoring the hat to his bald head. The other persons, whosoever they might be, artisans, small tradesmen, bank directors, editors, owners of estates, city commissioners, showed in their greeting the hasty eagerness which they felt that they owed Herr von Andergast's high office, as well as his dreaded personality. Accustomed to the reverence of a whole city, he walked coldly through it. His glance directed straight ahead did not concern itself with the scenes in the street. Not only that, his face denied so to speak its reality, as if this reality were a trap for him, as if it contained some painful intimacy, and his step had not only the characteristic, repressed gait peculiar to people who move for the most part in closed rooms, but also the casual manner characteristic of those who have constantly to protect themselves against importunities. And now there was this figure in his path. An unknown person who dared to stare into the face of Herr von Andergast, the chief prosecuting attorney! With a pipe stuck in his mouth! To stare in his face, and, as he felt without looking about, to follow him. Then, walking more rapidly to catch up with him, to stand again staring! With his pipe in his mouth. It was unparalleled. The next day the same impudence. Three days later again. Perhaps the man was crazy, one of the many soreheads known to the police and the courts, who went about with some unsatisfied request, trying thus to keep the authorities in suspense. The wisest thing was to ignore the man and sometime to give the policeman of the ward a hint. Then came the affront on the staircase. Entry into the privacy of the home—that was going too far, that required chastisement; the matter must not be permitted to occur again. At first Herr von Andergast did not heed the name which the suspicious fellow uttered. When he realized it he involuntarily turned his head back. He could not conceal his dismay.

The next day the petition was filed by the regular official procedure; it was by no means the first on the subject, but one of the many customary importunities of justice coming from the same source. Thus an apparently harmless explanation of the incident had been found, although the man's impudent manner remained none the less incomprehensible. In no case was the matter now worth any further thought.

CHAPTER II

I.

In Etzel's mind the appearance of the man with the captain's cap, particularly the encounter with his father on the stairs, which although unexpected seemed planned, and the image of the letter with the Swiss postmark and the handwriting which had an air of friendliness to him, became inextricably connected. In both occurrences something invited or challenged him; the difference was merely that the former incident remained quite external, the latter entirely internal, so that he seemed to himself like a pendulum swinging between the two. Both, however, confused him profoundly and drew his thoughts from his usual occupations and daily duties to such an extent that one morning, instead of turning his steps towards the Gymnasium, depending on the mechanical memory of his legs, he went in the opposite direction, constantly further as if lost in a dream, deposited his pile of books in the Bockenheim station and took the train to the Taunus. In Oberursel he left the train, strolled towards the Saalburg, paying no attention finally to path or destination, walked about in the woods, unmindful of the storm or the occasional bursts of pouring rain. When the downpour became too heavy he took shelter under a tree or in a woodcutter's hut. As if lost in a dream, but only "as if." For we are not dealing with a dreamer, by any means—this must be made clear from the start. He was in full possession of his five senses. He knew what he was doing and he accomplished what he was about without much ado; he engaged in no harebrained fantasies; he had the clock in his head and the time at his finger tips. The proof of this was that at one-fifteen he appeared punctually as usual, washed and dressed, at lunch. To dispose of matters, and to dispose of them with his intelligence, to be clear with himself, to perceive causes and consequences, to call a problem solved, this was his ambition; he practised this at every opportunity. He wanted to do it in this case too; this it was that had driven him forth. But he did not succeed this time, his bewilderment was too great.

The next evening during the routine conversation with his father he noticed that the latter's attitude was not the usual one. One could not ascertain in what way, nor what his intention was; a clairvoyant could scarcely see through his intentions and purposes when he wished to conceal them. He was more friendly than usual, he had something ingratiating in his manner; for example, he passed Etzel the cheese twice and inquired smilingly whether he were not going to have his hair cut soon. It was at once evident to Etzel that his father knew of his morning's expedition and of his staying away from school and that there would now ensue one of the veiled discussions which always terrified him. One could not expect this with certainty; it was worse if it remained a threat, a cloaked silence between them. This was then material, so called. Herr von Andergast was evidently trying as hard as he could to get Etzel to speak of it himself; he invited him by his mildness, as it were, to do so. But the more he tried the more uncomfortable the boy became, until finally he looked in tense silence, almost without moving an eyelash, at the imposing face across the table, which was to him so inscrutable, which always called forth in him a feeling of his own insufficiency. It was not possible for him to do what was asked of him under such strong moral pressure although silently; if it had been he would have been able to do it yesterday. He did not know why he had not done it, why he *could* not do it. No courage and no argument were of any avail. While he gazed curiously into his father's face, but in a way which apparently did not disturb him further, he racked his brains as to how his father could have found out so quickly about the excursion; certainly not from the class master—Dr. Camill Raff was not in the habit of making a commotion about every slight occurrence, furthermore he was indulgent towards Etzel. The boy wondered too why his father sought to entice him by roundabout approaches, to confess, instead of simply asking and taking him to task. Of course this was not new to him. Nothing was simple in their mutual relation. When he thought about it, his very ideas became confused.

Here, however, I must first explain, in order to throw some light on the relation between father and son, what I mean by their "routine conversation."

2.

They saw each other only in the house. Herr von Andergast, overburdened by his professional work, never took a walk, never went to the theatre nor to a concert. He disliked to show himself in public; with the exception of a few colleagues with whom he was thrown together in his official duties—Sydow, President of the State Supreme Court, and his family, for example—he had almost no social relations. He felt no need of sociability. Official entertainments which he could not avoid he regarded as a burden. Once a month he visited his old mother, the general's widow, as she was called for short, in her country house in Eschersheim. Sunday afternoons and holidays were devoted to the study of the accumulated legal documents.

To spend two hours daily with Etzel was nevertheless part of the routine of life just like the study of documents. To conceal that these hours were a routine educational measure was one of the tasks which he set himself. He could devote only the evening hours to this purpose. During dinner, which anyway was frequently omitted because of professional duties, they were simply strangers to one another.

Herr von Andergast's expression was set, the mind behind the strikingly intellectual and beautifully modelled forehead was occupied with legal disputes, the violent blue eyes with their fixed gloomy ardour had an absent expression.

Moreover, Frau Rie was present at dinner, and much as Herr von Andergast recognized her usefulness as the manager of his household, in the same degree she wearied him by her "unofficial" presence. Etzel was not much better off with her; he liked her, he could get on well with her but only when he was alone with her; in his father's presence, and especially at the table, she made him nervous to the point of hate. She sat so complacently on her chair, as if she were constantly praising herself in silence for the bringing about of a meal of such excellent quality, in view of the many difficulties which she considerately kept to herself. The appetite with which she ate was like silent praise of herself, and what she said was as banal as the maxims in a textbook for a young girls' seminary.

After dinner she remained in her room. When the table had been cleared Herr von Andergast lit his cigar and relaxed with a perceptible act of will. His bearing and expression lost their tension, never of course to the extent of letting himself go completely, far from it; but the violet-blue eyes no longer had their hidden glow, they reminded one strikingly of the eyes of a naïve young girl.

Generally he began the conversation with some harmless questions, skirmished about a bit, seized upon a subject, provoked Etzel to contradiction, took pleasure in the contradiction, parried with the skill of a duellist, defended that which was safe and sound against wayward innovation, suggested compromises, and after a heated debate was prepared to accept theoretically a revolutionary point of view. During all this, although Etzel went at the matter with enthusiasm, it seemed to him, as with his father's "playful" hand, as if it were all only a game, the sarcastic play of a partner who does not wish to take advantage of an incomparably stronger position. He's damned clever, thought Etzel furiously and full of awe, one can't get at him. In his naïve youthful eagerness he always transcended the bounds where there was no other help than paradox, and into this he then plunged madly, which would cause his father to express a Jesuitical deprecation.

"You are not only a fighting cock," Herr von Andergast would finally say, looking at his gold watch, "you are full of dodges and tricks, one must keep an eye on you." Then Etzel would stare at him with surprise and suspicion, for he was certain that he had not deserved this particular compliment.

The conversation generally ended in some such way; undecisively leaving behind a cruel vacuum—sharply at half past nine Herr von Andergast would get up with an expression which did not have the slightest relation to the words which had been spoken last; whereupon Etzel would turn to the door with somewhat silly haste, seize the knob and bow with the vague smile of a person who has been beaten by sharp practices. Yes, he felt duped, he could not say why; and every time he left the room he felt himself "dismissed," somewhat as after receiving a scolding from the rector.

If Herr von Andergast was obliged to go out in the evening he would appear in Etzel's room late in the afternoon, sit down at the table at which the boy was doing his school lessons, tell him to keep quietly at work, and observe him. After a while Etzel would become embarrassed, lose his thread and stop. "What are you working at?" Herr von Andergast would ask. When it was a mathematical exercise or a task in history he would show interest. With his superior gift of speech, "making every word tell," as the actors say, he one day praised the intellectual accuracy to which mathematics trained one, the magic of number, of pure number, to which they made one receptive. A lifelike conception of the laws of nature was among the advantages this science offered, he stated, and as the dome of a cupola unites seemingly divergent elements, mathematics could combine the highest and the most contrasting human forces. Etzel listened attentively, but looked like an obstinate little dog who was not minded to fetch. But on another occasion, when his father recommended the study of the science of history with the same gentle insistence, he became eager and obstinate, questioning particularly whether history was a science at all. One could by the same token call the copying of documents or the reading of newspapers a science. Where, in history, was there cognition, what were its laws, where did it rest upon a firm foundation? It was a burden of memory, arbitrary nomenclature and chronology, at best a romance. "Oh," said Herr von Andergast, making a gesture like that of an orchestra conductor when the kettledrum makes too much noise.

As a matter of fact these conversations were practice in dialectic, and the ground which they covered was definitely staked out by Herr von Andergast. Etzel knew that he must not overstep the bounds. The man who listened with so much friendliness to the experiences of his mental life, who even enticed them from his lips, who pursued his frequently immature, mostly quite pronounced, sometimes very passionate train of thoughts, would inevitably have changed into a lump of ice if the boy had permitted himself to think of speaking of external events, of daily occurrences, his relations with a friend or teacher, or had gone so far as to ask questions which touched upon his father's profession, his private life or his past. If he dared even to hint at such matters, yielding to a secret urge, knowing that he would be sharply reprimanded, Herr von Andergast would get up, frown and say with a sidelong glance, "We shall discuss that at a more suitable time." Etzel had reason to suppose that he had never yet been made to feel the greatest depths of his father's coldness; the instantaneous fall in temperature at the slightest slip made him anxious enough as it was. At times, when he thought that he was not observed—and such periods were even more seldom than he supposed, for Herr von Andergast's whole nature was watching and perpetually keeping his eyes open—he looked at his father as at a tower, a tower without an entrance, without doors and without windows, which simply rises majestically, filled with secrets from top to bottom. His deep admiration was mixed with an equally deep fear. A motherless only son he faced his father extraordinarily alone. This confrontation became for him a symbol of their relations and if he attempted to shift the symbol by approaching him more closely, his father retreated the same number of steps which he had advanced; if, however, the latter approached him he was seized with fear and compelled to be careful. His father's reputation for severity and inflexibility, and his iron inexorableness in matters of principle had penetrated to him in early childhood, for among the people Andergast was called "the bloody." This was, of course, very unjust, for a high consciousness of duty and the exaltation of office permeated his personality to the very pores, almost to the point of ossification. But such words circulate like poisonous bacteria and, although Etzel did not actually hear them, nevertheless he felt their reverberation and his dreams—for during his waking hours he closed his eyes and did not allow his fantasy to play with the subject—produced figures like those in Dante's Inferno. For everything is contained in us from the very beginning, even that which we have never seen and never known. Then he pictured his father in a blaze of fire, holding judgment over the hordes of the damned.

3.

Herr von Andergast sat in a dim light; he could not bear the full glare of the electric light, which usually inflamed his eyes; all the Andergasts had poor eyes, the general's old widow had suffered for years from a disturbance of the optic nerve. Perhaps there was a deeper significance; he who lives merely by his eyes suffers through his eyes. The intense violet-blue of Herr von Andergast's eyes was also somewhat abnormal. He sat with his legs crossed, his trunk almost violently erect; equally stiff was the pose of his long oval head, with its bald polished skull and fringe of iron-grey hair cut down to a single millimeter. There was something in his bearing—as if he were occupying a throne—and in his somewhat aloof manner, which drew Etzel's glance towards him, as if he were winding thread upon a shuttle, but he seemed neither to know nor to wish this. The boy was as familiar with the silhouette of his father seated with crossed legs, half detachedly, as with some lifeless emblem of daily recurrence. As a matter of fact, a cursory glance at Herr von Andergast, seated in a half-light, reminded one of a figure from an Egyptian temple. There is much harm derived from contemplating a rigid image; such familiarity has about it nothing of liberation or understanding. The timidity and the sense of distance always remained the same as well as the double resignation, first to a possible drop in temperature, then to the moment when one was "dismissed." He always looked over towards the half-light with the same tension; every evening, as today, he felt a timid astonishment at the athletic figure, the virile chin, the strong straight nose, the vigorous lips and the strong neck which the short-cut, carefully trimmed Vandyke beard, already grey, only covered in part. There was an indefinable aura of melancholy about his person, a secretive dissatisfaction which is peculiar to people who cannot pursue the destiny they believe in. Such people, diverted from the goal towards which they once aimed, at a time which they remember only as a phantasmagoria, hide their disappointment from the eyes of the world behind an armour of pride and reserve. The sense of isolation is what gives them value in their own eyes, and every experience, and every disappointment strengthens them in this. By finally losing themselves in this isolation they become so strange, so inscrutable, so aloof, that it seems as if the language no longer existed in which one could communicate with them. This was often Etzel's predominating impression; it is frightfully far to him, he thought, and when one finally gets there one is completely dulled by fatigue. Probably a somewhat exaggerated sensitiveness, but there was nevertheless so much which connected and attracted the two, that what separated and repelled Etzel became ten times more tormenting. He had seldom suffered as much from it as today. Several times he was on the point of jumping up and leaving the room under the pretext of a headache.

It would be difficult to say why Herr von Andergast took such an intense interest in Etzel's adventure of the previous morning. As a matter of fact he used the word "adventure," although the term did not fit a plain case of truancy and wandering about aimlessly in the rain. A lawyer had seen Etzel in the station at Oberursel and had casually mentioned the fact to Herr von Andergast this morning; such was the simple explanation of his puzzling knowledge of the adventure. Chance! And he was now making use of this in his own way. Whether he was driven to this by psychological curiosity, or by the fear that this was only the beginning of a series of arbitrary acts and omissions cannot, with his endlessly complicated way of thinking, be determined. Independent actions must be prevented as long as possible, but how and by what means? It was the spirit which must be tamed, the most dangerous explosive material in the world. He realized gradually, in the first place, that his artificial system of keeping his distance was defective; secondly, that it revenged itself spitefully upon him, for after using the same path so exclusively, only the bypaths remained to be travelled, for to pass through the barricades of the direct route would have meant a ridiculous waste of time. Prison wardens also have a pride of station. They feel themselves responsible not only for the prisoner, but also for the house, the wall, the door, the lock and the key. Finally the guardian himself no longer has any freedom left.

His sonorous voice filled the room. There was something compelling about it under any circumstance. His slowness of cadence—a barrier-language, one of his enemies called it—was rooted in the desire to find the most pregnant form for every thought. This at times made an impression of self-complacency, but he was not complacent, it was only a sense of superiority penetrating into the very circulation of his blood which in intercourse with people expressed itself as dry pedantry or consistent objectivity. In this he was extraordinarily German, that is according to the most modern conception of German. Almost all gifted speakers are inclined to regard their audience as minors, but this is never less justified than when the listener is very young. The more pains Herr von Andergast took the more irritatingly did he feel his words turning to dust. Not to meet with any resistance was the most unconquerable resistance. What was he actually advocating? Against what was he preaching? There were several things in the air besides the Taunus "adventure," there was the question of the letter and the meeting with the idiotic old man on the steps. Herr von Andergast felt latent questions which did not dare to come up, but he did not in the least wish them to be put. The evening before, the boy had dared to question the justice of a decision in a political case; extraordinarily bold of him, the breaking down of the customary ceremonial! His companions had argued heatedly about the case, Etzel reported; so far as he could perceive it looked as if there was a manifest incongruity between the offence and the penalty; the crime was slight, the punishment inhuman. To this conversation, which he had broken off brusquely the day before, Herr von Andergast returned today. It was undesirable that a legal case become the talk of the street. It was disastrous to confuse justice and sentiment, which meant to place the absolute at the mercy of the accidental. Right was an idea, not a matter of heart, the law was not an agreement between two parties, to be modified at will, but a sacred and permanent form. It was true, inviolably valid and so it had been since judges sentenced the guilty and a legal code regulated crimes according to articles. And what is it which nevertheless flashes such incredulous denial from the eyes of the boy opposite? Eternal form of the law? The lad starts restlessly in his chair and bites the knuckle of his finger with embarrassment. He has heard a whisper to the effect that the State has a right and a left hand, and a twofold measure, one for one hand, one for the other, and several scales, and for each scale various weights. What are the facts? He did not ask this aloud but his eyes asked it. Moreover, he had not doubted "right as an idea," but the justice of a specific decision, and the matter had nothing to do with his heart, only with his understanding and his powers of judgment. Here you are completely on the wrong tack, my dear father, but let's drop the subject, said his eyes.

Perhaps Herr von Andergast understands the silent speech which merely echoes from the sixteen-year-old boy, and expresses the doubting and denying spirit of his generation, a spirit sick to its very roots, unchained by the unchained. It was an attack of the anger which had been collecting which led him to the tactical mistake. Proof, example, explanation were in vain. Darkness does not become light because one mobilizes reasons against it. Light cannot convince the blind, cannot enlighten the misguided. This new spirit about which they are drivelling and drooling, where is it? In themselves, they say, there is nothing new; there is nothing old. Man, his life, his birth, his death, these things have not changed for the past six thousand years, indeed for the past sixty thousand, it was merely a short-sighted fiction to attempt to make an epoch of every lustrum. The less people are themselves the more they expect from their period, the same immemorial waters turn their windmill with the rest and they imagine they have changed its course because the water turns their wheel too.

He still considered his "casual" manner would assure him the accustomed victory, but actually his despotism was about to suffer shipwreck. Naturally, he was prepared some day to accept the alien nature of his son; perhaps the alien nature appeared so soon because in his frozen skepticism he had so long been prepared for it; fear creates what it dreads. But it was not the despotism of the father which suffered a defeat, but that of the official. To Herr von Andergast his service was a vocation, his vocation a mission. He was the agent of an absolute master, whose interests he represented and in whose name he operated and whose Asiatic absolutism could not be lessened by any loosening of the forms of government. The master, although he might disappear as a real person from the scene of action, remained as a symbol. And the servant too was a symbol, as a servant he had no history, no previous life, no private life. Every human tie was less important to him than the professional one. Immutability is his guiding principle, his period is every period, the religious belief in the hierarchy to which he belongs makes him a monk, an ascetic, under certain circumstances a fanatic. It was said of Herr von Andergast—at least his colleagues praised him for it—that his strong sense for facts had triumphed over the most difficult and obscure cases and won him an authoritative prestige which had not been shaken by any change or any innovations in the administration. This was easy to understand. Why should anyone be shaken by external matters who was so unshakable within himself?

4.

It was half-past nine. Herr von Andergast took out his gold hunting watch. Etzel got up. He made his bow, said good night and turned to the door with his accustomed gesture of flight. There he hesitated. He glanced at the wall, asked quickly and shyly: "Who is this Maurizius, father?"

Herr von Andergast remained standing on the threshold of his study door. "Why do you want to know?" he asked, measuring his son with a cold glance.

"Oh . . . only . . ." replied Etzel, "it's because—" He hesitated.

He had asked Rie too. She had thought awhile and shaken her head. At this moment he determined to ask other people, as many people as possible, above all his grandmother, with whom he was to have lunch the day after tomorrow, as he did every Sunday. He remembered that the man with the captain's cap had pronounced his name with a sort of consciousness of fame, almost as if one should say, "My name is Bismarck," though not triumphantly, but rather sullenly. The sound still remained in his ear.

"That is in no case a subject which we two can discuss," said Herr von Andergast, and rose like an inaccessible tower in a frosty cloud.

"I would like to write to her once," murmured Etzel as he walked up and down in his room. He saw a field in front of him, above it was a wood-covered hill with the setting sun above it, the earth was bent like the back of a giant. There was an itching in his throat.

He sat down and, snatching a sheet of paper out of one of his copy books, he wrote: "There is a great deal going on and I think over things a great deal. It's frightful that I don't even know you. Where are you really? It may be that some day I shall get into a train and come to you. Perhaps during the holidays. You may perhaps laugh over this schoolboy plan. Naturally, if I let out anything about this resolution it would all be over. Why, I ask? There are, moreover, many questions to be answered. A boy of my age seems to have his hands and feet bound with stout ropes. Who knows, perhaps when the string is once cut, one is already lame and tame. That is probably the purpose. One is to be tamed. Have they made you tame also? Can you not tell me what I should do so that we can see one another? I will do whatever you like, only it must remain a secret. You understand. He always finds out everything. This letter must remain an absolute secret. Of course, I am getting older with time. But the slowness of the process is enough to drive one mad. They will not succeed in taming me. Do you know, when I saw that letter in the hall, it was as if lightning had struck my brain. I would so much like to know what's the matter. I know you understand me. I have the feeling that you have had an injustice done you. Is that so? I must tell you in general that the injustices one hears of every day are simply frightful. You must know that injustice to me is the most horrible thing in the world. I can't give you any idea of my feelings when I experience injustice, whether towards myself or others; it's just the same. It goes right through me. It makes my body and soul ache, it is as if one had poured my mouth full of sand and I must choke on the spot."

He paused. He realized with dismay that he was writing to himself, or to a person of his own invention, not a real person. He could not even send the letter off. He had no address. He had neglected to look at the back of the envelope from Geneva. Furthermore, it was to be feared that his father would find out about it, as he did about everything Etzel did. As a child he had imagined that his father sat in the centre of the universe recording all the sins and trespasses of all the city's inhabitants on a marble tablet with a stylus of marble. Remnants of this faith still clung to him; from this image he still created internal scenes and imaginary conversations. His father stood in the room imperiously. As a magician, he had the power to pass through closed doors. In his capacity of magician, Etzel had given him the name of Trismegistus. Always when he thought of his father in his punitive function he called him so. The dialogue was something like the following: *Trismegistus*: "Etzel, where are you?"—"Here I am."—"Why do you hide from me?"—"I am not hiding, I have only taken the mask from my face."—"What! You have the audacity to appear before me without a mask?"—"Why, when a person is alone, father, he does not need a mask."—"But I can see into you. I am surprised, I am very much surprised, I wish I had not seen you without a mask."

He folded the letter, placed it in an envelope and wrote upon it: "To my mother; I don't know where." He placed it in a secret compartment which he had made for himself in the drawer of his work-table, and in which there were other papers, notes, records, and poems and, as special treasures, two letters which he had received from Melchior Ghisels. Then he sat down, his chin in his hands, his elbows resting on the table. He should have gone to bed long ago but there was an unrest within him which could not be quieted. From the street there resounded a long shrill whistle. The rain beat upon the trees. He jumped up, walked about, then remained standing in front of his book shelves. Every single book was a friend. He had bought them gradually one by one with his pocket-money, or he had gotten his grandmother to give them to him; some his father had given him. The place of honour was occupied by the writings of his beloved Melchior Ghisels, four handsomely bound volumes with an inscription from the author in his own hand. This man was to him a god and every sentence in the books a revelation. Only at sixteen can one thus reverence an author. Only an unruffled spirit can harbour such a passion. The admiration with which Etzel was attached to the man and his work was combined with tenderness; Ghisels, an author as profound as Kierkegaard, was to him a prophet and a leader. Often, before falling asleep he read half a page of a chapter which he had already read ten times, slowly with breathless reverence, then put out the light quickly and went smilingly to sleep. He did not know

Ghisels personally. He had written to him, once when he had asked him for the inscription and a second time very shyly to ask him the meaning of a difficult passage in a beautiful essay about the periods of life. Thielemann, Robert's father, who dealt in books, had given him the address, and since he knew that Ghisels lived in Berlin, the city had become a Mecca to him. He was jealous of Melchior Ghisels, as one can be jealous of a treasure, and it filled him with satisfaction that his writings were known only to a few. Noisy fame, which indeed the work was little qualified to call forth, would perhaps have disenchanted him. Camill Raff had been the first to open this realm of higher thoughts to him; the previous summer when he had been ill, Dr. Raff had come to see him and had brought him a book of Ghisels' out of which he had read to him one whole afternoon.

He took one of Ghisels' books from the shelf, lay down on the floor flat on his stomach, opened the book and began to read. Only in this way, flat on the floor, lying on his stomach, could he give his entire concentration to reading. But after a while his hand ceased to turn the pages, his forehead fell forward on his arm, his legs stretched out and he slept. He did not wake up until two in the morning, looked disturbedly about him, jumped up, hastily threw off his clothes, turned off the light and slipped noiselessly into bed. With his head already buried in the pillow he murmured some words of surprise and excuse to himself and like a ten-year-old urchin stuck out his tongue at himself in sleepy embarrassment.

5.

The widow of General Andergast was one of an almost obsolete type of feminine "characters." She was a woman of seventy-three, but she did not look her age. She was of small build, extremely animated, indeed a little impetuous.

Her features were vivacious, she had quick, inquiringly bright eyes, over which, when she was alone, she wore a green paper shade because her eyes were weak. She had the bright clear voice of a young girl. She had been a widow for twenty years; after the death of her husband, who had been a miserable tyrant and hypochondriac, she had begun to live; she had travelled far, had been to Syria and India and had spent several months with a married cousin in South America. She had knowledge of the world and diverse artistic interests; her favourite occupation was painting; in spite of her poor eyes she spent an hour each day in her studio and painted with devoted patience pictures in the style of the French impressionists, with taste and modesty. If anyone spoke of her pictures or asked to see them she blushed like a flapper and quickly turned the conversation. She did not get on well with her son, the solicitor-general. He was too eager for power and in this respect reminded her unpleasantly of her dead husband. Since he, obviously, though silently, disapproved of her unconventional attitude in society, her carelessness about money and her complete indifference to matronly dignity, she was always afraid of him and breathed a sigh of relief when he departed after ceremoniously kissing her hand. "I can't appear before a moral tribunal every day and give an account of myself; I am much too deficient and timid for that," she would sigh when he respectfully, in his soft voice, reproached her for some impetuosity, or an offence against social form. Since his divorce from his wife she had moreover become more profoundly displeased with him than because of his formality and his joyless principles. It had never been discussed between them, but Herr von Andergast did not deceive himself about it, and he always took due note of any failure on the part of others to declare themselves to be in complete accord with him and with his behaviour. The old lady had not forgiven him the harshness with which he had condemned his wife, the mother of his child, to spiritual death. The reports which one received of her spoke of a slow decline and pining away in foreign parts. The power had been entirely in his hands; he had used it to the very utmost, naturally with a conscientious observance of the law, which had been on his side. Whether the general's widow had felt any sympathy for Sophia von Andergast before the divorce, is uncertain, but in any case she had later, and long after Sophia had left the city, she spoke of her with undisguised sympathy; indeed one day, in the drawing-room of an acquaintance, she went so far as to express herself with indignation over the cruelty of separating a mother from all intercourse with her child and of making such a regulation unalterable and irrevocable. Those present did not know where to look. The matter had caused a slight scandal, called forth, however, by the tactless remark of a young barrister, who either out of shabby servility, or because he was a born "yes-man" could not sufficiently praise Herr von Andergast's "resolution." Naturally, the affair had become public to a certain extent, and had given rise to the usual gossip. The expression "resolution" in particular had driven the widow almost beside herself with anger. After she had with upright carriage and glistening eyes expressed her opinion, she quickly took up her shawl and her little bag and speedily left the disconcerted assembly, which could not for a long time decide whether to admire the old lady for her courage or to smile at her eccentricity. Two days later Herr von Andergast paid his mother a visit. Without any mention of this scene, or of any other expression of her opinions, without reference to Sophia or the divorce, after a brief discussion, he received from his mother the solemn promise that she would never mention Etzel's mother to the boy and remain absolutely silent about her existence. It was a triumph of his tactics. He had upon this occasion so intimidated her that she had kept her promise to this day, although it had sometimes been most difficult when the charming boy sat at her feet talking and asking confidentially.

Etzel as a guest on Sunday meant a beautifully set table in a well heated room. For herself alone the widow took little trouble, sometimes she forgot to eat at all; towards evening then she would feel hungry and send the maid—whom she had employed at scratching the paint off old canvases instead of cooking—across the street for a couple of sandwiches which she would then eat tripping tirelessly around the room talking and humming to herself. To Etzel his grandmother was a stimulating creature. To his mind she had more of the "mysterious" about her than most people with whom he came into contact. What he called "the mysterious" was his standard of value for people. Everyone, even the most boring, the most unimportant person, had something hidden and impenetrable about him which began to operate the minute he left Etzel's presence. Etzel would then wonder what he was doing now that he was left to his "mystery." Particularly he used to think about people in their solitude. How did this or that person behave when he was alone, what did he look like? One could never find out, for the eye that observes a human creature at once breaks up the mystery state, merely by looking at him. Of Trismegistus, for example, Etzel formed a picture that he sat with a compass, drawing big circles on a drawing board and filling the circles with figures. Of his grandmother he could imagine that she, defying the laws of gravity, would walk about the ceiling with her feet uppermost, or when she was out of doors and, of course, quite unobserved, that she would float daintily in the air like a balloon. This was her "secret"—what was impenetrable about her.

6.

Towards the end of the meal Etzel brought forward the question which he wanted to ask his grandmother. He had not seen the man with the captain's cap again, but his thoughts were none the less frequently occupied with him. Only it was not to be assumed that just his grandmother would know the name. She mixed up most names, even those of families with whom she associated, and had caused much confusion in this way. Far from regarding this as an embarrassing defect, she laughed herself half to death when she mixed up lineages, dignitaries and celebrities in entirely different fields. The maid who had been in her service fourteen years and whose name was Nanny, she called a different name every day, Bertha, Elise, Babette, whatever came into her head, for she was always the creature of the moment and in amiable roguishness seized upon any name she liked. Nevertheless, Etzel put the question to her and, in order to assume an appearance of indifference, to make the question seem unimportant, he examined the silver salt-cellar with feigned curiosity, as if it were a boat to which he was going to entrust himself for a long journey.

Maurizius; the name did not seem unfamiliar to the general's widow. She laid down her dessert knife, placed her arms upon her hips and with uplifted forehead, which gave her a somewhat silly expression, she too looked at the salt-cellar. It was a name redolent of blackness. When one pronounced it, or heard it, a mouldy cold blew against one as if a cellar door had been opened. Evil was called to memory, forgotten faces recovered their outlines and automatically called forth the horror which had once weighed upon the city, the county, indeed upon the whole country. It was as if the iridescent scum of a swamp once drained were to come swirling to the surface again through some carelessly made spade-stroke. "What have you to do with that, my boy?" she asked indignantly. "How does that concern you? How did you come across the name? The story is no longer true, it's so long ago." Etzel saw what an impression the name had made upon the old lady. "What is it then?" he whispered, mechanically rubbing the palms of his hands which he had stuck between his knees. "Do tell me, grandmother, what it all was, and then I'll tell you why I want to know."

"Impossible to tell it," the widow assured him. She had already said it was many years ago. "Wait a minute, let me think. Your grandfather was already dead. It must have been during the first year of mourning, perhaps somewhat later. Not much later, for a year and a half after his death I went to the Orient. That was eighteen years ago, two years before you were born. How should I still be able to tell you about it after eighteen years? What is it that interests you so about the matter?" Instead of replying, Etzel asked after a while in a still lower voice, "Was my father involved? 'Involved' is of course a silly expression, grandmother, but you know what I mean." Anxiously he fastened his glance upon the salt-cellar, which had changed into an ocean steamer and was already, as it were, nearing the dock ready to take on passengers. "Your father? Yes —I think—" was the hesitating reply, which had a slight undertone of malice. "I think he was. He was a public prosecutor at that time; it seems to me that it was this story which first made him eminent. I could scarcely be mistaken about that; it's fairly certain he distinguished himself greatly at that time; but for *him,* Maurizius would have gotten off unpunished in the end." She was silent, toyed with the ruff of her sleeve and laughed a little with embarrassment; at this moment she strongly resembled Etzel, her junior by fifty-seven years.

But Etzel urged and urged. With exquisite cunning he pretended that this burning desire for knowledge which permeated his whole being, kindled by an appearance and struggling towards a dimly adumbrated goal, was plain boyish curiosity. He moved his chair nearer to the widow, took her hand and placed it on his cheek. At the same time he begged with his tongue and his eyes. The old lady shook her head with surprise. "My boy, I tell you you have lost your senses," she scolded. "It seems to me that you've slipped off to the movies recently and have lost your head over the silly things they show. There are said to be boys who get quite wild from them. However, between ourselves, I go myself sometimes, but don't betray me. Now don't look at me so desperately. I am just trying to remember what I still know of the matter. With the best will in the world I can't remember it all. Such an old head as mine is a sieve with big holes in it. I won't investigate from what your interest springs; I might not be pleased in the end. All right, it was a frightful affair. People spoke of nothing else for weeks. The pros and cons agitated all the clubs and taverns. There were public meetings and the militia had to be called out on the day on which the death sentence was announced. I was over at Homburg at the time, and I remember that the doctor forbade me to read the papers. Even when the case was long finished and Maurizius—what was his Christian name? I have forgotten—and Maurizius' sentence was commuted to life imprisonment, the story did not end. Many believed strongly and firmly that he was not guilty. Perhaps only because he himself insisted to the last gasp that he was innocent. Moreover, he was no common criminal. No, he was not that. He was a learned man, many people insisted an authority on his subject. Others again said that he was a windbag. Anyway, in spite of his youth—I think that he was not yet twenty-six—he had attained a position of respect as an art critic. I even had a little book that he had written. I must look for it sometime; it's certainly in one of the cases in the garret. Now I remember the title: Concerning the Influence of Religion on the Plastic Arts in the Nineteenth Century. It interested me at the time; religion, art, people chattered about them in all the drawing-rooms. Who could regard such a man as an assassin? I could never quite believe that he was capable of it. To shoot his own wife in the back out of an ambush. And under such circumstances! A mixed-up story. A Godforsaken, pitiful story and I naturally no longer remember the run of it. I only know that everything was against him, persons, things, space and time. A flawless piece of circumstantial evidence, as the lawyers call it. The bringing together of this evidence was actually your father's work, that I remember well. He was very proud of his work, young and ambitious as he was. A bell-founder could not be prouder at the success of a difficult casting. He certainly had every reason to be pleased—I imagine that's much harder than casting a bell. Old Privy Councillor Demme, who was no man's fool, said to me once that to a criminologist a nice clean case of circumstantial evidence was what the correct calculation of the path of a comet was to an astronomer. I can understand that. To succeed in making an action speak more truly than the person who has committed it is no slight matter."

Etzel sat and stared. The man with the captain's cap became more puzzling all the time. Since he could not possibly be the Maurizius who was condemned to spend his life behind the walls of a prison, Etzel must find out what his connection with him was. What did the man want of him; why did he place himself in the boy's path, staring at him with his evil, squinting eyes? Had he instructions, a message? What kind of a message? Did he perhaps want to win the boy as an intermediary with Trismegistus? To get him to spy on Trismegistus? A frightful matter. If anywhere, here was "mystery." One had to be careful. One had to be prepared. Every smallest sign was of importance. While he sat there thinking thus, his face became white with a pallor which made it gleam like mother-of-pearl. Something began to tremble in the depths of his being and he ducked his shoulders as if a blow were threatening.

"What's the matter, boy?" the grandmother inquired in a stern tone. "I haven't been pleased with you for some time." She got up lightly, gave Etzel a pat on his cheek, and when he got up, placed her arm under his and went with him into the living-room. There she lit a cigarette and handed Etzel one, in a matter-of-course way, as though he were her household friend and shared all her habits. Then she took his arm again and walked up and down the huge room with him. "Now, confess," she began, "what's the matter? What makes you look like a shorn sheep? Are you having trouble at school? Last autumn it looked as if you were going to stand at the head of your class. Frankly, I don't place much value on that. Model pupils don't make model people. Industrious plodding does not make genius. Genius is industry, say the Germans. They might like to have it so. I think a good deal of you, you are my only grandchild, I am your only grandmother; if you had half a dozen brothers and sisters, perhaps I should have selected another among them than just you, for you are a little too crafty and a little too dreamy for my taste. One must have a lot in there"—she pointed to his breast—"if one has so much back of that"—she pinched the lobe of his ear. "Just the same I love you, only I am sometimes worried and afraid when I look at you."

She is a wonderful woman, thought Etzel. He smiled across at her—they were almost the same size—stopped short with a jerk and using the remnant of his smile in order to diminish the importance of the question, he asked: "Say, grandmother, where is my mother and why am I told nothing about her?"

It would be in vain to try to follow the complicated train of thoughts which induced him to make such an onslaught upon the widow's peace of mind. Perhaps it proceeded from the man with the captain's cap and the realm on the outskirts of which he had been browsing since his grandmother's story, perhaps it was a natural process, in which one of the pillars of his bridge of destiny quite naturally presented itself. In any case, the widow became stiff with fright and found him once again extraordinarily impertinent. Then her expression showed extraordinary irritation. He was certainly abusing her patience. It was only to trouble her that he had prepared a whole boxful of questions. Nothing was so distasteful to her as snapping question after question at her. One today, another tomorrow, the day after a third, so far she was willing, but a whole bombardment at once was beyond all bounds. Aside from that, she has eaten so much that she must rest, she must not gossip so much after eating, she feels oppressed if she does and can't sleep at night. Etzel is a nice little boy and is going home now. Love to his father, greeting to Rie. Goodbye. Then she pushed him, with an excess of bustle and loquacity, into the hall, took his head between her fine cool hands, kissed him on his forehead and eyes, with funny pointed lips, and closed the door noisily behind him.

CHAPTER III

I.

Dr. Raff seized the opportunity to talk to Robert Thielemann about Etzel. He was worried. Etzel was falling off disturbingly in his work. His lack of punctuality, his absent-mindedness, had given much cause for complaint of late. This had been hinted to Etzel but had not made any impression on him.

"It's a pity," said Dr. Raff, as they were walking up and down in the school hall. "I should be sorry to have to take measures about it. I don't like measures. What's the matter with him? Don't you know?"

Thielemann's chin protruded like a beak over his stiff, turned-down collar. The question flattered him; that he was unable to give an answer angered him; for about a week Etzel had avoided him as much as his other school companions. He admitted this hesitatingly. "I don't thrust myself upon him," he bellowed. "As far as I am concerned, let him do as he likes. Perhaps I am not distinguished enough for him and they've told him at home what to do."

"Shame, Thielemann!" said Camill Raff.

The unkempt boy ran his ten fingers through his shock of red hair.

His irritated contemptuousness was only intended to cover over his hurt feelings. "Perhaps the old man has gotten wind of my not being politically—well, how shall I put it briefly?—quite house-broken. At least for the baron's nostrils."

Dr. Raff repressed an ironical smile. "Oh, Lordie, these are our Marats and Saint-Justs," he thought. "I regret it very much," he insisted again in his Alemannic dialect, "very much. I thought that he had some confidence in me. He was always very confidential with me. That has changed. We ought to try to find out why. Perhaps you'll get some opportunity to get him to talk a little. Only don't be defiant, Thielemann. At the moment you are in the better position because he's in the wrong. Keep up some connection with him." He nodded to Thielemann and walked off. From behind he looked as though he himself were still a student, small, slight and flexible. Thielemann stared after him with irritation. No defiance, that's all very well, he growled to himself. Shall I throw myself on his neck? Fall on my knees and beg to be allowed to come to see him? He can wait a long time, he and his Andergast whom he seems quite gone on.

Boys of this age have their inviolable conventions of intercourse. These are adhered to the more strictly for having sprung up without discussion or agreement. Their origin is mostly as delicate and mysterious as their observation is a matter of course. It was a tacit understanding of this kind that Etzel should never go to Thielemann's house, that Robert visited Etzel Andergast, and never unless Etzel invited him. Etzel had only been a few times to the Thielemann bookshop. Now and again Robert had made some allusion to this, but only to keep up appearances. The fact of the matter was that he did not really wish Etzel to come, that he even dreaded such a visit. He had no room of his own at his disposal. He shared the room in which he slept and worked, with two younger brothers with whom he did not get on. That was, however, not the worst of it. There was no peace in the home in which he lived. There was constant strife between his mother and father. They offered their children the sorry spectacle of married people who could not be in the same room for two minutes without making bitter remarks and reproaches to one another. The thought that Etzel might some day be an eye and ear witness of this was unendurable to Robert. This explained in part the inequality of their mutual relations. The other part consisted in a feeling of social inferiority, doubly awake and developed in a spirit which was moreover rebellious by nature. The revolutionary attitude of a boy often has its roots in a disorderly household. In many bourgeois homes affection has been dead for generations. A heart must be rarely gifted if an unsatisfied hunger for affection is not to make it thirst for revenge. Such hearts are unusual.

2.

Etzel had discovered the petition of old Maurizius in his father's study. It was a petition for pardon. Peter Paul Maurizius, retired farmer and landowner, residing in Hanau, 17 Marktstrasse, requests the chief prosecuting attorney to institute and recommend the pardoning of his son, Otto Leonhart Maurizius, imprisoned for the past eighteen years and five months in the penitentiary at Kressa. Thus ran the superscription. The humiliating consciousness that he had lowered himself to prying, Etzel got over by means of some neat quibbling. He was sharply aware that the stealthy method he had chosen was dishonourable, but he justified it by circumstances which had left him no choice. It had been an animal-like scenting and tracking. The man with the captain's cap had played his part, similar to that of the ghost in Hamlet. Just look about carefully at home, his evil, inflexible, little eyes had said, look about and you'll find something. At each admonishment he thinks simultaneously of the writer of the letter from Switzerland. He would like to read the letter; secretly he hopes to find it in some drawer or folder. Look about and you'll find something; that thought does not leave him. The commanding hand of Trismegistus shows itself in the night, shining out plastically in the darkness. The picture of the chest of dynamite in the cellar constantly approaches nearer to reality. But there are more troublesome signals. Pedantic apparitions rise from the papers and blue notebooks with which his father's desk is laden and spread through all the rooms. Documentary ghosts have been haunting the Andergast house for some time, audible only to Etzel's ears, a nameless shadow-folk that only his eyes, which sometimes see shadows better than real bodies, can perceive. His sensitiveness in this regard has some of the characteristics of hysteria. There is danger that his constant preoccupation with the hidden and the secret will fill his mind with obsessions. But being a human being, equipped with the divine spark in his soul (though God knows where it came from), growing up in these surroundings, where human error and crime of every degree was daily called to account in atrocious numbers, where was afforded a forced resort to atonement, while a monstrous fist dragged the guilty pitilessly over it—he can in no case remain untouched by such visions. Probably the ghosts of legal documents already stood about his cradle and their lamentations lulled him to sleep. The very essence of destiny hangs over this house, and how is he, membrane that he is between the light and darkness of the world, not to feel it?

So he wanders from room to room in the quiet house under the command of the inflexible gaze of those astigmatic evil little eyes, tormented by a name, tormented by an undefined, legendary deed, hiding threateningly behind the name like a slimy mollusk behind the dark glass of an aquarium. He wanders again and again from room to room. It is a late afternoon towards the end of March, his father has telephoned that he is not coming home this evening, Hilde Sydow has announced her engagement and he has had his evening clothes brought to the office; Etzel must now distract and occupy Rie's attention. With unusual cunning he brings her his sport trunks, showing her a large triangular rent and appealing to her art in darning; at the same time he has wheedled from her a promise to make apple pancakes for his dinner, since the two of them will be alone. He knows that she will make them herself; she won't let the cook do that; she has a special recipe; moreover, she is glad that the boy, who has recently shown little appetite, should come to her to ask for some delicacy. "Yes, certainly I can do that, my boy," she says, and is thus made harmless for a couple of hours. Thoughtfully Etzel stands in the living-room; outside, twilight begins to fall, a bit of sky, like a pennant of pink and grey, glows through the window, the closed door of his father's study draws him on, he opens it and walks into the room with its smoky dark wall paper and disgusting odour of stale cigars, and remains rooted before the piles of papers. Pile on pile, they lie there in green and blue covers, each cover having an oval white shield with a neat penmanship label. He has never yet dared to open such a cahier, now he turns the cover of the top one over and finds the words "Petitions for Pardon" on the oval shield, and the first thing on which his glance falls is the name Maurizius. Such accidents are natural phenomena, elemental, conditioned by natural law.

The arguments of the former economist and property owner almost entirely lack the humility of the petitioner. A sullen, dogmatic tone is apparent. References to previous references in regard to alleged mistakes in the conduct of the proceedings. Very obviously, the reasoning is that of a layman. The petition seems to have been written without the assistance of a lawyer, perhaps because professional advice has so often been fruitless, and the writer wants finally to penetrate by means of his own logic. Thence the unadorned phraseology. What finally comes forth is far removed from logic, it is passionate statement, an obstinate reverting to the same point repeatedly, as if someone were knocking in the dark against a closed door, a convulsive impetuosity, appearing to spring from a delusion. At two points the name Waremme is mentioned. One can see that he functioned as a witness for the crown. The writer does not dare charge him openly with perjury, but one can read the accusation between the lines. More than that, it sounds as if this were something long known, a fact no longer denied by anyone, whereas possibly it was thus regarded only by the sick imagination of the writer. If the judicial authorities—so the petition went on—should decide to investigate the statements of this Gregor Waremme again, then there would still be valid reasons today, after almost nineteen years, for reopening the case. Perhaps then a different light would fall on a certain lady, most unfortunate of all unfortunates, whom it was superfluous to name. The words "most unfortunate of all unfortunates" were twice underscored and provided with two exclamation points in brackets, from which alone it was evident how little the author was familiar with the composition of an impeccable legal document. The head of the chief prosecutor's office had already written under it in red pencil: "Not to be recommended, Andergast." The former economist and landowner had no conception of how one ingratiates oneself; ten lines farther along he declares himself ready to tell the court where the witness Waremme, who has been considered as having disappeared, is now stopping, thus letting one perceive that he has been playing the policeman independently. Such amateur meddling is hardly calculated to increase belief in his trustworthiness in the eyes of competent authorities.

At the end, however, he rises to theatrical rhetoric. Is this Peter Paul Maurizius perhaps a religious crank who naïvely imagines that he can make an impression on the Prussian law by an imposing appeal in the biblical style? Aside from the ludicrousness of the assumption, there was nevertheless a note of truth which could not fail to be heard in the bombastic entreaty, at least subjective truth, and this made Etzel feel like Hamlet when the spirit of his father addresses him from the bowels of the earth. "Speak, poor ghost," he says with anxious dismay. The words engrave themselves upon his mind, he will be able to recite them; when he is roused from his bed at midnight and questioned, he will repeat them mechanically like a passage which he has learned by heart from the Gallic Wars: "By God and His holy angels it is a guiltless man who for more than eighteen years has mouldered alive in the stony grave of a penitentiary. He did not commit the deed for which he was sentenced, and if he had confessed it a hundred times (and he never has confessed it), and no matter how damnably the circumstantial evidence may speak against him, he was guiltless when his life was broken off in its full flower, guiltless when he took upon himself the yoke of atonement. And that I will announce to the world and for that I will vouch so long as there is a breath of life in my breast."

"Speak, poor ghost." . . .

3.

They were silly tricks which Etzel resorted to during the days that followed in order to deceive those who were observing him. With the same expenditure of energy and guile, he could have remained a satisfactory pupil instead of so falling off in his work that his teachers shook their heads over him. But just that was what he could not do. What he had been, to a certain hour of a certain day, now seemed to him useless and out of date. Something had taken place in him for which he himself lacked a comparison and a measure. A few days after the conversation between Dr. Raff and Thielemann the Easter holidays began; thus he gained time and was able for a while to withdraw his behaviour from public criticism. The only thing which he still had to do was to fool his father and Rie by pretending to be nonchalant, alert and good-humoured. As he walked along the hall he sang a little song to himself, in his room he could be heard humming a tune, when he met Rie he laughed at her pleasantly, if she asked him a question he answered gaily. When he was with his father he assumed a particularly willing and eager manner of listening and a way of agreeing with him with hearty eagerness and of saying obligingly,

"Yes, thank you; no, thank you," as if he were by no means harbouring purposes opposed to this hypocritical goodness and model behaviour. Even a person so profoundly familiar with human failings and surprising breakdowns of character as Herr von Andergast would have regarded the mere suggestion as a ridiculous slander. But if the apparently impossible did not constantly occur, everyone would be prepared for the possible at all times and life would be a simple matter. At present everything was still in the germ, perhaps the boy himself did not yet know much of it; what I have just called hypocritical was the result of a decision to attain clarity for himself, to illuminate the matter with intelligence and not to be guilty of any loose thinking and foolish enthusiasm. But in spite of all his "orientation towards mental freedom," as he expressed it with simple-minded scientific dryness, he could not keep himself from sinking, during school-hours, into deep water and becoming submerged in spite of his "clarifying" ideas. He could not help it; sitting half a day upon a bench and adjusting himself obediently to a presence which suddenly seemed to offer him no more space than a pea, was finally more than he was able to bear. Yes, on a pea he would have been more likely to find space than in these premises, among these men, while such a tremendous task was germinating within him. Thus it came about that on the street he would walk pedantically along the cracks of the pavement, keeping strictly to the mark only because of his wish to smother his "thinking," because "thinking" did not lead anywhere directly. He would count lanes of trees: an even number would mean, *wait;* an uneven would mean, *no time to be lost.* But wait; for what? Lose no time; in regard to what? What should be done? How begin? What indeed could be done at all? Who knew anything about it? From whom could he get advice? In whom could be confide? Who would not laugh, who would not be convulsed with laughter and say: Nonsense, boy, what's gotten hold of you? What are you thinking about?

You must be cracked, your brains addled. Really, seriously, who was there to whom he could turn? It was conceivable that a very noble young woman would understand what he was driving at and to what a decision he was being pressed slowly, unavoidably, necessarily. But he didn't know any very noble young woman. The world which he knew was in this respect ungodded, and such women and girls as he saw—for his grandmother was sexless—were as contemptible to him as the wax figures in the hair-dresser's window. It was in this respect a poor world, a masculine world, in which there was no Orpheus to regain Eurydice from Hades and Persephone. Nevertheless, one needs help, support, instruction, practical assistance, otherwise everything will become utterly senseless and come to an end before it has properly begun. And Etzel walks up and down his room, his left fist clenched against his breast, his right hand sunk in his trousers pocket, playing with his pocketknife and keys like a bank clerk. He is pondering, his brain is glowing and working in pictures, although he demands that it shall produce only logical thoughts. He does not always succeed, however, in compelling the instrument of thought to perform its natural function. He calculates that eighteen years and five months are two hundred and twenty-one months, or approximately six thousand six hundred and thirty days, and mark well, six thousand six hundred and thirty days and six thousand six hundred and thirty nights. One must separate the two; days are one thing, nights another. But at this point in his arithmetic he no longer sees, nor understands, there only remain figures which say nothing. It is as if he were standing in front of an ant hill and setting to work to count the crawling creatures. He wants to conceive what it means; six thousand six hundred and thirty days, he wants to form the conception. He thinks of a house with six thousand six hundred and thirty steps: too difficult. A box of matches with six thousand six hundred and thirty matches: hopeless. A bag of money with six thousand six hundred and thirty pennies: he can't get it. A train with six thousand six hundred and thirty cars: it does not become real. A book with six thousand six hundred and thirty leaves—mark well, leaves, not pages, for the two sides of every leaf would then correspond to day and night. Here he can reach some conception; he gets a pile of books from the bookcase, the first has a hundred and fifty leaves, the second a hundred and twenty-five, the third two hundred and ten, none has more than two hundred and sixty. He has overestimated them; he places twenty-three volumes on top of one another and then only gets four thousand two hundred and twenty leaves. With astonished eyes he lets it go at that. And to think that every day that passed for him meant one day more in the other place. His own life consisted of scarcely five thousand nine hundred days, and how long it seemed to him, how slowly it went! A week was often a trying tramp along a highway, some days stuck to one's body like pitch, one could not get rid of them. And at the same time, while he was sleeping and reading, going to school, playing his games, talking to people, planning this and that; and winter and spring succeeded one another, the sun shone or rain fell, night came and morning came—during all this passage of time the Man was there with the same passage of time, during the same time, always, always, always there. Before Etzel was born—an infinitely mysterious word, suddenly that: *born*—he was already there, that Man, the first day, the second day, the five hundredth day, the two thousand two hundred and thirty-seventh day. Etzel makes a gesture as if he were shaking off two iron hands clasping his shoulders, looks angrily, impatiently and wildly about him, seizes an ebony ruler and begins to "conduct." It is one of his games. As an eight-year-old boy he already liked to do this, now he returns to it seldom and only when he is ill at ease with himself and unable to master a mood of depression. He regards it as atavistic, a return to childhood and then has a fit of the blues as after a spree. His "conducting" consists in his singing at the top of his lungs a self-composed symphony consisting of reminiscences of all kinds of melodies, at the same time imitating the woodwind, the kettledrum and the brass instruments, swinging the ruler like a director's baton with fire and emotion. He is the orchestra, he is the music, he is the conductor; and the passionate enthusiasm, into which he sings and screams himself, finally draws the attention of Rie, who warns him with irritation to keep quiet; she cannot understand this stupid nonsense and draws his attention to the fact that his father is likely to return any moment. Covered with perspiration, very red in the face, the ruler still in his uplifted hand, he stares at her if he did not recognize her, then says with ill-humoured embarrassment, "Close the door, Rie, the hall is full of the smell of onions; it makes me sick."

4.

The next afternoon about four o'clock—it was a Wednesday—he appeared unexpectedly at the Thielemann house. He had himself shown into Robert's room, and suddenly stood before his amazed friend, who had not even heard him come in at the door. It was fortunate that Robert was at his school work, for at this time he had the room to himself. It was a large uncomfortable five-cornered room, with two windows looking out into the narrow court, and consequently so dark that one was already obliged to light a lamp in the afternoon. Thielemann needed some time to recover from his surprise; since Etzel had never yet been at his house, the situation was new, aside from the fact that he had reason to be angry at him on account of his recent inexplicable conduct. Moreover, there was a stormy atmosphere about the house today; Robert himself did not know quite what was going on. At lunch his parents had sat in icy silence, not one of the three boys had dared to open his mouth; at the last bite, Herr Thielemann had gotten up and left, his wife had gone to her room without deigning to glance at the boys; half an hour ago the father had returned, contrary to his usual custom; he generally played billiards until half past four and then went to the store. He was in the living-room; at times he left it, walked across the hall and banged the door behind him, then there was quiet again; but Robert did not trust this quiet, he knew that a storm might break forth at any moment. It was embarrassing to have Andergast come on just such a day as this, there were better days when one did not sit so on hot coals. He could not say a word; embarrassed, he looked for a blotter and stuck his pen behind his ear, a habit which Etzel hated because it made him look like a clerk in a drygoods shop; he had often told him so. But Robert had no mind to please Etzel. Matters were not to be as though there had been nothing between them. He blinked his eyes and stared attentively at the electric bulb which hung naked and unshaded from a cord in the ceiling. What he could see of Etzel by casting a few side glances at him propitiated him. The devil knows how that fellow does it, he thought, he's no sooner in the room than one forgets that one has anything against him. "Has anything happened?" he asked, while his glance wandered through the room as if he wanted to reassure himself that it did not make too objectionable an impression, and that the contrast to Etzel's pleasant room was not so noticeable to Etzel as to himself. "Has something happened?" he repeated. "You look so uncouth for your circumstances." Already involuntarily the considerate affection which distinguished his relation to Etzel from that to any of his other companions, showed in his voice, as he perceived to his own irritation.

Etzel took a breath. "I've been walking fast," he said, and seated himself somewhat shyly at the table opposite Robert. "I wanted to talk to you about something—that is, if you have the time? Not much; I haven't much myself; I must be home again by five. Only . . . it's a damnably delicate matter. You must be able to keep your mouth shut, Thielemann. Can anyone hear us here?" He looked penetratingly about. The corners of his mouth twitched like those of a child whose toy has been broken and who since then has believed he has discerned hostility in the world. It was always so with him, whatever his experiences might be and however decisive and mature his attitude towards them might be, something in his personality reminded one of an eight-year-old child.

"Go ahead," said Robert, more uncertain than he wished to show, "there aren't any listeners here." Etzel, with the palms of his hands pressed between his knees, was thinking with contracted brows. He did not know how he should begin. He bent forward and, lowering his voice, which was still immature and masculine in the middle register only, he said that in general it was repugnant to him when boys gossiped about their family affairs, it was the way of girls. But since at the moment he was in a difficult situation and had no more intimate friend than Thielemann, he had decided to appeal to him. Actually he only wanted an answer to a question of conscience. He did not want him to think a long time and to talk a whole lot; Thielemann was just to say yes or no, speaking from his instinct. It was the question of his mother. It was a question of the relation or rather the lack of relation between his father and his mother; this had recently become a source of painful conflict to him. "Do you understand me, Thielemann?" he asked with a bright friendly glance. Robert winced. "Not the slightest notion," he murmured with a motion as if he had gotten under the water-spout of a roof. His face became dark; he was not in the least prepared for such confidences and they seemed to him like irony, for he himself was completely under the pressure of a rift in his own family, and felt bitter over the evil of many years of strife and division. Father and mother, each filled with hate, each despising, hating, execrating the other, each endeavouring in blind delusion to get the sons to take sides. He was troubled by the suspicion that Etzel knew of this undignified state of affairs and was encouraged by it to unburden himself of the misery in his own family, out of pity as it were, and his petty middle-class pride rebelled at this. So distorted were his sick thoughts, such was the confusion of his soul. One must add, however, by way of an excuse, that he was not particularly intelligent, only kind-hearted and easily excited. His eyes had a pitiful hungry look as he gazed attentively at Etzel, he could not forget what was brewing outside in his home, but while he was trying to master his uneasy, listening absence of mind, his distrust towards his friend disappeared and the thought that Etzel spoke of the matter today for the first time suddenly moved him to tears. "I'll understand, all right, youngster," he said. "Get it off your chest."

Etzel nodded. "Listen," he said. He does not know his mother. He has never heard of her directly, or indirectly, he has only the scantiest information. He does not even know her address, only knows that she lives in Geneva, in Switzerland, or lived there until recently. Whether well or sick, rich or poor, alone or not alone, he does not know. He does not know why he knows nothing about her and is not expected to know. He does not know whether she is pretty or ugly, young or old. He has no picture of her, not even an internal one, since it is so long since she has disappeared out of his life, and every memory of her, for some reason that he cannot understand, has been obliterated, even all external marks, photographs, portraits. There has never been anything like it; she has been, as it were, erased: why? He cannot cease asking why. Certainly, she did not of her own accord give up her relationship with him, but what could have compelled her to do so? Had she committed a crime? Had she some feeling of guilt? It has never been known that a mother should leave her child in the lurch and forget it for such a reason. Therefore his father must be back of it. To ask him is out of the question. Two seconds afterwards, before one had noticed it, one would be out of the room. Rie is not to be considered. His grandmother, it appears, for some reason which he does not know, is kept silent. Decency forbids him to ask anyone else. Thus there is a conspiracy about the matter, a real plot. The centre of this plot or arrangement, whatever one may call it, is his father. It is he who has taken these measures, he holds the threads in his hands. He eliminates what does not suit him, in the way of knowledge, or inquiry or investigation. He is so, and he wants it so, and because he has the power, so it is. Etzel regards it as an injustice that is done him. He is undecided whether to accept the regulations any longer. At times it seems to him that to break this barrier with which he is surrounded is an internal command, it seems necessary to him too, in order to establish the balance which is lacking in his life. He makes a singularly intelligent comparison. He has the feeling, he says, that up to now he has only played one part of a musical composition, the bass; he knows quite well that he will never hear both hands playing simultaneously, but he would like to be able to hear the right hand play once so that he could at least put the two together mentally. The difficulty is that he would not care to deceive his father; he does not want to behave like a cad, he recognizes his duty as a son; obedience and duty are up to a certain point not merely empty words. His father has taken care of him in his way, probably has in his way a certain affection for him, one can't just simply ignore him; he is too big for that, too important, too much himself. "Now, tell me, Thielemann," says Etzel, getting up rather abruptly—and his eyes have those melting bronze sparks again—"you tell me what I must do. You are a just person; you feel and you think justly. And that's the point. Tell me. Shall I regard myself as bound, shall I endure it until some day it suits him to say to me: thus and so, this and that? Now choose, go to the right, go to the left, or remain in the middle; in any case, you know now. The clock has struck. But that will never be. That will never pass his lips. All right. Shall I stop bothering about it, shall I make myself independent and do— Well, as to the doing, we need not go into that just now. What it will be I don't know just yet, but in such matters one has to be prepared. What do you advise me to do, Thielemann? Don't think about it. You know the game: the table—is flying; the bird—is flying. There it's a case of raising one's finger quickly, tell me quickly what you think."

It was an unusually illuminating exposition, sensible and eloquent. It contained all the clearness and fearless honesty of a young creature who won't give up a halfpenny's worth of his moral insight. It was a question addressed perhaps not to Robert Thielemann only—he was perhaps merely a pretext, and the chance listener; it was directed rather to his companions in general, to his surroundings and finally to himself. The basis of it was perhaps the consideration that if he had once formulated the problem correctly and briefly, he could no longer fool himself about it. It was only a question of finding the courage to face the problem, that was the most difficult part. To have faced the problem squarely once meant to Etzel the attainment of a buoyancy, a freedom to act which were no longer related to the one particular question. This must be emphasized above all, and must be clearly understood on account of the many hidden strata in the boy's character, for all its almost lovable simplicity.

Robert Thielemann was in no hurry to answer. He got up awkwardly and walked around the table in his heavy boots, ran his fingers through his shock of red hair, struggled with himself and cleared his throat before he began to express himself. "There are two sides to that question: the heart side and the head side. Two horses that are not matched. I can't tell which horse will run better. You are in a certain way born in the silk. Silk does not tear as easily as sackcloth. You're a damned fine chap, but you nevertheless drag too many conventions or traditions, or whatever you want to call the stuff, around with you."

Etzel was no longer listening at all. He was smiling, silently. It was an intelligent, indulgent, disappointed smile. At the word "but" he had begun to smile. As soon as someone begins to say but he's of no use to me, he thought, and sitting down again, he took up a sheet of paper and a pencil and drew a horse with a stag's antlers, pawing the air excitedly with his forefeet. Thielemann had the same feeling that he had when he received his Greek examination paper back marked "unsatisfactory." His forehead turned red. "I want to tell you something," he said mysteriously, leaning over toward Etzel, "they keep us tied up short, that's the trick. And they haven't the ghost of an idea what's going on inside of us. We are moving forward and they are still in the eighteenth century. They don't know what's in store for them. Everything reeks of decay and demoralization. But they control the rations and that gives them the control of the situation. I'd like to smash a hole through the entire fabric, just like that." He snatched the sheet of paper on which Etzel was still smilingly drawing and angrily tore it in two.

At this moment a woman's voice was heard screeching shrilly and at the same time a man's furious shouting. It scarcely lasted three seconds. Then a door was banged. There was a silence just long enough to catch one's breath, then the door must have been opened again, for the woman's voice screamed louder than before, now complaining, then so shrill with rage that it broke. The man replied, from a greater distance than before, with frightful epithets and threats. Etzel jumped up; he thought there must have been an accident. He wanted to go to the door, but Robert seized him by the shoulder, and holding him fast with a distorted face, whispered through clenched teeth, "Don't budge, or you must deal with me." So it was this which he had feared to the point of trembling, which he had tried to hide like some disgusting rash on one's forehead, which had humiliated him and hung like a black cloud over his youth. He and Etzel were standing two steps from the door, he was still holding Etzel by the shoulder, his face was so white that his freckles almost looked black, like ink-specks on a piece of parchment. Etzel had cast his eyes down, and while listening to the revolting brawl he understood his friend's distress. He did not dare to look at Robert; then the voices ceased as suddenly as if they had been stifled by a torrent of engulfing sand, there was silence for a quarter of a minute, then someone began to play a waltz on a piano which was frightfully out of tune. There was nothing peculiar about this; it was one of Robert's brothers who was entertaining himself with music in the living-room, but the sequence, first the dreadful brawling, like a row in a tavern, followed immediately by the senseless waltz melody, showed such a lack of sensitiveness on the part of the player that Etzel could read the life story of this family like an open book. He shook hands timidly with Robert and whispered, "I must go now, Thielemann, it's getting late, goodbye." As he was speaking he was already out of the room, slipped shyly through the hall, and sprang down the steps. Mean of me to have run away, he thought, walking along Feyerleinstrasse in the rain, looking up at the sky with a wry mouth, but if I had stayed longer he would not have liked it either.

He walked more slowly, sunk in thought. After a time he stopped with a jerk. He pressed both hands against his breast, his heart began to beat quickly and he said aloud: "It's no use, I shan't be able to rest until I have been out to see the old man in Hanau."

5.

He wanted to go out on Thursday, but postponed it until Friday because his father was to go to meet some gentlemen that evening. He told Rie that he was going to the movies; please to put a sandwich on his table; if he came home late she was not to give him away, he certainly would not be home before eight. It was, however, almost nine before he returned, for he did not at once find Maurizius in his house; in fact, he had had to return for a second time an hour later. One of the occupants told him that the old man had gone to the Hare's Tavern around the corner, and Etzel looked in through the windows, but did not see the man he was after. He patrolled up and down the street in front of the long building in Marktstrasse and it was fully six o'clock before he saw the man with the captain's cap finally coming. The old man's rooms were on the courtyard, one had to ascend steps, resembling the ladder of a chicken-run, built on the outside wall, and when one had reached the first floor a narrow wooden gallery led to a door which opened directly into two uncomfortable rooms. Next to the door there was a door bell, under the handle of which there was a copper door plate with the inscription, "P. P. Maurizius, retired land-owner." When they had met in the street, Etzel had taken off his hat to him, but Maurizius had not returned the greeting; evidently he was seldom addressed, he probably had not many acquaintances in the city. Etzel followed him into the court, waited until he had disappeared through the gallery above, then he followed him, knocked gently at the door; when there was no reply he pulled the door bell, but he did not hear any sound, the bell itself seemed to be missing, so he knocked more loudly, whereupon the old man finally opened the door. He looked at his visitor distrustfully. With his head uncovered he looked so changed that Etzel at first thought it was not the same man. His skull was so narrow that it reminded one of the butt end of a gun and a frightful red boil stuck out like an incandescent light bulb through a few bristles of flour-white hair. It was uncertain, nor did Etzel learn later, whether at the first glance he recognized the young man whom he had followed about so obstinately for a few days. From his expression one could not tell. Etzel said, "I should like to talk to you," and the old man without saying a word invited him with a mumble and a wave of the hand to come into the room. Inside Etzel gave his name; Maurizius nodded and seemed in no way astonished; one might have thought that Etzel was a daily visitor. The old man pointed to a chair with his stiff left arm, took a tin tobacco-box from a drawer in the table and began to fill his short pipe. There was nothing striking about the furnishings; it was a lower-middle-class room, containing a table, bureau and wardrobe, a mirror hanging askew, all cheap department-store furniture. The only unusual thing in the room was the piles of old newspapers on plain board shelves, two or three dozen packages tied together with strings, on the front of which were labels on which was written in blue pencil: 1905, 1906, 1907; Preliminary Investigation, Proceedings of the First Day, Proceedings of the Second Day, etc., Foreign Opinions, Legal Specialists, Psychiatric Specialists, etc. There were pamphlets too, everything that had been printed about his son's crime and trial.

"I have sent in another petition," began Maurizius, sitting down on the sofa which was covered with black oil-cloth tacked on with white porcelain-headed nails, and convulsively drawing at his pipe, "so that the solicitor-general's office may not fall asleep. Of course, it's like spitting into the wind. Has anyone sent you, young man? Or have you come of your own accord? What the devil has prompted you to come? In former years, many people came. Even in nineteen-nine it was sometimes like the office of a fashionable doctor. Audiences given daily. Writers, lawyers, spiritualists, editors. Even Americans. For twelve or thirteen years there has been silence. Even battlefields are still when peace has been concluded, no matter how filthy a pretence of peace it may be. What do you want, young gentleman? So far as I can see you are a damned young gentleman."

His voice reminded one of the croaking of a crow, although he did not speak loudly but yapped out certain words hoarsely, opening his mouth wide so that his grey-green side whiskers with the unpleasantly naked looking ear lobes back of them seemed to grow directly out of his pharynx. Etzel admitted that he was young and gave his age, adding however, which sounded somewhat bold, that up to now he had not been able to convince himself that years alone sufficed to save the world from stupidity and meanness. Maurizius threw him an irritated glance; then he chuckled to himself and the chuckle ended in a long attack of coughing which only ceased after much spitting. Etzel was sickened, but he concealed his disgust and said with a pleasant attempt to begin a casual conversation that he hoped that Herr Maurizius would forgive him his youth. The wish had arisen in him, he did not quite know how, to hear the truth or at least the facts in the Maurizius affair, even though he could not promise that he would be in a position either now or later to be of any use or assistance. Who indeed would believe such a promise? Perhaps, however, it would not in the end be a waste of time; in any case after much hesitation he had come with the hope that he was not going on a vain errand. He brought forth his appeal with a mixture of embarrassment and naïve persuasive warmth which it is not easy to describe. If his grandmother, the general's widow, had seen him with his legs crossed and his hands folded over his knees, she would probably have broken into sarcastic laughter and would have called him, as she sometimes did, an illuminated dwarf.

The old man sank into profound silence. His pipe went out.

6.

His life had been a simple one which had become more and more sombre, to be sure, with the march of time, and had finally culminated in a single ruling passion, the struggle to prove the innocence of his son. His marriage with the daughter of a clergyman from the Upper Rhine had given him four children, three sons and a daughter. He had a property near Gelnhausen, the chief return of which was wine-grapes. He had lived a carefree life with his family. In the summer of 1900, an epidemic of typhus broke out which in the course of two weeks carried away his wife, his daughter and his two elder sons. The youngest boy, Leonhart, was at this time twenty years old and was studying at the University of Bonn. He had always been the favourite of his father, who regarded this Benjamin of the family as unusually gifted, and was partial to the point of weakness towards his talents and feminine delicacy. After the catastrophe of his fourfold loss, the father's preference and partiality had become idolatry. He was the boy's father and mother at the same time. If he did not receive news of him daily he became uneasy. He met all the boy's demands for money—not overmodest demands they were—although the returns on his property diminished considerably every year and the construction of a rather large wine press proved an unfortunate speculation, on which he was obliged to take out heavy mortgages in order to meet his obligations. Leonhart paid no attention to this. He was assured of a brilliant career, spoiled by his fellow students and professors, welcomed in the best society, and the expression of a happy conqueror had become disarmingly natural to him. His father did not dare to rob him of the illusion that as the only son of a man of property he had unlimited means at his disposal; on the contrary, he trembled at the idea that one day his son would come to recognize the true situation. Every distinction of Leonhart's, every examination which he passed, every aristocratic connection which he made, and which the conceited young man faithfully reported to him, gave him as much satisfaction as if he had begotten an amazing genius. The dreams which he had for the boy ran very high, far beyond Leonhart's own ambition, which perhaps culminated only in the desire to live well and pleasantly, to give himself up without effort to distinguished tastes, and to cut an imposing figure in the world, on the good opinion and approval of which he laid the greatest stress. Shortly after Leonhart began to teach at the university, the enlightenment which his father had so much dreaded took place. It was a question of a gambling debt of three and a half thousand marks which had to be paid within twenty-four hours. The old man did not have the money. He could only procure it with the greatest trouble. A money-lender lent it to him at a usurious rate of interest. Leonhart was dismayed. Father and son had at that time a long conversation—it lasted a whole night over a bottle of liqueur—in the rose-bedecked summer house in the garden. The upshot of it was that Maurizius formally begged his son's forgiveness for not being able to place at his feet the wealth which the boy rightfully demanded, for it seemed to him an almost unparalleled success to see the scarcely twenty-two-year-old boy teaching at a university and recognized as an authority in his subject. Two months later Leonhart's engagement to the widow of a well-to-do paper manufacturer, whom he had met while staying in Kreuznach, took place, and six weeks afterwards they were married. He informed his father of both events, the engagement as well as the wedding, in only a few hasty words. Maurizius' dismay was so great that when the newly married couple, towards the end of their wedding trip, came to visit him for a few days in his country-place he still seemed struck dumb and did not even take proper leave of Leonhart when they left. Leonhart, not without eagerness, seized this opportunity to feel himself offended, and withdrew himself from his father, pretending that he did not notice his father's disappointment and resentment. The fact was that he had become weary of his father's devoted tyranny and, moreover, he was ashamed of him, of his unpolished manners, his simplicity and his lack of culture. Like a bourgeois snob, he was glad to place a discreet veil over his antecedents. Also, he no longer needed the old man, for his wife had brought him a dowry of eighty thousand marks, the fortune which she had inherited from her dead husband, for they had not had any children.

Elli Hensolt, now Frau Maurizius, was a Jahn by birth. The Jahns at the end of the century had still been a respected family in the Rhineland; the notary Jahn had occupied the position of Mayor of Remagen during the last years of his life and was regarded as a leader of the Centre Party, which he had served with distinction during the *Kulturkampf* episode. He did not, however, succeed in making his pile. He did not rise with the dizzy boom of the country; he was perhaps too decent or not skilful enough to put aside for himself any of the golden superfluity with which he was surrounded; and after his death his family, though not poor, were limited to a modest income and slowly dropped back into insignificance. Besides Elli there were two other children, a son who fell as a first lieutenant in the African colonial struggles, and a second daughter, Anna, who was eighteen at the time of Elli's marriage.

There were many circumstances which fostered Peter Paul Maurizius' disinclination towards the marriage and his hatred of his son's wife. The first was that the Jahns were Catholics. Although he himself was not in the least a pious Protestant, not even a regular church-goer, Maurizius clung to the established traditions of his family with that puritanism which is a mixture of the pride of the peasant, obedience to family tradition and the consciousness of belonging to a progressive community. But he might have become reconciled to this betrayal, since he had done nothing to prevent it. It was worse that the woman was neither attractive, pretty nor elegant and had no advantages which struck the eye. Nor had she any distinction, either of birth, good connections, or money. Eighty thousand marks was a pitiful sum judged by Leonhart's worth, Leonhart's future, Leonhart's possibilities. The worst point, however, was that she was fully fifteen years older than he. A woman of thirty-eight and a man of twenty-three (and this man Leonhart!), there was no getting over this. Leonhart had thrown himself away, he had been snared by an intriguing woman, he had been taken to salvage a leaking ship and soon his magnificent youth would be a broken remnant of the past. This was how the old man looked upon the marriage and since he firmly believed that Elli had robbed him of his son, stolen the boy's love, hardened Leonhart's heart against his father, and condemned him to a frightful loneliness, soon his embittered mind knew no other passion than that of revenge. If he wished to continue to live it was only in expectation of the repentance and return of the beloved prodigal. He counted upon this, in his dark sorrow he hoped and waited eagerly for some tremendous revenging stroke of Fate. It came, but it came differently from the way he had anticipated; it destroyed him too.

7.

For the first two years the married life of the couple was unclouded. Leonhart's friends had always acquitted him of calculation in regard to his marriage, had even angrily denied every accusation of the sort, recognizing no other motive than friendship, inclination, attachment and gratitude. They said that the woman had saved the very volatile and easily misled youth from the dangers which his own character presented. They maintained that the woman held him with a firm hand and that it was due to her that he was less irritable and vacillating and had less of a mania for people. Love: who could penetrate into this remarkable relation and distinguish that which was "real love" from that which was mutual respect, mutual understanding and the exercise of those qualities which built up a harmonious existence. What indeed was "real love"? A theory for readers of novels, time had stripped this conception of its iridescent cloak of falsehood. The woman at any rate was attached to him, was capable of making sacrifices for him, had faith in him, was unceasing in her attentions; perhaps this was "real love" and the fact that his own was perhaps not quite so "real" was not very important and need not cause people to rack their brains over the situation. It is certain that it was at this period that Leonhart Maurizius published several of his most esteemed studies and that there was talk of his being appointed by the government to do research and travel in Spain.

But after a certain time public opinion changed in regard to the Maurizius marriage and there were rumours of discord. It was said that Elli had found out about Leonhart's relations with a dancer. This relation had existed a year before the marriage, but it had resulted in a child, a little girl, and one day Leonhart was warned by a lawyer of his duty as a father to support the child, the mother having meantime become destitute. Leonhart had kept the matter from his wife; she knew nothing of the whole incident; on the other hand, he confided the matter to his sister-in-law. Anna Jahn undertook to care for the now two-year-old child; with Leonhart's approval she took it to England, to a friend and distant connection, the superintendent of a home for governesses, who kept and brought up Hildegard Körner, which was the name by which the child had been christened. Curiously enough Leonhart loved the motherless child—the dancer having meantime died of tuberculosis in Arosa—with a kind of poetic infatuation, although he did not know her. This feeling grew and in later years never left him. Anna Jahn understood and encouraged this, whereas Elli, after she had been informed of the matter first by an anonymous letter and then enlightened as to the facts by her husband, fought jealously against it, and could not even bear to have the child mentioned before her. From this time on Anna Jahn appears inextricably bound up with Leonhart's life. After the death of her mother she had left Cologne, where they had lived, had spent a few months in various cities, had then come to Bonn, where she was soon a daily guest in her sister's, her brother-in-law's, house. Opinions differed as to whether the disastrous influence which she had on Leonhart, and on his marriage, began at once or only became evident after a time. One did not need to be a prophet in order to foretell a bad ending to such a situation. There are conjunctures of fate which are almost platitudes—although in this case there was a personality involved who, although at first in the background in the course of events, raised the situation above the level of the bourgeois commonplace. The astonishing beauty of his young sister-in-law could not leave a man like Leonhart untouched. Anna Jahn was at that time at the peak of her blossoming; whoever saw her was charmed. Students gave her serenades and sent her poems, the officers of the fort sought introductions to the families with whom she associated, when she appeared on the street people stood still and stared. For a time she was the subject of conversation, like a great singer or actress; young girls would say, "I have seen Fräulein Jahn," as if they were speaking of an exciting adventure. Elli should have hesitated before opening her home to her sister; she herself had advised Anna to settle in the city; she did not want to feel that a sister so much younger was unprotected and alone in the world. Thus she produced her own unhappiness. Leonhart at first was unfavourable towards Anna. He said that she was unsympathetic to him, that she irritated him. Anna at times treated him with a sarcasm which was so delicate that he did not dare to regard it as sarcasm, and so offensive that he would have died of shame, had he admitted that he understood it. Towards other people she expressed herself more openly, as for instance when she smilingly pitied him as a little schoolboy living under the supervision of a strict elderly lady. All too soon the division between the couple—created and widened by nature—became evident. Strangers occasionally asked whether the lady on whose arm they had seen Maurizius was his mother. No, was the smiling reply, it is his wife. Oh, the person would reply frightened, and remain silent. The malicious epithet of "schoolboy" was not entirely unfounded. Elli controlled her husband's every step. She supervised his appointments, his work and his hours of work, his reading and his mail, his conversations and his expenditures. She was not stingy, she even made him handsome presents, but she never let him have charge of large sums. She was too intelligent not to realize the mistake she was making, but the instinct to keep him in leading-strings as long as possible, at any price, predominated. When he went out he was obliged to tell her at exactly what time he would return. From the appointed time on she would not take her eyes from the hands of the clock, and if he were late, she began to tremble as if in a fever. While waiting thus she felt herself aging. She would sit before a mirror and see herself growing older. She would seek corroboration for this in people's eyes and deny it when she received it. Meantime there was already talk about Anna Jahn and Leonhart going on. They had been seen together in a museum, on an excursion, or at the house of a friend. There was whispering. Elli understood what had befallen her. She pretended not to have an inkling so long as she had a spark of self-control left. She realized that every day he drifted further from her and she clung to him with the strength of her despair. And all this was only the beginning.

8.

Meantime old Maurizius sat like a spider in a net, waiting patiently. For a time he hired a detective to bring him news of his son and of what was going on in the boy's house. Thus he discovered the story of the child Hildegard, had the traces followed and made every conceivable effort to obtain possession of the child. With his peasant-like cunning he thought that this would put a trump-card in his hand. But he did not succeed. He heard of Anna Jahn. He had the young girl watched. He heard of dissensions between Leonhart and his wife, of growing discord, of secret scenes and of the scandal gathering over them like a cloud. He was content. It was grist to his mill. But when one October night Leonhart appeared at his house unexpectedly—he had come as he said in a friend's automobile to say goodbye before a long journey—the old man was frightened at the distraction which he perceived in the face and bearing of his son. He at once had the impression that this goodbye visit, at an impossible hour of the night, was only a pretext. Why this polite consideration after three and a half years of brutal forgetting? There could not be a word of truth about it. Leonhart talked all kinds of inconsequential nonsense; finally he came out with it: he needed money. He did not dare to demand it, he only hinted at heavy obligations. But when he perceived the old man's stony face he gave up all further attempts, all further dissimulation; he only cared about getting quickly away again. The old man did not keep him. If Leonhart had fallen on his knees before him, he would not have given him ten cents so long as he did not hear from his mouth the words: I am free from the woman. And there was no very great degree of acting or pretence when he coldly accompanied his son to the door without shaking hands with him. This was the same man who, after his son's condemnation and while he was serving his time, worked to accumulate a fortune: for the son. There was no hope for him of ever seeing the idolized boy again during his lifetime, of knowing that he who was condemned to life imprisonment was enjoying the capital laid aside with such determination; nevertheless, he arranged his existence and took measures as if he could count upon it with certainty. He had succeeded in selling his property profitably; after paying off the mortgages he had thirty-five thousand marks left. With an incomprehensible prophetic foresight, he had deposited this sum in a Swiss bank—it is said of true maniacs that they fulfil their single purpose with outright clairvoyance—and he lived on a fraction of the interest. He lived as if in an almshouse, his flat was a pigsty, his suit was the same from year to year, his meals consisted of sausage, bread and cheese and in eighteen years the thirty-five thousand marks had become sixty thousand francs. He was seventy-four years old, the thought that he might die before Leonhart left the penitentiary did not enter his head; he did not fear death, for it had no reality to him.

9.

Etzel only later pieced together the picture of this past from the many details which he absorbed one by one. Later on he had several conversations with Peter Paul Maurizius; they met at an appointed place not far from the Andergast house. With senile feeble-mindedness, and because all plans and attempts up to the present had miscarried pitifully, the old man looked upon the boy almost as a divine messenger and paid no attention to the ridiculous difference of age, becoming more talkative than he had been in twenty years. Nevertheless, he still remained cautious. But the boy had him bewitched, as the saying goes, and he did not think it impossible that Etzel could help him in his great cause; and while he imagined that he was slyly enticing him onward, the boy, who was at least as sly as he, was sounding him about everything which he wished to know, and he was giving the boy important sections of his carefully collected material. Although Etzel thus obtained a fairly accurate knowledge of the events, as well as of the relations of the participants in the affair, and with his fresh clear vision could survey the confused interplay of interests, he understood equally well the demoniacal darkness of the world in the background, which in its totality seemed to him more insoluble than the acts of individuals. Very low; completely apart from all that had made up the "world" for him up to the present; this was why it was so insoluble. This was one of the reasons why he kept himself from any premature conclusions and behaved like an eager student in a police study course.

When the old man shook off the sleep-like torpor—into which he fell every day or every night, like a drunkard into intoxication—in order to decipher the past and to devise some comprehensible formulation, his first occupation was to thump out his pipe and fill it afresh. In doing this, his bony yellow hand trembled; meantime he began to talk. People who have spent a part of their life time thinking over one and the same material, eliminating all other events and bringing all of the people with whom they come into contact into a relation of dependence on this material, presuppose in their listeners a complete understanding and even become angry when they are confronted by their mistake. In addition to this Etzel at first did not understand the senile babble of Maurizius and at times fearlessly interrupted him with a friendly: "What did you say, please? How was that?" The old man would make a defensive gesture with his right hand, get up, shuffle over to the shelves of newspapers, pull out a pile and throw the yellow pages on the table. Then he would walk up and down with his hands in the pockets of his trousers. It became dark, the wretched lodging had no electric light; on the bureau there was a tiny oil lamp; Maurizius lighted it, it flickered and went out, he cut the wick and lighted it again, assisting himself with his stiff left arm, grumbling at the lamp-chimney, which had a crack in it. Etzel observed and listened with tense interest to the old man as he performed these tasks. His words became plainer, his coughing and spitting ceased. When the lamp was finally burning, giving not more light than a stable-lamp, he pointed to the papers, upon which the dust which had been raised began slowly to settle again, and said that one could read everything in them, how the matter had begun and how it had proceeded from the revolver shot to the arrest, from the twenty-fourth to the twenty-ninth of October of the unforgettable year.

"You can find it all there, young man. If you like you can also believe what you see printed. The whole world believed it at the time, the commission, the examining magistrate, the reporters and the readers. One person repeated what the other had said or wrote what another had written. No one asked himself: how could he have shot at her while he was still at the garden gate? That had been established by the witnesses. I entreat you to remember, young gentleman: by the garden gate. Eighteen paces away. At quarter of seven on the twenty-fourth of October when darkness had completely fallen. I entreat you to remember. Can one shoot a person through the heart with a pistol at a distance of eighteen paces in complete darkness? An honest answer, young gentleman! No. She was running towards the house when she was struck. Waremme testified to that under oath. A shot from behind. From behind into the heart. Moreover, the testimony of the maid, Frida Weis. His wife at first went towards him from the gate of the villa. As was quite natural. Just notice: he has returned home from a trip. He is carrying a leather suitcase in his left hand. The husband is returning from a trip, mark you; his wife is expecting him. What would the wife do? She would go to meet him. Or wouldn't she? Don't you think that his wife would go to meet him? Or not? Well, then. Nevertheless, a shot in the back. Enormously improbable, don't you think? The reports of the proceedings? They get around it. It is explained. It is explained against him. Everything is explained against him. He had the pistol in his right hand, it is said. And who saw that? Waremme. He saw it and swore to it. Waremme even swore that he saw him lift and point the revolver. And I ask you, where was Waremme standing, young gentleman? According to his statement, under the acacia, precisely three yards from Elli. What did Kleinmichel, the messenger boy with the telegram, who entered the garden immediately after the report, state? He said Leonhart stood at the corner of the house. In front of him, not behind him. In front of him, I beg you to notice that he stood in front of him, so he must have gotten there ahead of him. But the court was of the opinion that Kleinmichel must have been mistaken, otherwise the whole story does not agree, otherwise the net does not close. Or Waremme swore to a perjury. And what was Waremme doing in the garden? At six-thirty-five he was still said to have been seen in the casino. Various persons, persons whose word is incontestable, all agreed on that. From the casino to the garden gate is twelve hundred and forty-three yards exactly to an inch. You will have to admit, young gentleman, that one must do some tall running to cover twelve hundred and thirty-four yards in ten minutes. And how did Herr Waremme explain that? He explained it thus: that Anna Jahn had telephoned him to come at once, she felt so uncomfortable, there were suspicious figures wandering about the house. Suspicious people, a quarter of an hour before a murder, magnificent, isn't it? That's what I call seeing ghosts! Thereupon Herr Waremme runs as though the devil were after him because he can't find a carriage in the whole city—hi, hi! Of course, no one saw him running in the crowded thoroughfare in fine weather with one street-lamp burning close to another. The little bit of fog would not have prevented anyone from seeing such a huge man jumping along like a goat. Have you ever seen such a collection of contradictions brought together? Well, and the examining magistrate! He was not troubled by any misgivings, God forbid. Unswervingly towards the goal. For the goal he already knew, the path thither was for him to build. It went as smooth as silk. Motives as numerous as the sands of the sea. Evidence enough to feed the pigs. It all hangs together magnificently, there is not the tiniest hole in the net. It is an unimportant circumstance that the alleged murderer denies the crime. This certainly need not disturb them; they are sure of their work. But perhaps—I am of the opinion—I submit—one does not stand there with such angelic calm from the first minute to the last, O public and mighty court, one does not repeat two thousand times with such angelic constancy: I did not do it. To the judge, the lawyer, one's father, one's friends, the jury and finally from the penitentiary again and again: I did not do it. He should not have fled. I admit that. Colossally stupid. To run away like a schoolboy. To hide at a girl's in Frankfurt for two days, to go to Kassel, to Hamburg, to shave his beard; of course this was before, that shaving of his beard was done before, living in hotels under a false name. The boy lost his head; he could no longer tell black from white. When they arrested him up there and it was said: under a strong suspicion of murder, he stood as if struck by lightning. Then he exclaimed: What, gentlemen, me! Note that, young gentleman. Me! Like a person waking from a sleep. He does not know about the warrant for arrest, or about what newspapers are full of. This was then attributed to his craftily playing a part, just this. If a person has a clear conscience he gives himself up and does not wander around the world for a week, isn't that so? Formula F, as clear as ink! Ye almighty gods! They can hear the grass grow."

He ceased, panting. A frightful fit of coughing prevented his speaking further. Etzel stood up and screwed the smoking lamp; when the hideous sound of coughing died down, he remarked to his fingers: "Why, there must have been two revolvers—"

Maurizius stared at him with his mouth open. "Why that?" he stammered. Surprised at his surprise, Etzel explained: "The woman was shot in the back. She was walking towards him, he was walking towards her, it is said. He had a revolver in his hand. Who then had the other revolver?"

The old man closed his mouth slowly like a nut-cracker and began to swallow his lips. After a time he murmured with a dark smirk, "Quite right. But there was never any talk of that. That was never assumed officially. The assumption was that she ran first towards him, then away from him. A theory, isn't it? You know what a theory is. When a person has a theory ten horses can't drag it away from him. What does he care about the reality? The theory ran: When she saw him with the revolver in his hand, she was greatly frightened and turned and ran towards the house. Quite plausible. Two revolvers? No. The story is that not even one was found. Waremme maintains that after the shot was fired he wrested the weapon from his hand and threw it away. Tossed it into the shrubbery. Three specialist detectives searched the garden and the surroundings for two days and did not find it. Nothing. The revolver had disappeared. It never appeared again. What do you say to that? Inexplicable, isn't it? It's splendid how inexplicable all of that is." He snickered foolishly.

Etzel stared ahead thoughtfully. Suddenly he lifted his head and asked: "Who could—who then do you think—"

"Pst!" The old man interrupted him with a sharp sound.

He walked up close to the boy, squinted frightfully and said with the sullen severity of a village schoolmaster: "Not so prying. Not a sound. Where the devil would we get to? He himself, understand, my Leonhart himself never answered that question. Never. Not a sound. Not a syllable. He refused to. You understand, young man. What use for us two to ask about it? How could it even help us to know? Waremme's oath stands against it. Waremme's oath covers the whole matter. It is a strong refuge, such an oath. Just see, there was Anna Jahn, the beautiful, noble, unhappy Anna Jahn. Well, what makes you stare so ridiculously?"

As a matter of fact Etzel looked taken aback when the old man screeched out the three adjectives with furious contempt.

"That's what one read everywhere at the time: the beautiful, noble, unhappy Anna Jahn. Immediately after that evening she became very ill. Six weeks she lay close to death. So it was said. She had to be spared. No excitement, for heaven's sake, no excitement. After six weeks she was sent south. In Nice, or the devil knows where, she deposed her testimony. She did not reappear until the main trial. The whole court was dissolved in pity. It was a pleasure to see how considerate the presiding magistrate was at the examination. Put the answers nicely and palatably right into her mouth. And the solicitor-general, Andergast, was sugar and honey. For she too had almost become a victim of the monster. The pure virgin seduced by a good-for-nothing. Suddenly no one knew anything more about any gossip. It is only a marvel that the professors and clerks and officers and students did not get up a torch-light procession in her honour. All at once she was as pure as a dove, and he, my God, for him no word was bad enough. Only the people—the masses—thought differently. After the verdict matters looked bad for the Jahn woman for a few hours. Well, that's beside the point. But what was

I about to say . . . what did I want to say? Ah, yes: Waremme, but for his testimony—you understand—the matter would have ended differently. The man ruined us. The man, I tell you, goes under a curse. Or there is no God in heaven." There was suddenly again that biblical pathos; Etzel's head sunk. "The man—I hope his last hour has not yet struck. I hope it for our welfare and for his, for he is not to be envied his deathbed. Of the other person I don't want to speak. It seems to me that she already has her reward here below. There are all sorts of rumours. But the man—there is still judgment on earth for him. Yes, yes, yes!"

Etzel looked at the clock. "I must go home," he said, frightened. The old man nodded. Etzel asked him whether he might take some of the papers with him, he wanted to read them. The old man nodded. He helped him to choose them. When Etzel was already in the hall he ran after him, gave him a few pamphlets besides and implored him to take good care of them and not to lose any. "I'll be careful," Etzel promised, and set off at a slight run in order to catch the train.

CHAPTER IV

I.

ETZEL spent that evening and the afternoon and evening of the following Sunday reading the old newspaper articles. He said to himself: I must examine them and remain as cool as a moderately curious spectator. Since it was a question of newspaper writing he was doubly careful. It all sounded like a novel. He did not in general care for novels. An eager pupil of Melchior Ghisels, he differentiated sharply between poetry and vision, on the one hand, and facts which had been purposely bent according to will, on the other. In this regard he was dispassionate to the point of insensibility. The romantically adorned daily records were therefore an abomination to him. They were ghostlike, viewed over a gulf of eighteen years, a tricked-up corpse, dancing. . . . Many individual traits, however, remained untouched by this, these grew out of the truth of nature which no titivation can impair.

During the following days—for he still had a whole week of vacation before him—he developed a feverish secret activity in his attempt to get new facts and clues. He wanted to corroborate the accounts of old Maurizius, whose subjective point of view was unmistakable, to find corroborations for those newspaper accounts in so far as he suspected them of exaggeration or distortion in one direction or the other. But where look for such support or such corroboration? And if he did find them, what justified him in regarding them as more reliable than what he had discovered up to the present? He did not trust people's memories. He knew by instinct that every truth is forgotten in order to make place for a pleasing illusion. It was this which gave him his profound disinclination for history. He was always wont to smile when old people narrated incidents of their own past. It was so amusing, so easy to see how they "fantasied" and how much more pleasure they got from the half-lie than from the whole which they apparently no longer cared to recognize. The only person who might have helped him in these investigations, who might have assisted him in getting over his first doubts, was his father. But the mere idea of asking him, particularly him, was absurd. Never would Trismegistus acknowledge the justification of a single question; the violet-blue eyes would become frozen with surprise at such extraordinary audacity. So there was nothing left but to collect data in silence and to sift and compare the matter which was collected. Rie had an acquaintance who came to see her once or twice a week, a Distelmayer, Councillor in Chancery, who had been employed at the court and who had been pensioned since the war, a man who was badly off, because, like all retired civil servants living on pensions, he scarcely had enough to eat. Rie always kept lunch for him when he said that he was coming; then the same play would begin; he refused the invitation in the most decisive terms, stating that he had just had a hearty meal. Then apparently worn out by her persuasions, he would yield and devour soup, meat, vegetables and dessert to the last bite with a satisfaction pitiful to see. At times, Herr von Andergast walked through the hall when Distelmayer was just arriving, or leaving. Then the Councillor in Chancery would bow with a servility which was very unpleasant to Etzel, and Herr von Andergast would be affable, he would pat the councillor on the shoulder with two fingers and ask as one colleague of another, "Well, how are things going, my dear Distelmayer?" Although Etzel had not much hope of finding out anything useful from the somewhat talkative little man, he nevertheless made the attempt; he spun a web of candour around him, the effect of which he had tried out with grown-ups. He put himself on his level, and this was a different condescension from Herr von Andergast's, merely from the fact that a young man with intellectual pride must condescend when he deals with so worn and crushed a person as the councillor. Etzel began the conversation with jests, in order to give the old man confidence; he permitted him some little personal sarcasms and jokes such as older people like to express towards boys, then he easily turned the conversation upon serious matters, casually dropped the name of Maurizius and saw the councillor become attentive. He said that someone had told him a lot about the matter and that he was interested in it, he and a friend had had a discussion about it. The friend in question was a distant relative of the Jank family, or no, what was her name, it had escaped him; perhaps the councillor remembered the surname of the wife's family, the sister of Maurizius' wife? He had by no means forgotten the name, he only wanted to try the councillor out; the latter at once mentioned the name and showed that he knew far more of the case than Etzel had expected, that he had once been seriously interested in it. Etzel only wanted to hear about Anna Jahn and about her life after the criminal trial was over, for he had something particular in mind. As a matter of fact, Distelmayer was able to gratify his curiosity, it was a weakness of his to acquaint himself with the private life of people who had been the objects of public interest and been involved in a "case." Many people who have been connected with the law have this inclination, resulting from a mixture of the desire to pry and the fascination of an unsolved riddle. Distelmayer had even interested himself in the Maurizius case in the capacity of an author; he was half puzzled and half flattered at the keen interest of the young baron—he always emphatically addressed Etzel as "Herr Baron" which seemed silly to Etzel, who did not, however, dare to protest, for fear of putting the old man out of humour. Not less flattered was Rie, who sat quietly by during the whole conversation, taking in with eyes and ears the alertness, knowledge of the world and conversational gifts of her Etzel. At such times she claimed him with particular pride as her own, her property, the fruit of her care and would exchange secret glances with the councillor in order to get him to admire the boy. Etzel observed this and felt the ridiculousness of the situation, but what did that matter to him so long as his efforts were crowned with success? He realized anew that one cannot get anything from people by direct methods, not even from the most harmless, one always had to outwit them and deceive them about what one wanted; it was a constant setting of traps.

As to Anna Jahn. This had no longer been her name for a long time. In 1913 she had married the director of a big brick factory, a well-to-do man. Before that she had been abroad for a long time. No one had heard from her, she had not sent any news of herself to any of her former friends and gradually she had been completely forgotten. The death of her sister Elli had made Anna the sole heiress of Elli's whole fortune, but Heaven knew what she did with it, when she returned from abroad she had nothing left. The councillor knew this from a junior judge whose aunt had formerly been intimate with Anna Jahn. Over the whole of the inhabited earth there is a net of such relationships, so that no one can really stand outside of it, and only the impossibility of surveying the confusion of threads running from all to all places, puts the imprint of chance upon the laws of combination. To this aunt Anna Jahn had come one winter evening more than twelve years ago, broken in body and soul, inexpressibly tired, carrying a little trunk like a maid out of a job, lonely, silent, poor. From whence she came she did not say, what she had gone through she confided to no one, she had a panic timidity at meeting people whom she had formerly known; it was soon realized that she was in a dangerous state of mind. It happened once that someone, a guest of her friend, carelessly spoke, without recalling her presence, of Leonhart Maurizius and of the still—as the speaker thought—"unexplained case." Anna became white as a sheet, began to tremble and fell to the floor in convulsions which lasted for hours. After this she fell into a condition of depression and illness and was housed in a sanatorium. Then she recovered slowly and even regained some of her beauty and bewitching charm; in the institution she met a Herr Duvernon, from Lorraine, upon whom she made a deep impression, but whose offer of marriage she could not decide to accept until three years later. It then seemed that there was no reason to regret the decision, one heard little about her, for so few people knew of her existence, but what transpired was not disadvantageous, nor did it suggest a lack of Fortune's favours. She lived with her husband in the neighbourhood of Treves; she was said to have two children; a retired life was her greatest happiness; she scarcely ever left the house, had no social intercourse with anyone outside of her immediate family circle. The dangerous attacks of illness returned more and more infrequently, and gradually it seemed as if she had completely forgotten her dark and troubled past.

Etzel listened to the account with silent attention. With his usual clearness of thought he drew the conclusion from the old councillor's story that there was no opening in that direction, as far as could be seen, that the door was barred: and this was later on proved to be essentially correct.

2.

In the nature of things, the figure of a public prosecutor will arouse little sympathy, except from the lawyer, even when he brings the most damnable crimes to expiation. Probably this is because the prosecutor does not know the person, does not look at the person, must not know the human being, must not look at him. For him there exists only the action and the weight of the action and the necessity for retribution. He ceases himself to be a human being, the voice which calls the guilty to account is no longer the voice of a human being and does not wish to be heard as such; lifted above factions into a realm devoid of pity it is impersonal, it is the servant and the agent of the commonwealth. This is how he is regarded, this is how he thinks of himself; but only a character of great dimensions can develop in such an occupation and fulfil itself, while the smaller man by stretching and overreaching himself incurs a complete disparity with the task and only shows his own inadequacy. The countenance of the man who mercilessly demands retribution congeals into the grimace of the police official.

Never had Etzel seen the figure of his father so freed from fatherhood as while the boy was reading the reports of the law court of eighteen and one-half years ago. He was constantly obliged to keep before his consciousness: I was not even alive at that time, was so to speak not in the game, nothing depended upon me, nothing revolved about me, it all took place without the Etzel who was now undeniably thinking, sifting, acting and striding through the world with his eyes open. This made the time seem illusory and his father, whose participation in the incident which occupied Etzel, daily more and more began to rule all his thoughts; he was frightened by the boundless scope of his father's intellectual form, by his immense personal effect. He sometimes seemed to the boy's mind a sort of Comte de Saint-Germain who at the trial was already opposed to the apparently guilty Jean Calas, to the undoing of the innocent man. It was the first time that his father's professional activity had been made real and alive through the dramatic description of the whole legal procedure of investigation, pleading and verdict. Since his last promotion, which gave him dictatorial power, Herr von Andergast only appeared in the court room upon extraordinary occasions. Etzel could not grasp the picture, nor adjust himself to it; the recurrences of the name Andergast, which should now and again have reminded him of his own existence, seemed to the living eye to have no relation whatever to himself. There was a sinister hostility about it which no suffering could move, no exclamation, no outcry, no proof, no argument, no anguished face, nothing. The condemned man came in and went out, the metallic inexorable question addressed to him was not, Are you guilty or not? It was, Do you or don't you confess, do you or don't you submit? The passage of time, eighteen and one-half years, had in no way altered this; there was still the same passionate desire to catch the man, the same unshakable assumption of knowledge of the act, it cut into the present like a voice from the adjoining room and Etzel, as if the voice were addressing him, striking his ears, jumped up, rushed to the door, bolted it and ran up and down the room pressing his hands to his ears. He had to force himself at the table, during the "evening conversation," to remain unconcerned, to be submissive to cross-examination, to listen politely, to assume the appearance of one grateful for being instructed, instead of rising and walking up to his father to ask with all of the urgency and electrical tension which was in him: Were you convinced of his guilt? Did you really and truly at the time believe that he had committed the deed? His questioning eyes were fairly clinging to the big stern reserved face, to the forehead cased in armour. Of course in vain. There are human relations which would at once break if at the decisive moment a decisive understanding were reached. They only endure because this does not occur.

The opportunity nevertheless presented itself for him to see the participation of his father in the Maurizius case in a different light, and from this he could realize the opinion which had been created among some of the superior intellectuals. This information came to him through Professor Förster-Löring, the sociologist and economist, a man whom Etzel respected, whose merits he had often heard Camill Raff speak of with admiration. An uncommonly homely man, deformed, with a broken nose turned to one side. His two sons, twins, were classmates of Etzel's; he had often been at their house. Herr von Andergast approved the association. Just now they invited him again, the Ellmers and Schlehlein were there too. When tea was being served the professor joined the boys. His presence always started some fascinating conversation, something or other led to a discussion of modern legal administration, a subject which was just beginning to be a "burning" one; the young people felt that it touched the life and marrow of the nation. Etzel, full of only the one subject, like a hanging bell which responds to the touch of a breath of wind with a dull metallic sound, casually mentioned the name Maurizius as if he wanted to find out whether the professor knew the case and whether he were inclined to express himself about it. The professor looked up in surprise. "Curious that you should mention the case, Andergast," he said, "I alluded to it in a publication only recently." Ho-ho, he too, thought Etzel. "It seemed to me from the very beginning to be symptomatic. Yes, an extraordinary case in more senses than one. Have you looked into it, or heard anything special about it?" Etzel blinked, jerked about uneasily on his chair and made some flimsy reply, whereupon his companions looked at him curiously. "Well, the allusion is not remarkable," continued the professor in friendly tones, "the connection is quite natural, since it was your father who conducted the case at the time. It was said that he was actually its leading spirit. It required his strength, his courage, his superiority to overcome the difficulties with which he was faced. I admired him greatly in that struggle. For it was certainly a German *Hic Rhodus, hic Salta;* Germany was faced, so to speak, with a moral decision in which it could choose between ascent or descent. On the one side, there was frivolity, pleasure-seeking, thoughtlessness, irresponsibility, on the other, conscience, discipline and duty. Once again the better side was victorious. I still remember your father's closing speech. It was a remarkable performance and should have been posted on all of the walls and advertising pillars. I know that there were strong subterranean currents in favour of the accused; the movement has not entirely died down yet, just as there are still enthusiasts who regard Caspar Hauser as a martyr. But what does that prove? We older people who lived at that time and kept our eyes open have no doubt about the unfortunate man's guilt. For that, of course, is what he was, less a criminal than a weakling, unstable and lazy to the very depths of his soul."

Etzel kept his head bent. A superior stubborn little smile played about his lips. He might have spared himself the allusion to Caspar Hauser, he thought, he does not help his cause with that, we know better about that—he had interested himself in the story of the foundling and read much about it—only what he said about father was fine, excellent! He slowly lifted his eyelids and looked with his short-sighted eyes at the faces one after another. There were beautiful and ugly faces; the ugliest, although also the most expressive, was that of the professor. Just as in everyday life, at sport or at his lessons, for example, Etzel often found his short-sightedness trying, so at other times it was a source of pleasure to him in his intercourse with people, because he saw their features and even their bearing in a dim glow which made them better-looking.

3.

The question to put to old Maurizius was: where is Waremme? They met at a little coffee-house near the Guiollettplatz; it had been raining for hours, they walked on a few crossings to Christ Church and took refuge under the porch. It was the second time that they had met in this way in the city, by appointment, of course, but the first time Etzel had not been able to ask the question. The old man had held him breathless by the story he had told and afterwards Etzel had forgotten everything else; he had stolen away from the old man, stumbling along so absent-mindedly that he had gone into the wrong house on Kettenhofweg, and when he had noticed this and turned around, he had fallen down the stone steps by the gate, without, however, hurting himself. The story consisted in the account of how Peter Paul Maurizius had spent the five hours before the pronouncement of the death sentence with five of his acquaintances, all old men. God knows what it was which caused him to recall this episode of his past. He began it quite of his own accord, as though it were an occurrence of the previous week, which he had not yet had time to tell about. Absorbed in himself, with his pipe in the corner of his mouth, he told the story in a screeching voice, interrupting himself to spit frequently.

It was this. The solicitor-general had finished his plea, the second, which was even more damning than the first, and to which the lawyer for the defence—a poor, dried-up man—pitiful to listen to, after the ringing speech of "bloody Andergast"—had replied but briefly. The presiding judge gave instructions on the legal points of the case, the jury withdrew, the court room and the audience made up of all kinds and sorts fell into a fever of tension. Peter Paul, led on the right and left by two friends, who had already come with him from his home, left the seething mass, reeking with the venom of sensationalism. It was certain that the jury would take hours to consider the matter and cast their votes. The two men who accompanied Peter Paul insisted on his going to a hotel to await the decision. One was a revenue official from Lorch, the other a miller from St. Goarshausen. They asked a young junior officer, the nephew of the revenue official, to bring them the verdict without delay, as quickly as possible. The hotel was scarcely five minutes away from the court. The object was to spare old Maurizius, to help him over the period of waiting. The officer promised to remain at the court and when the verdict was reached not to fail to hurry. Peter Paul did whatever they pleased. He did not contradict, nor express a wish. In front of the gate of the court house—it was already evening, a cold August evening—two old men joined the other three with silent sympathy, one an optician also from St. Goarshausen, the other an insurance inspector from Langenschwalbach. All four followed Peter Paul into a large room in the hotel, in which stood an immense round table. At this table the five men seated themselves; Peter Paul Maurizius was by far the youngest; the revenue official, who was the next older, was sixty; the optician, the oldest, was seventy-eight. They ordered beer; a glass was placed in front of each man, no one touched it. Thus the five men sat five full hours in uninterrupted silence and waited for the verdict. When the fourth hour was over the miller got up heavily and opened the door into the hall. All understood him. He did it in order that the messenger might find the room more quickly, and that they might at once hear him when he came from downstairs. The last hour. There has not been such an hour since the world began, young gentleman. It was a small hotel, the stairs, of wood and uncarpeted, were right next to the entrance. Finally at twelve minutes of twelve there was a ring downstairs, after a time the door creaked, again after a time heavy boots sounded on the stairs; all five men, interpreting the slowness of the steps correctly, knew the verdict. It was as if death itself were walking up the steps. Then the young soldier appeared on the threshold white as a shroud, the five old men got up, one deep sigh coming simultaneously from all five: "Condemned to death."

4.

"Where is Waremme?"

Maurizius considered. He pulled his shabby cap deeper over his forehead. It seemed as if he could not decide to reply. "Nothing has been heard of him," he grumbled.

"One might well imagine that the ground had gotten too hot under his feet. He was in a hurry to disappear. Not a soul spoke of him again, nothing further was heard of him up to the present day. He had left the country. Just like Anna Jahn; she too had gone away. Where? Well, in 1908 it was said that they had been seen, he and she, in Deauville. Deauville, was that the name? A watering place? In France, isn't it?" The old man took the pipe out of his mouth, held it in front of him with his stiff arm and fixed a repulsive cross-eyed glance upon Etzel. The boy's eyes grew big. "What was that? That was new. A rumour; only a rumour? Seen him and her? Who saw them? Who was the reporter?" Maurizius shrugged his shoulders. "He is said to have worn a beard at that time," he added sarcastically. "Yes, one man shaves, the other provides himself with hair, that is the way of the world, young Herr Andergast." He chuckled hoarsely and spit upon the stone tiles. An old gentleman with a slouch hat, who came up in front of the ill-assorted pair, fussed with his umbrella and fumed about the weather in low tones. When he had gone on, Etzel asked what kind of man Waremme had been. "Had been?" Maurizius exploded, "had been? I hope to God there's no had been about him, that there is no breath of had been about him. Had been!! We certainly would be stuck in the mud then. Had been!" An expression of rage played about his blood-shot eyes. "I mean because it's so long ago," said Etzel, politely excusing himself. "It's hard to say anything about him," the old man said sulkily, rubbing his jawbone up and down like a horse whose mouth is being cut by the curb. "The devil knows how one's to describe him. It's incredible if one thinks what he was then and what he is today." He paused. He had evidently said more than he wanted to say and blinking and bewildered he looked for matches in his pocket. Etzel looked up with curiosity. Here he was on the trail of a discovery. His expression urged: on and on, and involuntarily he seized the old man by his coat sleeve. Maurizius had finally found the matches, but he pushed them back into his pocket unused. Somewhat helplessly he began to picture the Waremme of "that time." Etzel at once felt the incompleteness of the picture. The person was doubtless beyond the old man's horizon. He knew a lot of facts but had no conception of their meaning. Where interesting mental conditions mirrored themselves even in this vulgar account, every connection was lacking and events became improbable. Two years before the misfortune—the misfortune was the hub of all events—Waremme had turned up there and at once taken the whole university by storm. What was he? Well, a philosopher or something of the sort. A writer or scholar without any official connection. He never accepted an appointment, perhaps he was not offered any; he enjoyed his independence. He sometimes gave free lectures. People came from a distance to hear him. The professors were beside themselves, they spoke of him as a prodigy. When he went into society, men and women crowded about him and were completely bewitched by his talk. Waremme said this, Waremme said that, then there could be no contradiction. Particularly a few of the privy councillors and some of the big manufacturers from the Rhineland were quite crazy about him. The explanation lay in his having occupied himself, besides his own subject—in what particular science he worked Maurizius did not know—particularly with politics. "If I remember correctly, there were two things he threw himself into particularly, war with France and the Catholic Church. The Jesuits, of course, were behind that. Where did he come from? No one really ever found out. He said that he had come from Silesia, was the son of a baronial landowner, his mother had been of the nobility. But the estate was probably in the moon. When I investigated later no one had ever heard of any Waremme property. He had no fortune—he admitted that himself, even boasted of his poverty; but he could be seen in the casino at the gaming table almost every day. In spite of the fact that they don't accept anyone there who has not a handle to his name, they took him in. Sometimes he lost considerable sums without anyone asking where the money came from. If he had five hundred marks in his pocket today he would give a party tomorrow which would cost him a thousand and to which he would invite the entire city. They all came. They came, although in time remarkable stories about him began to circulate. There was a smelly story about some arrangement in regard to a loan. Then there was the suicide of Lili Quästor to whom he had been engaged, the daughter of the Quästors in coal. One fine day the girl took her life; no one discovered why. It was simply hushed up; we are great at hushing things up. So long as the privy councillors and the coal barons protected him he was safe. Finally, however, he was played out; those kind of people scent things, even before all the excitement they had silently withdrawn; and even if there was nothing against him at the finish except that he had been the friend of the murderer Maurizius, that was enough, that finished him, that was enough."

"Well, where is he now?" inquired Etzel with professional determination. Maurizius behaved as if he did not understand. It seemed as if he hesitated to show his cards about this point. His glance took the boy in shyly from head to foot. Then he whispered: "That's my secret and if I betray it to you now it must remain our secret. Give me your hand on it." God knows what he promised himself from the "secret," but Etzel strengthened him with a handshake. He continued still hesitatingly: A year and three-quarters ago he had found out that Waremme was living in Berlin. Under a changed name. His confidential man, a shrewd old fellow, who cost him a lot of money, had succeeded in finding him after great difficulty. They had only been successful because they had tracked him secretly and with great care back as far as Chicago, where he had lived eleven years, from 1910 to 1921. After much searching, through the intervention of a detective agency there, they had succeeded in finding several people who knew of his change of name and who had known him under his former name in New York, Pittsburgh, and Kansas City as well. Unfortunately there was not, however, very much that could be done with all this information. Of course, one must keep one's eye upon him, one could never know what might happen; in case anything should happen, it was well that one could seize him at once, but what should happen? As matters stood there was very little chance of seizing him, one could not get anything on the man, he was protected on all sides, he had nothing to fear; at least, nothing from him, P. P. Maurizius, certainly nothing from Leonhart. No, there was no hope, if there was nothing else scored against him and such a slick rascal would be able to take good care of himself; there was no way of getting at him. To watch him, yes, that was important so that he could be seized at any moment, and he had a man employed for that who, in turn, had people on the job; there was nothing besides that but waiting. The old man stared darkly into the rain. Was Etzel mistaken, or did he really hear a choked wooden sort of sobbing unlike any sound that he had ever heard before? "And you went to see him?" he asked with astonishing divination. The question had forced itself only because the old man had been trying to prevent it since the beginning of the conversation. And he started with fright, his face grew pasty and he obstinately remained silent!

"And what happened then?" Etzel continued, with apparent innocence, looking at Maurizius in a friendly way. He still refused to answer until Etzel gently pressed his hand on the old man's breast. "I made a confounded ass of myself," the old man said harshly. "What could I do? What did I want? I could have no peace before I had seen him. Well, so I went there. He calls himself a private teacher. And that's how he's registered in the City Directory. Private teacher Georg Warschauer

Usedomstrasse, corner of Jasmunderstrasse. On the first floor there is an eating-house. 'Frau Bobike's Lunch' is the sign on the door. He takes his meals there. He doesn't need to pay anything because he gives Frau Bobike's two sons lessons. He lives on the third floor. His pupils come to him there. Other people come too. He teaches English, French, Spanish, Italian, Portuguese, writes obituary notices, articles for newspapers and business advertisements. Well, then, I went there. And I saw him there. Then I stood up on my two legs and thought: *'Oh, Christ!'* And when he looked at me I said, 'I think I have made a mistake.' I turned around and went at once to the station and took the train home, fourteen hours at a stretch. There wasn't anything to be said. Anyway, what can one say about it? How can one engineer the matter? With what can one begin? And supposing he did throw one down the steps, what then? One can't intimidate such a man. And if I say one careless word it will spoil everything at one stroke and he'll disappear again. I didn't so much as mention my name. There wasn't even the possibility of intimating to him: man, human being, or anything of what has been burning up in me all these years. I realized that too late. Dear Christ, no!" He began again to search for his matches with uncertain movements and Etzel looked ahead as if distrait, he might have been making observations about the weather.

"I must run along, good night," he said suddenly, and ran out into the rain, leaving the old man standing still in surprise. When he had turned the street corner he retarded his pace, stuck his hands into his trousers pockets and began to saunter along easily. Twilight came, the lights were burning in the shop windows, he stopped at every third show-window and looked at the display, humming to himself like a street urchin. What was the reason of this good humour? It looked like an unbridled desire for enterprise, accompanied at times by little outbreaks of gaiety. When he entered the hall of the apartment house from Kettenhofweg, he ran into the two daughters of Dr. Malapert, the oculist who lived on the first floor. They were young girls of fourteen and seventeen; he knew them well and greeted them intimately and as they walked up the steps together he began a lively conversation, asking them whether they had been to the Städel Museum yet to see the exhibition of ancient Greek sculpture, whether they had gone to the automobile races, and whether they were going to Professor Coué's lecture, at the same time making them laugh by standing on one leg like a stork in order to tie a shoe lace which had become undone. Above, Rie was just opening the door for him, he almost threw himself on her neck, said that he was frightfully hungry and danced about her chattering, his eyes gleaming the while as if he were rejoicing over some successful prank. Rie made him understand by some huge winks that his father was already home, and at work, pointing to a door over which hung a cloth portière and putting her hand over his mouth. "I'll be quiet, Rie," he whispered, "walk up and down with me a little to make the time pass." He took her arm and pulled her into the back part of the hall. "Why should the time pass?" asked Rie in astonishment. Etzel replied: "Because it's unendurable how long it takes until one is a month older." "Silly," replied Rie. "With you time is already beginning to run backwards," Etzel jested; "my time and yours will probably meet somewhere, I think, and be rude to one another. Neither will want to give in, like two stubborn mules on a bridle path." During this conversation they walked up and down comically keeping pace with one another. "Just listen to me, boy," said Rie suddenly, and looked about carefully. "Because you are so nice today I'll tell you something." She was only whispering the words now: "I believe that your mother is no longer where she was; a letter has come from her from Paris; she seems to be in better health; I have the feeling that she may soon come to our neighbourhood. But what they are writing to one another about recently"—she pointed with her thumb back over her shoulder somewhat fearfully towards Herr von Andergast's study—"I don't know. For Heaven's sake, don't betray me." Etzel stood still, freed himself from Frau Rie's arm, looked at her earnestly and let forth a long shrill whistle. "Oh," he said—nothing further—and sank into thought. All that can't alter anything, he thought, pressing both of his fists against his breast. Whether it was on account of the whistle, the noise of conversation, or because he was finished with his work, Herr von Andergast appeared upon the threshold of his room and looked with frosty surprise in his violet-blue eyes along the hall towards the pair standing opposite one another. Rie quickly turned away towards the kitchen. She regretted her communicativeness. She had only wanted to see what the boy would say. His expression and his silence made her uneasy. She was full of jealousy towards the unknown woman who had "forgotten her duty" and who could call herself mother without being so in anything but name. She had wanted to feed her jealousy and was dissatisfied because she had been successful. "Good evening, father," said Etzel shyly. Herr von Andergast let a few seconds go by in observation before he answered slowly in his deep voice, "Good evening. You seem remarkably cheerful, my son."

It was no longer true.

In his room Etzel tore a page out of a notebook and wrote upon it, "Bobike, Usedom-Jasmunderstrasse," and hid it under the lid of his watch.

5.

Etzel was already clear in his mind about the practical feasibility of his plan when he tried to discuss its moral justification—its theoretic side, as it were—with Dr. Raff. Camill Raff was waiting for Etzel to approach him. When the boy telephoned to ask whether he might come about eleven o'clock, Dr. Raff nevertheless felt it suitable to postpone the meeting to a later hour in order to appear somewhat less willing. Also he did not ask him to come to his house, which would not have been very convenient anyway because his young wife was sick in bed, but arranged the meeting in Miquelstrasse at a spot near the Palm Garden. Only when he saw the boy hurrying towards him—it was promptly at half past three—did he realize how fond he was of him. What interrogatory force there was in those sparkling eyes! When someone questions me thus, I am an idiot if I imagine I could answer him and he is an amiable hypocrite if he behaves as if the answer were profitable. Camill Raff knew a lot about the young persons with whose guidance he was entrusted. Unfortunately, it was a guidance which could not satisfy him, it was only a partial sort of thing because he was fettered by so many subterfuges and regulations from those in control and there was so much distrust and so many reservations on the part of the boys that the time was perhaps not distant when his machinery of thought would get rusty, too—up to now he had not been swamped in sterile pedagogic dogma, he had as yet no sacerdotal sense of infallibility. He had imagination, and whoever has this gift is constantly receiving when he gives and striving where he teaches. Therefore, he did not need—like so many of his older colleagues, who wanted to keep up with the times while they were panting behind them—to fear being suspected of being an eye-servant; people believed in his fellowship because he had the courage to keep away entirely from whatever was equivocal or mendacious. He lacked only one thing: good health. He had delicate nerves and was not equal to any exertion; during the sunless winter months he walked about like a shadow, depressed and unable to work.

Etzel Andergast had long been one of the few favourites with whom he associated personally. Some natures have a brilliancy like fresh polished steel which has just been hammered in the forge of God. They are pleasing by their newness and a sublime kind of fitness, as if they were intended to attain something quite special. Camill Raff had only recently become aware of what was new about Etzel. It was about a month ago that he had had a discussion with him about a painful incident. Karl Zehntner, the son of a bankrupt salesman, had during the gymnastic lesson taken a five-mark note out of Etzel's jacket, which was hanging up among a lot of other articles of clothing. The thing was quickly discovered, for fat Klaus Mohl had observed the thief and the money was at once found in his pocket. The matter was reported and Zehntner was expelled from the school. Etzel went about for days devoured by doubts. He had rather liked Zehntner, he did not regard him as bad—not as worse than most of us—as he somewhat cuttingly observed to Robert Thielemann—then, too, his parents, as was later discovered, were in desperate straits. He thought that he should not at once have made a row about it, that they could have settled the matter between themselves, that with the help of his colleagues a sharp penalty might have been inflicted without destroying the boy's future. He asked Camill Raff directly whether he had behaved properly. Raff replied that he did not see how he could have behaved differently; the tribunal of schoolboys which he hinted at would only have led to unpleasant results. Then he dropped the remark: "You must be careful, Andergast. Certain events in life are flattened by our becoming too emotional about them. Emotion is a rolling machine; it makes everything broad and soft." Etzel was taken aback. The word reminded him of the leitmotif of Trismegistus and surprised him, coming from this source. He felt himself decidedly misunderstood. His danger did not lie there. He rather imagined it lay in the opposite direction. He shook his head and did not speak of the matter again. Intelligent Camill Raff was not particularly proud of himself when he thought of the conversation later on. He feared that he had lost ground with the boy. who could be as resentful as only low, or at times really great, natures can be. He did not at once find out wherein he had erred, probably he did not trouble himself too much about it, it was too difficult to listen to the many voices and to do justice to the many demands made upon him, as well as carrying on his own life with its suppressed ambitions and financial limitations. Sometimes the face of the boy would rise up before him, always in profile, his head always up, boldly cut, with lines of obstinacy and no trivial softness, and he would have an inkling that he might have been wrong in his pronouncement. Today he became certain of it in the first five minutes. The boy was strikingly changed, in quite a different way from that which he had seen when he had warned Thielemann; perhaps there was even some impertinent superiority in him, something which made fun of the teachers who frowningly gave him a bad mark.

But what has happened to him? Quite a job to pump him! He is sly and reserved. Camill Raff does not want to scare him, he is feeling his way over thin ice. When the boy with his questioning and assistance decides to make certain revelations, he seeks at first to avoid disapproval as well as limitations. It's useful to reach a clear understanding about matters, to work out things clearly, to take a position, to weigh and measure. Then when one has to act one seizes the matter from the intellectual standpoint and proceeds methodically and gradually. "Yes, all right," says Camill Raff, repressing an ironical gesture, "certainly, certainly." He's still tacking about rather hopelessly. One can't reach a determined goal unless one can eliminate passion, Etzel brings forth with the expression of an analyst, steeled against all the storms of thought—he is once again entirely the "illuminated dwarf." "Of course," admits Dr. Raff a little anxiously, placing his hand upon Etzel's shoulder as if to hold him back from some break-neck plunge, "of course. That's how one saves oneself trouble, above all one saves oneself from the unforeseen. An excellent method for getting out of the way of phantoms. Talking, dialectics, you are becoming more and more attracted by both and consequently there is also something—how shall I call it?—something unlonely in you. Yes, I'll call it that. The unlonely. But this unlonely state is at the same time the unconscientious. I mean from a broad standpoint. Because responsibilities accumulate. Because the original perpetrator of a deed is lost in the crowd. But that would not be so bad. Anonymity is in many respects a fine thing. But, you see, Andergast, conscience is in turn related to science, with a particular kind of knowledge, therefore, too, with judgment and with law; language is so deep, so wise; who is to determine how much conscience is necessary in order to act—there are so many inaccessible depths?" He stopped, frightened by the boy's eager, thirsting expression. The "break-neck jump" was evidently a jump into ice-cold waters. Not all organisms can stand icy cold, and certainly not a sudden plunge, thought Camill Raff, made tense by Etzel's manner. They all live with their heads now, at least they want to; that's their official motto, if you like. That's why the reproach about too much feeling irritated him the other day. That's the solution of that. Fine, fine and well, better than living without thinking, better than living by means of tepid, worn-out feelings, by means of which my generation still think they are models of progress. We have not gotten very far with the politics of the heart, that's a fact; the so-called heart has become a debtor who can't pay. These youngsters with their methodology, with their "working things out clearly," with their "taking a stand"—horrible words—they have handicapped us for the time being, as they put it, and we must be glad if they still accept a bit of bread from us. And I'm not sure that they'll thank us if they do it.

He sighed. And Etzel smiled while Dr. Raff was expressing his thoughts aloud. Perhaps he only smiles because the other has sighed, perhaps, however, he has felt and understood everything, for he has a delightful understanding. He feels and spans the whole wide world, he knows everything and has grasped everything, that is why he smiles. He looks up again confidentially at his teacher and takes pleasure in his handsome young face. For a time they walk along silently side by side. In his confidential effervescence Etzel suddenly drops some tentative hints which throw some light upon his condition and betray the fact that he is undergoing a serious crisis. He speaks of a dilemma in which he finds himself which forces him to a decision, a determination which would involve the serious adoption of a principle. It is a question, he continues with lively, gesticulating eloquence—it is a matter not of resistance; one cannot resist the air which one breathes, one can only withdraw from it, and that is a ticklish matter because one cannot tell beforehand whether one will be able to breathe better in the new air which one will then breathe. Therefore, it is not a question of resistance, still less of contradiction. Camill Raff, noticing at times the eager gestures and the quick change of expression in the boy's dark face, wonders whether he has not some Jewish blood. "When nothing is said there can't be any contradiction; understand, Dr. Raff, what I mean to say. I am between the devil and the deep sea and I must try to get out of the dilemma." He stood still, pressing one fist against his heart and putting the index finger of his other hand upon his nose, an amusing gesture of helplessness.

"Come now, let's have the whole story," said Camill Raff encouragingly. "Up to now you have only spoken in riddles, my dear boy."

Etzel made a dash, turned to Camill Raff and asked: "Tell me, doctor, is there ever a conflict of duties?"

Raff perched his head to one side. "Hem, you're touching upon an ancient and much debated problem in ethics," he replied smilingly.

"You are dodging," continued Etzel earnestly, almost

imploringly, "but I want to know. Are there conflicting duties, or is there only one duty?"

"You must explain yourself more clearly, Andergast," said Camill Raff, driven into a corner and astonished at the boy's categorical tone.

"All right," nodded Etzel, "all right. But you may not accept the explanation. You will naturally hold it against me that I am only sixteen. Yes, all right. By now, sixteen years and four months. You're twice as old, aren't you? Thirty-four? Thirty-five? Really. Frightfully old; thirty-five. Good heavens, when it comes to the point I have been sixteen years in the same spot, in the same house, in the same room, I'm not a dunce; I already know people pretty well except for that trouble of being short-sighted. I'll have to get a pair of glasses, although Dr. Malapert is not in favour of it. As I see it, what does it matter, sixteen, or nineteen or twenty-five? One can't fold one's hands in one's lap and wait, what's gained by getting older? There are cases where it's a question of now or never." He became involved in his own words. Camill Raff, more and more astonished, stared at him. "What are you driving at, Andergast?" he inquired in a low voice, feeling as if he must take the little boy who was all aglow by the hand and say: "Calm down, child, don't hurry so. One thing at a time, don't rush."

"Just answer me this question, Dr. Raff," began Etzel again, snatching as he eagerly talked at Camill Raff's sleeve, as he had done a little while before with old Maurizius. "Just answer me this one thing. A man has been many years in the penitentiary. It is possible that he was unjustly condemned. It is possible that one can get the proof of this. Can one permit oneself to be held back by any circumstance? Dare one hesitate or consider? Could there be any other duty in such a case? Answer me that, doctor, answer me yes or no?"

Yes or no: again he was seeking the unconditional, the

enthusiastic unconditional, a moral dictatorship, and again he wanted an unpremeditated answer just as he had wanted poor Robert Thielemann to give an unpremeditated answer. "The table is flying, the bird is flying." How could one do such a thing; how could a Camill Raff throw his experience and knowledge of the world to the wind and support an inexperienced boy in Heaven knows what sort of dangerous idiocy? Nevertheless here was something which moved this experienced man with his knowledge of the world to his very depths. Everything began to tremble, precaution, consideration, fear of the consequences, knowledge of the futility of his answer, all collapsed as if shaken by an earthquake and only this ardent young boy stood there with his yes or no. So Camill Raff, almost against his will, somewhat overwhelmed in a burst of defiance against his own common sense, replied: "Whether one may, Andergast . . . I don't know . . . I can't tell . . . whether one may or should. You perhaps . . . perhaps you may and should." He paused. Etzel looked at him beaming with a burst of gratitude. Silently they walked along a little further together; they parted with a silent handshake.

What's going on there? thought Camill Raff, becoming sober and doubtful. What is the boy planning? Should not a conscientious teacher warn the father? This, however, would mean sacrificing forever the friendship of this remarkable boy and appearing like a liar and maker of phrases in his own eyes. What has he in mind, this half-child? A jump into the ice-cold. Camill Raff fears that the plunge into the ice-cold will injure the delicate vessel irreparably. Impossible to find out what has so obviously driven the boy from the net of circumstance in the direction of a goal. A sixteen-year-old boy must revolve freely, he says to himself, must move in the illusion of infinity. If he is compelled to give up the freedom of dream and play for the paths of purpose and utility, suffering inevitably commences because he soon senses and comes to realize that he is being forced to give up a happy confusion and the joy of immeasurable abundance for which life can never again compensate.

6.

The general's widow had such a fright as she had not had in a long time when Etzel asked her for the three hundred marks. He came on an ordinary week day, surprised her in her studio when she was painting some flowers, threw his arms around her neck and without preliminary or preparation brought forth his request in one breathless sentence. For a time the old lady did not know what she should say. She put down her palette and stared at Etzel in dismay. "Are you crazy, child?" she asked with white lips. "Where shall I get so much money offhand? And what do you want it for? And even if I could give it to you, if I could do without it, how should I justify such recklessness to myself? I should feel as if I were taking part in some wicked plot." Oh, all right, said Etzel's eager, impatient face, I knew, of course, that you would have to say all that, let's wait till the little speech is over. When she had finished speaking, he knelt down, took the old woman's slender white hands in his equally small and delicate, although browner ones, and the impatience in his features changed into an earnestness which the widow had never yet perceived there, and which at once robbed her without further effort of the comfortable superiority with which Nature had invested her through the start of fifty-seven years. If he does not state the reason for his request—this is about how Etzel begins—it is because she could neither understand nor approve of the reason. Because she would be obliged to prevent him from doing the thing for which he needs the money. Of course, she could already now go and report him, since, by his mere request, he has already put himself in her hands. But she will not do that. She would never do such a thing. It would never occur to her for a second that he needs this money for an evil purpose. She merely has to look at him as he kneels here before her: does she think anything bad of him? No. He has no debts, he does not want to buy himself anything. Shall he swear to this? No! Give his word of honour? No. He has no other honour towards her than is apparent in his kneeling before her. Well, then. "Listen, grandmother. Listen carefully. We won't waste a syllable about it. You are going to lend me the money. When I am of age I shall return it to you. Don't laugh. It's an eternity till then, of course, but I am sure to pay, in spite of the eternity." He probably had the idea that he could get on five years with the three hundred marks, an amusing collision of the conceptions of time and money, but the widow did not laugh, she merely shook her head gently. He finished: "You see, I am not flattering and I am not begging; I have simply come to you because I don't know of anyone else in the world."

The old lady placed the little finger of her left hand straight across her lips and did not move for several minutes. Then she got up, beckoned Etzel to follow her, and went into her bedroom, which was furnished with white-enameled furniture, with a canopy down to the floor over the bed, and which looked like the apartment of a seventeen-year-old girl. She tripped over to a secretary in the wall, opened it and took out a little box incrusted with mother-of-pearl, unlocked it with a little gold key which she wore on a ribbon about her neck—the whole episode reminded Etzel of a person in a fairy story—pulled out five one-hundred-mark bills, counted them and handed the boy three. "The five hundred is my money for the whole month, including the rent," she said, with downcast eyes. "It's hard on me, boy. I am quite limited financially, I must tell you, but no more nonsense about returning it or anything of that sort. I think that you . . . I want to believe . . . It's curious, the whole business. It makes me feel rather queer, little Etzel. . . ." Etzel went up to her almost humbly, took her face between his two hands and kissed her right on the mouth. Then he looked her in the eyes with that indescribable seriousness which had once before disturbed her, and whispered: "Farewell, old grandmother." When she looked up he was already out of the door.

CHAPTER V

I.

THREE days after his visit to his grandmother, Etzel left his father's house and the city. It was the last day but one of the Easter holidays, a Tuesday. On Monday evening he told Rie that he had arranged an excursion to Hohen Kanzel with Thielemann and the two Förster-Lörings. They were to start at six o'clock in the morning and return on Wednesday afternoon, Rie was to prepare food for him to take along. It had been raining since noon and to Rie's remark that it would probably rain tomorrow also, he replied that they had decided to take the walk no matter what the weather. "If it depended upon you, Rie," he said, looking teasingly at her, "I should always stay nicely in my room. The thing you'd like best would be to tie me to the leg of a chair." As a matter of fact she was not friendly to "enterprises"; any deviation from what had become sacred through daily routine was abhorrent to her. But since Herr von Andergast had already given his consent, she was obliged to yield. But it struck her as peculiar that Etzel, after he had packed his knapsack, bustled about his room until late at night, opened and closed his drawers, rustled his papers and was unusually silent the while. Moreover, the size of the knapsack surprised her when he left his room the next morning. It was the size of a bale and he was scarcely able to lift it onto his back, so big and heavy was the thing. Surprised, she asked him why he was taking so many things for the one day; he replied, blushing, that there were books in it which he had borrowed from the Förster-Lörings and which he wanted to return to them, since he had to pass by their house anyway, also a coat Robert had recently lent him. His face betrayed that he was lying; Rie knew it; she always knew when he lied; but she thought nothing further about it, and was even touched that he reproached her for getting up so early, for they had agreed the evening before that he was to breakfast at the station. She had wanted, however, to show what a sacrifice she could make for him, that this show of affection had not remained unnoticed lessened her dismay at the dark and rainy morning hour. In addition to his other provisions, she gave him four sausage sandwiches; he thanked her, turned in the hall once again, gave her a hearty kiss on the cheek and then left.

On the same morning, Herr von Andergast left on a professional trip to Limburg, saying that he would be back Thursday for dinner. When Etzel had not returned late Wednesday evening, Rie became uneasy. At eleven o'clock she decided to telephone the Förster-Lörings. The Thielemanns had no telephone in their apartment, otherwise she would have applied to them because she knew Robert, who came to the house frequently, better. It took a considerable time for the call to be answered. Her consternation was considerable when she found that the two boys were at home, that they had gone to bed long ago, and that they had not been in the country either that day or the day before; there had not even been any talk of it. In her dismay, she dropped the telephone, hurried into the maid's room and woke up the cook to consult with her. Finally, she allowed herself to be reassured, could not, however, go to sleep, but wandered about the apartment till half past one, peering out of the window every ten minutes, watching and looking, a prey to every kind of anxiety, thinking of every possible catastrophe, of crime, accident and abduction. Not until her legs would no longer hold her did she go to bed, where in spite of all her anxiety, she slept quite soundly—a fact which the truth forces us to note—not waking until rather later than the usual hour. Daytime with its accustomed duties calmed her somewhat, every time the bell rang in the hall she gave a sigh of relief and, although she was disappointed each time, she expected the boy's return with certainty. Only when towards ten o'clock she sent the maid to the Thielemanns and the girl came back with the same report that the Förster-Lörings had already given, did she become anxious again; in order to forget her fears she dressed and went into the city to attend to some matters about the housekeeping. When she returned, it was one o'clock. Her first question was: "Is he here?" The answer was no. Before she could conceal her dismay, the hall door opened and Herr von Andergast stood before her. She turned to him with folded hands: "Etzel has not returned, Baron." Herr von Andergast handed the maid his little travelling bag, hat and coat and said with perfunctory surprise, "Really? That's strange," cast a penetrating glance at Rie's white swollen face and went into his room. There on the desk among the other letters which had come during his absence was a letter from Etzel.

2.

He read it. Not a line in his face changed. He leaned back in his chair and looked into the air. He seemed interested in a fly moving about on the ceiling. After a time he took up the envelope and looked at the postmark. It was postmarked in the city Tuesday morning. After a time he picked up the telephone, called the office of the chief of police and had the president informed that he would call on him at quarter past three. During lunch he was completely silent. It was in vain that Rie made several attempts to turn the conversation upon the subject which lay so near her heart; Herr von Andergast did not seem to notice her and was completely occupied with his thoughts, just as on any other day. But when they arose from the table, he asked her to come to his room and dryly requested her to tell him what she had observed in regard to Etzel's leaving the house. The course of her narrative suffered under the disapproving expression of the violet-blue eyes. It seemed as if Herr von

Andergast were wearied and overburdened by her flow of words. She brought forth the circumstance of the voluminous knapsack like a discovery which she had just made with "oh, yes," and "of course" and "who could have thought of such a thing?" Herr von Andergast agreed earnestly: "Certainly no one can always think of everything, one can't ask that." She looked at him perplexed. Her mouth quivered as if she were going to cry. Herr von Andergast wanted to know which of Etzel's clothes and books were missing. He would expect a report that evening. Then he gave her to understand that the audience was over.

The conference with the chief of police, Herr von Altschul, took the form of the meeting of two colleagues. At first the official statement that the boy was missing and his description was given. In the further course of the conversation, after the president had expressed due sympathy and some sort of astonishment, Herr von Andergast showed that he would like the authorities to show a certain consideration in the matter of the pursuit and seizure of the fugitive, as well as all possible secrecy, especially in regard to information for the press. The chief of police understood. He said that he would give the necessary orders. The question as to whether any reason existed which could have caused the young man to run away, Herr von Andergast answered in the negative. I need scarcely point this out, for one could see from his behaviour towards Rie, to whom he said not a syllable about the letter which he had received from Etzel, that he was determined not to mention it, simply to act as if it had not been written. Had the boy made any preparations? The chief of police continued his examination, which, of course, in the case of such a man could only take the form of a series of friendly inquiries. Only the most necessary, replied Herr von Andergast. Had he confided his plans to anyone in the house, or to any of his comrades? Herr von Andergast shrugged his shoulders. Not so far as he knew, he replied, but so short a time had elapsed that he had not yet been able to make any comprehensive inquiries. But had the sixteen-year-old boy a supply of money adequate to a long stay, to a stay obviously calculated to be of considerable duration? Herr von Andergast was not able to reply to this either; at the bottom it was probably a silly boy's prank, but the possibility that had been mentioned did make the matter somewhat disquieting, he did not conceal that from himself. Was there any idea as to where the boy might have gone? Had he had any secret connections? any secret correspondence? Did he belong to any political society of young people? Nothing of the sort was even conceivable, replied Herr von Andergast, coolly. Were there any family influences which might have had some secret power over him? The chief of police naturally knew the situation in the baron's family and put the question hesitatingly as if asking forgiveness for the indiscretion. Herr von Andergast dropped his eyelids and replied with somewhat undue sharpness. "No, not that either. In no case that." He reached for his hat, got up and said, "There is something to be added to the personal description. My son is very short-sighted; to such a degree that he cannot distinguish faces more than ten paces away. The condition has remained stationary in recent years so that the doctor has advised against glasses for the present. This defect will, I think, facilitate his arrest."

"I think so myself," replied the president, putting his notebook aside and getting up also. He remained thoughtful after the solicitor-general had left. Men of this profession have an extraordinary sense for the completeness, or the gaps, in the declarations which they hear, for the slightest suppressions, for the least mental reservation. He could not get away from the impression that Herr von Andergast had failed to be completely honest and had found it necessary to throw a veil over important details. However, he said to himself that he need not worry about it. If, however, he was of the opinion that it would not be difficult to seize the fugitive and return him to his father, he was thoroughly mistaken. The official apparatus operated with its usual precision, the guards at the railroad stations were informed, all of the police stations, border guards, and the gendarmerie force were set to work; nothing was omitted except the public notification. But this would probably not have had any better result. The boy seemed to have disappeared from the face of the earth.

Etzel's letter, which has been several times mentioned, was not calculated to put Herr von Andergast in a mild frame of mind. He was profoundly hurt as a father, his sense of authority was offended. He also felt that as a man, a human being and a friend—for he had deceived himself to such an extent that he regarded himself as completely his son's friend—he had been disgracefully hoodwinked and cunningly cheated of the fruits of the confidence which he had so generously offered. The very first sentence was laughable: "I cannot stay with you any longer; my decision to leave your house is not a light-hearted one; I have struggled with it conscientiously." So he has struggled, has he? Leave the house; a decision: what justifies, what empowers you to make decisions, impertinent urchin? Who has taught you to judge, how do you know what conscience demands or forbids, who has asked you for reasons? Then the next. "I cannot say that anything stands between us because everything stands between us. I am defenceless against your contempt for my youth, but perhaps I can reach the goal that I am setting myself and thus compel you to respect me in spite of my youth." The impudence of it! Much insight into the affairs of the world prevents one from making the banal lament of parents that one's children are ungrateful even if one does not fear to be regarded as old-fashioned, for saying that they are without peers in a tactless exaggeration of all they do and are and aspire to. However, the tone: I cannot say that anything stands between us because everything stands between us, does raise the question as to whether one has not failed in salutary chastisement, however lightly such educational methods may be regarded today. Then the culmination: "Since I have known about the case of Leonhart Maurizius and of his fate and the rôle that you played in condemning him, I can no longer rest. The truth must come to light. I wish to find the truth." Such a sentence in spite of its silly presumption only makes one shrug one's shoulders pityingly.

The complete letter ran: "Dearest father, I cannot stay with you any longer; my decision to leave your house is not a light-hearted one; I have struggled with it conscientiously. I beg you with all my heart not to regard what I am doing as a lack of deference; I am quite conscious of what I owe you. But we have no access with one another and it is useless for me to look for any. I cannot say that anything stands between us because everything stands between us. I am defenceless against your contempt for my youth, but perhaps I can reach the goal that I am setting myself and thus compel you to respect me in spite of my youth. Thought generates thought, it is said, but the truth is beyond this and one must achieve it like a product of labour, I believe. Without a lever one cannot lift a heavy weight, and a certain name has become a lever for me. Since I have known about the case of Leonhart Maurizius and of his fate and the rôle that you played in condemning him, I can no longer rest. The truth must come to light. I wish to find the truth. I have one great request; I scarcely dare to write it, scarcely dare to hope that you will grant it: do not pursue me, do not have me pursued; leave me free, I cannot say for just how long, but do not be my opponent in this matter. Your son, Etzel."

Charming, was Herr von Andergast's sarcastic remark; in addition to all the rest he would like to enjoy the luxury of my silent approval. But one must go on with the day's work no matter how painful and irritating the matter is. Since I did not foresee the matter and allowed myself to be taken by surprise and have been fooled by a fool—twofold folly is my mistake—I must get used to the idea of having been led by the nose by a young scamp.

The letter could be ignored. The thought of it aroused a sensation like that of having a sharp stone in one's shoe, without being able to remove the painful object decorously. But it was not so easy to forget. Herr von Andergast had fought against using the police force of the state on account of a "silly boy's prank." He could not accept the boy's flight as anything but a silly escapade and could only ignore the reasons assigned. Consideration of the reasons he regarded as ignominious. He had the gift of keeping his thoughts away from a subject which he did not wish to think about. It was a question of self-control. As the days went by and the measures he had taken remained fruitless in spite of their usual excellence, the "silly boy's trick" took on a new light and compelled an attention which it did not deserve. This brought with it a feeling of discomfort, as if one were suddenly to see that the hands were missing on looking at a clock from which one has been wont to tell the time with mechanical indifference. In addition to this, there was Rie's attitude of grief, complaint, question, reproach, surprise, all in silence, importunate and shy, enervating by its repetition. Moreover it was necessary to telephone to various people, to the headmaster of the Gymnasium, to the class teacher, Dr. Raff—taking this opportunity to ask him to call in person on Sunday because he noticed the embarrassed reserve in the teacher's tone—to all sorts of acquaintances who had heard of the boy's mysterious disappearance and who could not refrain from curious and sympathetic questions. It was all very annoying and inconvenient, so much so that Herr von Andergast thought of taking a vacation and going off on a trip for a few weeks. But he did not carry out this plan.

3.

The general's widow had telephoned to Rie on Friday and found out everything from her. That evening she called up her son. He had expected her call, he suspected his mother of having given the boy some assistance in his transgression. Since it was not to be assumed that the boy had gone away without a cent of money and since his grandmother was the person to whom he could best apply, her often proved indulgence making success fairly certain, the suspicion seemed half a certainty from the very beginning. The old lady said in a trembling voice that she was ill, that she could not move out of the house, that she had telephoned to the office in vain, he was please to come out at once, that very evening. Herr von Andergast ordered a taxi and drove out. After he had chatted with her apparently at random for five minutes, she had already admitted that she had given Etzel three hundred marks. The playful assurance with which he brought this about surprised her, she stared at him helplessly with her mouth open. She lay in bed, a satin cover over her delicate figure, her little head resting mournfully on the embroidered pillow; Herr von Andergast for his part reserved the politest countenance in the world. He had taken up an ivory paper cutter from the little table near the bed and held it between the fingers of his two hands, and no expression of any feeling could be seen on his face. His tactics doubtless consisted in expressing by silence everything which he scorned to say in words, which might be refuted or discussed. He knew the weight and the effect of his silence in such cases and could calculate them just as an artillery officer calculates the trajectory and incidence of a hand grenade. What he expected happened. The old lady lost her self-control, her eyes gleamed with anger; she rebelled against the torture administered to her by his ominous and pregnant silences; and she shouted out that he had ruined his relation to the boy himself; it was his own fault;

it all came from his military discipline; the child had probably run away . . . well . . . to find his mother . . . and, well . . . my God . . . why not! . . . to have her caress him a little. Perhaps that was just what he had lacked, being a little petted. Herr von Andergast looked up with interest: "Oh, really, mama," said he in cool surprise, "this is the first I have heard of it. Who would have thought of such a thing? I should never have hit upon that idea. How did you come upon it? Is it a mere assumption, or have you some special reason? How in the world should he have found out . . . There would have to be the most contemptible treason . . . Have you had any communication? I mean, have you any details about . . . about where she is living?"

His violet-blue eyes rested with steely composure on the face of the old woman, whose frightened expression recalled a chicken who knows that a hawk is circling above it and is seeking a refuge. She made a gesture of protest. "Oh, no," she assured him with an expression of regret, which sounded too genuine for Herr von Andergast to be able to doubt her words, "how could I know? How should I tell? You and your system have succeeded in bandaging the eyes and closing the mouth of everyone around you. Who would dare, even if he knew? Sometimes, Wolf, I ask myself whether you have any heart left in your body like other people. You frighten one. When you come into a room, one begins to be afraid." Herr von Andergast stood up, smiling. "I hope that your indisposition is only temporary, my dear mother," he remarked in a tone of careful consideration, mixed with fatigued indifference. "I shall in any case ask Nanny to let me know how you are tomorrow and what the doctor prescribes." He wanted to kiss her hand and leave, but she was offended to the point of indignation by his arrogant evasiveness, irritated by his imperturbable calm, and said commandingly: "Stay! Not so fast! We are not through so quickly. Where is Etzel? Where is your son? You don't know? How should I know? You think that I am in league with him? I told him that, just that. I know the way your mind works. Now what's to be done? What are you going to do? Of course, set your policemen to dog him. Put his back up still more. That's your last word about everything, the police. Have you any idea what kind of a boy he is? what he has in him, what's going on inside of him? No, you don't know anything, not a single thing about him, nor anything about anyone else. You drove poor Sophia out into the world like a dog and her . . . her lover to perjure himself so that there was nothing left for him to do but put a bullet through his brain. And even if everything was according to law and the code of honour and as correct as a military parade . . . well, I won't say anything, I won't say a word, but at times it sears my soul, when I lie quietly and think it all over." She stopped, suddenly frightened, seeing that her son had turned pale. She had allowed herself to be carried away. Her concern about Etzel and all of the things which she had suppressed for years had kindled her inflammable nature, and she had thoughtlessly thrown aside the curtain from past evil and pointed to the spot which—aside from all the other occurrences—certainly looked like irremediable guilt. But back of this there was a life, there were destinies. She regretted her words, they had scarcely slipped out before she pressed her hands to her eyes and sobbed quietly. Certainly Wolf von Andergast's face had become white as chalk. He raised his left hand slowly and tugged at his grey beard, he quickly wet his lips with the tip of his tongue and his reddened eyelids sank, until only a thin slit of his eyes was visible, then he said very softly: "Very good, mama. It is not my intention to correct your romantic notions. In the future, be so good as to omit all allusions to my person and to my past, if you care about keeping up the sporadic intercourse between us." A typical "restraining" Andergast speech.

The old woman repented and repented. But of what avail was that? The people who impetuously say the wrong thing get into a far worse situation than those of whose actions they complain with good reason. The slightest grain of injustice gives the other a tenfold advantage and they are left to repentance and shame—from both of which the general's widow suffered abundantly.

The next morning Herr von Andergast summoned Rie to another audience. He could not get the words of the widow, "He will have gone to his mother," out of his head. Since the old lady maintained, credibly enough, that she had refrained from any prompting, it could only have been Rie, with her stupidity, who was guilty. But where could she have gotten her knowledge? That the boy could not go to his mother was evident; he would have difficulty crossing the French border; moreover, it was not to be assumed, however romantic and incomprehensible the adventure was, that the reason expressly stated for his flight was a falsehood. The thing did not look so, and that was not the boy's way. Nevertheless, Herr von Andergast did not want to drop the thread which he had accidentally picked up, if only in order to get to know his subordinates. According to him, everybody, even the most irreproachable and unassailable, had a corner in his soul which contains the germs of crime; this was why one never knew people entirely! And as for his wife who had changed her residence in so disconcerting a manner, and whom it had recently pleased to importune him with letters about Etzel, one could not tell to what methods, contrary to the agreement, she might resort in her suddenly awakened, so-called yearning for the boy. So he asked Rie to come to his study.

She was so broken by his merciless pressure that she could not deny that she had obtained the knowledge of his wife's change of address from the envelopes of the last letters, and admitted with tears that she had spoken to Etzel about it, but she had not meant to do anything wrong. Herr von Andergast said: "I regard your behaviour as a breach of confidence. If I do not act accordingly, it is due to the fact that you have been in my house so many years." He retained a bitter taste in his mouth after this conversation; he felt as if his "system" were turning its spikes towards himself, as if his spies were walking at his own heels, as if his creatures had turned traitors. An irritating interlude, that was how the whole thing had looked at first—a young man with some overwrought idea in his head runs away from his father's house, he is caught and disposed of for a while—and that was all. However, there was something different, it was perhaps a little different. But how? Why? What was it that was "different"? What had gone wrong, what was the odd and depressing thing about it all?

He had determined to call up Herr von Altschul to inquire whether any trace of the fugitive had been found. But he did not do so. Every time that he lifted the receiver of the telephone, he pressed his lips together as if seized with some distaste and would sit at his desk for a time sunk in gloomy thoughts.

4.

Herr von Andergast purposely greeted Camill Raff with a tone of cordiality. He pressed his hand as if he had long wished to have a confidential meeting and as if he assumed this desire to be present in his visitor also. In truth, he regarded him merely as an unimportant little school teacher, in spite of his reputation; many people thought a good deal of his intellect and his culture, but Herr von Andergast did not share this opinion. He did not think much of school teachers of any sort; he concealed this carefully, but it was the way he felt, a survival perhaps from feudal times, or the fact that strong personalities often show a certain intolerance towards the generally accessible stock of knowledge, which is bound therefore to be somewhat diluted. Camill Raff at any rate was surprised at the friendly reception. He knew Herr von Andergast only from his professional visits, as it were, at the Gymnasium. It was his custom to inquire of the teacher, two or three times a semester, about his son's progress. Camill Raff had always been glad when this dry, ceremonious call was over and he had preserved his good manners. Now he faced an agreeable gentleman who could sit and chat delightfully. People in limited circumstances are always charmed by the polite advances of those more highly placed; no philosophy and no democratic pride can save them from this. Dr. Raff was much too intelligent not to know this, and was on his guard. Nevertheless, he succumbed to the charm of the man, who in versatility and knowledge of people was infinitely his superior, and did not notice the trap which Herr von Andergast laid for him. For the baron had some reason to suspect—he was suspicious here, too, suspicious all along the line: the net was breaking and everywhere his subordinates were unfaithful—that Camill Raff's influence upon Etzel had not been exclusively educational, that a harmful and perhaps even culpable toleration of dangerous tendencies had been the rule.

Camill Raff for his part had a certain intriguing provocation. He had a fairly accurate knowledge and a still better conception of Etzel's personality and nature, and he said to himself: this father has probably no real understanding of what his child is like; if anyone can give him this conception, it is I, and I shall do it in a manner that he won't soon forget. He was impelled to do this for two reasons, first, by something akin to vanity, a feeling from which even the most candid narrator is not free under such circumstances; and, in the second place, he felt a need, in spite of the friendliness which Herr von Andergast showed, to soften the latter's perceptible pressure by means of self-revelation. So each, absorbed in his own interests, acted with apparent amenity towards the other. Raff told how he had come to know Etzel at the school camp in the Odenwald, a year and a half ago, how exceptionally much he had liked the boy, so that when he had been called here to the Gymnasium, he had rejoiced at the fortunate chance which had made Etzel his pupil. He had given much attention to the boy, especially during the last six months, when he had been in the upper second form, which he, Raff, had taught. Herr von Andergast leaned forward a little, his hands over his crossed knees, his bearing and gesture expressing a courteous curiosity, which flattered Camill Raff and led him on to a thorough analysis of Etzel's character, full of delicacy, full of sympathy, full of the secret intention of telling the father something new and unexpected about his son. He speaks of the clearness and transparency of Etzel's nature. It is not transparency in the usual sense, not what one simply calls open. Open, no, Etzel is in no way open, not reserved, but rather provided with a series of layers. What Camill Raff means by transparency concerns the inner make-up, the clearness of his whole personality, a kind of orderliness of soul. Everything always rings true. In dealing with him, one always has the pleasant feeling: that's all right. It can only be this way, this is how one speaks, this is how one does thus and so, this is how one acknowledges a friendly service or an insult, when one is in an embarrassing situation, or angry, so and only so. One does this because that is the sort of person one is, because one has the gift of being what one is, and does not need to appear to be what one would like, an advantage which is so rare that only a few people can appreciate how unusual it is, although most people speak of it incessantly. Of course, this requires a certain sort of courage. But courage in such cases is only a question of tempo. Some things in life which we regard as the result of an ethical inclination are only a result of speed. Camill Raff has at times compared the speed reaction in boys. He has found that the slow minds, which may be housed even in quick elastic bodies, tend more to evil than the quick and fiery ones. How, for example, does a love of justice differ, the expression of it, differ from a lightning-like kindling in the brain, the glowing shock of an association of the imagination? He has observed Etzel in quarrels with his comrades and in games, in situations where decency, silence, readiness to help, chivalry were at stake. He was always astonished at the justice and the strength with which he took a stand in regard to himself and to others. Once in the classroom, they had played a nasty trick on the professor of mathematics. This man loves sweets, and always carries a bag of candy in his coat pocket. The boys, of course, knew this and one day mixed some strong laxative tablets with his candy. The professor came to the class the next morning furious; he said that he did not intend to take any steps to determine the guilty party, they were all involved and therefore it would suffice him to call one boy to account and punish him, the boy could escape punishment by reporting the real culprit. So he selected one boy at random, asked him to make the admission which, as you may well imagine, was not forthcoming and dictated a severe punishment. The procedure roused Etzel's anger. He could not bear to have an innocent boy—and the one hit upon was really the one least involved in the prank—suffer for the guilty, so he got up and denounced himself. He had done it, he was the one to be punished. This made a great impression upon the class; the boys would not permit such a thing, contradiction ensued, a real little revolt broke out. Fortunately, the professor had enough sense not to push the matter to extremes, his examination of Etzel was somewhat tepid and he left the classroom to consult, as he said, with the teacher in charge. Camill Raff sought to calm him and took care that the matter should blow over, partly in order to spare the man himself and save him from further ridicule. Afterwards, he had had a long talk with Etzel. While he described this conversation, an enigmatic, an almost roguish smile played over his handsome melancholy face. "I had great difficulty in keeping him at a distance with his ridiculous indignation, with the unabashed coolness with which he demanded of people that they act according to justice and common sense towards themselves, in order not to create confusion and trouble in the world incessantly," said Camill Raff. "That was just about his meaning; I am repeating it in somewhat more complicated form; but that was the gist of it. People should act consistently, the person who carries on a business must understand the business; a judge should only condemn a man when there is no shadow of doubt as to his guilt. I felt obliged to reply: My dear boy, heroes and martyrs have bled to death over these truisms."

5.

Herr von Andergast had dropped his lids over the violet-blue eyes. He looked as if the curtain in a theatre had been dropped over a change of scene. He scarcely moved. At times, he dropped a half obligatory, half skeptical "Hem." Camill Raff, without any idea of the man's real character, of his icy pride, of his intellectual sensitiveness, of the inflexibility of his point of view, thought that he ought to continue to explain the boy still more fully. He wanted to convince Herr von Andergast—the culmination of *naïveté*—to convince him of what? In the end he no longer knew himself, he only felt the stony, silent contradiction and he resisted it. He tells the story of what had taken place with Karl Zehntner, of the theft of the five-mark bill, and how Etzel had confessed his scruples at having gotten a comrade into trouble by acting too hastily. Herr von Andergast did not know this incident either; he listens, but his face shows only the same polite curiosity. Camill Raff remarks: "Such a delicate sense of proportion is extremely touching. I myself do not know of anything that moves me more. I mean the sense of what another person can stand and what it is permissible to load upon him . . ." "You have really studied the boy down to the last jot," interposed Herr von Andergast dryly. "Certainly, baron, I regarded it as one of my duties." "At the same time you seem to me to be trying to place a halo of virtue around his head. You will forgive me if I regard this as a little exaggerated. The boy has his good points, he is not lacking in thoroughness in some respects, moreover, he is not entirely ill-bred, rather impetuous at times, rather audacious, and—let us not fool ourselves—has a goodly share of cunning when he wants to put a thing through. Or do you think that I am going too far?" Camill Raff felt rather that Herr von Andergast was offending him by the malice in his tones. He replied that he could not agree, that he had never observed any cunning about Etzel, but something certainly different, a striking sharpness of sense or acumen; *that* he certainly had, a kind of Indian instinct when it was a case of bringing some hidden thing or circumstance to light. At the Odenwald camp, an incident had occurred which brought upon the then fourteen-year-old boy the epithet of a "pocket edition of Sherlock Holmes." There was a seventeen-year-old boy whose name was Rosenau, he was a room-mate of Etzel's. He was not particularly liked, in the first place because he was a Jew, then because he was distrustful and unfriendly, and finally because he wrote poetry. Since what he wrote was trash, a lukewarm rehashing of famous models with an unpleasant erotic touch, the boys were not entirely unjustified in their teasing. But this, of course, made him all the more bitter. For the rest, he was a decent fellow, with no harm in him. But he had gotten himself thoroughly disliked; there was nothing that could be done about it, and most of the boys wanted to get rid of him, or at least to spoil his stay at the camp. One day, one of the teachers asked for a book at the camp library. They looked for it for a while, then someone said: Rosenau probably has it; he did not, of course, borrow it; but he always takes the books from the other boys. Rosenau was not in the house, they decided on the spot to open his closet, the key of which was hanging on a nail, the teacher rummaged about, opened a drawer and suddenly stood shaking his head with gloomy expression. In the drawer there lay half a dozen photographs of the most obscene sort, such as one generally can see only after all precautions have been taken in a house of ill fame. With the exception of Rosenau, all of the boys were in the room; it was shortly before dinner, and all of them witnessed the horrid discovery; a few jeered and sneered, but contempt and anger predominated. While the teacher sent for the director of the institution and asked him to come down, Rosenau returned. He was ordered to approach the closet and the pictures were pointed out. Etzel stood close to him and at once had the impression that the boy knew nothing about them, and that someone had played a dirty trick on him. He only needed to look at Rosenau's face to be strengthened in this conviction. It was impossible to pretend such frightened astonishment and helplessness. No one else had the slightest doubt. Rosenau's protestations were received with contemptuous silence. The director of the camp had gone to Würzburg in the morning and was not expected back until the next day. The horrid pictures were for the time being confiscated and Rosenau was locked in his room until they should decide what was to be done. All of his comrades conspicuously avoided him. He sat brooding in a corner of the room with his face in his hands. Etzel meantime had made an observation which seemed to him important. He had noticed that the photograph lying on top was spotted with blood. The blood had run in a thin streak along the whole length of the leaf. He asked himself where the blood came from. He went quietly up to Rosenau's closet and pulled the drawer out; he found a nail close to the lock with the point protruding, furthermore that the bottom of the drawer was also bloody. Then he said to himself: whoever put those pictures in the drawer was evidently in a hurry and hurt himself on that nail; he must have lost a good deal of blood and one should still be able to see the wound. A little later, when the room was empty, the boys having gone out to play football, he went up to Rosenau and said: Show me your hands. The boy looked at him in surprise and obeyed, he showed him his open hands. There was not a scratch on them. Then Etzel thought for a long time. Finally, he reached a conclusion. He asked for two hours' leave of absence, walked to Amorbach, which was not far distant, and bought a bagful of hazel nuts. Towards evening, when all of the boys were again assembled in the room, he brought forth the bag and announced that he was going to distribute the nuts, this evening nuts were going to be cracked by way of entertainment, that was great fun and made a devilish row, one after the other was to reach out his hand and he would give each one a few nuts. This was done amid much laughter. At the ninth boy, Etzel perceived the wounded hand; it had a long red scratch on the inner side, just as he had supposed, for the wound could not be on the back of the hand, if it had been inflicted as he supposed. The boy with the wounded hand was Erich Fenchel; he was the oldest boy in the group, almost eighteen years old, and hated because of his brutality and love of fighting. He tyrannized over the boys, had his favourites and his aversions among them; Etzel occupied a medium position, Fenchel did not dare to attack him; all of them curried favour with him except Etzel, —since the boy had once told him that he had assaulted a deaf and dumb girl, his mere proximity made Etzel shudder. He could have told on Erich Fenchel, but he wanted to be sure, and therefore did not give the slightest indication of what he had learned. All of them cracked their nuts gaily and he along with the rest. When the boys had gone to bed and the lights were put out, he remained awake. He lay still for hours and waited. It might have been one o'clock in the morning when he got up noiselessly, convinced himself that all of the boys were sound asleep, slipped between the beds to Fenchel's closet and unlocked it. The evening before he had hidden a little tin lantern, which he had bought in the city at the same time as the nuts, under the closet. Scarcely making more noise than a mouse, he began to search the cupboard, screened by the open door from the room itself; it did not take long before he found what he was seeking. Again his assumption proved correct; again his logical considerations had triumphed: Fenchel had only slipped a few of the pictures into Rosenau's closet; the others were in his own, beneath his books and papers. Etzel closed the closet, slipped into bed and slept until morning. Immediately after breakfast, he went to the teacher and told him the facts and how he had come to establish them. A quarter of an hour later, Rosenau was reinstated. Fenchel, who was furthermore a rabid anti-Semite, had taken the opportunity, when the book was being looked for and no one was paying any attention to him, to smuggle the photographs into Rosenau's drawer. He was expelled from the camp in disgrace. Rosenau from then on was attached to Etzel with an almost silly devotion. The following year he was sent to South America by his parents, who did not know what to do with him.

Herr von Andergast looked down at his hands. He seemed extraordinarily attracted by something on the nail on one of his middle fingers, he lifted his hand to his chin and looked carefully at the nail while he asked, seemingly with no purpose: "You knew, of course, of my son's plan to run away?" Noticing the expression of uncomfortable surprise on the face of the man opposite, he added in a kindly manner: "I should understand that. You were the person in his confidence. I did not stand so well with him. I did not have the advantage of his confidence to such a degree. Not that I wish to complain: I have no talent as a father confessor. And frankly not the slightest inclination. I do not value secrets of the heart very much."

"'Secrets of the heart' is scarcely the right expression," Camill Raff ventured to interpose. The conversation changed from the narrative to the dramatic, he suddenly saw the noose which was to be thrown around his neck.

"The relation never went beyond the bounds which I myself drew," he said calmly.

"You have not answered my question," continued Herr von Andergast, opening his eyes almost with the expression of a woman who is complaining of being neglected.

"He came to me in his trouble," said Camill Raff. "As an older friend, I was obliged to try to help him. He said the situation is thus and so, what shall I do? Or rather can I do otherwise than thus and so? I did not know what he had on his mind. I could not tell from his hints. In any other case, I should have shrugged my shoulders, would have consoled him, would have evaded. With him that would not have been possible. Not at that moment. I admitted to him at that moment what I would not have admitted to anyone else, namely that he should do what his own feelings prompted. I do not deny—I am speaking always of that one moment—that I did not try to keep him from the decision with which he was struggling. I did not, of course, have any idea that it was such a far-reaching decision."

"Doubtless you would in that case have hesitated to support him in such a very nebulous project?" inquired Herr von Andergast in the same soft voice, with a sly little smile.

"That . . . I don't know," replied Camill Raff with hesitation. "There was something about him . . . I should have been ashamed to pour water into such wine . . . it is so seldom . . . You should just have seen him, baron. . . ."

"To be sure. And were you not afraid of the responsibility?" continued the gentle voice.

"No," said Camill Raff, "not for a moment."

"That surprises me," replied Herr von Andergast, as he rose. "Not so much your personal attitude—that is no concern of mine; but rather—how shall I put it?—the moral latitude which you showed as an educator." Camill Raff, who had also gotten up, changed colour slightly. "In regard to your personal attitude, I can only deplore that you failed to warn me. It would have been your duty . . ."

"I could not betray him."

"A boy not of age? Can you speak of betrayal in such a case?"

"I think that one can, baron. Not being of age in such a case seems to me only a legal conception."

"Is the legal conception not sufficient when a crude impropriety may be forestalled? Is there a higher conception? I am open to conviction."

"It does not suffice, baron. There is a higher."

The dramatic dialogue had become tense, but without any sharpness, without voices being raised; on the contrary, there was complete politeness on the one side, modesty but firmness on the other. At the close, as he accompanied his guest to the door, Herr von Andergast asked, with apparent casualness, whether Camill Raff knew where Etzel was; Raff replied that he had been extremely surprised at the boy's flight, he did not, of course, know where he was. Herr von Andergast nodded earnestly, shook Raff's hand and assured him that his call had been most pleasing. But when Raff had closed the door the baron stood a long time with his underlip drawn in, sunk in thought. The next day he sent a letter to the school authorities in which he drew their attention to the serious omission which Dr. Camill Raff had been guilty of towards his pupil Etzel Andergast, and requested an investigation. The investigation so categorically demanded by one in so high a place was started without delay. The consequence was that Camill Raff was relieved of his duties as a teacher for two months and was then transferred to the gymnasium of a small provincial Hessian town. For him, to whom his sphere of action, up to the present, had already been too limited, the blow was a crushing one, one which meant mental and physical disaster to him.

6.

Several days after Camill Raff's visit, which had left an impression of something humiliating connected with it, from which he had not yet rid himself, Herr von Andergast invited President Sydow to supper. The president had asked him to do so, as his family had gone to the opera and he wanted company. The food was good, but the conversation dragged. The president was a sociable gentleman, fond of telling anecdotes. Herr von Andergast had no predilection for anecdotes, but people who insist upon telling their jokes are not concerned whether the listener is interested or not; they provide the applause as well as the amusement, so the president did not even notice how absent-minded his host was. Herr von Sydow had the name of being a "good judge," but the reputation was based rather upon a mixture of epicurean laziness and general contempt for mankind, than on any superior sense of mission. He did not like to get to the bottom of things, and was still more reluctant to scale any heights, he only felt at home when taking the middle course. In many cases his "kindness" was based upon the coarse sociability of a moderately temperate alcoholic. Himself as heavy as a barrel, he deplored the heaviness of the judicial system, regarded the jury system, without ever protesting against it, as a ridiculous farce, and, so long as he had been a criminal judge, had shown his finest qualities when confronted with a criminal who had confessed. He would have loved to shake such a man by the hand and give him a reward. Such a man does not waste one's time, he used to say, as if a judge were intended to spend his time in dreamy enjoyment in a comfortable wine-room. Professionally he and Herr von Andergast had differed seriously, personally they were on excellent terms, for the difference between them was so great that there was no possibility of any friction.

He left early. They had sat in the study. When Herr von Andergast was alone he opened the window in order to let out the cigar smoke. It was a warm, damp April night. The trees were dripping, the dark street looked like a great open rubber-hose. Herr von Andergast stared into the darkness. He rested his chin upon his crossed hands and stood as immovable as a pillar. When he had closed the window, he sat down at his desk, took one of the legal papers from the pile lying before him and opened it. But his eyes went down the page listlessly. He was holding a pencil in one hand and absent-mindedly scribbling words and signs on a sheet of blank paper. Suddenly he started. There stood the name Maurizius. He had written it without thinking or knowing what he was doing. He tore up the sheet of paper, threw it in the waste-paper basket, tossed his pencil on his desk and got up unwillingly! For a time he walked up and down, stood still, seemed to be thinking about something, left the room, stood in the hall, at the edge of the patch of light which shone from the room, with an undecided expression on his face, took a few steps until he reached the door of Etzel's room, opened it and went in. He pushed the button of the electric light, carefully closed the door, looked about with his eyebrows contracted and, breathing deeply, sat down at the table. It was the first time since the boy's departure that he had entered the room.

With his back to the window he leaned back in the chair in his accustomed manner, crossing his arms over his breast. There was something singularly silent about him. His face looked sad and lonely. The tension which never left it, perhaps even in sleep, lessened. It seemed as if the mask which his face generally wore gradually relaxed. His eyes took in everything in the room, the brass bed with the worn yellow silk cover, the old embroidered canvas in front of the stove, the two straw chairs along the narrow side of the table, the bookcases with the empty gaping spaces. The books which were missing the boy had taken with him. An indescribable sadness permeated the room; Herr von Andergast could not help feeling it. A room which its occupant has left reminds one somehow of a corpse. The top of the table was covered with square-checked linoleum and full of spots near the ink well. At one place, the profile of a head had been cut into the material; it was an awkward attempt. He never did have any talent for drawing, thought Herr von Andergast. The drawer of the table was slightly open; it appeared to be empty. Boys are always careless, thinks Herr von Andergast, closing the drawer. The drawer reminds him of the incident with the photographs at the camp. He smiles a little. It was a shy smile, mixed with the feeling of being uncomfortable, which Camill Raff's narrative had left in him. How is it that he should never have heard of such episodes? How is it that such a child only stands before one in the present, never in the past? that the words of yesterday die away, the figure of the previous year fades? Are the human senses too lazy to retain a series and sequence of events, are they always sustained only by the moment and consequently cheated? For the moment is deceitful. Impossible to get a picture of how the boy looked at the age of ten. Or earlier perhaps, at eight, or at six. Photographs Herr von Andergast never had made; he regarded photographing children as a terrible nuisance! Nor is that the point; the point would be that the picture should exist in one's memory. Etzel was a beautiful child; thus much Herr von Andergast thinks he still knows. He remembers too that he was irritated every time that people praised the boy's pretty face, his smart appearance and attractive manners. While he sits there, seeking like a robber who slips into the house at night, to break in upon the past, he thinks of the lantern which the fourteen-year-old boy bought in Amorbach along with the nuts. An astonishing gift for putting things together, which he would not have attributed to the boy! Then he suddenly sees the fifteen-year-old and, as if rising out of dusty grey veils, the brown curly head suddenly appears. "Father, look at the big atlas with me and tell me about the sea and about Asia." How prettily the little white teeth gleam in the fresh mouth! The clear open glance, what confidence there was in it, as if Asia and the ocean presented no secrets to the father's omnipotence and omniscience! That was the "present" then. "Present" means timelessness. No, little curly head, father hasn't the time, he must work. Curly head does not dare to contradict, but he is sad and puzzled: can there really be anything more important in this wistful moment than the atlas and Asia and the ocean? Not to have the time is an incomprehensible conception, since there is so immeasurably much time lying about that one scarcely knows how to master the length of it between waking up and going to bed. The whole riddle of life is contained in "not having the time."

Where can the boy be now? It is night, the trees are dripping, the street lies there like a piece of rubber-hose cut open—where can he be at this present hour?

The clerks the next day noticed their chief's extraordinary silence; also that he seemed inattentive to the questions which they asked. The latter was particularly unusual; sometimes they cast glances of astonishment in his direction. A little before twelve, just as he was starting to leave, he sent for the clerk of the chancellery. When the man entered, it seemed—or was it merely assumed?—as if he had forgotten why he had sent for him. "Ah, of course, my dear Haarke," he said in friendly tones, "have the Maurizius records of nineteen hundred five and six brought in from the county court and sent to my apartment today."

At three o'clock the musty records extending over two thousand seven hundred pages, many of which had already turned yellow, were lying on Herr von Andergast's work table.

7.

He began reading that same evening. Since he had once made up his mind, he wanted to do it conscientiously. Made up his mind? Looked at closely, the matter was something different from a decision, something that had little connection with a voluntary decision. Nothing of the sort had ever happened to him before, it was an irresistible compulsion. So the thing did exist, this condition in which he had never really believed, which he had in truth regarded as a lawyer's ruse, invented in order to paralyse the arm of justice and smuggled into law books in order to flatter the superficial laity. It had begun with the word Maurizius that he had suddenly found on a sheet of paper, which he had himself written and did not know how. When he had given the order to the clerk, he had scarcely dared to look him in the face, he thought that people must be able to see by looking at him, he suffered as he continued to act under this compulsion, as if in the grip of some unknown disease of the nervous system, and was ashamed as if from the consciousness of some secret dissipation.

Not less curious was what went on within him while he was reading. He only remembered the rough outline of the events and the attitude which he had taken towards them at the time. All of the separate incidents were blotted out, the counter play of destinies at first seemed almost incomprehensible; the development and outbreak of passions appeared as if viewed through an inverted opera glass. The people seemed like corpses, their motives, their actions, their justifications, their statements, their accusations, explanations, excuses and observations also had something putrescent about them, something disgustingly stale, formless and flat. Yes, it was all hopelessly flat, the accounts of the servants, the men who lit street-lanterns and sold firearms, the policemen and railroad conductors, the hotel porters and florist-women and boarding-house mistresses, the hairdressers and coachmen, and even the reports of the doctors and professors, and of professor's wives, of students and tradespeople, of manufacturers, baronesses and countesses. There was an army of witnesses, a flood of hearsay evidence, of rumour, of examination, of reports, of statements, of pleas, investigations, documents and *corpora delicti;* of nonsense of all sorts and efforts of all sorts. Every form of human suffering, of human baseness and human weakness was preserved colourless and bloodless in this mountain of papers. To examine it was a business far less fruitful than that of the anatomist who studies an army of shadows. But Herr von Andergast had experience at this work. He had known beforehand that to penetrate into this world of catacombs would not be a pleasurable undertaking and would put his patience to a severe test. But to be patient was his calling, and to enjoy any sort of pleasure did not enter into his scheme of life. He began at first by separating the essentials from the unimportant, by selecting the chief characters from the chaos. There had always been a great deal of dissatisfaction at the verdict. Not only had the habitual grumblers remonstrated, and all of the muddle-headed enemies of law and order protested and dared to speak of an appalling miscarriage of justice, and expressed doubts of the procedure and doubt about the man's guilt, but the better elements of society had also expressed themselves as dubious. Indeed the people who felt that a new trial was desirable had not been silenced and had continued to make themselves heard. But there was not the slightest reason for this, the proceedings had been correct, according to law and to form; Herr von Andergast had refused to sponsor the last of these requests for a new trial six years ago, he remembered it distinctly. The more absorbed he became in the study of the case, the clearer the recollection of it became, as if the cobwebs had been swept away from his brain, as well as from the dirty covers of the records. This did not happen all at once; it was a gradual process and late one night the face and figure of Leonhart Maurizius seemed suddenly to appear before him.

He had closed the record and was walking up and down the room smoking a cigarette. He looked tired and there were dark shadows around his eyes. But the tired mind, just because it has shaken off the idea of purpose or goal, often produces without effort the thing which the most determined struggle would not have brought forth. Suddenly he saw the young man before him as he had stood behind the bars, eighteen years before. A handsome fellow undoubtedly, of good carriage, elegant, and when he sat with his legs crossed, above his immaculate shoes one could see his grey silk stockings. It was only just beginning to be fashionable for men to wear silk stockings. His wavy chestnut-brown hair was carefully parted, his features were frank and soft, almost feminine in their sensitiveness, the hands narrow and unpleasantly small, his whole appearance something between a man of the world with artistic gestures and a spoiled, obstinate, self-seeking woman's man. The stereotyped smile never left his well-formed sensual lips. Herr von Andergast remembered what repugnance the smiling sensual mouth had always roused in him. Why? He had never been able to fathom the mystery of this smile; it suggested inaccessible depths which contrasted with the handsome brown eyes, disfigured, however, by frequent winking, in which lay an obstinate determination and profound inscrutable sadness. There he stood; five minutes before Herr von Andergast would not have been able to say how he had looked, or carried himself, or behaved and now, here he was down to the very crease in his trousers, and the minute exactness of the picture almost frightened him. He wanted to get rid of him, he turned his eyes away as if from something obscene, but the apparition was obstinate, it seemed as if his will were not strong enough to banish it, as if it could only be exorcised by another picture of still greater clearness. And this second picture appeared. It was that of Etzel.

During the whole of his preoccupation with the papers about the Maurizius case, the picture of Etzel kept getting into the sad muddle, and gradually rising out of the bog and mire, it spread a light over it and mercilessly compelled him to continue his concentrated reading. How this came about, it is difficult to explain in the case of a man who was not given to hallucinations, whose capacity for presentiments was nil and who had as little interest in metaphysics as an ever so efficient rotary-press. There is not the slightest doubt that thinking about Etzel's flight, about his absence and the reason for it had partly influenced Herr von Andergast when he had, reluctantly, with the feeling that he was wasting his time, ordered the Maurizius records to be brought forth from the oblivion of the record office. What had occupied him chiefly up to then had been the offence to his vanity, whether in the upper regions of his consciousness he called it dignity, authority, paternal responsibility, social position or public opinion, or in some secret recess of his soul the feeling of having been disdained, of shattered hopes, of the failure of his own strength. Even though he carefully avoided the latter feeling, and roundly denied it to protect his own pride, he nevertheless suffered from it, as if from some physical disability, which one dares not attempt to cure for fear of discovering some more deeply seated ailment. In his effort to direct his thoughts towards the more external circumstances, these became the source of his anxiety. A sixteen-year-old boy exposed to a world he did not know. How could he protect himself from the daily dangers, from coarse overtures, from mountains of filth, from the crimes which might be perpetrated against him, or which he might be led to commit? He was gambling with his future, his name, his honour, his health and lastly even with his life. One has brought up a child with care, prepared him for the position which is his in life, taken the most careful measures to protect him from the general demoralization and suddenly he strikes the hand which leads him, is sought by the police, and wanders about the world with the stigma of an adventurous fugitive upon him. Incredibly bad from every point of view. I have done my duty completely, says Herr von Andergast to himself, and the feeling of how badly he has been used in this matter brings a smile of bitter contempt to his lips. I was a true counsellor to him; he was properly cared for; he had every attention and consideration, all the freedom which was due him. What had he to complain about? In every serious difficulty he could confidently come to me. He was in decency bound to do so. Would I have reproached him for being immature, would I have been hard upon his youth? I? Have I not rather wasted too much care and too much conscientiousness on a bad egg? Probably he has inherited some moral taint from his mother. I could not, in spite of all my care, eradicate the poison entirely; nature was too strong.

During this exchange of complaint and self-justification, of penetrating retrospection and moody anticipation, his spirits sank lower and lower. If he had had a friend—had a man like himself been capable of friendship, of which he was as incapable as a eunuch of propagation—he would have gone to him and have tried to talk matters out and perhaps have found relief. But he had no one. There was no such person. He was as much alone among the half-million people in this city as on a boat in the middle of the ocean. He was only now beginning to grasp this fact. When he had once struck a path which freed him from himself for a while—freed him insufficiently, because he never could get really free from himself—it would lead him (rarely, and then always by night) in quite another direction.

CHAPTER VI

1.

NIGHT after night he would sit until late over the papers, so dusty that one could fairly taste the dust, copying, noting, comparing and examining. It is a work of burrowing and digging; and although he struggles against it, with an unconquerable aversion, he gets deeper and deeper into it. What he is doing is not in compliance with any order, he refuses to give any reason for it, at the same time he sticks to the work and becomes a puzzle to himself. He must find pretexts in order to make this inexplicable situation plausible, and persuades himself to admire the magnificent accomplishment which the case represents, once one has worked one's way through the chaos of words and the muck of facts. The separate details are welded together with iron consistency, forming the complete picture which in the end was crowned by the verdict. There were jewels of legal art, the lapse of years now permits one to see the imposing structure for the first time, the firmness of the foundation and the fine mechanism of its internal operations. The specialist takes in the whole of it with æsthetic appreciation and his own efforts seem to him now to have a dash and vigour which, when he judges himself honestly, he would not be able to put into it today. Such is often the case. We frequently look back upon the efforts of our youth, upon which we have poured forth our whole passion and imagination, with a sort of tragic envy of our former selves.

2.

Nevertheless, it was undeniable that there was one flaw in the case: the man had not confessed. Neither at the time of the proceedings, nor in the preliminary investigation, nor at the trial, nor in the penitentiary, had Maurizius admitted that he had done the deed. On the contrary, he had answered every question as to his guilt with the same abrupt, determined negative. He had been equally abrupt and determined in his silence when asked who, in that case, had committed the crime. This, of course, could not alter the verdict, for the chain of evidence had been too strong, there was no possibility of escape. The most gifted counsel could not have broken down this evidence. How hopeless for the mediocre Dr. Volland—long since dead—whom Maurizius had chosen to represent him! Herr von Andergast still remembered the man quite well, a quibbler and a dry little provincial with an impudent walrus moustache and black pince-nez which always sat askew on his large bony nose. He by no means believed in the innocence of his client, he depended upon the psychiatric experts and took refuge in formal objections. The accused could not have had a weaker supporter. Nor did Maurizius pay much attention to him; he treated his interruptions and questions with impatience and contempt and even ordered him to be silent once before the whole court. He might easily have obtained a better lawyer. Why had he not done so? Among the papers there was a letter from old Maurizius to the court to the effect that Anna Jahn had urged Leonhart to take Dr. Volland, he was the only lawyer in whom she had any confidence, he had always given her father satisfaction, was honest and dependable. No attention had been paid to the letter at the time, they had not investigated at all, it was really not the duty of the court to pay any attention to the quality of the counsel for the defence; today in the loneliness of his study, a certain ambiguity attached itself to the slighted incidents. It was at first like a tiny hole in a huge vessel out of which a well-preserved and long kept liquid runs, without one's needing to fear, of course, that the hole would grow larger. At first it all seemed absolutely water-tight. Herr von Andergast felt neither doubts nor uneasiness. He put out the lamp on his desk and stood for a while in the darkness, uncertain whether to go to his bedroom, or into Etzel's room. He did not dare to decide upon the latter. He felt as if he were returning from the scene of the trial upon a dark and narrow path back into the present. He had at first to remember where he was. For these events were, after all, eighteen years behind him. He considered these eighteen years thoughtfully. They embraced the most significant years of his existence, an immeasurable number of days. One just like another, one following upon another. Eighteen years of a man's life that had passed with nothing to show for it. Externally, yes, profession, career, position, but what had he to show for it? Regarded seriously, it was an endless period of time. There is a kind of boredom which steals upon middle-aged men of the bourgeoisie which is as destructive as the voracious tropical ant; the object which it preys upon remains untouched upon the surface, but the interior is completely rotten. One stroke, one blow and the framework, indeed the whole building, collapses in a formless heap.

But something existed during this endless period which could have broken this level monotony if he had paid any attention to it. That something has disappeared. It was overlooked, and it is gone. During all those countless days it had grown up beside him and, if he looks into the past, he does not know much more about him than the steward, the office boy, the letter carrier might under certain circumstances have known quite as well. Is that what the comical little fellow was like, who long ago—while Sophia was still in the house, a fact which his thoughts avoid—would run up and down the nursery making a senseless noise? The picture rises as if from stagnant water, surrounded by iridescent rings; what a curious piece of machinery the brain is, why does it call up just this picture among the thousand possible ones? The boy is not more than three years old.

He is naked, just before his evening bath, and runs screaming after a blue rubber ball. How pink his flesh is, how clumsily the tiny feet move along the floor, straight ahead like those of a little bear, what a deep sparkle in his eyes, as if this knee-high creature were drunk with the joy of life! Play with me, daddy, I'll find you! Why don't you want to? Are you going away again already? Do stay! Do you know something, you are the big engine and I am the conductor. He's whistling and puffing already, yelling: get in! He changes frantically and completely into what he represents, locomotive, cars, passengers, all in one. The father has only cast a distrait glance at the miniature magic world at his feet, he closes the door behind him and betakes himself again into the realm of serious affairs.

The way in which the pictures and faces produced by his preoccupation with the case became confused with those from Etzel's childhood gradually became an irritating nuisance. It seemed as if he had taken one of those drugs which paralyse the will and precipitate one's mind into unbridled fantasies. In spite of this, he was quite capable of thinking logically. Only he constantly had a feeling that his reflections were shattered against an invisible wall behind which was going on something which he could not find out. One night he lay in bed with his hands crossed under his head staring in the air. Lying in bed for men of the stamp of Herr von Andergast has something peculiarly senseless about it. There are figures, bronze and stone monuments which, with the best will in the world, one can only think of as upright; in a horizontal position they would seem disorderly and disturbed. An unpleasant bodily sensation overcame him. He was aware of his toes and his back, he felt painfully tense all of a sudden. His thought was: There's something wrong about the case, but what is it? There's something wrong about the structure of it somewhere, but where? He went over the course of events. He began at the beginning. Suddenly the marriage between Leonhart and Elli Maurizius became extremely clear and present to him. This was new and in a certain way disturbing. One had always been of the opinion that a too vivid comprehension would cloud one's detached judgment. Every sort of participation of the imagination was taboo and even a tendency in this direction in another person aroused distrust. Never in his whole practice had it occurred to him to see people and things. Was this condition perhaps responsible—it seemed like the condition of a man who has been drugged—for his being compelled to see also the past life of his child, instead of merely knowing it as he had done up to the present? Was there here as well as there, behind the truth which he knew so well, another truth, more mysterious and at the same time more real? In any case, it was not uninteresting to watch the course of the events in this unusual way. While he lay motionless staring at the ceiling of his bedroom, it rolled off before his eyes like a cinema picture.

3.

Elli Hensolt had not consented with a light heart to become the wife of young Maurizius. She had refused him three times before she finally consented. She had said: I am a mature woman, tomorrow I shall be old, you are a boy and will remain young another twenty years—what would such a marriage lead to? What charmed him in her? Is it this maturity precisely? the calm which emanates from her? the firmness of character for which she is known and which is evident in all her actions? Has he had enough of temporary adventures, does he long more for leadership than for seductiveness, more for permanence than for temporary passions? Is he at four and twenty already longing for a settled home-life? In addition to all this the fact that Elli Hensolt is a rich widow certainly plays some part. He had, however, as he later found out, greatly overestimated her fortune. He had thought that she had at least two hundred thousand marks, but her deceased husband had left her only half of his fortune; the other half had gone to a charitable institution. The whole estate had not amounted to more than one hundred and sixty thousand marks. This Leonhart discovered only a few days before the wedding. Whether he felt disappointed, or even showed it, no one knows, in any case he can't withdraw. Moreover, Elli is not a woman whom one takes or leaves, according to a whim. She is dignified, still handsome and if one sees her on the street or in the drawing-room, one would take her for thirty at the utmost; she knows how to dress, has excellent manners, and although she is not beautiful, she has charm, and one can well understand that a young man like Leonhart Maurizius would not be indifferent towards her.

What he needs and seeks in her is clear from the beginning. He has reached the end of his tether. He is tired of too much speedy and greedy enjoyment. He has snatched at every hand which was extended towards him, and each and every time his whole person has been seized, and he has been dragged resistless off his path. He lacks a mainstay. He sees his own danger and looks about for support. Men of his sort fall hopelessly if they are not seized by a stronger person at the decisive moment. He has been made irritable by too much society, blasé by too much admiration, and uncomfortable by having aroused too many expectations which he fears he will no longer be able to fulfil. It is a case, to put it bluntly, of saving him. Elli realizes this, she takes counsel with herself, weighing what she has to win or to lose, and resolves upon the salvation. She has confidence in herself. The task, scarcely formulated, will demand her whole life, she realizes this. One thing she demands as a condition: confidence. Without complete, unreserved, measureless confidence, she cannot undertake the venture. She must know everything, in every situation and under all circumstances; there must be no secrets and no secrecy, concerning either the past or the present. She wishes to have confidence, then she can give confidence, complete, unreflecting, measureless. He regards the demand not only as just, but as natural; he himself cannot conceive of any other relationship; it is exactly what he longs for. He eagerly takes the vow which is his moral stake in matrimony. He is convinced that he will never break it, she believes him because forthwith she doubts his heart still less than she doubts his honour. Her love depends, as it were, upon an act of creation. She has the feeling of having created him for herself.

4.

When she discovers through the anonymous letter, after a year and a half of marriage, in the midst of their harmonious life together, about Leonhart's relation with the dancer Gertrud Körner, and learns of the existence of their child Hildegard, she regards it as a slander. She destroys the letter and tries not to think anything more about it. Soon, however, she notices from Leonhart's restlessness that everything is not as it should be. He had gradually confessed everything to her, his communicativeness in this regard had at times even amused her, there was something of boyish boasting about it. She knows about the apothecary's daughter, who carelessly threw herself at his head, and of whom he had gotten tired after one summer, of the wife of the silk manufacturer in Krefeld, who had made scenes in the public thoroughfare when she was jealous, of the little Viennese pianist, who had almost persuaded him to go to America with her. She knows of occasional liaisons of a less serious nature, which had been over in one night, of women picked up on every hand; there was always something new, another stolen heart, another woman expecting and disappointed, another successful assault upon matrimonial peace. Of a Gertrud Körner not a syllable. He did not, however, care anything about silence, he had said often enough: Thank God, all that is past, all of that muddling is over, since you know everything; since you know it all, I am really free from it for the first time. How glad this had made her, how much more serious and manly it made him seem, how much more legitimate her feeling, and how much more secure her life with him! She can't understand it, the name is there, the name can't be made up out of thin air—who would be so mean, or so envious, as to invent such a story? She can't get rid of the thing, she must talk it out; one day at the table with downcast eyes, she tells him about the letter. For a while he does not answer, then he admits the fact, and begins by confessing that he has written the letter himself. He has written it on the typewriter.

He treats it as a joke; her eyes wide open with astonishment make him realize that she does not understand such jokes. Well then, he wanted her to be prepared when he should tell her the story. Why? He was still the silly boy masquerading as a university teacher, a schoolboy playing pranks. The idea was that that was over. A relapse, unfortunately. To write an anonymous letter to one's own wife. Well, let's forget it, act as if it had never happened; go on with the story. He admits further that he has had a liaison with the dancer, he has spent the holidays with her in Mürren; he was fond of her, perhaps she had meant a little more to him than his other sweethearts; he can't say accurately any more; they parted as friends; then in the winter she had the child. He admits that too. Not so openly as with all his other confessions; he is oppressed, dodging. She wants to know why he has kept just this affair a secret, or at least has postponed telling about it. He replies shyly, just because of the child. At first, she does not understand, then she grows white and still. She is a childless woman, condemned by her body to remain childless. It is unalterable. In a minute she has considered the dangers of the situation. Her position as a woman and a wife requires the sharpest attention during every second of her life, the clearest presence of mind. In a marriage between a man of twenty-five and a woman of forty, there rests upon the shoulders of the woman not only the fulfilment of the most secret demands, but also the most difficult task that exists, that of pretending that what is contrary to her nature is the thing that she most wishes and desires. So in a moment of despair she thought of adopting the orphan, and would have discussed the plan had she not been surprised by an unfortunate remark of Leonhart's which probably sprang only from his embarrassment. The conversation was mentioned in Record Number Fourteen of the preliminary proceedings, as well as in a letter of Elli to her friend, Frau Professor von Geldern, which was among the papers relating to the case; the plan for adopting the child appears only in the second document, as may be imagined. Leonhart says: Anna knows about it, I could not think of anything to do except to confide in her. Elli stares at him. Suddenly the only impulse which she has left in her is one of hostility and the instinct to defend herself against the child. She gets up silently and leaves the room. How has it happened that he has confided in Anna before confiding in her? What has happened? What was said? She must get to the bottom of this. She feels that Leonhart has an affection for the child, which he has not yet perhaps admitted even to himself, but which is all the more dangerous for that reason. Does Anna know that too? Has she approved? Has she encouraged the feeling? Has she played the guardian angel? Without a doubt—and she does not have to wait for the evidence of this—Anna took the child to England; Anna has undertaken to care for the child; Anna has charge of the correspondence; Anna watches over this treasure which has suddenly turned up. What induced her to? Was she asked? A helper in need? Was she, Elli, of no use in the emergency? Had he been afraid of her objections, or only pretended to frighten her? Anna's face takes on a different expression in Elli's eyes. She has loved her sister. She has admired her beauty. She understands that it is a joy just to look at her. God creates such creatures only at rare intervals. She considers Anna pure, a proud girl; she expects much of her natural gifts and knowledge of the world; she knows how to adjust herself to any circumstances without losing her dignity as a lady. Elli therefore does not think that her sister has been guilty of any indiscretion, in such a provincial little town where everyone from the street pedlar to the colonel's lady indulges in backstairs gossip, one is compromised if one merely smile at a man in public, although every kind of crime and dishonourable action goes on behind the demurely painted curtain. Anna will therefore be careful, even if she likes her young brother-in-law better than she should, thinks Elli, and she can understand that she should like him—what woman could remain indifferent towards him? But the matter of the child Hildegard has created a bond between them far stronger than a little incidental flirtation, or a chance proximity, could create; far more intangible since they could allege duty, service of friendship, and all those things which might appear harmless and protect them from Elli's distrust. But then Anna is not in the least a coquette; but every woman has her wiles and those who are not flirts are all the more dangerous when it comes to a serious issue.

But Elli did not dare to be suspicious. She did not dare on her own account. Matters must not be allowed to go so far as to make her doubt, or even regard it as possible to doubt, on a mere adventitious provocation, the most sacred assurances that he had ever made. For the fact now is that she loves him. Up to her thirty-ninth year she had not discovered what love is. She had never known the joy of exclusive monopoly which changed her previously joyless existence to a daily repeated miracle. Is it not natural that she should begin to tremble at what her eyes do not yet perceive, to shudder at the nightmare which she prevents her senses from taking in? Nevertheless, anxiety is her teacher and permeates every virtue which she shows in her married life. For it is a marriage with a man who is at the beginning while she is at the end, a spoiled child of fortune to whom everything has been given which others strive and contrive for; a man who has been met with kindness, indulgence, promotion when others, his contemporaries and his colleagues, found themselves knocking at closed doors. Her husband was a man who had only to take where others begged in vain, only to speak to find people in agreement with him, only to work in order to receive recognition, only to beckon and he had a following. Thus every hour became a test and every minute of their companionship made its special demands upon her. He, of course, must not dream of this; everything must appear easy; he must not notice when she is tired; headache or nervousness must be heroically concealed; for she has time to nurse herself and to rest when he is not present; in his company she is easy, fresh, gay, discusses his plans and drives away his moments of depression. He has attacks of despondency, although up to the present Fortune has favoured him in every way; like all persons who are inwardly uncertain, he regards himself as misunderstood. At such times she uses the most subtle powers of persuasion; the situation begets in her the greatest intellectual tenderness, by means of which she brings him back to a more peaceful relation to herself and the world. These conversations often last until well into the night, and when she has finally succeeded in getting him to laugh, she knows that she has prevailed. She is permitted everything except to be boring, and actually she entertains Leonhart so well that during the first eighteen months of their marriage he sits at home, alone with her, night after night. To the surprise of his friends he does not appear either at the club or at any other social gatherings, nor has Elli the slightest desire to go to the theatre, nor into society. Three or four times in the course of the winter, they invite people to the house; now and again they accept a few invitations, that is all. For a time it looks as if the "genius Maurizius," as his friends call him, or the "unscrupulous romanticist," as he is sometimes referred to by scoffers and doubters, has developed under Elli's influence into a clean-cut personality.

5.

The records are precise enough to show that the trouble began shortly after the discussions about the child Hildegard. At this time Anna Jahn is already visiting her sister's house almost daily. It is a comfortable house, tastefully furnished, well run, a pretty villa in the suburbs, a place where one feels at ease. Anna lives in a crowded pension, she complains of the bad food and the tiresome company. Groups of uninteresting students, elderly females who criticize all the families of the city, old bachelors who bombard her with feeble flattery; the whole thing makes her sick with nervousness. Moreover, she is uncertain about the choice of her future occupation; her financial situation is distressing; during the last few months she has been living on the small capital which she has inherited. She is hesitating between studying the history of art and preparing for the state examination in French and English. She asks her sister and brother-in-law for advice; both endeavour to help her but she cannot decide. She lacks all interest; she feels that she is unfitted to support herself; she has no gifts; she cannot subordinate herself; she cannot serve. She cannot give up what was at that time called "life," by those who were skirting the outer confines of life. Leonhart, who at first had been rather unsympathetic, understands her hesitation and strengthens her in it. In her contempt for earning he beholds an aristocratic trait with which he sympathizes under all circumstances. Elli, on the other hand, warns her against following the career of a creature of luxury, which, unless one has adequate means, involves a loss of self-respect, a far more essential lowering of oneself than that required by a life of bread-winning. Moreover, Anna does not intend to retire to a convent, it is probable that she will find a husband soon enough, who will offer her the kind of life she wants. Anna shrugs her shoulders. Her beautiful face grows curiously dark. In the diary which Elli keeps at this time, the fact is expressly noted as an interesting observation. Later on Anna expresses herself scornfully to Leonhart, saying that her sister is afraid she will ask her for money. But he can safely reassure his wife; Anna would rather cut off her hand than accept anything from Elli; despicable though a stingy man appeared to her, a stingy woman always seemed like a miscarriage of nature. The poisonous word has its effect. He cannot refrain from an irritable remark about Elli. One of his best qualities is generosity, he can't bear to see people clinging to their pennies. Elli calmly rejects the assumption that she wishes to forestall her sister's possible requests for money. Was it not you, she said, who always most disliked Anna's ladylike inclinations, indeed, made fun of her appearance, so little in harmony with her social position; did you not regard her ambitions as exaggerated? This was true. Leonhart was silent. As a matter of fact he had never lost an opportunity to make fun of "Miss Have-Nothing" who put on the airs of a princess, and for whom no society was good enough. As things developed later, it is fair to assume that he wanted to pay Anna back for her haughty, or at least indifferent, attitude towards him. She was at first convinced that he had only married Elli because of her money, that he had from the beginning speculated on the fortune of the dead paper manufacturer. Ought she perhaps to have particular respect for a young man who shamelessly harnesses himself to the gilded yoke of an old woman? Shortly after he had appealed to her in connection with the child Hildegard; they had a curious discussion. It appears that the decision to appeal to her feminine sympathy and to make her his confidante was entirely spontaneous, without any preliminary, without his being able to know whether she would listen to him, or throw him out of the room, at the first mention of the subject. Perhaps he had wished to take her by surprise, having long been secretly irritated by her coldness, not at all conscious of what he was risking in so doing. He was simply a creature of instinct and allowed this to drive him. Then, at the second or third conversation concerning little Hildegard, the question of his marriage came up in the course of the conversation. He was passionately bitter at the nasty suspicion which he forced her to confess. In his defence there was a tone of veracity which could not be ignored. How does a man defend himself against such reproaches? He will point to the unselfish friendship which the woman has shown him, he will say: only a mature woman, whose character has developed, and whose point of view can no longer be influenced by cheap delusions, can so understand a man, especially one who has not yet found himself. He will praise the peace of mind which the relationship has given him, the feeling of confidence like that of a captain when he knows that there is a safe hand upon the rudder of a damaged vessel. But one must go deeper; these are commonplaces; they contain nothing of Elli's strong personality, her sensitive heart, her incorruptible judgment of persons, her courage in self-sacrifice, the richness of her soul. Leonhart becomes eager and enthusiastic, Anna Jahn listens with bent head. So much superiority in another woman is almost a reproach to her who hears it expressed, especially if it be one's own sister. He explains what he meant by a damaged vessel; it is characteristic of him to seize the opportunity to speak of his endangered character, although mostly in rather favourable colours, suggesting that he was a problematical nature. He was putty in the hands of the first comer; he might have given up at any moment, deluded by his erroneous ideas, disheartened to the point of despair; it was pure chance that this did not happen; only his almost impertinent faith in his lucky star kept him from sinking. If he has not yet known a great love and his marriage to

Elli means a conscious renunciation in this respect, he has nevertheless gained something else, nobler perhaps, more enduring in any case. She cannot refrain from an ironical smile. What does it mean not to have come to know love, a "great love," as if there were a great love and a small? Besides being the flowery language of a high-school boy, it looks like a very clever trap. It is the way to entrap eager young flappers, whose sensuality is nothing more than a vain nibbling curiosity, to which one casts resignation as a bait. Nevertheless, the apparent truth of a confession which sounds painful, the kernel of which is a sugar-coated lie, is a recipe which seldom fails to take effect.

Anna does not fall easily into the trap. She looks at her brother-in-law with somewhat different eyes, but she does not trust him very much. He is so eloquent, he talks so skilfully in the unceasing attempt to rid her of a prejudice, from which she no longer needs to be freed, she believes that he has not married Elli from mercenary motives; she is not so stupid that she cannot give up a superficial judgment when she has learned better. Why then the constant conversations, the effort to secure a hold on her, the many questions, so much persuasion? She has finally done as he wishes and gone to Switzerland with a nurse, fetched the child and taken it to her friend Pauline Caspot. This Mrs. Caspot is the daughter of a physician in Düsseldorf; she had married an English merchant, who died shortly after the wedding, leaving her almost destitute, whereupon she had opened a home for unemployed governesses in Hertford, a few miles north of London, and thus made quite a decent living. Anna corresponded regularly with her about Hildegard, gave accurate instructions for her education—the single woman had taken an eager interest in the deserted child—and each month sent the money for her care which Leonhart gave her for this purpose. All of this, of course, required certain arrangements and agreements, particularly since Elli's flat refusal to have anything to do with the matter made it to a certain extent Anna's duty to assist Leonhart, who was very awkward in practical affairs. But he never tires of speaking of the thing; once each week she must go to town with him to buy a present, a little dress, some toy or other, for the child. He begs her to get him some photographs; he wants to have Hildegard's portrait painted by an English painter; he implores Anna never to give up her interest in the child, saying that she was her real mother, and other things of the sort. It is hard to refuse him anything; his graciousness is so captivating; they get to know each other better; their relations become gradually and naturally more informal; each step follows so naturally on its predecessor. Elli behaves like one who tries to look agreeable with a rope tight around her neck. Where are you going, or where do you come from, she asks smilingly. Anna feels that she is being watched. She becomes obstinate; a sarcastic remark, an expression of boredom suffices, and Leonhart turns upon his wife with irritation. Are we in a kindergarten, he asks; are we forbidden to speak to one another? Elli smiles apologetically. She can no longer find the right words. It is as if a veil had been drawn between her and Leonhart; they can no longer be innocently together, every conversation contains a hidden element of hardness, a secret trap; the loneliness and separation which has come upon them gets to be unendurable; when Elli disagrees about something which he has said, Leonhart at once ceases to speak, and withdraws into a silence lasting for hours. Then when she looks at his face she knows his thoughts and becomes more and more afraid. One day, he asks her for an advance of money. He is in financial difficulty; Anna's trips, the care of the child have eaten up considerable sums; he is hard up; he needs six hundred marks. She writes out a check on her bank; he looks at it; the check is for four hundred. I asked you for six hundred, he remarks coldly. She replies that no other interest is due. Interest?

Do you wish to limit me to an income, are you treating me like a schoolboy who has overstepped his monthly allowance? I know what I'm doing, she replies with an averted glance, her fingers working nervously; if we begin to use up our capital, we shall be done for in ten years. He laughs in her face. In ten years I hope to have gotten so far that I can dispense with your generosity—or do you wish to play tutor to me all of my life? Elli winces; a quiet, fierce expression, which he has never seen before, comes over her face; placing her hand upon his shoulder, she says: You wanted this guardianship yourself; it protects you from yourself. If necessary I shall protect you from yourself against your will. He stares at her and becomes silent. She has never spoken so before. It is a threatening program. He suddenly realizes what he must be prepared for.

He now commences to spend his evenings out of the house. She neither protests nor complains. She is careful to avoid an open rupture. She sees at every step that she is on the brink of an abyss and trembles at each successive move. She does not inquire whom he is visiting, does not ask where he has been when he comes home late, but his complicated explanations and unmistakably false accounts of meetings, conferences, professional duties, which he asserts are very irksome to him, fill her with fear and anxiety. Once she catches him in an open lie. The people whom he pretends to have called upon left the city on the previous day; he has overlooked the fact that she could easily find this out. He conceals from her the fact that he goes to the Casino almost daily to play poker, but she is aware of it. He has sunk again, as before his marriage, into endless drinking and smoking, there is no pretence of regular work. Not until Waremme's overwhelming influence takes hold of him does he begin to talk—but it is only talk and stops at beginnings—of disciplined activity, which does not keep him from wasting nights in the company of this dangerous man in discussion, gambling, and drink.

6.

In the diary, already referred to, Elli frequently mentions Waremme, sometimes with a casual jotting, sometimes in long descriptions, and she also mentions him in a letter to Frau von Geldern. She could, of course, not comprehend him any better than could most of the people who came into contact with him. Everything that was said about him was just as correct as the exact opposite would have been. No one could make him out. For a time the whole town discussed only him, particularly at first, in the winter of 1904 and 1905, when he really created a great stir. A gambler, a social lion, a hero among the ladies—it is a well-known, not very exciting type; but then Waremme was also a poet, a philosopher, a philologist and a politician, and of what dimensions! Here was no cut-and-dried dilettante, no mnemonic acrobat, but a productive mind, a first-rater, a universal genius. He was working at a new translation of the whole of Plato, said to be magnificent; at times he would read some of the best parts to his friends. He would give private lectures on Hegel and the Hegelian philosophy, which was just beginning to flower again. He publishes a book of German odes, reminiscent of Hölderlin, and writes a profound article proving that the Parsifal legend is not of purely French origin, but rather has its roots in the old Germanic mythology. It was said that he was *persona grata* at the palace of the bishop of Breslau, who recommended him warmly to high clerical circles in the Rhineland. A convinced Catholic, he attends Mass regularly, but is divorced from his wife. He has no fortune and no regular income, but he refuses to accept any sort of teaching or salaried position. Is this because he wants to remain independent—when he asserts this one believes him implicitly—or does he receive money from some obscure source? This too one could believe. His forte is philosophy and politics. With all of the passion of which he is master, he proclaims Germany's mission in the world, declaring that Germany will be stifled in its own stuffiness, be destroyed by the disturbing elements within the state, unless she obtains breathing space by means of a war. This war is to him a tenet of faith; he considers it sacred and regards himself as a Peter of Amiens. By basing his contention upon the historical tradition, which was interrupted, towards the close of a happy medieval period, by Latin-Celtic migrations, he constructs in his mind a German-Roman empire extending from Sicily to Livonia and from Rotterdam to the Bosporus. Everything must be made to serve this idea, poetry and art, the Gothic and the Baroque, the Renaissance and the Ancient World, Christ and the Fathers of the Church. Either this thought really makes a fanatic of him (if he is one) or fanaticism (if that is what he may be said to have) is one of the ingredients of his nature, giving birth to this idea because the time for it is ripe. Supporters are not lacking, nor admirers either, surrounding him, eager to learn, even though their number is never sufficient for his hungry vanity. The assumption of some cool-headed observers that he is supported by more important people than university professors of chauvinistic tendencies, retired generals and a group of inflammable students, may have some foundation; that these people know what they want and are quite indifferent to a medieval empire, except in so far as they can in some way do a profitable business with this intoxicating dream. An intellectual giant like this Waremme was unquestionably very useful for this purpose, whether he was absolutely convinced at the bottom of his heart or not. This was why people were indulgent about his affairs with women, his constant money troubles, his personal unreliability and the uncertainty as to his origin, about which he constantly told different stories, like one who lies unskilfully, because he lies too often.

It turns out that he is a friend of Anna Jahn's, or at least that he knows her well. He met her a year before in Cologne and coached her so well for the rôle of Pierrot for an amateur theatrical performance during the carnival, that her performance met with unqualified admiration. This is the story; how much of it is true it is difficult to find out; Anna herself has never discussed it, for Anna never talks about her experiences. It is striking, however, that since then she does not go to the theatre and abhors everything connected with it. She is silent also with regard to Waremme, at least she never mentions him to Elli and she certainly did not introduce him to Leonhart. It seems as if Waremme took the initiative in this matter, as if he had sensed from far off that this young man would make a suitable victim. Soon the two are inseparable, Leonhart goes to Waremme's house early in the morning; in the afternoon, he rides with him; Anna is frequently with them; the trio naturally make quite a sensation in the streets and finally Leonhart introduces Waremme into his home. Some remainder of intuition has made him hesitate a long time before doing this, and the first meeting with Elli is painful enough. Her dislike of the man is elemental. She feels unwell when she merely looks at him; his sallow face with the lower jaw of a negro boxer, the watery blue eyes with their bold gleam, the fat neck, the fat hands covered with rings, his sarcastic staccato politeness, which at once draws a sharp distinction between a man and a woman, and the sovereign lightness of his conversation—everything about him is indescribably hateful to her. It is true that in comparison with him, Leonhart seems like a lackey in the audience chamber of a prince, but that is no reason for her to see him humiliated; position does not make people; it is established by God; only what Leonhart means for himself should concern her. She implores him to drop this person. He behaves as if she has asked a thing incompatible with his honour. You don't seem to have any idea who Gregor Waremme is. Oh, yes, she has an idea; as the man walked towards her, her heart stopped; she had a feeling of inevitable fatality; but she is careful not to say this. And moreover, he continues, Waremme is the only person who really takes an interest in Anna. What should she reply to this? She stands still and her head swims. It had been agreed that he should go with her to a tea at Mrs. Privy Councillor Eichhorn's; he had promised to call for her. He does not appear; it gets to be nine, ten, eleven; she stops expecting him. The next morning he excuses himself, he had not gone, Waremme had read him an article he had just completed. Two hours later she called up the councillor's wife. Why didn't you come, Elli? It was a delightful evening, we even danced and the handsomest couple was undoubtedly Dr. Maurizius and Anna. Elli stammered helplessly into the telephone; she feels her very heart's blood turning to gall. She is already so unimportant to him that he does not even trouble to devise a lie that will hold water. She does not dare call him to account, matters have gone too far, like a fire which scorns a stream of water; her hands tied, with frightened staring eyes, she sees him sinking deeper and deeper, but she can scarcely believe that it is all over; she still hopes and waits, thinking that it may only be a temporary cloud; he cannot possibly have forgotten all of the promises he has made, promises on which she has built up her life. But while she is still deceiving herself in this way, the demoniacal forces are already gathering within her, the forces with which she fights for him and for the possession of him and destroys him and herself.

7.

One afternoon at dusk, returning from an errand in the city, Elli opens the door of the living-room, and Leonhart and Anna, frightened, move away from each other; they stand disconcertedly staring at Elli in the doorway. Anna takes a few steps to the window and arranges her disordered hair, which is hanging down over her forehead and cheeks, and hides her flaming face; Leonhart remains as if rooted to the sofa and turns to Elli with a gesture of entreaty. Not a sound is uttered. When Anna has somewhat collected herself, she seizes her hat and coat and walks to the door with furious steps, casting at Leonhart as she hurries by a glance of such withering contempt that he, white as a sheet, now addresses to Anna the same gesture of entreaty which he has just made to his wife. But her eyes merely blaze scornfully at him, as if it were a disgrace to be in the same room with him, which she therefore leaves as quickly as possible. Let me pass, she explains to her sister in tones of command; Elli steps silently aside and Anna disappears. Her light quick steps can still be heard when Leonhart walks up to his wife and says entreatingly: By our Eternal Father, Elli, it is not her fault. When Elli still remains silent, for the room and the furniture are turning in a dizzy circle, he sinks upon his knees, clasps her legs, repeating: Believe me, Elli, you have nothing to reproach her with, she is as pure as the daylight. His behaviour is theatrical, Elli feels this; nevertheless there is honesty and truth in his voice and face. What could disturb Elli more than just this?

There were two reports about the incident which were essentially in agreement; one was Leonhart's own, the other was that of the maid Frida, who had played eavesdropper. It apparently was a valid characterization of the situation among the three persons concerned. What happened was approximately this: Leonhart, the sensual, stupefied weakling, was so fascinated by his beautiful sister-in-law that he thought only of how he might ensnare her, and she, entirely dependent, uncertain as to her future, defends herself as best she can against his passionate pursuit, trying as hard as possible to bring him to his senses; but, being an inexperienced girl of nineteen, she is fascinated by the man's undeniable charm, so that in spite of her reserve, she must appear in an ambiguous light to her sister. She does not want to be unfair to Elli, even if she cares for Leonhart; she would not estrange her sister's husband from her; even if he were to get a divorce from Elli, she could not bear to have interfered with her sister's life. This was quite out of the question. In the first place, he is, like herself, dependent on Elli, only to a far greater degree; he is a person far too dependent upon the small luxurious pleasures of life to be able to make up his mind to return to an uncertain and unrestricted bachelor existence, dependent upon the humours of a despotic father. Then it would jeopardize his position in society, which he values very highly, as well as his intellectual career. In the circles into which he has ingratiated himself, any secret offence is pardonable, but never a public scandal. He sees himself forced to shift and compromise, for he is not man enough to give up the one thing or the other. Renunciation requires a clear recognition; but such half-baked characters are seldom clearly aware of their situations or of their secret impulses; they prefer to flounder about in uncertainty. And here begins the enigma in this otherwise uninteresting triangle.

In spite of his increasing and unbridled passion for Anna, a feeling which scarcely leaves room within him for anything else, and which in the end is no longer concealed from anyone, he continues to live with Elli as his wife. Perhaps one can understand this in him. Perhaps he seeks oblivion in her arms, but it is hard to believe that she can give him this, since she, in her agony, cannot see her own way clearly. Perhaps he wishes to deceive himself as to his own condition, if we presuppose that such a woman as Elli could be deceived about such a matter. Perhaps she simply does not deny herself to him, hoping perhaps, believing perhaps that some magic in her blood can win him back; perhaps something of the sort really exists, and it is not merely the pity of the woman which drags her into an abyss which seems like a fire-filled fissure in a glacier; perhaps it is not merely the compassion of the maternal beloved who gives to the last drop because everything is demanded of her. That he should require this, that he should take it, having so perceptibly and evidently only the adored picture of the younger sister before his eyes, that what is for him a dream of happiness, is horrible to Elli, makes this picture of him almost repulsive. The voluptuary treads the darkest paths in the world.

Nevertheless, it appears furthermore that he cannot escape from her. She has some incomprehensible power over him which holds him. He could probably not explain this himself. Possibly it is something which he is ashamed of. Sometimes a woman, and she need not even be remarkable, sees through a man in a way which ties him to her more than sensuality, or interest. There are men whose sinews of action are paralysed if one guesses their thoughts before they have converted them into action, because they are so constructed that they can attain external truth only by concealing their inner selves. If now the same woman, in addition to this intellectual gift, has a certain power over a man's senses, she is doubly, trebly or ten times more dangerous, just in proportion to her strength. This creates the most profound form of dependence that we know. He has bound himself by having sworn to confide in her. Like many weak natures he is morbidly sensitive about his honour, so sensitive in fact that he would uphold his integrity if necessary by the most shabby self-deception. He would obstinately deny having done wrong to the very last, even in the face of crushing evidence against him. The point is that he does not want to fall in her eyes. Her admiration and her delicate understanding have gradually elevated him to a mood of being pleased with himself, which he finds necessary to living, and thus he still has the gestures, the glances and even words of his former confidences, when for a long time he has no longer dared make his confessions to her. It is as if a wheel in a machine should run without any transmission belt. He is afraid. He prefers to have her find him out gradually and indirectly, without his doing anything about it. Thus he wins time. One can never tell what may happen between today and tomorrow. He is afraid of the change in her feelings, of her knowledge, of the inevitable decision, and above all, he fears what he calls her jealousy. The idea of such an outbreak makes him wish to run away; her passion threatens his foundations, and there is something about it which seems barbaric to his sensitive nerves.

Jealousy is not a conception that means very much in this case. It is a question here of a hopeless disease, a cancer of the soul, for which there is no physician and no remedy, no relief, not even pauses of exhaustion. She listens eagerly to all rumours and there is no lack of tale-bearers. Here and there Anna has been seen with him. On Sunday they were at the Art Club for two hours. Night before last he called for her at her pension and they took a walk along the bank of the Rhine. He sent her a book from the university library with a letter in it. On Wednesday she went to his lecture, sat in the second row and looked at him continually. One snowy night he walked up and down in front of her house from eleven to half past twelve. Then again she was in the garden of the villa while Elli was in the city; Leonhart went down to her and they walked up and down over the straw-covered beds in animated conversation, she with bent head, merely whispering, he gesticulating with excitement and at times wringing his hands. Waremme called for him yesterday at the Casino in a carriage; back of the parish church, Anna got in. The maid Frida tells with a grin that Fräulein Anna had already called up at half past eight and Frida had said that her master and mistress were still asleep. Elli is unequal to the effort of any sort of activity. There is no heat in the house, she pays no attention to meals, the tradespeople have not been paid for weeks. She remains in bed all morning, with her windows darkened; when she finally gets up, she who was once so smart and careful of her appearance, now is unkempt, her hair in disorder, with an old shawl over her shoulders, as if she were cold to the very bone. She sits at the window, she sits at the stove, she sits and stares into space. Her face is covered with deep lines, her skin is a leaden grey; if she happens to look into the mirror, she shudders. If Leonhart does not come in to lunch, she commences telephoning, calls up his friends and acquaintances, inquires whether he is there, whether they know where he is, sends Frida to inquire of others who have no telephone and to the Casino and various restaurants. Of course he finds this out; people make fun of him; Waremme makes a *mot* about a bold runaway stumbling over the apron-strings. Angrily, he takes her to task; she maintains that she was frightened; she imagined he was lying ill somewhere. Sometimes in the evening she can no longer bear being alone, she rushes out of the house, scarcely taking time to slip on a coat, hurries into the city, wanders distracted through the streets, staring at people outrageously, follows a young couple thinking them to be Anna and Leonhart, and causes passers-by to shake their heads with disapproval. Then she runs home as if in mad flight and waits and waits and waits. Finally he comes, at midnight, often much later, tired, silent, evasive. He does not dare to withdraw, her commanding demand upon his presence makes him cowardly. Has she no sense left, to humiliate herself thus, begging for a glance, begging for some slight show of affection, that he should take her hand for just a minute? How helpless she is, how completely abandoned! Cowering before him, she sobs upon the floor, suddenly what he has dreaded takes place. She begins to rage: You have dragged me into the mire, into the dirt;

what about your promises, what are you keeping from me, what is it your intention to do? And she curses her sister, and threatens to kill herself, first that woman who has betrayed her, then him, then herself. Don't imagine that you can treat me as you have the others, I am not a woman who lets herself be put off, with me it is a question of everything, of life, of eternity, and you knew that. And he, like a beaten cur, consoles, pacifies, denies, swears, pretends affection, friendship, pretends to be moved. He can't get free, he can't make an end; he wants to get to bed and sleep; all of this is so unpleasant, so repulsive to him; he forces himself to bestow a mendacious caress in order—as he excuses himself to himself—to keep her from raging anew and she says: Kill me, then at least we shall have peace! Does it not look as if this "Kill me!" had at some dark hour taken root in his soul? Is it not probable that she has read in his eyes the wish which was already in him before her desperate entreaty, and as if the frightful forebodings which she is always a victim to, when her tired heart seeks to recuperate for a moment, proceeded from this?

Night after night the same scenes took place, more pointless, more embittered, more hellish, each time! He shudders at his house, at the very steps, at the light. Once, on the way home, he throws the key to the garden gate into the Rhine and is then obliged to climb over the gate. He already knows the words, the gestures, the tears and demonstrations by heart, and finally the pitiful entreaty not to leave her alone in the room, for they no longer sleep together; then her restless wandering about the house when he has finally torn himself away; then she takes veronal, and tormented by ceaseless fear, tries to fall asleep. At times she knocks once more at his door as if she wishes to assure herself that he is really there. Lights were frequently seen burning in the couple's living-room until four o'clock in the morning, and one night the woman screamed so loudly that the policeman on patrol rang at the villa to ask whether anything had happened.

8.

One afternoon Elli goes out, pays a visit to her dressmaker, takes tea in a pastry shop, where she also drinks two glasses of cognac, and then goes to Anna's apartment. Anna moved out two weeks before; she has rented a fashionable little apartment from the widow of a major in the army. Where she obtained the means has never been discussed, nor explained. Of course, Gregor Waremme engaged her as his secretary a few weeks ago; she works three hours every morning with him; but the salary thus earned would scarcely be adequate considering her extravagance in shoes and stockings; moreover, this was only to be for a short time. Towards the end of the month there is to be a so-called German Congress; the most distinguished patriots have been asked to take part. Waremme is the soul of the plan, which is to be representative in character. He is much occupied with the preparations, the correspondence, and with raising the necessary funds. He devotes himself the more vigorously to this affair because recently another scandalous story has become attached to his name, a homosexual affair in which some young noblemen of a distinguished fraternity are involved, and his supporters are busy trying to suppress the matter. They were, however, only partially successful; a socialistic paper published a somewhat alarming article, for the time being without giving any names, and it was decided as a precautionary measure to postpone the congress until the autumn. Then, in consequence of subsequent events, the congress was abandoned entirely.

Evening is coming on; in the darkening room Elli is waiting for her sister. She walks restlessly up and down, sometimes stopping to listen at the door, then she stands at the window, looks over the papers on her desk and walks up and down again. Then she opens a drawer of the desk and the first object that strikes her is a photograph of Leonhart which she has never seen and under which she reads the words: "May 18, 1905, seven o'clock in the evening. Since this hour I know that I have an immortal soul, Leonhart." She stares at the picture. She bursts out laughing. In one of her last letters to the friend we have frequently mentioned, she writes: "I felt as if there where my breasts are I had two deep open wounds." Her whole body shakes with laughter. Then Anna comes in. What are you doing there, Elli? The hated, harsh, melancholy voice. Elli tears the picture in four pieces and throws them at Anna's feet. How much further do you intend to carry this revolting comedy? she screams into her face. Either you or I, one of us must go; and if I must be the one, you know where I shall go and your troubles will be over. You can then be congratulated upon having the conscience of a swineherd. Anna leans against the wall spreading her arms out as if to support herself against it, she turns deathly pale and falls over. Without paying any attention, leaving her lying there convulsed as if with epilepsy, Elli starts to go. But she has not yet reached the door when Leonhart and Waremme stand before her, both in evening clothes. They have come to fetch Anna, a gentleman has invited them to dine with some other friends at the hotel. Waremme goes over to Anna, bends over her and, seeing the photograph torn in pieces, he gets up, shaking his head, and turns to Leonhart with the words: You see, my dear Maurizius, you should not have let matters go so far. At the same time he motions to him to look to Anna; he himself curiously enough goes towards Elli, who stands facing her husband in trembling silence, offers her his arm, which she still more oddly accepts, and thus he leads her through the hall, whence the major's widow, who has of course listened and heard everything, whisks off like a bat.

There is a carriage waiting below, he steps in after her, drives home with her, accompanies her to her room and talks to her for perhaps a quarter of an hour. She has the feeling that a great doctor, or a priest that knows the human heart, has taken over her case. Her antipathy has disappeared, she cannot speak herself, but still weeping, she gives herself up to the charm of his presence. He is so gentle, so kind, so wise; he grasps her whoie misery; how can it be, she thinks, that such a man exists, and one thinks one should hate him? She silently approves of his advice that Leonhart shall keep away from her for the next few days; he will provide quarters for him at his own house; nor is he to see Anna. The best thing would be for Anna to come here to her sister; he will strongly recommend it to her; it is important, if only to stop the evil talk. He protests that Anna is guiltless, saying that in a short time he will bring her the most overwhelming evidence of her innocence. What his plans are cannot be misunderstood. Elli in unconquerable excitement seizes his hand, wishing to kiss it. For heaven's sake, he exclaims, and presses his lips upon her brow. That night Elli sleeps a dreamless sleep of thirteen hours. The great physician has helped her. Leonhart remains at Waremme's a whole week. One morning in the beginning of October, he strolls into the garden, cuts some roses and sends Frida to her with a bouquet. She is so moved with joy that she throws her arms around the girl and kisses her. Everything can again be well, she writes to her friend, in her incomprehensible delusion; the bitter part of the situation is that the last ten months have aged me ten years; I am today an old woman. Meantime for Leonhart the situation has become terribly acute. Anna, in his own house, is more effectively separated from him than by a ten hours' railway journey. Waremme back of every step he takes, Waremme, to whom he has promised to avoid Anna, indeed not even to see her before she goes to England in November, to stay a year. That, however, is not the worst of it. He owes Waremme two thousand eight hundred marks. It is a debt which he must pay within a very few days, no matter what happens; Waremme in order to help him, and relying upon his word of honour, has taken the money from the funds of the German Congress. Certainly an unparalleled proof of friendship, and one cannot take it ill in Waremme that he presses Maurizius to pay him, as he would otherwise be called to account as a defrauder. The sum is replaced two days before the murder, not of course by Leonhart, who never knew of its return, but how and by whom was a question that did not come up at the trial. It may be true, as he afterwards asserted, that Waremme offered him the money of his own accord without his first having to ask for it. Waremme is regally generous in money matters, in this regard Leonhart must have seemed to him almost degenerate because he was so involved in petty financial cares. At the same time, he knew of his friend's difficulty. Leonhart's bill at his tailor had grown to be seven hundred marks, he owed a hundred marks at the riding academy, and four hundred to a little money-lender; and there was a gambling debt of twelve hundred marks, the payment of which could not be postponed. He had not dared apply to Elli during the daily nerve-racking discussions with her; now, of course, it is out of the question. Perhaps a remainder of pride keeps him from it; perhaps he considers that he must not just at this time sink into deeper material dependence upon Elli; perhaps it is only the old fear, his mystical fear of her as his judge. Yes, he sends her roses, but he does not dare appeal to her generosity, he does not wish to seem to have sent the flowers for this reason only; this would make him appear too unmasked and contemptible in her eyes. So he plans the journey to Frankfurt. There he has some rich friends. He only thinks of his father after they have turned him down, with all the friendliness customary in such cases. He drives by car that very evening to his father's place. The young son of a jeweler, to whom he had last applied, had placed the motor at his disposal, in order to make his refusal of a loan less unpleasant. During these hours his brain must have become confused about everything. He can no longer stand being without Anna; he does not live when he does not see her. He sends her a telegram from Frankfurt to which she does not reply. Now, during the trip, he telegraphs Elli announcing his arrival for the following evening. He wants to go home because Anna is there; he cares about nothing else, not even the financial catastrophe which awaits him if he returns without money. In order to put his father into a yielding frame of mind he tells him a whole series of lies and yarns, for example that he is on the point of starting for Italy, he wishes to finish a study which will give him the title of professor, and wished to say goodbye before leaving and a lot more of the sort. However, even he, with his slight powers of perception and his ability to deceive himself, observes at the third sentence that he will get nowhere with the old man, that tears and entreaties will be of no avail, that he might as well try to get something out of the table which stood between them. Thus one path after another is closed to him. What remains but the mad and frightful deed with which his idle thoughts may perhaps have played in a cowardly and greedy wish? He drives to a hotel in Königswinter, sends the motor back and sleeps until noon. When he gets up he shaves his beard, buys a long yellow English ulster with a turn-up collar, telegraphs Elli again, recalling the telegram of the day before; could he have acted more succinctly, have sought more planfully to free himself from a hopeless situation? However, later on he stated that he had first wanted to talk to Anna, he had intended to have her called into the garden, and had made himself unrecognizable, so that she would not know him at once and refuse to see him. The night hour would have favoured this plan, he would then have suggested that they should fly that same night. He had been obliged to buy the overcoat because he had only had a summer coat with him and the weather had suddenly turned cold. A pitiful explanation. The connection, the whole chain of events, lies clear before one.

9.

Which does not prevent Herr von Andergast from being overwhelmed with doubts. It is almost as if he were being torn into the tiniest pieces. The same construction whose solidity seemed at that time to defy all attack now appears to his sharpened glance full of flaws and defects. Is it only experience and time which have sharpened his scrutinizing gaze, now free from professional preoccupation and partisanship? Has not a certain little lantern bought at Amorbach come to play a part, not as a figure of speech, but actually, tangibly, although regulated by an unseen hand? Its bright light falls upon the figures and the action, following them into still uninvestigated shadows and darkness. And a pair of eyes are at work too, a pair of fresh, bold sixteen-year-old eyes, and back of them a will which knows how to express itself and which becomes irresistible in inverse proportion to the bodily absence of its owner.

Indeed it is absence which makes the appearance so clear, and an absence indeed, both in time and in space, upon which one's own will has no influence, and which makes everything which the memory can call forth turn into an obsession. There he is again among the waving shadow figures, a boy of five perhaps, with brown curls, dressed in a sailor suit, his mouth set for a pert whistle, standing at the top of the stairs, puzzling about the problem of how to get down without using the steps. One can see by looking at him that he scorns steps, he has recently announced that he is convinced that he can fly, but that this requires a complicated magic formula which one can pronounce only after having looked into the sun five minutes without blinking. He tries this once a day and expresses the greatest impatience at not succeeding, and is greatly embarrassed when he maintains that he has done it and it is proven to him that he has cheated.

Herr von Andergast sees the following picture before him. It is a Sunday morning and he has taken Etzel to the Liebig Museum with him. The boy is standing before an antique Venus, staring at her with curiously frightened, deeply astonished eyes. A young lady walks up to Herr von Andergast to speak to him. Etzel fastens an absorbed glance upon her, then upon the statue, then stares again at the living woman and Herr von Andergast thinks that he can hear every word of the hesitating voice: Are all ladies like that, father, so wonderfully beautiful? There is a mysterious fear in the question, the shining eyes cannot hide this, the fear of the angels perhaps, when God's outstretched arm points to the accumulated guilt of his creatures and the path they must tread, a path full of woes, watered with tears, leading from earthly love through death to divine love. But this knowledge or foreboding is one of second sight, of today; at that time, he ignored it. As he ignored everything. The manifestation of life is a matter of course. If a person exists he simply exists. Childhood is an imperfect condition, to develop the child as much as possible is the parents' and teachers' duty. The father dominates; he attends to the business of the world, and the creature he has brought into the world has nothing to do but take him as a model, and walk obediently in his footsteps. The individual day does not make any impression, the hours do not invite one to pause, they must be added up, the sum of the figures runs: promotion from class to class, confirmation, a certificate for the semester, a certificate for the year; the final sum gives the content and the value of life. A problem in arithmetic.

Herr von Andergast remembers a serious illness which Etzel had when he was eight years old. One evening, quite late, he goes into the nursery and up to the child's bed. His mother has left the house long ago. The child's face is scarlet, his eyes shining; his hair, covered with perspiration, sticks to his forehead; a high fever. When Etzel sees his father, a curious expression of fright comes over his features, he turns his head away, stammering inarticulate words. The nurse tries to calm him, stroking his forehead and saying softly: Why, look, there's father, little boy! But the boy struggles as if he were about to be punished and his dry lips murmur: I want Rie. Rie is brought; she kneels by his bed, taking his little hands in her own. Then he calms down, merely whispering. I don't want to die, Rie, do you understand, tell my mother I don't want to die. His "I don't want to" was uttered with so much determination that Rie instead of her usual indulgence in melancholy replies: That is well, little Etzel, if you don't want to die you won't, and then you know too that we need you. The silly fool, thinks Herr von Andergast. Although he was touched and seriously worried, these words seemed to him at the time as silly as they were inappropriate. One may love a child, even when one carefully conceals it—and has "one" not concealed it to the point where there is not much left to conceal? But one can't speak of needing a child. And of course one does not "need" children: one needs kings, generals, officers, judges, lawyers, soldiers, workmen, servants, but children must first be brought up to the point of usefulness.

No, actually one could not speak of love either, scarcely of one of the many variations of the conception. As things have turned out today, after the complete collapse of his so-called private life, there is no longer any basis for deceiving oneself.

He ponders and ponders, seeking endlessly.

Illnesses like that attack of scarlet fever are mostly important stages in the development of a child. Herr von Andergast remembers that shortly afterwards he lost sight of the boy in a remarkable way. He lost sight of him in the sense that he became uncertain of his godlike sway over this human being, the motions which he has been in the habit of commanding having gradually become spontaneous and productive of humiliation for the self-esteem of the educator. He finds it difficult to understand the boy. He often feels in him such a curious unspoken obstinacy. One can't even point to any misdemeanour, to disobedience, it is just obstinacy in the abstract. He remembers a Whitsuntide holiday when he took the ten-year-old boy to the country. They are sitting in a first-class compartment, Etzel keeps sticking his head out of the window; Herr von Andergast tells him to stop doing that and to sit quietly in his place. There is, however, no special reason for this prohibition; it has just occurred to him that he wants to read his paper quietly and he thinks it unsuitable for the boy to get excited and poke his head out constantly. Whereupon Etzel sits up straight as a candle opposite his father with emphatic politeness and stares him in the face. And his look—although Herr von Andergast pretends not to notice it—is somehow irritating, it is penetrating and surprised, showing a secret unpleasant curiosity about the man who is his father; there is even a secret glow of sarcasm in the bright, short-sighted, sharply peering eyes. For a minute Herr von Andergast is furiously angry, he is on the point of lifting his arm and striking the boy. He remains taciturn and ill-humoured the whole day, feeling the boy's bright glance resting upon him and taking him in.

What a lot of mystery there is in such a child! It always seems as if Etzel walked about absent-mindedly in the normal channels and were seizing every opportunity that offered to dodge around the corner in order to execute some secret undertaking of his own. When he reappears he looks as if he had stolen something and were quickly and slyly secreting his booty. And indeed it is all stealing, the experiences which he seeks and which cannot be examined, the words and thoughts which he is accumulating, the pictures with which he is storing his insatiable fantasy. Everywhere he finds accomplices, every door opens into the world and all new knowledge of the world sullies this untarnished soul. Learning is either a fever of eagerness or a burden, knowledge either is presumption or is characterized by obtrusive doubts. Once Herr von Andergast had a talk with the rector about Etzel and the worthy gentleman remarked: That boy has a restless spirit; really he will only believe what can be proven as clearly as daylight, and he enjoys looking for a needle in a haystack; even God Himself would not have an easy time with him.

But at the same time the reverend gentleman smiled as they all smiled when they spoke of him, or when they merely looked at him. Even the registration clerk, worn down by bending over his papers, had a smirk about his faded lips when he caught sight of the boy. Even ill-humoured Dr. Malapert smiled whenever he met him in the house. And it was always a friendly, cheering, unexpected, happy smile with which people greeted him. What could the reason be? Probably external. There are whipper-snappers who move as if they were giants, and the effect is extraordinarily amusing. He certainly had something of the roguish gnome about him, of the little rogue who looks you steadfastly in the face and then makes a long nose at you as soon as he's out of the door. A few years ago an old hunch-backed great-aunt used to come to the house; she was in the habit of kissing the boy with the most unpleasant slobbering demonstration of affection; when she had gotten through Etzel would carefully wipe his face, bow gravely before her and say dryly: Thank you so much, Aunt Rosalie! Was it the amusing contrast of his courteous respectful bearing against the background of pranks either planned or executed, which won him so much general favour? Doubtless he possessed a natural grace, a quick pleasing sort of impertinence, both of which he had probably inherited from his mother, who as a young girl had had the same kind of gracious pertness, and who had also been hard to understand. Or did the answer lie a little deeper, did the attraction lie in what Dr. Camill Raff, in his estimable psychological discussion, had called his "sense of proportion"; did people feel clearly that he had taken their measure, that he did not demand too much of them, so to speak, and allowed them to stand for what they were?

Whatever it might be that was particular about the boy, which everyone seemed eager to acknowledge, Herr von Andergast himself had felt little of it. If occasionally it forced itself upon his attention, he would not accept it since he felt himself bound to pay no attention to it. He could not have reconciled it with his fundamental principles. It would have disturbed their foundations. It would have injured the orderliness, contradicted the rules and one would have had to give up one's general "guiding lines."

Only when he thought back, it seemed to him that in all this he had renounced some quite different thing. Perhaps a certain permissible sense of well-being. Perhaps he had renounced something which one might call a willingness to love. Thinking this over, it appeared to him that he had found an adequate, pregnant expression for a condition of sterile abstinence which he embodied. Furthermore, it seemed to him . . . well, what, what of it? Well, it was too late, much too late from every angle.

CHAPTER VII

I.

TOWARDS the end of the week which had begun with the perusal of the Maurizius record, Herr von Andergast came home one afternoon at tea time, and as he walked through the corridor, he heard low voices proceeding from Etzel's room. The door was ajar; he remained standing and saw his mother sitting at the table, with Rie opposite. They had Etzel's copy books in front of them; Rie had probably collected them together from the drawers and shelves. The widow was turning the pages, here and there reading a few lines and at times making a remark in low tones. Perhaps she hoped to find something there, a note, or a forgotten letter, which might give some indication of the boy's whereabouts. All of her other efforts had been in vain. A cloud of sadness hung over the two women. The widow in an old-fashioned lace mantilla, with an equally old-fashioned cloth hat on her small head, looked woebegone. She still could not understand Etzel's flight; still less could she understand that he had not given her, whom he had flatteringly convinced of his affection, any sign of life. She was consumed with worry. Herr von Andergast noticed her chin, sharp and small like Etzel's, and heard her saying to Rie: "We must not be discouraged, dear Rie. I have the most distinct confidence. The silly part of it is only that I am so old. But that too has its advantages. The absence of the people one loves gradually accustoms one to death. There is so much absence and the world is so big."

Herr von Andergast, who had on overshoes, on account of the rain, went back through the hall, without being heard and without having taken off his coat, descended the stairs and left the house. Suddenly the thought of greeting his mother politely, of looking at Rie's sad, humble, reproachful face, with anxiety written in every line of it, had seemed unbearable to him. To be condemned to sit at a desk loaded with legal papers, till evening, till late at night, with no company but an inkwell, notebooks, the chairs, the sofa, the horrible pictures on the walls and the books exuding taciturnity, was unendurable.

He walked rapidly till he came to an open field near the the Dammheide. There the wind was doubly wild, the rain beat in his face and the descending sheets of water flashed like whips. Since he had no umbrella (he objected on principle to an umbrella), he became wet through and through. He paid no heed to this. It was an entirely deserted region, no house, no hut anywhere about. After walking a few steps he would stop repeatedly; holding the brim of his hat he would struggle for breath and look carefully about, but his attention was not on the landscape, the storm, the whirling leaves of the lane of trees, the low threatening clouds, it was directed inward. The strain of intense thought was visible on his forehead. His brows contracted more and more every minute. Gradually he seemed no longer to be aware of anything in his surroundings, seemed to forget where he was and where he was going, and at times he would utter parts of sentences and detached thoughts aloud to himself, which was so different from his character and habits that the expression of his face would change, like ground which loses its hard upper crust when it is tilled.

2.

He cannot deceive himself about it. There is a flaw in the network of logic. And now considerations begin to make themselves felt. Up to a certain point he considers it excusable; the evidence was crushing; from the first moment they worked only in the one direction; an old empirical law of criminology declares that every crime has a suggestive force all its own. An error of justice is not to be thought of. Not in this case. If a flaw in the structure should appear, now after such a long time, one would have to investigate under cover. "In no case any official step. To direct the eye of the world towards a long closed trial would be a piece of blasphemous stupidity." "If I say, 'The whole truth has probably not yet been discovered,' I have already said too much. Perhaps . . . well, perhaps . . . we shall see."

He bit his lip and fixed his glance upon the dripping crown of an elm. He is willing to admit that they should have watched Gregor Waremme at least for a time after the sentence, although it would have been purely a police activity. But if at that time they had paid attention, had been able to pay attention to what occurred after the trial, they would probably have gotten useful information concerning his previous life. This was not done; incomprehensible omission, as Herr von Andergast now thinks. Nothing was known about this man's past, nothing was mentioned. And indeed, why should it have been mentioned? It was neither the duty nor the interest of the court. The witness for the crown is valuable to the court, which will avoid any active steps to undermine the credibility of his statements. Strictly speaking, the case stands and falls with Waremme. Without him, in view of the perpetrator's insanely persistent denials, the case would not have been brought to a successful close, or at least, only with much difficulty. A "successful close," of course, meant a verdict of guilty and the passing of the sentence.

"Undoubtedly, there are weak points. Let us look at them calmly." Herr von Andergast diminishes his impetuous stride in order to collect the weak points. There must be more than he has supposed, for after a time he presses his lips still more tightly together. Any satisfactory explanation is lacking on the subject of the relations between Waremme and Anna Jahn. Something must have occurred, as early as the Cologne days, which cast a shadow upon their connection with one another. Her practising a part for the play, under his guidance, her pathological aversion for the theatre and theatricals had not been investigated at all. There was not a hint as to the nature of this friendship, whether there was any erotic basis, whether they thought of marriage in the future. His one remark to Elli Maurizius—that he would soon bring her striking proof of Anna's innocence—proved nothing at all. What did "innocence" mean from his lips, what might the term mean to such a man as this? One ought to know about their relations after 1906. But the scene is covered in complete darkness. After sentence has been passed, the actors disappear from the scene. The law knows only the case as such; it has no right to interfere with the course of life after it has been resumed by the protagonists. "What I know as a private person, I have no business to know." But Herr von Andergast in private life knows nothing of the actions and omissions of witnesses or condemned persons; in this regard he is like a chemical substance which permits another substance to act upon it only in a certain physical condition. He ponders: if the intimacy between Anna Jahn and Waremme had been more than friendship, he would certainly have taken a firmer stand against the importunities to which she was subjected by her brother-in-law. On the other hand, he calls upon her quite informally at her flat, takes her to parties and athletic contests and acts decidedly like her cavalier and protector. If she does not give him this right, it is again inexplicable that after the last worst scene with Elli, she was persuaded by him to move to her sister's house, to take care of her, into the lion's mouth, as it were. One must assume that she has been robbed of her own will, to forget overnight the crude way in which Elli slandered her. And what about her financial condition? Certainly hopeless. She assists him as his secretary; he probably pays her for that, but if not, if her assistance is voluntarily rendered, then more than ever one must suppose an intimate relation. Which she, however, utterly denies. Who gives her the means of livelihood, since she nevertheless leads the life of a lady? Who pays for her luxurious apartment? Leonhart? He maintains not. Waremme? The question has not been discussed. A curious situation, one way or the other; certainly not a clean-cut one. But let us proceed. Since she is the cause of the upheavals between her sister and Leonhart and must undoubtedly know it, even if she feels herself guiltless and probably suffers as much as anyone, why does she remain? If she has a horror of her obstinate pursuer, why does she constantly receive him again? If she is tired of the man who endangers her reputation, why does she constantly show herself with him in public places? If he permits himself to be so carried away by his passion as to make such shameless overtures to her, in her sister's, his wife's house, that she is beside herself with indignation and contempt, why does she resume her relations with him? Why telephone, attend his lectures, keep his photograph with a passionate and quite unmistakable inscription in her desk? She was not able to protect herself against him, she states, she has put the best face on a bad business so that he should not lose his head completely and in his raving plunge herself, Elli and him into destruction.

Is that plausible? "At that time it seemed plausible enough. Dear God in heaven, a child of nineteen, so inexperienced that one pitied her, such youngsters often get themselves involved just because of their profound innocence; possibly this passion has flattered her, she is basking in the blaze which she has kindled; who knows women entirely?" Herr von Andergast unwillingly shakes his head. This is too lax a standpoint, it seems to him. She should have left the city, the reproach that she has remained, daily offering fresh fuel to this criminal passion, one cannot spare her. She should have disappeared into the night, should rather have gone forth to any uncertainty than have remained kindling this mortal dissension between the two, all unwillingly, let us assume. But what if she had played a double game? What if both men had merely been her pawns? Or if—let us go to the very limit of possibility in our imputations—what if she had been in collusion with Waremme and had manipulated the situation to its final catastrophe according to some preconcerted plan? Can one admit such a hypothesis? No, it is not admissible. It is not admissible under any circumstances. It is a silly, romantic hypothesis. Even the boldest slanderers did not dare at the time to advance such an insinuation; even the people busiest in whitewashing Maurizius refrained from expressing such an idea. Nevertheless, let us consent to follow even this thin thread down into the abyss, let us consider that this had been the case; then the two must have been very certain that the eighty thousand marks which were Elli's fortune—for this was what must have been at stake—would be inherited by Anna Jahn. What about the will? Herr von Andergast decides to inform himself as to the existence and the wording of the will. There was, however, no testament and since the husband was ruled out of the inheritance as unworthy, and the marriage had been childless, the sister was the lawful heiress. But we cannot venture so far. In the case of such a calculation, which defies all human clairvoyance, they would have had to be absolutely certain that Maurizius would put his head into the noose, that the noose would only have to be tightened, that everything—crime, evidence, witnesses—that absolutely everything would mesh in together and work with the accuracy of clockwork. "Nonsense! Damned nonsense! Things like that don't happen. One would have had to notice something about it. A web so carefully woven becomes coarse and snares the weaver."

Herr von Andergast stood still. Either from the exertion of walking, or the struggle with the storm or the burden of the thoughts streaming in upon him, an unhealthy red had come over his face; the veins of his forehead stood out like blue cords, and his dark eyes were drawn together; there was an expression of terror in them that he had never known before.

The picture of Waremme, no longer to be gainsaid, rushes in upon his memory. He sees him clearly before him. The bold forehead, his glance fixed diagonally upon the room, the protruding jaw of a fierce shark, the large head with the short bristling hair, all reeking of brutality, the somewhat corpulent figure. It required a man of a different calibre from this nervous puppet of a Maurizius to stand up against him. Nevertheless, those who knew him well spoke of serious neuroses, depressions and attacks of weeping to which he was not infrequently subject. This body, which produced an impression of immensity, in spite of its normal proportions, may be an arsenal of destructive functions, as in the case of those who have quite another age, in the light of the ages, than towards the period in which they live. He gives his age as twenty-nine, but it seems as if this were the mere accident of a birth certificate. When he begins to speak, everyone listens carefully, even to the most indifferent remark he makes. What compels attention is neither the voice nor the choice of words, but the precision of the expression, the superiority of his bearing. The court room has the feeling, "There, he knows what he's about," as if up to now it had only seen bunglers at work and now had a master-craftsman before it. Between him and all of the other witnesses there is a difference like that between pitiful fragments and a well-rounded whole. His appearance is such that the chairman at once obviously pulls himself together and the counsel for the defence, helpless little Dr. Volland, presents the appearance of a collapsed zero. The usual attempt of the witnesses for the prosecution and the witnesses for the defence to dodge the issue with sarcastic remarks, affable catch questions, the triumphant discovery of contradictions which must then be apologized for with, "one heard badly," was "mistaken," or that the prosecuting attorney "heard wrong" or "made a slip" are of no avail. Here there is no need of any of the reminders, or aids to memory, of tricky cross-questions, which can finally reduce seamstresses, coachmen, letter-carriers and even persons of the higher bourgeoisie to trembling and stumbling, but would be utterly out of place on this occasion; for Waremme is as professional, cool and collected as a glass of water. During his examination Herr von Andergast can't help saying: Thank Heaven that he is not the accused; we should not be equal to him. The presiding officer became more polite and respectful at each question, the room became so quiet that the hum of the ventilators above the window became unendurable. Every word is now decisive. To the chairman's questions about his opinion as to the behaviour of the accused before he was arrested, Waremme replies that he thinks he can be sure of the approval of the court, in saying that it is not for him to express any opinion, that his sole duty is to state what he saw and witnessed. This is accepted curiously enough; they acquiesce, although it sounds like censure. The judge, the solicitor, the attorney for the defence, and the jury all seem subordinate to him, he himself by his mere presence appears to be in a judicial capacity and his statement has the weight of a judgment. The emotion in his features transfers itself to the whole assembly. They understand that he struggles against giving up the unfortunate man, who was his friend, to the hangman, but what he knows and has seen prevails; the oath is compelling; this is what I saw, this is how matters went, here I stand and I cannot do otherwise. And back of him Leonhart Maurizius, his face shining with a transparent white, staring at him with eyes opening wide with deadly horror, springs up, stretches out his hand to him imploringly. Waremme turns towards him, sways, and the court officers catch him; he loses consciousness. He, not Maurizius! This scene makes a tremendous impression, and seems like a ghastly corroboration of his statement. . . .

Herr von Andergast stood still again, pulled his handkerchief out of an inner pocket and wiped his forehead. The cloth was at once wringing wet. His beard was like a sponge dipped in water. His eyelids were swollen and he could only open them with difficulty. Of all this he took no notice.

A thorough study of Gregor Waremme would certainly have led to interesting results, Herr von Andergast continues his ruminations, and struggles on into the storm. We have learned nothing of his background; and of the surface, only what he cared to show. There was a sombre atmosphere about him and a theatrical suddenness in his appearance and disappearance. Nothing further was heard of him. Curious. Such a distinguished mind, such a will, a man who had such an effect upon people, who raised such expectations and, after a short star rôle, he disappears leaving no trace of himself. Most extraordinary, a phenomenon of his time. Shall one take seriously old Maurizius' statement that he has found out where he is now living? Herr von Andergast pauses at this thought, which leads him to a decision which he utters aloud: "I must send for the old man the next time I get a chance. He must have a sharp warning. That fellow goes too far in his nasty insinuations as to Anna Jahn. . . ."

Anna Jahn. . . . Her figure appears, and Herr von Andergast makes a gesture in the air as if he wishes to ask her to wait a little, he will soon give her his attention. Just be patient a moment, he seems to say. Waremme has almost convinced him completely, just as formerly; the complete picture leaves nothing to be desired, no further questions; however, if one studies the details carefully, things get mixed up, the lines become blurred. In the first place, what has become of the revolver? Did Leonhart

Maurizius own one before the murder occurred? They were never able to prove it. Waremme saw him take it out of his coat pocket. He saw him aim it. It was, however, never found in the garden, nor anywhere within a radius of one hundred yards. Theoretically, under such conditions, it was conceivable that someone had shot from the outside, a possibility which was sufficiently emphasized by the attorney for the defence. But who could have fired the shot? Who in the whole world? Secondly: what happened when Maurizius came into the garden? Elli, after the second telegram recalling the first, could no longer have expected him. From whom did she find out that he was coming? Of course, from Anna. He had not recalled the telegram to Anna asking her to meet him at the station, either because he had lost his head and already forgotten all about it, or because he secretly hoped that she would perhaps come nevertheless. Thus Anna, who probably at once understood that the second telegram to Elli was a blind, in order to gain time, told her sister that Leonhart was on the point of arriving. Fine. She does not reply to the telegram he sent and pays no further attention to it, but rather makes sure of the assistance of her friend before the return of the man she fears. Quite logical. But why does she not go away? It would be the simplest thing to do. She has merely to leave the house and go to some acquaintance in the city. Why does she stay? Stay, stay and stay again. If it is her intention that he should find only Elli, that Elli, restless and eager as she is, should receive him—for before this trip he did not even say goodbye to her—the wisest thing she could do would be to disappear and there is not the slightest necessity to send for Waremme. The reply to this is that she must watch her sister, that she cannot leave Elli, in a condition of excitement bordering upon madness, alone. If this was only the case! There had been a reconciliation between the two sisters, but it seems to have been of brief duration, or Elli could not yet bear the sight of her rival, for after she had lain sobbing and crying uncontrollably the whole afternoon, she had rung for the maid Frida and asked her to keep her company; she was so terribly afraid. During this time Anna was playing the piano. Herr von Andergast remembers that this fact had already puzzled him at the time. She had explained it, to a certain extent plausibly, in connection with her disturbed frame of mind; upstairs was her sister in a state of mind in which she was scarcely accountable; she downstairs, alone, shuddering at the prospect of the arrival of the desperate man whose attempts to raise money have probably been pitifully unsuccessful. So she plays Schumann's Carnival, meantime having frightening visions of suspicious characters prowling about the house. Leonhart will be there in a few minutes. She can't stand it any longer, she rushes to the telephone, imploring Waremme to come. All very well, all fine and good, only it might look as if Waremme had been waiting for the call. Everything fits together too well. One might become suspicious that Elli had become frightened at the very last minute; and the question of the attorney for the defence to the Jahn woman, how she explained that Elli in her condition of ill health, in spite of the heart attack which she had been suffering from since morning, left the room and the house in order, not merely to go, but to fly to her husband, had not been a random shot. It was a critical moment, the jury raised their heads, the remark of the chairman that Fräulein Jahn could scarcely give any information on this point, since she had not acted in the capacity of a trained nurse, had met with the disapproval of the public. But then there was old Gottlieb Wilhelm Jahn, an uncle of the sisters, who was called upon to testify in regard to his nieces, and who had a great deal of influence on the opinion of the jurymen, when he turned towards the bench where the accused was sitting, and with upraised hand exclaimed: The wretch not only physically murdered the one, his wife and his only friend, but he killed the mind and soul of the other. The curse of all mankind rests upon him. As the old man with the imposing white beard spoke, Anna crossed her hands and closed her eyes. It was like the fainting of Waremme, one of the great moments of the trial.

Herr von Andergast walked more rapidly and with longer strides. It seemed as if it were yesterday that she stood there in her tight black dress, with the white pleated collar, and the white lace sleeves coming down over her slender white hands. He had shortly before seen a portrait of Mary Stuart, by Clouet, and he still remembers how surprised he was at the resemblance between Anna Jahn and the picture. One could not forget the pain of the mouth, the eyes "whose glance was endless," as an excited journalist wrote at the time, the nobility of her motions and the delicacy of her figure. Outrageous to think that such a creature could even be aware of lies, why, she lived in a world apart, frozen into some unapproachable element! The court and the jury regarded her as a martyr. "She stood out from the trial like a white flower from a black curtain," the same excited journalist wrote. Moreover, judicially viewed, she was the axis of the proceedings by which the crime was proved; if Herr von Andergast had allowed the emphasis to be shifted, the ground would have disappeared from beneath his feet. And in God's whole world there was only one possible perpetrator anyway. No one except him! No accomplice, no confidant. Where should one have looked for them? "From this it is at once evident that the path was traced for us, was shown me, with a diamond stylus. . . ."

He defended himself against a gust of wind as if it were a last onslaught of doubt and said, standing still: "Therefore too the judgment is unassailable. At every point." And standing still again after a few steps: "I take the whole responsibility upon myself." And again, after walking on a few steps he almost screamed: "No, the judgment is unassailable."

But the pronouncement, however final it sounded, did not smother a slight doubt. The fright in his eyes spread like a spot of ink on a blotter. He avoided the fright within himself and treated his thoughts shyly. It was a lack of candour towards himself and it troubled him like a disturbance of the equilibrium of life. As a child he had for weeks observed a clock with growing uneasiness, the pendulum of which swung badly and irregularly. He was forced to think of it constantly. On the Rödelheim Road he called an empty taxi and drove back to the city. Half asleep, wet to the skin, he leaned back in a corner of the carriage. Where can the boy be? suddenly shot into his mind. His thoughts no longer obeyed him. For a second he understood the wish of some children to be sick in order that they need not go to school. Of what avail would it have been to him to be sick? What was there for him besides school? Yes, he could withdraw into his repulsive bedroom, like some remote hole; from time to time that repulsive Rie would trip up to his bed, and he could not even send for little Violet.

3.

Violet Winston was a young Californian, whom he had met three years ago after a stag dinner at the Russischer Hof. She was sitting in the hotel hall trying in vain to make a waiter understand her. Herr von Andergast offered his aid as an interpreter. She had only arrived a few days before from the other side, intending to study in the Stern Conservatory; she did not know a soul in the city, was entirely alone in the world and had means of livelihood for another half-year only. She became his friend, and he rented a modest flat for her, very far from his house, on Pestalozzi Square, where she received him two or three times a month. The relationship had been clothed in the greatest secrecy;

thanks to the rigorous watchfulness of Herr von Andergast all talk had been avoided up to now.

It is a delightful task to construct the picture of his lady love from the character of a man whom one knows. In many cases one can be approximately correct without indulging too cheaply in mere contrasts, or making a scheme of simple attractions. If we bear in mind that in this case the sinister side of this man's character cannot be resolved by any erotic experience, that the increasing frigidity of his being cuts him off from everything except the hollowness of life, forming a barrier against any warmth, that life's aspect is known to him only by its appearance, the choice which Herr von Andergast made in the young American will no longer surprise us. She offered him nothing, she was nothing to him, she had nothing to give, she was nothing herself. And this nothing was just what he needed. Mind, piquancy, moods, cultivation, why should these mean anything to him, since he sought neither excitement, nor recreation, scarcely that which we call distraction? What he wanted was a kind of opportunity for rest which would incidentally allow him to function as a male being when the need asserted itself. These advantages were more compatible with ignorance and banality than with distinguished qualities. For he had been living ten years without a wife and he knew that the desires of the body cannot be permanently stifled without danger to one's mental balance. He was not in any sense a used-up man. His grey beard and bald head marked the passage of time, but no internal decline or weakness. He came of a family whose men and women reached eighty and ninety in vigorous health, and he had the physical freshness of those who have never been guilty of dissipation and are aware of their unspent strength. After his separation from Sophia, he had given up every attachment, every expectation from women. He simply excluded such sensations from his life. But he acted thus not merely from principle. He had had an experience which had wounded his pride almost mortally. The wound had not yet healed; it could never heal. It was impossible to think of it without sending the blood to his heart and making him boil. The idea that such an experience might repeat itself, in any form, was enough to keep him away from any feminine attractions. For him there was no more belief in this respect —nor indeed in any other. Who could know better than he what people mean by love, what they cover over with this term, and what this love actually amounts to? He could have written a large dictionary of the forms of degeneration, the pitiful compromises, the wretchedness and miseries, little and great, which formed the content of his working days, the intolerable repetition marking all other days, year in, year out. A word, a record, and the individual is no longer anything but his previous record, his reputation and an indicated punishment. Although the thumb print is not registered in a book, his forehead and his eyes none the less are a brand of equal weight. No matter if they read Faust, or some at times say our Lord's prayer, or disfigure their walls with maxims as pious Jews nail verses from the Scriptures on the door-posts, none of this will keep a single one of them from cheating, embezzling, stealing, perjury or assault, if he has the slightest prospect of evading responsibility for the matter. There were strictly speaking not good people and bad, honest and dishonest, lambs and wolves; there were only people with good reputations and with bad, those who had been punished and those who escaped, this was the whole difference; and that they were the one or the other was determined not by some quality or defect, but by some accident beyond their control. He did not inquire about the man or the woman. There did not exist for him any Mr. So-and-so, or any Mrs. Blank. He knew the position, the class, the profession, the occupation, the groups, the antecedents, the social ramifications and habits, the conditions and frictions of life, people's proportionate strength and weakness, their powers of expression. His familiarity with these reached the point of easy mastery so that he could talk as well with a locksmith, a peasant, a prostitute, in their own language, as with a countess or a minister. Of the real person and of his indissoluble entity he knew nothing, and did not wish to know. And so it was proper and suited him that Violet Winston was a female, as a whitefish in the ocean is a specimen of his tribe, like a hundred thousand others whose capture was the result of an accident unworthy of any special attention.

She was pretty, friendly, good-natured, complaisant and harmless. She had a white skin, a white inexpressive face, corn-yellow hair, the washed-out colour of which seemed expressive of nothingness, also little round clumsy hands, like a baby's, and pretty, slender legs. Her silly big blue eyes, when their glance rested upon him, reminded him of nothing at all. When her lips, painted brick-red, parted in a smile showing her tiny white teeth, these too seemed to wish to share in the sweet vacuity of her whole personality. If one had cared to dissect her in order to see what her inner feelings towards her big sombre friend were, one would probably have found, besides a certain moderate animal-like affection of a creature in need of protection nothing but a little silly fear. And on account of this fear, she admired him. Yes, she admired him much in the same way that a little whitefish admires a monstrous greedy pike which does not devour it merely because it feels too much contempt for it. When she sat upon his lap, absorbed in making sheep's eyes at him, she could not speak without calling herself "poor girl" and "poor little Violet." There was always a stupid little outbreak of surprise at the dissimilarity of human creatures. The conversation between them was mostly on the subject of things. She had a picture of Sacramento, the city which was her home, over her bed. Herr von Andergast was of the opinion that the picture hung fully three inches too low. The conversation on this point lasted over a quarter of an hour. She was fond of flowers, but did not know how to arrange them; this offered an opportunity for endless discussions whether, for example, to put pink lilacs and red carnations in the same vase. Although she dressed well, her taste was slightly barbaric, also she liked perfume which was a little too strong. Herr von Andergast instructed her, and reprimanded her constantly, seriously, dryly, patiently. He would have regarded impatience towards such a dear little nonentity as a waste of energy. She would give him an account of her expenditures and when there was a superfluous item on the list he would scold her gently until her silly blue eyes would fill with silly tears, whereupon he would smile indulgently. She had many faults, she was forgetful, flirtatious, greedy, rather careless. But it was all so little! She, including her faults, amounted to so little one could not be angry at anything so unimportant. A little whitefish. Sometimes she would sit down at the piano and sing the songs of her home. Her silly little voice would fill the room like a little insect chirping, and she would accompany herself with her silly little baby hands. It was a perfect idyl.

4.

Herr von Andergast still felt his walk through the storm all over his whole body when he got to Violet's. He had eaten at home and had changed his clothes carefully. She complained poutingly. She felt neglected, his visits had recently become more and more infrequent. In her amusing broken German—he had insisted on her learning German—she said that she felt deserted "like a single shoe." Herr von Andergast quieted her as easily as one puts out a burning match. She had had a bad day. She had lost her gold wrist-watch. She said that she would never know again what time it was. "Poor little Violet has lost the time." At night she would wake up every hour afraid lest she should miss the daylight and would wait for the horrid big church clock to strike. Herr von Andergast looked as if he were considering a problem in chess and said that a new watch might be purchased for her, but she must notify the police about her loss. He described how to get there, the building, the necessary formalities. Meantime she sat opposite him, looking at him with unbounded admiration. She had bought a brand of cigarettes for him which he particularly liked, she brought the box with quick steps, gave him a match, lighted a cigarette herself, after which they peacefully and minutely discussed the aroma, the price, and the fact that the tobacco was a little too strong. As Herr von Andergast rubbed his hand over his forehead several times, she finally noticed how tired he looked and in reply to her worried question, he admitted that he had a pretty bad headache. She opened her eyes wide in dismay, as if the thought that such a big creature could become ill, or even be indisposed, had never occurred to her. In a scared piping voice, she suggested various remedies; when he mildly but decidedly refused them she began to scold him and he permitted her to. She said that he must lie down and rest. He admitted this and obeyed. He lay down upon the sofa and she covered him up with a big shawl, put out all the lights, except a shaded lamp in the corner, and said that she would leave him alone, she would go into her bedroom and not disturb him. On the threshold she turned around again, and stroking the sleeper with a fat little finger, she said with an affectionate little mew, "You are a naughty boy," nodding her head precociously. "You work too much and you think too much. Sure!" He smiled pleasantly. He accepted her sympathetic displeasure with the seriousness with which one accepts a make-believe coin from a child, which it declares to be a gold-piece.

He lay for a long time with open eyes in the half-darkened room, curiously devoid of any thoughts. How much time had elapsed when he got up he did not know. He looked at his watch, but was so distrait that he had forgotten the time when he had closed the lid. He gently opened the door into the adjoining room. Violet lay in bed asleep. At the foot of the bed there hung a reddish swinging lamp. Violet liked swinging lamps and she never slept in the dark. She was afraid of the dark and impervious to instruction in this point. Herr von Andergast stood by the bed looking down upon the sleeper. Since nature erases all mental activity from a sleeping face, it is in this state completely in harmony with her. In the case of little Violet there was as little erasing to do as with any mortal creature. So she lay there, entirely a vegetable, slightly aglow from the sentimental lamp which hung over her, and from the youth and health within her. Sometimes an expression of fear flitted across her face, making her for a few seconds a few years older, but it seemed like only a slight wave, not indicated by any visible disturbance of the water. A sigh, her breast would rise and then her body lay still again. Herr von Andergast, like all people attached to consciousness as the only power in life, did not like the sight of people asleep. He was indeed always obliged to overcome a slight revulsion when he saw a sleeping face. He walked over to the toilet table, sat down in the armchair and waited, his face turned a little away from the bed. The position of the mirror above the table enabled him to see the sleeper when he looked into the glass. It was a situation in agreement with his nature. The indirect was characteristic of him. Gradually, however, he seemed to forget where he was, his chin sank slowly upon his breast, his eyes stared penetratingly, indescribably hard, indescribably sinister into some hidden depth, and thus he sat hour after hour. It was dreadful the way he sat there silently staring, the powerful figure, the strong forehead, the stony impassivity of his face. When he finally lifted his head again and looked into the mirror, he saw not himself, not Violet asleep, but he saw . . . Waremme. That is to say he saw a person whom he at once assumed to be Waremme, but who bore only a vague resemblance to that

Waremme whom he had last seen only eighteen and a half years ago. Now, of this person he saw only the upper part of his body, which was somewhat over life size, had his right arm extended—the left being supported against his hip—and upon the palm of his hand stood Etzel, very small indeed, but very brave, perhaps indeed with a somewhat impertinent expression. He held a lantern in his hand and the light of the lantern fell upon the face of Waremme—or whoever the person really was—and completely illuminated it as if the skin and bones were made of gelatine, and in such a way that the brain, upon which the light chiefly fell, was completely exposed. The whole mass of the brain with its channels, convolutions and convexities, its endless veins and arteries contracted constantly under the effect of the light from which it could not defend itself, which acted upon it like the knife of a surgeon; and as the beams moved hither and thither, directed by the sinewy little fist, as if to discover a certain spot, gradually the whole jelly-like mass, quivering painfully like a disgusting jellyfish, became clearer in its minutest detail. What's happening to me, thought Herr von Andergast with irritation, I am seeing apparitions, seeing apparitions with my eyes open. He pressed his fingers upon his eyes and the next time he looked into the mirror he saw nothing but the young girl asleep, with the rosy light of the lamp upon her, smiling under the influence of some pretty and certainly unimportant dream.

Herr von Andergast got up noiselessly and returned into the living-room. He sat down at the rickety, thin-legged, little desk, took some paper and an envelope out of a writing pad, held his pen towards the light before beginning, and then wrote in a big hand with letters inclined forwards, the l's and t's and f's looking like telegraph poles in the wind: *"Dear Violet: This evening has been the last which I can spend with you. The standing bills will be paid and your monthly allowance of one hundred and fifty marks will be paid until the first of July. Wishing you much future happiness on your path in life. W. A."* After he had put the sheet into the envelope, addressed it to "Miss Violet Winston," he placed this against the electric lamp, turned off the switch, went very noiselessly into the narrow, cagelike hall, slipped into his coat, pressed his stiff hat upon his forehead, and went into the public-hall, closing the door slowly. As he strode down the street, he noticed after a time that it had ceased to rain and that a brilliant starry sky was spread over the city.

5.

The servant announced that Peter Paul Maurizius, who had an appointment for eleven o'clock, was in the waiting-room. Dr. Nämlich, state attorney, stuffed his documents into a brief case and disappeared. Herr von Andergast sat for a time with his head on his hand, an open notebook before him. He wanted to be clear in his own mind about what he wished to learn from the old man. He would have to weigh every word. It would be necessary to occupy him for a while with his own affairs in order then to take him by surprise with his question about Etzel. Up to what point he could mislead, confuse and set the old man on a false scent, would have to be determined in the course of the conversation. In what an annoying and tormenting manner the two situations had suddenly condensed into one! How annoying and tormenting was the mysterious puzzle: Where is Etzel? It had become mixed up with that fruitless puzzling about a criminal given over to a just punishment. Only now, as the name Maurizius struck his ear, did Herr von Andergast realize that he had sent for the old man "to warn him," and at the same time to get something out of him. This was the weaker impulse; the essential point was to ask about the boy, to hear about Etzel, to lessen the silly uneasiness which, as matters stood, he could no longer talk himself out of, to get rid of something else, something more unusual, more troublesome, a longing, an emptiness, a discontent, an impatience, something that worried and gnawed at him as if some visceral organ had suffered a lesion.

Old Maurizius remained standing at the door after he had made a profound bow. He wore a kind of hunting-jacket with bone buttons. On his stiff left arm rested the inevitable captain's cap. Herr von Andergast, from underneath half-closed eyelids, cast a sidelong glance at him, the glance of the criminologist, which discovers in a second what a long investigation at times fails to reveal. But in this instance, he gained little. A weather-beaten, pinched, obstinate, impassible face of an old man. However, the sullen immovability of the old man was only a controlled dissimulation. Back of this external rigidity, expectation was pounding like an iron hammer in his breast. He felt that finally the great turning-point had been reached. How was anything else possible; what other reason was there for the invitation; why otherwise the mysterious dealings with the boy? He scarcely dared to think. Since he had received the notification from the solicitor-general's office, he had neither eaten, nor slept, had forgotten to fill his pipe, or when he had filled had forgotten to light it. There he stood now ready to listen, ready to speak. But he distrusted his tongue, he feared a mistaken, a premature, a harmful word. He felt as if he were standing not on the floor but in the air, and that if he took a step, he must fall. Control yourself, man, he kept repeating constantly to himself, that fellow too is made of flesh and bone. "I have asked you to come in order to put an end to your written importunities. Take care, you may get yourself into trouble." The voice sounded cold. There was no note of promise in this, nor of a change of mind. Ah, well, this is just a beginning. These lawyers, when they want to go to Rome, act as if they were on the road to Amsterdam. Maurizius bowed. That was all. The sides of his nose flattened against the bone, his nostrils became quite concave. He was immensely intimidated by the majestic appearance of the man at the desk. He felt himself as dependent upon this man as the bell is upon the beam from which it swings. He trembled at every fresh word, but betraying nothing of this, stared straight ahead like a helmsman with his eyes upon an approaching reef. The man who controlled his fate held a pencil in his hand, which he turned up and down constantly, so that the point was now turned up and then down again. This was curious, one ought to know why he did this, he certainly could not wish to frighten one in this way. "I should like to take this opportunity to ask you some questions, but please note that the conversation is not official and does not bind us to anything on either side. Take a chair."

This sounded better already. Well, well, so we are on the way. He did not act upon the invitation to sit down. That might be a pitfall. He merely replied with his stereotyped bow. It was the politeness of a penguin. What had led him to assume that the lawyer, Dr. Volland, had been forced upon his son at the trial? Maurizius rubbed his lips one upon the other in order to moisten them. A ridiculous frog leaped quick as a lightning flash before his eyes. If only the man would stop turning the pencil up and down. It was enough to drive one crazy. The pencil got constantly longer, it became as tall as a tower. Now don't let me lose any of my precious thoughts. "It was not a mere assumption, sir, Leonhart said he had been asked to." That pencil, that damned pencil! Moreover, a diamond gleamed on the man's finger. All right, all right, one must simply look out of the window, although it was better to keep one's eyes upon the danger, the danger in which all hope lay. Had he said that correctly? Had he spoken comprehensibly? He felt as though his mouth were full of sand and he could not speak properly. "By whom was it desired?" "It had been suggested to him." "By a certain person?" "By a certain person." "You are probably mistaken about the real state of affairs." "Very improbable, sir." To himself he added, That's as sure a thing as the Cathedral of Cologne. The suggestion might have come from the family. That of course was possible, but there had only been old Jahn, Gottlieb Wilhelm Jahn. "Well then?" "Six of one, half a dozen of the other, sir." "What do you mean by that?" "He had no other intention than the destruction of my child."—"Nonsense, man! Leonhart had destroyed himself! The worst lawyer could not add anything to the situation, nor the best detract." "Moreover, Leonhart had given Anna Jahn a free hand to choose the lawyer whom she thought best." "Well then, she considered Volland the best."—"Very good, sir, but one soon saw what kind of man he was." "Others offered their services. It is for the accused to select his lawyer; he must have known from the first that he was not in good hands." "Sir, he did not care." "Did not care! How can anyone not care when his head is in the noose?" "Nevertheless, sir! If a person is innocent and does not see any possibility of proving his innocence, then he does not care what kind of sophistries a man who rides the letter of the law brings forth. In that case the Lord Himself would have had to plead, and who knows whether He would have fared better?"

There was a minute of silence. It was a heavy silence, pregnant with thought. Maurizius' body swayed a little like the top of a tall tree in a considerable breeze. He cast a shy glance at the solicitor-general. Something is going on in that man, he thought, and his heart ceased to beat for a moment. Herr von Andergast stroked one side of his face with the four fingers of his right hand and the other side with his thumb. It aroused a curious sensual pleasure in him to feel the skin of his cheeks. Innocent, he thought, and expanded his lungs in obdurate pride, innocent! A mad and impertinent phrase when the law and the court have spoken. Innocent, when the criminal has been found guilty and is still expiating his crime, and human and divine justice is being enacted. Innocent! He felt as if the old man had struck him in the chest with a stone. But Maurizius had perceived correctly, something was going on inside of him. There was one means of making his conviction still more unshakable than it already was. He could see with his own eyes: to do so lay within his power. He could assure himself how this Leonhart Maurizius bore the burden inflicted upon him. It was not out of the question that, confronted by him, Leonhart might break the eighteen years of silence, that he would relieve his soul, become submissive and confess. Such a triumph would be worth some trouble. This was what was going on in Herr von Andergast and what the old man, who was the creature of his hopes and his delusions, felt by a mysterious transference. "Do you perhaps remember what you and Leonhart spoke of that October evening when he came to see you the last time?" Maurizius shook his head, not because he was answering the question by a negative, he was only surprised that anyone should think that in this matter it was possible that he should not remember the very slightest detail. At the same time his face seemed to cloud over with a grey veil. The man there back of the desk knew how to aim and to hit. Now he had finally laid aside that devilish pencil, but to make up for that he was looking at one with his blue eyes as if he invited one to walk right into them. Good Lord, how blue the man's eyes are; it seemed as if everything which had taken place at that time was mirrored in them. He snatched at one of the horn buttons of his jacket and turned it convulsively. It is superfluous to tell how the boy treated him with lies, a host of lies, he merely implies it with bent head. The lie about the study trip for the government, the lie about the twelve hundred marks which he should have been paid for his last piece of work, if the publisher had not gone bankrupt, the lie about Herr von Krupp's asking him to give an opinion on a disputed Dutch painting. Finally the lie that he had intended to come the next day to say goodbye, but that someone in Wiesbaden had told him that his father was sick, whereupon he had asked Count Hatzfeld to lend him his motor. He had not been in Wiesbaden at all and a jeweler's motor had not been good enough for him, it had to be a count's. What pathetic lies; they never had two legs to stand upon. Sick—he? No, Peter Paul Maurizius was very careful not to be sick then when he was waiting for his day to come, just as he was careful not to get sick now when still more he was waiting for his turn to come. Oh, those pitiful stupid little lies intending to say: "Just look at me, see what a fellow I am, how many honours are conferred upon me, how far I have gotten on in the world." If only his face had not itself given him the lie, looking as though he had been drinking and carousing three days and three nights, or as if he had been dragged out of a burning house and the traces of the scare were still upon him.

The bone button was torn off. Maurizius held it in his hand, looked at it with surprise and let it slip into his pocket. His narration had been a monotonous murmur, scarcely comprehensible. Now he took two steps into the room as if for what he had now decided to say he needed to be nearer to his listener. "He had probably supposed that I would overwhelm him with questions and coax him. He had probably thought that after he had for days and years . . . well, it was so, sir . . . about this marriage, there was no friendship any more, everything was over, his name might as well have been Leonhart Schulze. He had probably supposed, when he came of his own accord in the night and sat in front of me there talking as if he were about to be sent to a lunatic asylum the next day, he had supposed that I should give him my hand. That was it, honoured sir. And that I did not do. I saw what way the wind was blowing, but I did nothing of the sort. And that, sir, that remains a load on my conscience. And that will be reckoned against me. A human being is a rotter. When a man does not want to do a thing and gets his back up he becomes a rotter. And that at once.

What was at stake, I ask you." He walked a step nearer, placed his hand flat upon his head, the big naked lobes of his ears grew blood-red. "Two thousand marks. Put it at three thousand. If I had given him the money, if I had not in my contemptible superiority insisted, not only that he should humiliate himself before me—for that he finally did—but that I should remain in the right, in the situation with Elli; if I had overcome myself and given him two or three thousand marks, and I could have managed it, that's as certain as that I am standing here now, then everything would have turned out differently. Then he would have freed himself for a while; he would not have returned to his damned house with despair in his heart; he would not have fallen into the trap like a blind bird. Then he would have seen what was going on about him and have been able to protect himself. That is the story, sir. His life was at stake that night and his life was not even worth three thousand marks to me. Think what a life is worth. Think, honoured sir, how valuable a life is. Can its value be calculated? One cannot estimate the value of a human life any more than one can estimate heaven, and for me three thousand marks was too dear!" He drew his hand down from his head and bending over, placed it with a loud bang on the desk under Herr von Andergast's eyes, as if as a visible token and sacrifice. And when Herr von Andergast looked up he saw that tears were pouring over the weather-beaten face.

He got up with a jump, strode through the room and remained standing at the window. "You see matters in a false light," he said in a broken voice, and without turning his face away from the window. "You have twisted the facts thus, all that has nothing to do with reality." "I don't know what reality is," replied the old man darkly. Then, after a period of silent brooding, with his head drawn in and downcast eyes: "Sir, do help me." Herr von Andergast turned around and went towards him. The old man's forehead reached exactly to his shoulder and Andergast noticed the red protuberance with disgust. "What have you done with that boy, with my son?" he asked sharply. Maurizius blinked and seemed to withdraw into himself. "The boy came to me of his own accord," he said after a long silence. "Afterwards, it always seemed to me as if I had merely dreamed. In all my life I have never had any visions or anything of that sort. I have been at bottom a dead man for eighteen years and way deep down there is only a spark burning. But I wanted to say . . . I wanted to say this: The boy always seemed to me like an apparition. One can't express with ordinary understanding what there is about that boy. Well, yes, we talked two or three times, I believe. He was interested in the case. Read everything that I gave him, all the material. One day I got back a whole package and a note with it. The note ran: '*I am going away now, I must go to Gregor Waremme; when I come back we shall know one way or the other.*' Not another word. I laughed so. Or no, I really didn't laugh. You angelic little boy, I thought, you angelic little fool. I had such a remarkable feeling at the time, as if the hand of God were finally at work."

Herr von Andergast returned to the window. He stood like a black battering ram against the light rectangle. "You do not know where he is?" "I don't know and I should not like to say what I assume about it." "Why not?" "It's a superstition, sir." "He has not written to you since then?" "No, sir." "And you know . . . or do you not know where this Waremme is?" "May I ask, sir, whether that is an official or a personal question?" "It is . . . for the present . . . a personal question." "Then, sir, since I have this superstition, I should like with your permission to leave the question unanswered for the present." "Very well."

This was a dismissal. But Maurizius did not move. Herr von Andergast, with an expression of suppressed aversion characteristic of him alone, beneath which there might be feelings hidden, which he had only too much experience in keeping from the surface, threw out: "So far as the other matter is concerned, I advise you not to have any high hopes. We shall see." The old man raised his eyes with an expression of terrified pleasure. "Certainly. That is a matter of course, that one. . . . What could one hope for under the most favourable conditions?" he stammered hoarsely. "Under the most favourable conditions? . . . One might propose the pardon which you have asked for." The silence with which the old man moved away had something ghostlike about it. He feared perhaps that the words might be taken back if he made himself noticeable any further.

As Herr von Andergast walked down the monumental stone steps fifteen minutes later, he felt as if he were walking through a huge sea-shell, the roar of which was hurting his ear. The halls and steps were already empty, but the air vibrated with absent steps and voices. Behind the walls, clerks sat, bending over deeds and proclamations, writing. With their pens they were intervening in the fates of human beings, but their expressions were as indifferent as if they had merely been ordered to transfer a certain quantity of ink to a certain quantity of paper. Doors slammed; electric bells sounded; peremptory voices dictated into machines, or shouted into telephones. Complaints were brought forward, oaths were sworn, verdicts were given and laws were interpreted. It is a well-built construction and everyone in it works obediently, conscious of his duty; the barristers, the assessors, the solicitors, the lawyers, a respectable hierarchy, only dimly and shudderingly aware of the mind and spirit dominating it all. But are they aware of it, do they within the shell know? Do they shudder at it? That is the question. The shell certainly seems to contain the ocean if one listens to the sounds inside of it, but the sound of the ocean's perpetual organ-tones is deceiving, for the shell only roars because it is empty.

Part Two
INTERREGNUM

CHAPTER VIII

I.

ETZEL did not need to fear pursuit during the journey. He knew that his father would not come back from his trip until Thursday; by that time he would be in Berlin. The question was only, what then? Where could he find shelter; where could he hide? He did not deceive himself by thinking that his father would fulfil the request he had made in his farewell letter not to have him pursued. He was obliged, however, to have a free hand, so that he could move as the conditions required, otherwise the whole enterprise would come to naught. At any hotel, any pension, any inn, the police would have to be notified of his presence. To give a false name would probably not help matters much, since, if they were seeking him, they would have a description of his person; and they were skilful in such matters. He had no acquaintances in Berlin, not a soul whom he could apply to, except perhaps, perhaps—a timorous sigh accompanied this thought—Melchior Ghisels. However, it was to be assumed that a Melchior Ghisels could not attend to such unimportant matters, even if he were inclined to pay any attention to an Etzel Andergast. Where should he go? He was greatly worried.

Chance came to his aid. As he sat upright in a corner of the compartment, weighing as the hours passed the difficulties, which seemed to him insurmountable, his glance fell upon a woman between forty-five and fifty, who was occupying a seat opposite him and had been looking at him for some time with something like sarcasm. Sunk in his own thoughts, he had paid little attention to his fellow passengers; the carriage was fairly full, all kinds of bourgeois were travelling, salesmen and small tradespeople, women, children, young girls; only at Kassel did the seats begin to empty, and up to Hanover but few new passengers got in. The woman, however, remained and at once began to talk to Etzel. She was uneducated, gossipy and fairly good-natured; at the same time her face had an expression which one often perceives among women of the lower middle class, something worn and harassed, which reminds one of horses which fall down on the pavement and then lie there with an obstinate questioning pain in their eyes. After the first few words he knew her name, and her family circumstances and her financial situation were not long withheld. Her name was Schneevogt; her nineteen-year-old daughter Melitta also went to business; her flat was in Anklamerstrasse in the north of Berlin and consisted of three main rooms and two little ones, the latter of which she let out to gentlemen. She said that she was returning from Mannheim, where she had buried her brother, her only brother. He had gotten on in life, had been a bookbinder and an expert chessman and the secretary of a choral society. When she had gone there she had hoped to inherit something, at least a little something, but the hope had been vain; there was not the black under one's finger nails left, nothing but broken-down furniture and debts. It was so hard to get on; she had secretly hoped for some assistance from the dear departed, it was such a damned struggle and no ray of hope in sight. Her husband was always sickly, and as for his salary, the Lord knew it was just sufficient not to starve; no one had expected when he was a baby that he would have to live on herring and potatoes when he was fifty-seven years old. Unfortunately he was too decent, that was no way to get on in the world today; Melitta gave the chief part of her monthly earnings to the household; but there was not much to be done with seventy marks; such a youngster wanted a little fun, too, and so on and on. Her voice ran on like a waterfall with an even shrillness, not only as if pity and understanding were expected of Etzel, but as if he were also partly to blame.

Misfortune is for such people exclusively the result of guilt, never one's own but either of the community which has not adequately appreciated the gifts and services of this offended ego, or of certain individuals, who at decisive moments have failed them out of malice, weakness or stupidity. She could not indulge sufficiently in bitter reminiscences, comparisons with the lot of this or that acquaintance, contemptuous remarks over the inefficiency of a Herr Schmitz, even though he had become the director of a factory, or bitterness about a Frau Hennings, the daughter of a man who repaired shoes and who, as true as I sit here, had once sewn children's shirts in the most wretched part of Marienburgerstrasse, and now resides in a villa in Grünewald and drives about in a motor. If, for example, the dead man had had any gumption and had taken the opportunity and sold his business three years ago, how would she, Frau Schneevogt, be off now? How? Why, it was a shame that cried to heaven! While talking thus, she really screamed aloud and, bending over towards Etzel, glared reproachfully and threateningly at him. He nodded. He was entirely of her opinion. He considered the Schneevogt family far more worthy of riding in a motor-car or living in Grünewald than Frau Hennings, who had sewn children's shirts; was of the opinion that the dead bookbinder had committed an unpardonable sin of omission. Full of frank sympathy, he gazed into the woman's face, ready for every concession which she might demand of him, prepared to admit that Herr Schneevogt was a genius of business enterprise, and that Melitta, who in spite of her charming voice, had not been engaged by any theatre director, or agent, was a great singer, and Frau Schneevogt herself a quite unequalled example of female virtue and ability. The woman was elated by his insight. She took him into favour. When she took half a dozen sandwiches out of a greasy package, she invited him to share them. She had dry, trembling, hard-working hands. Her hands interested him. He said to himself: Those must be stingy hands. He gave her all the more credit for the sandwiches, of which he ate two. He watched how the woman ate. She ate greedily, but without enjoyment. Her eyes were close together and had an unsteady look. Her face could never have been pretty. But it was worn with worry, greed and dissatisfaction. Under these feelings there slumbered an almost incredibly high estimate of her own person. If things don't go well with me, with whom should they go well? Etzel made use of the pause during which they were eating to hint carefully at his dilemma. He was seeking lodgings; price was not the important factor, although he did not lie on a bed of roses; but he must remain hidden for a few weeks. Household dissensions had driven him from home; he must wait until everything had settled down again; meantime he has accepted a position as a private secretary; his name is Mohl, if he may introduce himself, Edgar Mohl. Why he has chosen the name of this schoolfellow, particularly that fat glutton, is a puzzle to himself. Particularly clever of him not to have called himself Klaus; it occurred to him at that moment that his linen was marked with an E. The whole thing was a momentary inspiration.

Frau Schneevogt's eyes became slits as she took him in. Business having become the topic, she became more reserved for a little while. Her glance appraised him, his character, his antecedents, his means. The result seemed to satisfy her. A nice boy, an open countenance, probably of good family. The situation was promising. Both little rooms were at present unoccupied. During the winter two mechanics from the Borsig factory had occupied them, both excellent people. She only rented at pension rates, breakfast and one other meal, midday or evening. That remark about wanting to remain hidden probably meant that he did not wish to be registered with the police. There was a serious fine for that, as he probably knew; they were very nasty in such matters. But when he remarked that in view of this difficulty he could perhaps pay a little extra, she interrupted him hastily, as if she did not want to make any undue demands, saying: "Oh, well, we can talk about that, in any case come along and look at the place. It will be midnight before we get home, but you can sleep as late as you please tomorrow." He for his part was thinking: what luck! At the house of a bookkeeper in Anklamerstrasse they won't look for me; to do that they would have to make a house-to-house search. He was content. The train was ploughing through silver-grey mists; the horizonless plain rolling like the sea. But it is spring; everything is strange; consequently everything is inviting; even the slight fear, fear of the world, fear of people, quickens his blood rather pleasantly.

2.

The room which he occupied opened into a dark court; it was five paces long and three wide and contained a narrow bed with a bag of straw for a mattress and a woolen cover, a rusty iron stove, a shaky bureau with only three legs, a round tin washstand with a bowl the size of a shaving-bowl, a wooden table, and two chairs with straw seats. On the grey lime-washed wall hung a gaudy chromo of the battle of Vionville, near the bed there were suspicious blood spots which Etzel observed questioningly for a while, till it occurred to him that they suggested bedbugs. He had never seen bedbugs. From the ceiling hung a gas-jet, with an incandescent burner and a chimney of isinglass. The only window had no curtain and one could see into the opposite tenement which seemed occupied by countless people; new faces whisked by the windows constantly. It certainly is not pretty here, thought Etzel as he unpacked his knapsack, but that need not matter to me. I am not here for the sake of finding things pretty.

The worst part of the situation was that the room had no entrance of its own, in order to get into it one had to go through the room in which the daughter of the house slept.

The bed indeed was hidden by a thin stuff curtain, but the situation embarrassed Etzel. It doesn't matter, he said to himself, that's the situation; it would be easier if it were different; but so it is. Frau Schneevogt hesitated a long time before fixing the price; she was obliged to calculate beforehand; then she must consult her husband; so far as meals were concerned she could estimate the cost exactly; he must of course realize that when he gave notice that he would not be in for a meal he would have nevertheless to pay for it; again a long-winded sermon culminating with a hymn in praise of her own honesty. Finally she produced the figure, sixty marks a month for board and lodging, seven marks fifty for service, light and laundry. Etzel did not think of bargaining, he counted out sixty-seven marks fifty of his capital and brought it to her with a promptness which gave her a high opinion of him. From that time on she regarded him as "a superior young man," but was at the same time the victim of conflicting emotions; on the one hand she took him into her withered heart with a certain rough affection because he was so alone in the world; on the other hand she regretted not having asked for more and considered how she could get more out of him, sensing, moreover, a secret, the discovery of which would not only produce tangible profit, but also transform her whole existence. One can often observe in life that it is the inferior natures which incline to look for fantastic experiences, and give their attention to unreal situations; sympathy and self-interest are like two unequal sisters who would like to get on together and do not know how. Frau Schneevogt, of course, searched through all his belongings, but she found nothing which gave her a hint. He had been on his guard and had himself examined every scrap of paper and the inside-cover of every book. Fortunately, she had no method in her spying; her mind was occupied with nothing but her daily misery. She quarrelled constantly with the other occupants of the house, with her husband and daughter, with the police, the government, and with heaven itself. When she could get hold of Etzel she would overwhelm him with complaints of how cruel Fate had been to her, how kind to others; the conclusion was a burst of tears and a little bill, forty pfennigs for the repair of the lock, eighty pfennigs for a new water pitcher, the old one having gotten cracked, about which he knew nothing. He never contradicted, but drew out his purse and paid the money. A thrill of pleasure always flitted over her face when she felt money in her poor bony hands, whether the sum were forty pfennigs or, as the first time, six ten-mark bills and some silver. Etzel could not see his fill of those hands, the confused gestures of her greedy fingers; they fascinated him like the behaviour of animals of prey when one shoves food into their cages. He wished that he had enough money to satisfy the greed of those hands, just in order that they might rest in peace. But he would probably never have so much, nor earn so much, and at night when he lay awake thinking of Waremme—he often woke up at night for there was a dancing-school in the house opposite, it soon turned out, and a horrible mechanical piano played until two in the morning—his thoughts would turn to the woman and he would ask himself whether the hands were quiet at least while she slept. The light from the dancing-school across fell into his room, so the second night he hung his overcoat across the window, but aside from that he could not go to sleep for a long time because the bedbugs worried him. . . . Sleep, half-sleep, awaking, dream, half-dream, half-waking, he was continually gliding from one to another. What shall I do? he would think. What is the wisest, what is the safest, how shall I go about it? Commencing meant believing in his success; he believed in his success because he was bound to. Only in his most despondent moments, at times when he was half sleeping, half dreaming, when there was no ray of light in the world outside, not even in the dancing-school, did he have doubts, and once the idea struck him like a blow in the face: What if he were dead? Suppose Waremme had died yesterday, or last week. Then he would stand like an ox before a new gate, unable to go through. But when he considered the matter clearly he decided that this could not be. Then he himself would not be regulated by any law; then he would be a zero in the scheme of creation, he said to himself; for there is a deeper truth in all things than we can perceive or grasp; and how could Waremme be dead since Maurizius was still in the penitentiary? That was what kept spurring him on, the thing he could never think through clearly: that man in the penitentiary, and that every day that went by here was a day more spent for him, too, and that one could not hurry sufficiently to make an end of this situation, in order that the world might cease to be a disfigured and crippled thing, a running sore which it hurt one and made one ill to look at.

The next day he went to Usedomstrasse on the corner of Jasmunderstrasse and ascended up to the first floor; on the banisters hung a cardboard sign on which was written in large black letters: *Mathilde Bobike, lunch, per week four marks fifty.* It was one of those houses into which no fresh air had penetrated for years, and in which the air from the front hall to the garret smelled of roast mutton, boiled cabbage, baby linen, leather and dish-water. He asked to see Frau Bobike and there at once appeared a lady, six feet high, with bony features and ice-grey hair, who stared down upon him in silence. After he had said that he would like to eat lunch at her house for a month she silently pushed a bill in front of him and he paid eighteen marks, whereupon she, continuing to be silent, handed him a small book containing four leaves, each of which consisted of seven meal tickets.

3.

A serious, inviolable decision on any subject produces elevated thoughts even in a child. But Etzel was a child only in stature and years; furthermore, the conception "child" when applied to a person of sixteen, is only an expression of embarrassment on the part of those who have lost their childhood a day after it ended. They point to the lack of experience in youngsters, although their own experience is only a pitiful mosaic, not a picture, but rather a laborious addition of figures which seldom yield a total, because very few people are capable of having real experiences, because there is no sap in them; the tree only bears wooden fruit because they have no hearts capable of remembering. It is his idea of life which makes man creative, his innate, undying idea, which he creates for himself. In such a case youth is only an interval and what one lacks in retrospect and the summation of comparisons is compensated for by internal life and a passionate interest in the present. Desiring to undertake the seemingly impossible, Etzel first undertook to inspect fearlessly the world which he entered at this juncture. The eating-house of Mathilde Bobike flourished under the title of "lunches for superior ladies and gentlemen." This meant that between twelve and one o'clock, in a large, musty, barnlike room and two smaller adjoining ones, there were collected from thirty to forty people of doubtful character, people who had stumbled and failed, people tired of swimming against the current, persons of shabby elegance and badly disguised poverty, salesmen without jobs, travelling virtuosos, actors from the suburbs and actresses without jobs, those about to attempt a daring venture, or those who had just failed, bartenders and professional dancers from the surrounding pleasure resorts, people from the provinces, who had come to the capital as a last hope and were now stranded like wrecks on a sand-bank. A few were political suspects, there was a wife who had fled from home, and a young girl, the daughter of a clergyman in the east, who wanted to work in the movies. Etzel made a point from the very beginning of not offending anyone, and of winning favour by his confiding, modest and talkative manner. He quickly made friends with his neighbours at the table and between potato soup and vegetable pudding engaged them in a conversation which greatly increased his knowledge of the social transition states. They at once began to talk of an embezzlement which someone had committed, the name was mentioned with a wink, and how with a little cunning one might escape all the pitfalls of the law. They spoke of a certain man, a piano player in the Victoria Café, named Cabaret Erich, who had run off with the wife of the proprietor and four thousand marks besides. They spoke with a mixture of admiration and envy, such as Etzel had only heard used in connection with important artistic successes, or at most in regard to an athletic record. Back of him people were talking about the stock exchange; at a table on the left a tubercular painter was explaining how much money was being made today by bogus paintings; at the right there was an animated discussion about how large a bribe a housing commissioner had accepted on a certain occasion. He listened with interest, eager to learn, with the smile of a beginner who is taking a lesson. Secrecy was of the utmost importance; he would have liked to hide from his own self as if his association with himself were a trial, as if one ought not to feel or know anything about oneself under circumstances like those in which he was placed. He was two people anyway, Edgar Mohl and Etzel Andergast, and he played with his duality, in order to get a little fun out of the strict task which he had set himself, by setting the one upon the other and pitting them against each other. Only Etzel Andergast, who was the real person, sank more and more into the insignificance, whereas Edgar Mohl, the shadow, constantly gained in substance and did not permit any interference with his dangerous duties.

He had already looked about frequently with care, but none of the guests seemed to be the one whom he sought with such tense interest. Finally, it was already quarter of one and most of the diners had already finished, when a man stepped in whose appearance left no doubt whatsoever. He was a medium-sized man in a long grey, old-fashioned overcoat, grey baggy trousers and a somewhat shabby velvet vest, patterned with blue flowers. His gait was careless, slow and heavy. He took a few steps before he removed his broad-brimmed felt hat and showed a head covered with a few wisps of ice-grey hair, but such a powerful head that from that minute on his body looked five inches taller. One could not see either his eyes or their expression, on account of the dark glasses which he wore, and these black circular spots threw the ghastly whiteness of the massive, heavily lined, beardless, flabby face into such sharp relief that it looked like an artificial mask, painted for the purpose of arousing terror. Etzel involuntarily lowered his head over his plate. He felt as if something biting had been poured into his throat, and he was obliged to swallow hard several times. He dared only cast furtive glances towards the man, but he felt him weighing upon him like something monstrous and heavy. Most people knew him, some nodded to him as he walked to his table, for he ate alone and even had a table-cloth; others said: "Howdedo, Professor." He was commonly called professor, even by people in the street who knew him only by sight.

4.

A week from today I shall speak to him, unless there is some good chance before then, Etzel decided. But there was small hope of that, for the "professor" spoke to no one. Even when the tables were crowded and one could scarcely hear one's own voice, he would sit at his separate table, taking no part in the conversation, reading a book which he had fished out of the back pocket of his ridiculous overcoat and held open near his plate. He seemed to see no one and not to understand what was being said.

I shall speak to him, Etzel decided, and ask him to give

me English lessons. Not astonishingly daring, one would think, since it was generally known that to give lessons and take pupils was the man's calling. Nevertheless, Etzel was glad that he had some time ahead of him. The blood ran to his head and his heart beat like a triphammer when he thought of meeting the man and being in his presence. It was not cowardice, it was only that he became aware with a shudder of the task that he had undertaken. When he grasped this completely, through and through, to the tips of his fingers, and his soul was filled with the thought, he would smile, somewhat like a person standing on the roof of a burning house, measuring the distance which he is bound to leap, and fixing the spot on which he must alight without fail, if he does not want to make sure to break his neck. He must, of course, be a good jumper and something of a magician besides.

Meantime, he made careful use of the interval he had allowed himself. The plan was to make himself popular at the Bobike eating-house, to be known by everybody as a good fellow, to do little favours for people. He wanted everyone to feel he was one of them, to have the appearance of cheerfulness, to participate in the fun with all kinds of pranks, and in this way unobtrusively to force the "professor" to notice him and form a definite opinion of him. He wanted the "professor" to think that he was a good-natured clever boy, worthy of confidences, needing guidance, and useful in all sorts of ways; this conception would be fruitful later on. He soon saw that the "professor" lived quite a solitary life—to himself Etzel always called him Waremme; for him the name Warschauer did not exist—he did not seem to have any following or any relations to people, but Etzel said to himself, not entirely without reason, that there was no life so shut off that one could not find access to it, if one were skilful and clever. It was not enough merely to offer himself as a pupil, it would be better if favourable presumptions were also at work. He posed here, too, as a "private secretary" and furthermore, he invented the tale of an uncle, his guardian and only relative in the world, who had supported him and had administered the small capital which he had inherited. The man had absconded with Etzel's money. He had been looking for him for several weeks, he had reliable information that he was in Berlin and indeed in this neighbourhood. The sentimental story was believed. It suited the surroundings perfectly. He knew how to emphasize effects by reticence, he had the ability of convincing people by a word. He made all understand that he had their best interests at heart; therefore they gave him what he modestly demanded for himself: liking and the admission that he was rather a good chap. His laughing eyes calmed even the most vulgar lout. His charm was of a popular sort. When he wished to, he could make people laugh by the depressed gesture with which he shoved his cap down over his forehead. Travelling salesmen for rubber goods and vagabond artisans are not people who assume much social reserve; the dental surgeon out of a job who makes eyes at a box of tuna-fish in the window of the corner store, and then buys ten cents' worth of cheese for his supper, is glad if he is spoken to. What these people liked about him was his dry matter-of-course manner. If he talked to a cocaine addict, he seemed surprised that everyone did not take cocaine; if he was dealing with a drunkard it seemed as if he admired his capacity for drink, and looked at him kindly, as if such a condition were the most natural in the world. One day a rouged young man made tender advances to him; when he understood he promised to consider the matter. When he was most profoundly moved he could look like a buffoon; when he was dealing with an angry person he would look like a nursemaid whose duty it was to soothe a crying child. No degeneracy astonished him; no baseness offended him; he was disgusted by no vice and presumably not even the sight of crime would have changed a feature of his contented smiling face. To such an extent could he control himself. He was like a man playing a game behind his own back, and although he was suspicious of everything romantic, and dismissed all dreams with contempt, there was nevertheless something akin to romance and dreams, some rudiment of them in all this, though often only in the form of resistance. For at bottom he was the same Etzel whom his grandmother had noticed when he was three years old, sitting on a rug trying to eat a ray of sunshine with a spoon, and who, when he found that he was being observed, threw the spoon in the coal-scuttle in embarrassment and anger.

What was the name of the uncle who had absconded, they asked? Mohl was his name, the same as his own. Ah? Mohl? An agent for cigars in St. Matthew's Cellar had heard of a Mohl. Someone else recommended him to the so-called "Half-Silk," who was a permanent guest in Marburg Hole; he was a walking bureau of information; there was in all the Wedding Section not a soul whom he did not know and whose history he could not recite by heart. A third advisor with a saffron-coloured complexion and a scar over one eye, who was said to have had some connection with the navy, recommended him to ask at some of the dance halls in the Wintergarten and at various betting places and in ninety out of a hundred cases searching in a certain coffee house near Alexander Place was successful. Furthermore, he named several hostelries in Oranienburg, Alsace and Lorraine streets, where common people lodged, and in case of danger quickly changed from one to another, people who wished to disappear from the public eye. One must, he instructed the respectful and silent listeners at the table, know how to differentiate between respectable, semi-respectable, lower middle class, and proletarian places of refuge; one must know the difference between a shelter for the night, a lodging house and a cellar. The person who was under police surveillance naturally selected a different place from one who was pursued because of a crime; one could sound out the former in moderate depths; for the latter one must look deeper. A person who merely wanted to disappear for a while generally did not go very far from the surface, even if he was sailing under false colours, which one would have to fear in the case of Uncle Mohl. Sometimes inquiring of the ladies brought quick results (he bleated a citation from Goethe's Iphigenie: "Address thy quest to noble womanhood") ; recently he had caught a boy, whom he had fished for in vain for a long time, by going to the clairvoyante Salome in Landsburgerstrasse. Etzel thanked the speaker effusively for his prolific information. In order to let his own light shine also, he developed before the wondering auditorium, which after this superb feat did not hesitate to declare that he was "no man's fool," a kind of popular philosophy of the social groupings, proving that people of a certain social class, by reason of their close proximity, as well as those engaged in the next move up or down the scale, all knew each other. Every tailor knew twenty tailors, every retail trader twenty others; there are callings which may be regarded as sister callings, or cousin callings; the locksmith knows the bicycle dealer; the glazier knows the builder; the chief of an office supervises a couple of dozen clerks; a waiter serves two hundred guests a day and knows not only their names but also their personal lives; the shopgirl is interested in the people she waits on, knows who most of them are and what they do; chauffeurs know the people who live near their stands; street-car conductors know their morning, noon and evening passengers. Most people walk through the same streets at the same hours, it is not a question of how many "acquaintances" a person has, whether the *professor,* the member of parliament, or the manufacturer has two thousand and the poor student, the beggar, the petty clerk or *the man with a prison record* only fifty, or ten; nevertheless, everyone is surrounded with acquaintances, and on every rung of the ladder of life, there is an "acquaintance" to lead one on to the next rung. Everyone belongs to his own guild of fate.

Young people, when they think that they have something clever to say, are fond of talking for the gallery. Etzel was fairly free from this form of vanity. He had a different motive for speaking with a raised voice and for compelling his audience to listen silently; he simply wanted the "professor" to hear him, and while talking he observed Waremme-Warschauer like a lynx. He could not see his face or expression clearly because of his short-sightedness, but it seemed as if the man were interrupting his reading in order to listen, and at the end of his dissertation he noticed that the man had turned his face a little to one side as if to see what was going on and then ground his hypertrophic lower jaw. It looked as if he wished to defend himself against a wasp, but was too lazy to raise his hand. Now he knows my voice, thought Etzel, now I am so to speak an acquaintance.

5.

Not only his friends at the table asked Etzel to do various errands; for example, on his way home, would he make a détour to the Linienkeller and tell a gentleman who looked thus and so, and was waiting there, this or that; or would he tell Fräulein Else Grünau, 27 Gollnowstrasse, that Heinrich Balle could not call for her that evening; or would he go out to the Sport Palace—here was the money for the underground—and have someone call the runner Paul and tell him that if the thing which he knew about were not delivered by four o'clock that afternoon, he would have Christoph Jansen to deal with; but even Frau Bobike herself entrusted him occasionally with errands, such as warning someone who had failed to pay her, or putting off some butcher or grocer whom she had failed to pay; or she would ask him to tell a young lady who two years before had taken a gramophone on the instalment plan and was at the moment sick at the hospital, that she must return the instrument because she had not kept her bargain—there were two more instalments to be paid. Then there would be a corset to be taken for repair, a bottle of gasoline to be bought at the drug store, or an address to be sought at the registry office, or information to be gotten at Schönhauser Gate about a candidate for the ministry, and other errands of the sort. He did it all willingly. His good spirits were always the same. He went absolutely wherever he was sent. He seldom used a conveyance, first because he wanted to save; then, he was fascinated by what he saw as he walked about. He would go from crowded sections, where countless people coldly and angrily shoved by one another, into deserted quarters where gas factories, prisons, hospitals, factories and graveyards made one feel as if one were in a torture chamber containing gigantic instruments of torture, and near-by dungeons and graves were already yawning. He went into rooms where dampness trickled down the walls, into lodgings in cellars where candles were stuck into the necks of bottles in the evening and where someone always lay sick of a fever on a sofa covered with rags. He saw children with wrinkled faces who had perhaps never seen a tree, nor a meadow, and when he spoke to one of them he felt as if he were making fun of himself because he was not equally starved and neglected. Once he was obliged, in front of a Salvation Army structure, to force his way through a group of homeless and unemployed persons, and he walked through this silent and frightful company as innocently as if he were walking across a playground among his schoolfellows. The above-mentioned Fräulein Else Grünau took a liking to him, and it required all of his shrewdness and innocent loquaciousness to slip out of the net. Nothing mattered to him; nothing was worth looking at so long as that man was in the penitentiary. This thought operated inexorably as the clock, turning the hours into wheels of stone, under whose grinding the life of the world was expiring with a sigh.

He got up daily at seven, left the house at eight, and did not return till six or seven in the evening, and sometimes later, for he was obliged to keep up the fiction of his occupation as a secretary. He was, of course, asked for whom he was working; for an author who lived in the Kastanienallee, he said, giving a name which he had made up. It was careless, for Melitta Schneevogt had a characteristically Schneevogt notion to look into the directory, and one day she sarcastically asked him how his employer was. He understood. I must not get red, he thought, replying impertinently that the name was a pseudonym. "Are you a political worker, or perhaps a spy?" the girl asked angrily. "If so get out of here before we get into a mess with the police." No, he had nothing to do with politics, he replied with a disarming smile, withdrawing from the sight of the unamiable young woman. What did he do with his hours from early morning on, until it was time to go to Frau Bobike's, and from half past one until evening, for the errands which he ran were always quickly disposed of? He simply walked and walked. He had brought two pairs of shoes with him; after a week the soles of one pair were worn through and the heels of the other so crooked that both pairs had to be repaired. His feet were worse off, sore and covered with blisters, and only gradually did they harden and become callous. As he never crept into bed before midnight, this mode of life would have injured his delicate constitution if he had not been as tense as a taut spring. He walked and walked, thinking and pondering, recollected himself and kept on walking. If he was tired, he would sit down on a bench in front of the public hospital or in the Humboldt Park, or when it rained he would seek refuge in one of the many railroad stations. Sometimes he would take a Latin or Greek book out of his pocket and study; sometimes he would recite poetry, which he had memorized, aloud to himself, verses of Rilke or George; sometimes he would read a volume of Melchior Ghisels. But suddenly he would be tormented by the fact that there was no longer a disembodied spirit behind the book, but a tangible man whom, if he wished, he might see that very day, perhaps even speak to. But he pondered his visit to Ghisels as a pious person plans a pilgrimage; even the conception of a "decision" was not significant enough, it must be like a flight without any effort of will, as if he were carried thither by some element; only thus could he overcome his fear, that stage-fright of love, for the eye of such a man was like the eye of heaven itself.

Among the patrons of Frau Bobike's table there was a down-and-out student named Schirmer. He had been an assistant instructor for a time at one of the non-sectarian schools, but had been dismissed because of a scandal, and he wished only to buy food and shelter. He had begun to take his meals at the house the same day as Etzel and sat at the same table with him. He was a blond, smallish man with bits of brown beard on his face, which looked like spots of dirt; he drank a good deal and did not appear to be very intelligent. He was wildly enthusiastic about "little Mohl," as they all called him, and when Etzel made one of his dry remarks, talked about the condition of the world, or played some prank or other, for example an imitation of an omnibus driver in a bad humour, or of a man who called out the names of newspapers with a stammer, Schirmer would howl with laughter, strike his fist on the table with a bang, and look triumphantly about the room as if seeking applause. When such an attack was over, he would wipe the tears from his eyes with a tremendous blue handkerchief. One day at noon—Etzel had been eating at the house for just a week—Schirmer in conversation with the naval man somewhat complacently used a Latin quotation. Etzel laughed and added the second line of the couplet. It was from Horace, which was quite amusing under the circumstances, and of course comprehensible only to the student and himself. Schirmer was overcome with the usual attack of enthusiasm and then said: "Mohl, it seems to me that you did not go to school in vain. What a pity about your talents!" "Why a pity?" replied Etzel. "Talents can't harm, if one has them. I know more than that," he added with a tolerably good pretence of conceit, "I know whole poems of Catullus by heart, for example. Do you want to hear me?"—"Attention, gentlemen," exclaimed Schirmer, wiping his mouth off with a paper napkin, for they were already at the last course. "Attention, little Mohl is going to recite a Latin poem. Go ahead." Etzel gave a curious smile and began:

"Quid est Catulle? quid moraris emori?
Sella in curuli struma Nonius sedet,
Per consulatum perierat Vatinius,
Quid est Catulle? quid moraris emori?"

The listeners looked puzzled; it sounded to them like Hindustani, and even if they had understood that here Catullus was calling upon himself to die because Vatinius could commit perjuries and go unpunished, what would they have been able to make of this? But the boy continued, and his cheeks flamed with the significance of the poem, as if he were too astonished for thought:

"Risi nescio quem modo e corona
Qui, cum mirifice Vatiniana
Meus crimina Calvus explicasset
Admirans ait haec manusque tollens:
Di magni, salaputium desertum . . ."

"Ye gods, how that chap has the gift of gab!" Etzel threw in a translation of the last line and they all grinned appreciation while silly Schirmer did not cease bawling bravo and applauding loudly. Oh, heavens, if I only had some glasses now, thought Etzel, and with good reason, for the "professor" turned his face to one side as he had done the other day, only a little more, and ground his frightful lower jaw as he had done before. However, the fleeting interest that the curious scene had perhaps aroused in him—one could not be sure about it—seemed of short duration, a few seconds later he appeared to be once more sunk in his book. And a few minutes later Etzel, who had finished his meal, got up from his chair and spoke to him. He would like to take English lessons, the professor had frequently been recommended to him; he was going to emigrate next year and wanted first to learn the language thoroughly; what would the professor charge for lessons? Waremme-Warschauer fixed his black glasses as slowly upon Etzel's face as if he were seeking to place an object in the field of his opera-glass. "One mark an hour," he replied with a cutting, somewhat hoarse voice. "How many hours does the young man want? Three? Four? Monday and Wednesday from four to five, Saturday from four to six. What was the name? Mohl? M-O-H-L? Very well. Goodbye."

"He looks," thought Etzel quite down in the mouth, "as if he had not paid the darnedest bit of attention to me up to now."

6.

Warschauer occupied, in the third floor of the same house, a single room which was so big, however, that it was divided in two by sliding doors. The bed stood in a windowless alcove behind the door. Two or three hundred books were stacked in piles, like pilasters along the walls; they were mostly paper-bound, strikingly many books of a technical nature, on the Jewish antiquities, Semitic philology, Hebraic dictionaries, various editions of the Talmud and the Bible, and yearly reports of Oriental societies; also cabalistic writings. There were no shelves; there was no atmosphere which suggested a "home," it was a storehouse of objects which did not apparently belong together and seemed collected by chance. There were cobwebs on the ceiling and in the corners. The window-panes had not been washed for so long that one could scarcely see through them. Ornaments, pictures, anything that made for convenience, except an old carved sofa, seemed unknown to the occupant of this room. It was the saddest, most neglected, barnlike lodging that Etzel had ever seen. After feeling his way along a pitch-dark hall, along which five or six other people lived, a street-vendor, a washing woman, a male nurse and a photographer with many children, he had knocked and no one had answered; and he then found himself in the desolate room as lost as a needle in a haystack. After a while Warschauer came from behind the folding doors and nodded to his new pupil with a friendliness which made his clay-grey face look for a few seconds like that of a grinning old woman.

His person was as clean and neat as his surroundings were dirty and disorderly. At times he would get up, snatch a brush hanging on the wall and brush his coat and vest. Every fifteen or twenty minutes he would disappear behind the folding doors and carefully wash his hands, then he would return to his place, grinning like an old woman, and place his fat white hands, the nails of which were so closely cut that the ends of his fingers protruded over them like hats, with a prelate's deliberateness, upon his knees, and continue his teaching.

His method is simple and practical. He places his chief emphasis upon phonetics and the imparting of stimulating data, at times giving examples of grammar. He emphasizes what is visible and audible and writes certain words with chalk on a blackboard which he has on a stand near the table. After a little while he perceives that his pupil is a young man of humanistic culture and that he may presuppose a certain foundation, so he abridges his method and redoubles his grimacing friendliness, in which only his epidermis takes part. He points out etymologies and the qualities of the English race, the results of which may be seen in their pithy words and speech. This stamps itself on the memory. His remarks issue forth as carelessly as pennies dropped from the hands of a millionaire. But he speaks without his eyes, without a glance, and his black glasses are the external corroboration of this situation. I would like to tear off his glasses, thinks Etzel, he seems to wear them to annoy me. His eagerness to learn and his mental quickness fill Warschauer with obviously pretended astonishment, at times it even seems as if he were trying to parody the enthusiastic outbursts of the ridiculous Schirmer. Etzel feels embarrassed; the man's jesuitical exaggeration angers him; during the second lesson he asks why the professor is making fun of him, as he is not at all conceited about his own meagre knowledge. Warschauer replies with a frightened and imploring gesture intended to convey the notion: For heaven's sake, young man, what do you think of me, how could I think such a thing, who am I? But this is acting. It is a comedy like everything else. The harder Etzel tries the more Warschauer's sanctimonious joviality increases. He notices, of course, that he is dealing with an unusual boy, whose good bringing up is unmistakable; his politeness and desire to please betray some secret purpose; where does he come from; what is his game? But it is not disquieting to have a little dog sniff at one's feet; let it sniff; there is always time enough to give it a kick; meantime one gives it a little piece of sugar, or now and again a bone; let it sniff and let it gnaw. This about expressed Waremme-Warschauer's attitude, and Etzel understood it well enough. Nevertheless, he knew how to flatter his way into the man's habits of life; he did it like a parasite fastening upon its host. His toadying manœuvres begin by his arriving ten or twenty minutes before the appointed time, even when he finds another pupil having a lesson—the professor has not any too many pupils—and remaining after the hour, even when Warschauer begins to work. As far as Etzel can make out, he is busy compiling a bibliography on Arabic sculpture for the director of a museum, under whose name the work is to appear, for a pitifully small sum; for the director is a famous expert on the subject, and could do the thing himself if he had a little more time. Etzel busies himself with the books, which are covered with inches of dust; he dusts them and classifies them, and decides to make a catalogue, without asking Warschauer too carefully whether he wants one or not. He notices that Warschauer, who neither drinks nor smokes, has a great liking for strong black coffee which he makes himself over a little alcohol lamp. He takes to making it for him. Chance, which he believes is favouring him, helps him along. Warschauer runs a nail into his foot and can't leave the room for several days. He has no one to wait upon him. The curious thing is that in spite of his miserable circumstances, he does not seem to be poor or have anything of the beggar about him, rather the contrary—the way in which he lives often makes the impression of a camouflaging for some secret purpose or other, which, of course, rests upon an allusion—he makes his bed himself and cleans his shoes himself. Etzel fetches his lunch from Frau Bobike's kitchen and his bite of supper from a store in Demminer-strasse. Of course, he changes the arrangement of his days to fit in with these altered circumstances, but he has been waiting to have his days governed thus. He gets lysol and bandages from the drug store, washes the wound and bandages it correctly, and is as skilful as if he had completed a course in first aid. The conversations which take place between them, for it is clear that they cannot live like two clods in such close proximity, become more and more animated on Etzel's part; he becomes a tireless chatterbox whereas Warschauer seems to grow more inaccessible and to withdraw into the background as if embarrassed. He spends himself in hypocritical thanks and hypocritical dismayed protests, as if a person like himself were in no way worthy of such kindness or such sacrifices. There are moments of tenderness. Etzel cannot help being frightened, and trembling to the very depths of his being, when they occur, although at the same time he says to himself that nothing could further his cause better, saying it, however, like someone who reaches into a burning stove with set teeth in order to pull something out of it. These outbursts consist of nothing but attempts to touch him, and a sparkling of the eyes behind the black glasses, and the funny empty grinding of the hypertrophic lower jaw. Etzel feels as if a clay image were suddenly to awake with a snort and claw about, because it had an appetite for human flesh. One day he was chatting in a manner which was half assumed, half a genuine boyish characteristic of his, about what he was going to do when he got to America, for his desire to emigrate is his fictitious reason for taking lessons. He wants first to become a cowboy and then to earn enough to buy a big estate with lakes and woods, cattle and game, and to live there in freedom. "To live in freedom" has in his mouth a sound of determination and enthusiasm. Warschauer lifts his head and emits a hoarse chuckle. He stretches his arm out and pulls the boy so close to him that Etzel, with a mingling of revulsion and instinctive resistance, which he can only overcome because of the purpose which possesses him, feels the man's breath caressing his forehead and hears him say, nodding his head didactically: "To live in freedom? There? There? To live in freedom! Boy, boy, boy!" And he emits a laugh of bitter amusement which seems to proceed from his entrails. Etzel breaks away and shrugs his shoulders with displeasure. "I know," he growls, "I already know . . . you," and he hesitates, glances defiantly about him, and stands obstinately shaking his hair off his forehead. The eyes behind those black glasses are fixed upon him with the expression which Etzel describes to himself as that of a cannibal, although they are neither cruel nor evil, only they have the curious sleep-drugged prurience of the image coming to life. Perhaps, memories of old fairy tales are stirring in Etzel's soul, day before yesterday he was still a child. . . .

Warschauer wants to go out tonight for the first time to a beer hall near the Stettin Station, where there is to be a mass meeting, Etzel has suggested that he will accompany him, for he is not yet quite safe in walking. Warschauer has a passion for all congregations of humans, whether they be movings, public spectacles, demonstrations of strikers or just common street meetings; the crowd draws him irresistibly. He feels happiest in closed spaces, when he is packed in among thousands of people and skilled speakers are rousing the crowd to fanatic demonstrations; he has explained to Etzel that this makes him perfectly happy, he feels an intoxicating state of depersonalization and anonymity. Etzel has not quite understood, but he consoles himself with the thought that the man will probably speak of it often. They are to start at half past eight, Etzel is to fetch the cold supper from Demminerstrasse before then. He starts on his way whistling with his hands in his pocket, on the way back he can only keep one hand in his pocket, he needs the other to carry the package, which is fairly bulky, because he has bought a pound of cherries; but nevertheless he can whistle.

Already on the steps he hears Warschauer's sonorous, lazy deep voice. Oho, thinks he, the professor has company. However, it is only Paalzow's boy; Paalzow is the photographer next door. Paalzow's boy is just Etzel's age, but he is a low chap who has had several run-ins with the juvenile court. He had already been there that morning—Warschauer had hinted at it with irritation—he wants money and Warschauer designates as an attempt at blackmail the reason which he has seized upon with cynical audacity. A few days before, Warschauer had expected some books from the director of the museum; he was obliged to go out and wanted, before going, to ask mother Paalzow to take the books for him, if the messenger came while he was out. But there was no one at the Paalzows, the room was empty. This much of the story was true; the Paalzow boy, however, maintained that the professor had left the door of the Paalzow room open on this occasion, and as a result someone had stolen a pair of shoes which the professor must replace; he did not demand the full value of the shoes, but modestly enough only three marks. But three marks he must have, otherwise he would make an ugly row about it and the professor would regret it. When Etzel entered, he was standing in the room with arms akimbo, his hat on his ear, impudently demanding "his money." Warschauer sat at a table holding a pen in his hand, only glancing awry at the place where the boy stood. He was ridiculously cowardly about such attacks. Etzel went to the open window, passing behind the Paalzow boy, and laid the package on the window ledge, first taking out a handful of cherries. It was a warm May evening and he hung out of the window, as if he wanted to have it understood that the matter did not concern him and that he did not want to side with either of them. Deep down in the courtyard there was an empty wooden box standing upright under the window, and he busied himself for a time trying to spit the cherry-seeds into the box, at which he was not very successful. Meantime, Paalzow's boy became more and more impertinent; Warschauer's contemptuous silence gave him courage, and in the most colourful Berlin dialect, he vociferated that he would know how to get his money, if he were obliged to set fire to the idiotic room. Hereupon Etzel turned around, walked over to him and, poking him with his elbow, said, "Just see that you get out of here." Paalzow's boy spun around as if he had been bitten and stared at him nastily. "Outside we'll discuss matters sensibly," continued Etzel, winking as if he regarded the professor as an idiot, but must not let this be noticed, and as if he were engaged to settle his affairs—particularly such difficulties as that with Paalzow's boy—in a gentlemanly fashion. When he had gotten the rowdy out of the door he said, "Now, listen, Paalzow, the story is a stinking lie. You need not pretend to me! I understand that you are trying to turn a neat trick, but the thing is not worth a whole thaler. Be satisfied with a half, here's one mark fifty; the professor and I will settle matters between us, now beat it." Hesitating, distrustful, not quite knowing what he should think of Etzel, but altogether uncomfortable, Paalzow's boy took the money and shuffled away down the hall with an obstinate and sombre look.

When Etzel got back into the room, Warschauer had lighted the lamp over his writing table and the scratching noise of his pen could be heard. Through the open window the tooting of motor horns and the ringing of the trolley-car gongs could be heard dully over the roofs of the houses. Etzel sat down upon a pile of books and, kicking one leg, began once more to eat cherries. Suddenly Warschauer turned on his chair and asked: "You gave that rascal money?" Etzel nodded eagerly. "Why? It is stupid and wrong to give such a dog of an extortioner money. Why then did you do it? Have you such an awful lot of it?" Etzel spit some cherry-seeds in a wide circle out of the window. "I haven't a lot at all. But in the first place there should not be a row here. In the second place, what do you mean by a rascal or a dog? A pitiful chap. One can wind him around one's finger for one mark and fifty pfennigs. I wanted to see whether he is really as pitiful as that. All that's positive about him is three marks with a reduction of fifty per cent. Is it my fault?" Warschauser turned around a little further on his chair. "The positive, what do you mean by that?" he asked. Etzel kept spitting cherry-stones assiduously. "Oh, well, the positive is what one needs if one does not want to go under," he replied indifferently, "some little ideal, for example, a belief, a person, a cause. They none of them have that." He made a vague gesture with his hand towards the door in order to designate all of the Paalzow boys outside who were yearning for the "positive."

Warschauer was silent and returned to his work. But after a few minutes had elapsed, he put down his pen and turning again he rested his right elbow on his left hand and covering his chin and mouth with his hand, looked thus for a while at Etzel, who did not appear to be at all disturbed. "The devil take me if I understand you, Mohl," he finally said in low tones. "Perhaps the end of the business is that your name is quite different. Now come, show your true colours." He did not sound either suspicious or threatening, but rather kindly, hypocritical and again there was the "cannibalistic" undertone.

Etzel got off the pile of books with a jump. "Perhaps my name is no more Mohl than yours is Warschauer," he replied pertly, "perhaps. Who knows?"

Warschauer got up very slowly. He walked slowly towards the boy. "What, boy?" came from his chest in a new voice, which had been lost as it were. "What, boy?"

"I merely said perhaps," insisted Etzel growing a shade paler and keeping the penetrating glance upon the gleam behind the black glasses, which was necessary for his short-sighted eyes, "perhaps my name is . . . now what could it be? Perhaps my name is Maurizius. There are still some people of that name. Why couldn't my name be Maurizius?"

Warschauer-Waremme looked as if someone had called to him away across the roofs from the street. His features became convulsed with an expression of tense gloomy thought. "Maurizius?" he repeated broodingly. He slowly wiped his forehead with his fat white hand. Suddenly he took a step towards Etzel, took his glasses off and looked with surprised curiosity intently into his face. For the first time Etzel saw his eyes; they were colourless, watery, almost dead eyes.

CHAPTER IX

I.

The general's widow had received a letter from Sophia von Andergast which had caused her to send the following answer promptly: "Dear Sophia: It seems to me right that you should come here. However, you need not ask me and I should not advise you. But I think your decision is so proper that I am asking you to live here with me and if you accept I shall be glad. I hope that you are not already on the way, and that this letter will reach you. Who could understand your despair better than I? I myself have been in a frightful condition since the boy left. We will talk over what you should do. From me, of course, you cannot expect much help; I am a useless old woman and hampered in my actions not only by this sad fact. Your son is my son's boy, *voilà tout*. But this time, Sophia, I am on your side, and as long as my courage and strength hold out, I shall stand by you. Of course, I tremble at the idea of a meeting between you and Wolf. But it will have to be; you are right. He must give an accounting to you; before God and man he is bound to do so. You must ask him for your child. Even though he cannot, unfortunately, tell you where he is, he will have to give account to you how it could come about that he does not know. Your friends have not informed you falsely; no one knows where our boy is. Oh, heavens! I no longer sleep at night. I am constantly worrying my head with whys and wheres. Your letter shattered a last silly hope of mine that he had fled to you. Recently he spoke of you often, but I was not permitted to listen and what was the result? He stopped talking about you. Then I really felt like a useless old geezer, no good to anyone in the world. Oh, not to get old! or if one does get old not to feel old! After all this, you will be all the more surprised at this letter. But the fact that you, his mother, had to hear first from strangers—even if you call them friends, in such a case they are strangers—that your child had left him and could not be found, that was the drop that made the bucket overflow. He ignored the three letters which you wrote him during the last few months, all right; at a pinch I'll still understand that; but not to inform you, not at least to have his lawyer write you what has occurred, which concerns you as much as him, and perhaps a thousand times more, that is too . . . consistent for my brain. You young people are so curiously logical anyway, you, too; there are some things about you which I cannot understand. But I don't want to become garrulous, at least not on paper; perhaps you will explain things to me. I have not seen you for nine years, dear Sophia, or is it, God forbid, ten? And I do not know what has become of you as a human being; as a woman you are closer to me than formerly; I believe that we shall understand each other without much talk. I don't take much stock in words, but about people, provided that they are human, I care all the more for that. Believe me, yours affectionately, Cilly von Andergast."

In order not to be accused of conspiring with his opponent behind his back, the old lady considered it necessary to inform her son of the correspondence. She did so in a letter which was considerably shorter than the one addressed to her former daughter-in-law and added that Sophia would come tomorrow or the next day and live in her house. This was an unexpected blow for Herr von Andergast and brought the uselessness of many years of precaution clearly before his eyes. He found his mother's letter lying on his desk in the afternoon. He read it, folded it and put it aside. He took it up again, read it, tore it in four pieces and threw it in the waste-paper basket. Ten minutes later he picked the pieces out of the scrap basket, threw them in the stove and watched them burning up! Then he walked up and down; finally he lifted the receiver of the telephone and had himself connected with the Palace of Justice, asked for Director Günzburg and told him to inform the supervisor of the penitentiary at Kressa that the solicitor-general would call there the following morning. Whether there was a causal connection between the letter which had been so incomprehensibly destroyed and this professional decision may be conjectured. Certainly Herr von Andergast had not previously set any date for a conversation with the prisoner Maurizius. If it was not fleeing from Sophia, it certainly looked like a flight, an internal defence which he was demonstrating to himself by this move. At least he would not be there when she came. Escape he knew that he could not. This time he would have to face her.

2.

Kressa towers high between wooded hills, an old fortress, the ancestral estate of a royal house. That the nation should keep the dregs of humanity confined for expiation where the cradle of its princes formerly stood is a ghastly commentary on the passage of earthly glory. Herr von Andergast's service motor, smoking oil, dashed up the steep incline to the recently added wing, where Director Pauli was waiting at the gate. He is a pale slender man of thirty with a pince-nez and a little blond beard; he was formerly a teacher in the village of Kressa. He receives the solicitor-general and conducts him to an office on the left, a painfully clean room, something halfway between a bourgeois living-room with covers on the sofa and chairs and photographs on the walls, and an office with a filing cabinet, a desk and telephone, and a signal apparatus. At the desk a man is writing, a favoured convict who is breathless with excitement over the distinguished visitor, for his eyes are glazed and his hands snatch senselessly to the right and left to put papers in order. Herr von Andergast sits down and requests Pauli, merely with a gesture, to make his report to him. He calls him director and is politely dry. Pauli explains that since the last attempted escape, which occurred ten years ago, the institution has been peaceful, certainly there is no particular ground for complaint. Herr von Andergast wishes to hear the details about the unsuccessful outbreak, which was frustrated by the watchfulness of the night guard in the upper yard. The superintendent's bloodless face colours slightly at the recollection of the unfortunate event; he is ashamed of it, embarrassed at the criticism of the officers of the court, and finally expresses the thought that one is never certain from day to day that it will not occur again. There is only one thing worse, and which has more evil consequences, and that is an open revolt. They have had that, too. It seems unavoidable. One does for these people whatever is possible, they have their regular meals, their regulated hours of sleep, their religious services, their recreation and rest, one treats them decently, eases matters for them where one can; and yet they have no insight; they never cease plotting and conspiring in culpable collusions. All this is mirrored in the features of the young superintendent, as he tells the story of the last attempt at insurrection, a dull and sad narrative, rendered remarkable only because the men had succeeded—it was the occupants of dormitory twelve—during two hours of the night—in silently breaking through a wall sixty inches thick and making a hole through which they could easily slip. They then let themselves down on hemp ropes, which they had gradually taken out of the work-rooms and hidden, it was incomprehensible where and how, in the dormitory. Five men! A distance of twenty-five yards! "It was senseless and it was useless," continued the superintendent in his low sad voice, with downcast eyes, "for there they had again thirty feet of climbing in front of them and for that the ropes were not long enough; they would have had to jump the last five yards. Simply madness!"

And aside from this, inquired Herr von Andergast, carefully, as if to spare the man's feelings; so far as he knew there were some difficult men here. Yes, certainly, admitted Pauli with resignation, above all there was Hiss, the murderer of the police gendarme Jänisch; the baron would remember, it had been an attack by night on the street. He was a difficult customer, there was no way of taming the man and accustoming him to the regulations; he had been in the house six weeks and every day he made some groundless complaint. He had been at Dietz three months and there he had written entreaty after entreaty; he wanted to get away; he could not stand it; finally they had moved him to Kressa and now he wanted to get back to Dietz at any price. He was lazy to a degree that was pathological; his only desire was to write; he wanted to write the story of his life and thereby, at the same time, to adduce proof of his innocence. He had not committed murder, but had been thrust into the greatest misery by the brutality of his father, an incurable drunkard who had begotten him in a fit of intoxication. At the time of the so-called murder, one winter night, he had begged the gendarme for cigarettes, whereupon the man had made a movement towards a revolver in his trousers pocket so that he, Hiss, out of fear of being shot, had pulled the trigger himself. That could not be called murder; one could not shut up a man for life for such a thing; it was self-defence, nothing else. Unfortunately, continued Pauli shaking his head, a lawyer from Aschaffenburg had turned up who had taken up the cause of this deceitful liar as a just one, and was constantly asking for consultations with his client, and was flooding the courts with requests to have the case reopened. "You will see him, baron," continued the superintendent. "Three days ago we granted him the solitary cell which he had asked for, with paper, pen and ink so that he could write, but up to this time he has not written a single word. That's the kind he is." He cast a glance at the man writing at the desk, who understood directly and pulled a blue copy book out of a drawer, which he handed to Pauli. On an oval shield was written "Recollections of My Youth." "Hiss wrote that," said the director, handing the book to Herr von Andergast, who opened it and glanced through the pages for a while. The quick flowing handwriting suggested a commercial clerk; the style varied between insufferable elegiac pompousness and boastful self-admiration; at the same time there was an astonishing accuracy and a quantity of not uninteresting details. "Yes, they are very serious about themselves and very nonchalant about the rest of us," said Herr von Andergast, putting the book aside and getting up. "I should like, superintendent, to walk through the institution and at three o'clock this afternoon to see the prisoner Maurizius alone." Pauli bowed and rang for the inspector. "How does the man behave?" asked Herr von Andergast in a casual tone, with his hand already on the door knob. Pauli smiled with upraised eyebrows. "Oh," he replied, "if they were all like him, Baron! Then life here would be easy." The inspector, a well-preserved old man, with a friendly intelligent face, came into the room.

3.

An iron grating is unlocked and they enter a dark court surrounded with walls towering towards heaven. The inspector walks ahead, followed by Herr von Andergast and the superintendent, and the rear is brought up by two watchmen in uniform. The court has been swept clean; everywhere one notices a degree of order which is perhaps not entirely usual. Herr von Andergast, of course, knows all about such prearranged visits; he is aware that everyone who has arms and legs has been set to using them in order to avoid being raked over the coals, and when something is foul they hope for indulgence by pointing to long established habit or to the failure to allot funds. But the baron knows that the employees are faithful and perform their hard calling with understanding and patience. It is not as it was in former times, not so long ago, either, when penitentiaries were notorious infernos, the horrors of which people dared only allude to in hushed and frightened whispers, when the directors were irresponsible tyrants and the wardens were the true torturers. We are living in a cultivated state, and the execution of punishment is carried out according to humane, one sometimes fears too humane, principles. Kressa, moreover, has in this respect a particularly good reputation.

However, he has not come for the sake of one of the routine inspections. He has used this official pretext in order to draw as little attention as possible to his real purpose. He does not want to have people saying that the solicitor-general has been seeing Leonhart Maurizius, that he is evidently interested in the case and that something is afoot. He does not want any talk. No, there is nothing going on, one can be quite reassured. This is his conscientious pretext for his visit.

The five men silently mount a steep winding wooden staircase, the inspector opens an iron door and they proceed through a long, almost circular corridor, high up in which there are small barred windows, narrowing towards the outside; then the inspector's keys grind again, a second iron door opens and they enter one of the work-rooms. Herr von Andergast involuntarily pulls out his handkerchief and presses it to his nose. A smell strikes him like that from a cage of animals. He knows that smell. As a young man he suffered from attacks of oppression before such visits, because the odour caused him almost to faint every time. The smell was of musty clothes, of warm mildewed glue, of rancid fat, of musty walls, of human perspiration and foul breath. The weather is bad and the windows in all three rooms are closed. About a hundred and fifty men are moving about, some free, others crammed into pens, separated with hemp cords. They are weaving straw mats, making ropes; some are cobbling; a few are working at a planing bench. A bent-over man approaches with stealthy steps so that one is scarcely aware of his presence, and with a secretive expression plucks at the director's sleeve and whispers in his ear that the trouble with the bore-worm in his brain is not getting better; his pain gets worse every day. The superintendent looks as if he were treating the complaint seriously and exchanges a glance of understanding with the inspector, who shrugs his shoulders. There is no doubt that the man is simulating, however; he becomes dangerously excited if he is not believed and one reproaches him.

Perhaps he has merely established the idea of the bore-worm in his brain in order to obtain notice and some importance in his own eyes. The inspector summons a certain Buschfeld, who has been guilty of insubordination this morning and in a gentle and pleasant manner, as if in the name of common sense, takes him to task. Buschfeld, during the 1918 revolution, had shot General Winkler in Darmstadt, after previously boxing his ears for no other reason than that he was a general; otherwise he, Winkler, had been a harmless man, not at all unpopular. Buschfeld smiles peculiarly, while justifying himself almost like a boy who is reproached for being obstreperous; his smile is half embarrassed, half sarcastic, and shows his magnificent teeth gleaming in his well-cut face, with the strongly developed chin disfigured by bristles of beard. Herr von Andergast approaches and listens. Like everyone else in the place as soon as he is merely permitted to speak, Buschfeld after three sentences begins talking of his offence and sentence, proving with many obviously carefully considered arguments that he is innocent. Seeing a public before him he goes at the subject with a vengeance, depicts the situation, explains the misunderstanding of which he is the victim. He smiles constantly, showing his magnificent big teeth, and Herr von Andergast looks into his great eyes, like the kernels of brown nuts. There is a passionate longing which drives him mad at the slightest hint of the thought: outside. When he says "outside" he means the world, life, freedom, trees, grass, women, sky, taverns: a glowing conglomeration of lovely things. The strange gentleman in front of him comes from "outside" and consequently has a halo about him, an intoxicating odour, incomparable possibilities. He stares at him and seems to ask in amazement: What, you come from "outside" and are going "out" again, and you are not beside yourself with happiness? They all have this devouring, maddening conception of the "outside" in their eyes, which is something different from yearning, which is more, far more, something beyond yearning, something more exalted, more sombre and starry than any yearning on earth can be. There are eyes in which this thing has almost died; too much time has passed; the mind has lost the pictures; they rustle about like withered leaves, for the man himself is withered. There is a man of fifty with his grey, soap-coloured, shining face framed by a black beard, like a charcoal-burner. He has been in the place nine years. He killed his employer because the man withheld from him the two thousand marks which he had saved during many years of labour and confidingly entrusted to him. When asked, he tells the story in his Rhenish dialect; a deep breath raises his chest; the powerful bent body relives the unendurable injustice again like a distant echo which shakes him and penetrates through him; he tells how he needed the money and asked for it, once, twice, five times; how the peasant tried to talk himself out of the situation, beat about the bush, put him off and how he was obliged finally to admit to himself that the money was no longer there. What can be of any use then; neither God nor judge can help; that man must be done in; otherwise it will eat out one's heart. A disturbed spirit. A broken distracted soul. Next to him works Schergentz, a boy of twenty-five, an incendiary; no one had ever found out why he had set the place on fire;

he had been a good son and an industrious workman; one night he had set fire to the neighbour's barn and three people had been burned to death. Why? No one knows. Since the hour of his arrest, he has not spoken a word; his father, his mother, the witnesses, the investigating attorney, the policeman, the judge, the lawyer for the defence and the jury have all tried in vain; not a syllable, he remains mute. He does not even speak in his sleep, nor when he is alone; he never forgets himself. The manager talks persuasively to him again now, but from the expressions on the faces of the inspector and the superintendent, one can see how useless the attempt is; Herr von Andergast places his hand heavily on the man's shoulder and looking penetratingly with his violet-blue eyes into the obdurate burning ones of the prisoner he says: "Come, man, what is the meaning of this? Certainly it's not for your own good; come then!" But his lips remain sealed. Months ago a man imprisoned with him, one from the "intellectual cell," expressed the opinion that the first minute the man is free he will speak, and not any sooner. And so his hands perform their accustomed work, while his sombre closed eyes—for they, too, are silent—gaze past the men. There could be no greater contrast than that between him and his nearest companion, who committed murder by means of poison. He had done away with his bride's father because the father had tried to prevent the marriage and had refused to give the girl a dowry. His limbs, his joints, his muscles, his lips and his forehead all tremble convulsively, and his cheeks flush hectically when he thinks of the incomprehensible injustice meted out to him when he was found guilty. Nothing had been proven against him; he had had no thought of evil; the witnesses had been his enemies and the court prejudiced. He quotes the testimony of the chemical expert, the testimony of the druggist; all false, all perjury; they had been silent about this thing and had invented that thing merely to destroy him. "Why?" asks Herr von Andergast dryly. He shrugs his shoulders passionately. A plot on the part of the whole world. His words tumble over one another as he weaves quickly, pounding the mat with a flat mallet and wetting his lips with the tip of his tongue, protruding like an adder's. He keeps his eyes constantly lowered and the whole man is the embodiment of a lie. But what a pitiful lie it is, skulking slyly off, how transparent and how sick! The body only has the appearance of belonging to the will, it is a broken-down mechanism, a machine whose wheels and pipes are out of order; that it still breathes, swallows and digests is a hoax. In the third cell there is an old man of sixty or sixty-five, he himself does not know exactly, he has spent thirty years with short interruptions in the institution, a typical recidivist. He was taken again for the last time eleven years ago. He looks like a jolly vagabond, with his little grey beard over his chin, his squat little figure with its short neck, the little round head, the small turned-up nose, the small mouth and the little protruding forehead. Herr von Andergast inquires for what crime he is there. He smiles complacently to himself, "Oh, for such a leetle bit o' thieving," he replies, examining the edge of the plane with his finger. "Come, Käsbacher," says the inspector, reproachfully, "thieving would not have meant eleven years." "Certainly not," admits the old man, "a leetle morality got mixed up with it, too."—"Well, and are you satisfied with the treatment you are getting?" asks Herr von Andergast. "Oh, yes, there's not nothing to kick about, now the humane establishmints is established; get along good now in these here institutions. Humanity is a grand thing anyway. Only there could be a little more fat. Fat a fellow does miss." Then with elegiac downcast eyes, "The twenty-third of May is my birthday." "Really, and what would you like to have then?" asks the inspector knowingly. "Liver-sausage, I suppose you'd like that." "You've guessed it, boss. For the life of me I do love it." And the thought of liver-sausage beautifies the shrivelled old face as sunset the face of an enthusiastic girl. For him the "outside" no longer exists.

4.

They climb one flight higher to the solitary cells. Herr von Andergast wishes to see a few "specimens" only. In the first cell, which has the shape of a tower-room, there is a man who committed murder from jealousy, a slender man with sad features, in the first stages of consumption. They had looked through the peek-hole and had seen him sitting at the table in a state of complete collapse; when the door opened he jumped up and stood at military attention. It is that which they call good behaviour and he is much liked for it. He is a marionette who knows how to conceal his inner despair to the point of self-effacement. The inspector closing the iron door remarks professionally: "One often hears him sighing for hours, through the whole night." The next "specimen": a gigantic creature, one who was guilty of violent assaults; he was one of the men involved in the attempted insurrection last October. He had succeeded in getting hold of an iron bar, with which to kill the watchman on the way to the bath, which was to be the decisive signal for the other conspirators. It happened, however, that the watchman on duty that day was the one who had secretly given him a piece of chewing-tobacco a few weeks before, so he could not strike him, the bar simply fell out of his hand. He stands against the wall blinking. From the window of his cell, far off in the landscape, he can see an apple-tree in blossom at a bend in the river, delicately outlined in the distance against the gable of a house. Sometimes the man stands from morning till evening, leaning motionless against the wall and staring at the distant tree, and if the warden opens the door he merely turns his head as if drunk with sleep and continues blinking and gazing. . . . While he was "outside," he never had such impulses; what did he care about an apple-tree in blossom?—he never even looked at one; now it is something tremendous; the embodiment of all that he has missed and neglected, like the bird for the man in the adjoining cell, which he is permitted to keep and take care of. He is there for life; he strangled an eight-year-old girl and then practically chopped her to pieces; but he loves his bird so dearly that his eyes fill with tears when he looks at it. The walls of his cell are filled with all kinds of photographs and illustrations from newspapers and a small coloured lithograph of a Madonna; each one of these things is dear to his heart and he can look at it for hours. He greets the visitors with a childlike smile. There is something very suspicious about this smile; even though it seems so winsome and natural, it reminds one of the delusions of a delirious person. He has tied a cloth around his head; the manager asks why, what is the matter, and he answers humorously that during the night he had been to Kressa village to attend the kermis, and he laughs. He presses his lips against the wire of the bird cage and wheedles the bird, which has been well trained, to kiss him. The little animal flutters up and presses his bill into the man's mouth. One is transported into a cheap scene in a dime novel where the human side of a debased criminal is supposed to be shown, and perhaps the inalterably godlike germ in human nature. But how frightful it is, how far removed from the illuminating word; can God know anything of it?

They reach the dormitories. The manager shows Herr von Andergast the window which eight and a half years ago two convicts broke through; the third remained stuck between the bars, he had pushed his head, chest and arms through, but his hips were caught and his comrades could not free him, so he hung from midnight until the next morning with his naked greased body hanging out like a beam over the depths below and groaning with pain. The other two had run naked along the street through the winter night and had broken into an empty country-house, where they had stolen clothes and gotten away. The manager, measuring the narrow space with his hand, says that it still remains a mystery to him how grown-up men could pass through those bars which a cat could only slip through with difficulty. Herr von Andergast remarks: "It seems that the urge for freedom gives these people supernatural powers." The manager and inspector silently agree. But Herr von Andergast is aware of the banality and feebleness of his remark; since he has entered this building he feels an almost pathological inadequacy; he cannot remember that he ever before felt quite so dubious to himself; and this shows itself in his pallor and the uncertainty of his gait; he walks as heavily as if his joints were filled with lead. Forty beds in the one room, sixty in the next, he suddenly sees, beds one over another, beds standing next to one another like twin beds; he perceives this suddenly and says, heavily and unwillingly, pointing to the beds, that that arrangement could not last; the two watchmen grin to themselves, the manly earnest features of the inspector show that he is not a stranger to solicitude on this subject, and the manager murmurs: "The focus of infection of many evils." The superficiality of these remarks irritates Herr von Andergast, his forehead flushes with anger, and he continues to gaze at the mounds of beds as if struck by a vision of horrors. He presses his hand to his forehead as if to shut out the sight which causes his feeling of inadequacy to grow into some dawning of responsibility; he wants to stop seeing those beds, they make his conception of mankind unspeakably disgusting, slime inflated into malice and sensuality and the inside of the human breast a limited purlieu of darkness with a quivering muscle in the centre of it which it has always been the vain business of poets and religious enthusiasts to turn into a container of all the virtues. "Example is our teacher," says Herr von Andergast to himself, as he walks into the cell of the dangerous Hiss, which does not need to be unlocked, because the prison rector is in it, and a warden, a young man with a brutal face, disfigured by a red birthmark, is acting as sentry before the door. The pastor of souls greets Herr von Andergast. With his weather-browned features and white mane he looks like a Norwegian fisherman. But the appearance of religious force which puts a shining halo around the heads of these men is deceiving in regard to him, as it is in the case of many others. The strength which has given them wings is mostly used up, they have come to perceive that they can only remove a few grains of sand from mountains of human misery; that the shaft which they are digging collapses daily over their own heads; they have grown tired; they no longer believe in their calling, and function as officials because they are paid by the State. "A hopeless case," he whispers softly to Herr von Andergast, shrugging his shoulders towards the prisoner, and over his features there spreads the insipid annoyance of a man who is asked for the hundredth time to pull a tree out of the earth by its roots. Hiss stands there with the upper part of his body bent over; his mouth in his citron-coloured face is distorted with rage, and his retreating chin is covered with beads of perspiration, his eyes, yellow like those of a panther, are fastened upon the priest with boundless hate, and when the manager speaks to him, asking whether he has begun to write, he looks at him with the same measureless hatred. "Couldn't," he growls bitterly. "How could a fellow write here? That one over there in the cage yells all the time so that one has no head for writing." The glance of hate sneaks around the room, seeking every face, the back bends more forward, the dangerous panther-beast in which there is little of the human being left, may break out any moment. Herr von Andergast involuntarily recoils a step and leaves the cell in silence; the guard has already opened the next one; its inmate is the one who yells in his cage; he is a prisoner condemned to discipline; he has been locked up in an iron cage for three days and cowers in semi-darkness, shaking the bars from time to time like a gorilla, screaming from time to time, lowing like a cow bellowing for its calf which is being slaughtered. Sternly the inspector calls to him, "Lorschmann, if you don't keep quiet, nothing to eat tomorrow," whereupon a grinding noise comes from the man's interior as if its occupant had rusty entrails of iron. There is a "human being" totally destroyed, vaunted "man," even what is left of the outer form is merely a caricature; Herr von Andergast stands at the door of the cell as if he were himself imprisoned; why is all this new to him, something frightfully unprecedented for him? Is there something in his eyes which was not in them before, or has the reflection of the lantern—Etzel's lantern—fallen upon them as it did recently upon the brain of the creature in the mirror?

5.

Three o'clock. Herr von Andergast has lunched at the inn in Kressa, that is, he has paid for several dishes; he has only consumed two cups of black coffee. The cell of convict number 357 is unlocked and locked behind him again. A man gets up from the table with the military swiftness which the institution demands and remains standing and waiting. He is half a head shorter than Herr von Andergast, and the grey convict suit hangs loosely about his lean figure. He stands erect and his head is not bent. The greyness of his face scarcely differs from the greyness of the walls, over his high forehead his chalk-white hair hangs uncut. The cell is a five-cornered room, containing the iron bed, the bucket with a lid, the wooden chair, the wooden table and a rack with a few books. The window opens into a court; below, five convicts are moving silently in a circle. It is the prescribed "walk." There is not room for more than five in the court. It takes five hours for eight sets to perform their daily exercise. One hears the scuffing of the feet on the stone pavement. It sounds like the wind flapping in slack sails.

"You will scarcely remember me," says Herr von Andergast, beginning the conversation conventionally. He does not seem to care about securing any understanding, nor to be sounding the man's mood. Maurizius, who up to now has not moved, lifts his chin a little as if he had been struck. Since he is standing with his back to the window one cannot tell the expression of his eyes, which stand out like two dark circles in his long face. Herr von Andergast sits down on the chair, indicating by a gesture of his hand that he is waiting for Maurizius to sit down on the bed opposite to him. The latter, however, hesitates. He inquires in a husky voice what the reason for this honour is, from whose sound one can tell how seldom he speaks. Herr von Andergast sits bending forward with his hands folded between his thighs. The violet-blue eyes have regained their brightness. He cannot answer in one word. He repeats the gesture requesting Maurizius to sit down, and folds his hands again. A silence falls. Then Herr von Andergast, looking at the floor, remarks that his visit is quite unprofessional in character, he has come entirely for personal considerations. Maurizius finally seats himself upon the bed, carefully, as if not to lose a syllable. Now when the full daylight falls upon his face, it looks ghastly. One might suppose that white blood was flowing in his veins. His nose is sunken, and his mouth, whose curve is extraordinarily pleasing, indeed charming, is pressed together in a hard line. The eyes are no longer black circles, but coffee-brown, and have a mild, steady, joyless expression.

Personal considerations. What could they be? Herr von Andergast attentively contemplates the nail of his right middle finger. Then, opening his eyes in a straightforward manner—decidedly, even though it is forced, it is Etzel's manner—he says that it is a matter which concerns future measures. "Measures of what sort?" "About that there could scarcely be any misunderstanding." He asks if Maurizius has given up all hope. Maurizius slowly lifts his hand and places it on his head, a gesture which causes Herr von Andergast to see father Maurizius before him, as he stood with his hand upon his head. There is something of the mysteriousness of inheritance about it; the external things which Nature transplants from father to son are often more telling and real than the internal ones. Maurizius replies dryly, but firmly, that he has never at any time, under any circumstances, given up his hope of rehabilitation. Herr von Andergast twines the index fingers of his hands about each other. Rehabilitation? That was scarcely to be thought of. Certainly it was very far away. Such a possibility, even if it existed, would not have moved him to undertake this interview. One had to take the real situation into consideration. And this showed only one single way. And one could go along this path only if a certain condition was fulfilled, which was as indissolubly attached to it as a fishing cord to its rod. "I understand," said Maurizius. "I believe myself that we understand each other," said Herr von Andergast. There was a pause.

"It is another attempt upon an unsuitable subject," begins Maurizius in his unaccustomed tones, looking at his knees with his brows drawn together. "Since I have been living in this place many have tried. They were quite wild with eagerness for their end, directors (for a superintendent is a new arrangement), four directors, among them a former colonel, then various court officers, also a gentleman from one of the ministries, and above all the clerical gentlemen, of course. The clergyman Porschitzky, whom we have now, is the seventh who has come to me"—he counts them over in his mind. "Yes, he is the seventh. One—I don't remember whether it was the third or the fourth, his name was Meinertshagen—did not leave my cell once for two days and two nights. During the same time and with less exertion he might have converted a village of negroes. In the end I felt as though my head had been bashed in. Then in my despair I said to him—at that time I could still feel despair about something of that sort: 'Herr Meinertshagen, when Moses struck water out of the rock he performed a miracle. You want to perform a miracle with me; but you will first have to conjure into me what you want to conjure out of me. How shall a man confess to a deed which he did not do?' Then he gave it up, but from that day on I no longer existed for him. He did not believe me. No one believes me."

Herr von Andergast's face expresses a certain formal regret. He does not want to appear as if he too did not "believe," but Maurizius probably knows that he does not "believe." For the present they agree upon a basis of polite conversation. Much has already been reached by letting a man come to the subject himself, and he would not wish at any price to disturb him in his outpourings. Herr von Andergast knows that these people condemned to loneliness for decades, at the slightest provocation, the encouragement of a glance, fall into automatic communicativeness. They regard it as a release and a kindness if one merely listens, and scarcely count on answers. But Maurizius seems to sense the thoughts of his visitor. You may know this and you may know that, a quick twist of his mouth seems to say, but what do you know of "decades," what do you know of "time"? That time exists you, none of you, know; merely, that there was time. The present is for you a magnificent lightning flash between two periods of darkness, for me it is an unceasing darkness between a fire which has sunk in the horizon and another for whose rising I am waiting. Perpetual, perpetual waiting is my present, and the time during which I must wait on into the uncertain and the unseeable is the present for me. Only he knows hell who has found out what the present really is. Maurizius raises his eyelids like the wax lids over a doll's eyes. It is as if he only now realizes that the man sitting in front of him is the same who formerly, a long, long time ago, unrelentingly and superhumanly pushed him into this abyss. How is it possible that you are still alive, his glance, boring and penetrating, seems to say, while the unusually small white teeth of his lower jaw gnaw his lips; how is it possible that you are in my presence, you who are without a present? It is approximately as if Attila, or Ivan the Terrible, were sitting before one and those outside were as immortal as oneself. Since Herr von Andergast retains his challenging silence, and depends upon a magic whose force he knows from analogous cases—as if up to now his self-assurance has not been in the least shaken and as if he has not felt how incurably it has been undermined, Maurizius returns to the last word, which recurs to him. "No, no one believes," he says to himself, "the accusation had merely to be made, and I was already guilty. I had many friends; at that time I could call them friends; from the standpoint of my life at that time they were friends; but from the day the accusation was made they seemed blown away. I constantly looked for them, I could not understand it, such a falling off. . . . I had not injured any one of them, I had not betrayed anyone, I thought that they must know me. Every man has a moral standard, as it were, we had confided so much in one another, no crevice had remained hidden, so one thought . . . and no one . . . not a one, as if one had suddenly appeared under a different name . . . in a new world." "You forget one," Herr von Andergast reminds him. "I think that your father never lost his faith." It is not easy for him to decide to make this reference, which is too familiar, but in the first place he says to himself that he is here to dissimulate, secondly his opponent is beginning to fascinate him; there is a mixture of decision and breadth, of coldness and presumably of resolutely suppressed warmth, which compels his attention and causes the distrustful indifference with which he has come to evaporate. Maurizius nods, scarcely perceptibly. "Yes, that's true," he replies, "father, yes . . . he; but father does not count. There is a difference between the tie of blood, between the affections of relatives and others. If one belongs to a man it does not prove anything to the world to stick to him. Possession effaces guilt. Elli too would have . . ." He stops, shaking his head. It was certainly a remarkable "too," a remarkable example which he suppresses. Herr von Andergast pulls out his cigarette case and offers it open to Maurizius who, surprised, takes one with greedy eagerness. Herr von Andergast gives him a match, lights a cigarette himself, and for a while they look at each other in silence, smoking. Herr von Andergast is thinking hard. Finally, as if he began to have doubts and wanted to be put on the track, he throws out the question: "If I am to assume that you did not shoot—which, note well, I may not assume; I am only trying to get your point of view—who from your point of view could have shot?" A friendly, encouraging smile plays about his lips, the violet-blue eyes beam in an almost kindly manner. Maurizius stares at him. He raises his eyebrows contemptuously, cutting a deep groove in his forehead. About a minute and a half goes by during which his face is black as if with something like silent fury. Is it the question which has been asked thousands and thousands of times in the same tone, with the same skepticism, with the same triumphant manner of judge and executioner, which so transforms him? Scarcely. He has learned patience. He has learned to know the patience of the questioners. He has become hardened and deaf towards it. The question no longer strikes home, it no longer entices him, or releases anything in him. Never to answer it, under no torture of body or soul to answer it, not with a glance or a breath or a gesture to answer it, has been his determination for eighteen years and seven months. They are biting upon granite. But it is not that. He suddenly understands: there sits his opponent. Three feet away from you is the condemner, the destroyer, superhuman and unmerciful, not merely his representative—there were many such who came—but actually the man himself. A disposition of Providence, an incarnation of Fate. All the outside condensed into one individual, the world, humanity, court, condemnation, everything he has suffered, and that he has brooded over in this room, all of the perpetual present, all the sleepless nights, the humiliations, the deprivations, the despair, the fear of death, the desire for death, the greed for life and the greed for flesh, the whole theft of life, all of it embodied in one man. He feels him to be frightfully close, as close as one's brain-born opponent sometimes appears to be in a dream. To settle accounts with him is like the fulfilment of a desire unconsciously cherished for eighteen and a half years. But he must calm down. He must not allow the person who was once in him to rise. He feels that with this man he has time. He says quietly: "A judge must prove my guilt to me. That I should prove my innocence to him when I can't is contrary to the meaning of the world. There are nations who have recognized this long ago and therefore they are the greater. Better laws, better people."

6.

Herr von Andergast got up and walked to the window. While crushing his cigarette end against the sill, he planned his further behaviour. He felt confused, to a certain extent even helpless. With well-assumed anxiety he said: "We won't get any further in this way. You have fortified yourself, as was to be expected. I don't expect to outstrip the clerical gentlemen. It would be a mistaken undertaking, as matters lie. As my visit, as I have already said, is unofficial, I do not allow myself to doubt your statements. Otherwise I could reply: A fiction with which one has determined to live is a tyrant who has lost the power to see and to hear. But let's drop all that. I had thought of coming to an understanding." He remained silent a few minutes, to study the effect of his words, but Maurizius neither budged nor said a word. Therefore, Herr von

Andergast went on, and one could hear from his voice that he was greatly irritated. "In regard to the administration of our laws, you are mistaken. Like most laymen. That the evidence of guilt is to be produced by the judge is expressly stated in the law. Everyone is regarded as innocent so long as his guilt has not been indisputably established. That is one of our fundamental legal tenets and there is no court which would disregard it."

Maurizius lifted his head a little. His bearing and expression were full of silent irony. He smiled. Perhaps at the judicially embellished phrasing of "in regard to" and "the administration," perhaps at the didactic tone in which an institution was defended whose bloodless semblance of life existed, except in dusty digests, only in the heads of men who constructed conceptions out of letters with which they then entered into a spectral symbiosis. He said, shrugging his shoulders: "It is written thus. Can't be denied. A good many things are written. But will you assert that it is carried out? Where? When? To whom? On whom? I hope you don't think that I am talking of my own experience, that I am judging from my own fate. I don't matter here at all. My delusion, well, all right. Do you really regard this delusion as a process which makes one blind and deaf? It must be a consolation for you to say to yourself that this so-called fiction has prevented me for eighteen and a half years from seeing clearly what went on and goes on around me. In this world. In such a world." He had spoken completely dispassionately, rather with exhausted coldness than impetuously, but he had gotten up and came a step closer. In such a world; it sounded as if it came out of the bowels of the earth, out of total darkness, yet without any exertion, because the cry had already been repeated a million times and no longer had any hope of being heard. Lacing the middle fingers of both hands together like links in a chain, a movement which seemed habitual and proceeded from his brooding, his coffee-brown eyes stared constantly at Herr von Andergast's chin, not higher than the chin, which was extraordinarily unpleasant to Herr von Andergast, almost as if he were being measured too low. "As I have said, I am not referring to my personal circumstances," began Maurizius again. "For me, of course, my fate is as important as the solar system; as an experience it is nevertheless only a single instance. But I have not only had my own experience, I have had a thousand. I have heard of a thousand judges, I have seen a thousand before me and I have been able to observe the work of a thousand, and it is always the same thing. From the first he is the enemy. For him the deed has been done, he takes the human being at his lowest. The accuser is his god, the accused his victim, punishment his goal. If one has gotten to the point of appearing before a judge, one is done for. Why? Because the judge anticipates a later excommunication. With incredulity, with sarcasm, with contempt, with pollution. If his victim is not tractable, he places him under a moral pressure which ends in stigma. It is the work of a virtuoso. The law demands that he use fair scales, yes, but he throws his whole weight into the side where the deed lies, without hesitation. Who has empowered him to make one of the deed and the doer, and what permits him not only to condemn the doer—all right, let him condemn, it is perhaps his function—but to take vengeance upon him? Judge! That formerly had a high meaning. The highest in human society. I have known people who have told me that at every trial they have the same horrible feeling in their testicles that one has if one suddenly stands over a deep abyss. Every cross-examination depends upon the employment of tactical advantages which one mostly secures just as dishonestly as the subterfuges of a victim at bay. But the judge and the state attorney demand that they shall be regarded as omniscient, and to question their omniscience means unchaining their desire for revenge to the point of hopelessness, so that only the hypocrite, the cynic or the completely broken man can have mercy from them. How then can one have a just decision? How can one obtain the protection which your law demands? The law is only a pretext for the cruel organizations created in its name, and how can one be expected to bow down before a judge who makes of a guilty human being a maltreated animal? The animal howls and rages and bites and the people outside shudder and say: Thank God that we are rid of that. It is a frightful way in which they are rid of it, so much they admit, some of them at least; but they maintain that it cannot be changed. It all comes to the fact that those who live in heaven have no conception of hell, even if one tells them about it for days. There all fantasy fails. Only he can understand who is in it."

"You are going at the matter with hammer and tongs," said Herr von Andergast, with a slight displeasure in his tone. "The consequences which his crime brings in the soul of a criminal cannot be made a reproach to society. The justice of a punishment cannot be measured either by how subjectively bearable it is, or by the behaviour of the organs which dictate it. In the end, every human institution is drawn, by the persons who administer it, out of the realm of ideas into that of imperfect practice; we must seek the nearest possible approach, that is all. The suffering that lies between these two, even the most pitiful, perhaps justifies indignation, but it cannot destroy the whole structure. Since you cannot expect to win me over to your side, you are wasting your time in such outbursts. Or rather you are wasting my time, which is in this case much more regrettable." Maurizius' lips twitched sarcastically. His expression seemed to say: I know that words are in vain, why all of this? At the same time there was an arousing quality about the man at the window. He was obliged to look towards him constantly, he did not dare to turn his glance for a second in another direction. The voice which came from there sounded as if it came through a megaphone, which, of course, was a deception resulting from his sick, irritated nerves, his pathologically distorted sense of hearing, for Herr von Andergast spoke with a restraint that took into account the smallness of the room, yet with a coolness which was only the more evident for his attempt to appear benevolent. "What do you want then?" asked Maurizius hoarsely, letting head fall on his breast as almost all convicts do when they are about to receive a decision from their superiors. Herr von Andergast replied eagerly, as if really relieved by the question: "I will tell you. Little as I am interested in your theoretical point of view, I am all the more interested in all that concerns you personally. To be frank: I have during the last few weeks gone into your case rather thoroughly. I had naturally quite a definite picture of you. I had naturally opportunity enough at the time to make definite observations. My recent study of the records has not altered the picture in any essential. Now I come here and I see a man who has not the slightest resemblance to the Maurizius of nineteen-five. Let us not go into the reasons. We could only consider the time which has elapsed as a factor if I knew what had changed in me. Assume therefore that I have not much resemblance to the prosecuting attorney Andergast of those days. I should only like to know whether you remember your own picture and the relation of that picture to reality. I should also like to know how the fifteen- or sixteen-year-old Leonhart Maurizius is mirrored in the man of today, or what between the two, the man of twenty-five thinks about the youth of sixteen. I should like to know that very much. From that, from my point of view, something serviceable might be deduced. It would be enlightening from the standpoint of a personal evolution."

Maurizius listened intently. Why does he say "something serviceable," was the first idea which shot through his head, with what reserve and lack of clearness he expresses himself! The man at the window became constantly more mysterious. Suddenly, he looked right into the heart of him. He perceived a mixture of self-assurance and uncertainty, of autocracy and weakness, of impregnability and dull reluctant resistance, which surprised him extremely. People like Maurizius possess a sensibility of quite different acuteness from those who are dulled by constant contact with others; the atmosphere alone transmits to them the most recondite mysteries. He considered for a while. "There was at that time a famous French novel, *Peint par eux-mêmes,*" he then said. "Waremme brought it to us. We read it. We, that is to say . . . but that has nothing to do with the matter. I remember it described very prettily how the individuals revealed themselves crosswise in letters. Without really wanting to do it, all that happened ran on them like toothed wheels; a crime impinges upon a virtue; desire for revenge drives cowardice forward. It is generally so. The best mirror is the one in which one betrays oneself while luring another into the net. Excuse this talk, I always have to think of so many things at once. When I begin to talk my thoughts come flying from all directions, like pigeons scattered in flight. What you are asking really surprises me. You really don't need such circuitous means to obtain knowledge of me. At that time, so far as I know, you got hold of all that was worth knowing about my life; that is, the facts; the rest was a remarkable deduction. You could easily dispense with me, myself; on the contrary, I should have disturbed your mental labours." The cutting sarcasm of these words caused Herr von Andergast to raise his head haughtily. But since Maurizius was standing before him with his head lowered, the warning remained unobserved and the latter continued. "There is a portrait of me at twenty-six which I can outline for you faithfully and which you will recognize, for it was drawn by yourself. On the twenty-first of August, nineteen-six, in the court room, it was—shall I say exhibited?—exhibited. But it was made of words. Do you wish to hear? Listen. A man of great intellectual force and complete culture, surrendering with the least conceivable resistance to the seduction of an epoch of decay and of threatening moral collapse. Let us mark the signs, gentlemen of the jury. Let us not permit the individual to deflect us from the symptom nor the specific crime to delude us as to the far more dangerous tendency which it embodies and against which you must erect an effective dam. Rarely will there be so favourable an opportunity to strike, and if not to heal, at least carefully to prevent the spread of the disease of a nation, the destiny of an epoch, yes, even of a continent, by a decisive operation. Am I accurate? I believe I am. There is no comma lacking, as it were. But that was only the frame. The face itself was far more frightful. You are probably marvelling at the perfect functioning of my memory. There aren't many people, you are probably saying to yourself, who are capable of repeating an oral judgment after so long a time word for word. After so long a time. Yes. If someone were to assure me that it had been eighteen hundred years instead of eighteen, I should scarcely wish to quarrel about the difference. Those are conceptions which are burned out; months . . . years . . . they don't play any rôle. Well, formerly, when they kept books from me, particularly winter nights, when the lights are put out at six o'clock, I would lie till three and four in the morning digging around in the past as in a house which has collapsed, then I would take pains not to forget that speech, I could have written down every word as it was spoken, but I could rely better upon my memory than upon anything else. When I had repeated all that I knew by heart of Shakespeare and Goethe, then came the speech. Well, to continue. We must see clearly. The purpose requires of us the greatest concentration of our inner eye. There must not remain in us the slightest psychological doubt about the person and make-up of the accused and, without presumption, solely because it is my ineluctable duty, I maintain that I can settle every doubt of the kind in you; for this key to the situation, which may not appear quite clear to you—I have received it from the personality, the point of view, the moral development of the culprit himself. Faithlessness and irresponsibility are the motors of his behaviour. These plunge him into the maze of his lusts, which was probably also a garden of torment—I assume for the honour of human nature—which cut him off from all ties, of society, of family and of the order of society. Enjoyment is the token which has fascinated and stunned his senses; he pays for this enjoyment with all that he has earned and all that he has struggled for, with all that he has become, with his heart, with his intelligence, with the hearts of those who loved him, and when finally he stands there unable to pay, he becomes a murderer. We do not wish to discourage and offend those people in this country who are honestly struggling; only those who have broken as adventurers into the garden of the spirit and exchange their vanity for the treasures preserved there which the unsuspicious guardians permit them to get at, waste its prizes thus. Every aspiration towards a noble goal was to him a rung on the ladder of his ambition; under his frivolous touch the most sacred things turn into lucre with which to augment his meretricious prestige. Science is for him merely a carnival in which he dances in a masque intending to provoke confidence; nothing is serious to him; nothing has a deeper meaning; and when finally he marries a woman, infinitely his moral superior, he is shattered against the pure metal of her character like friable stone. This is an obstacle to him; the shame which he feels before her is in his way; the latent reproach which she constitutes for him destroys his self-assurance; the sight of her grief when she is forced to recognize that her struggle to save him has been in vain, that she is defeated in this conflict, poisons his blood. The malignant weaklings who appear before the world in a varnish of beauty do not want anyone to see through them; they want to be taken for the mysterious and seductive comedians which they are in their own self-enamoured eyes. And so things happened—as they happened. The unfortunate woman was destined to be destroyed by him; it lay in the physical and social constellation; and he would have gotten rid of her even if his hopeless material circumstances had not made him snatch at the last horrible means, even if his crazy and hopeless passion for her sister had not robbed him of the remainder of his sense and honour. . . ." Maurizius took a deep breath. His temples were covered with little beads of sweat. "Am I quoting correctly?" he asked with excessive sweetness, as his head turned to one side. "It was a bold turn and a master-like stroke to expose the motives where they were least likely to be seen by the populace. That you treated them to such an exalted point of vantage flattered them and made them pliable. Up to then they had thought that this . . . this passion was the only motive. Now they saw something far more infernal, now they saw a murderer chosen by Destiny. A settled matter; one did not need to think about it at all. You also spoke of God, did you not? You felt the necessity of summing up once again the separate parts of this beast, of proving philosophically the disorganization of his soul, as you so neatly put it. What are we headed for with such a body of men aboard, you exclaimed, and, referring to a certain superstition among seamen, you prophesied the anger of Heaven if that rotten member was not cut off. God has cast him out, you said; why should we spare him? Very presumptuous to state such a thing; you could not possibly know whether God had really cast me out or not. But under the influence of your remarkable oratorical powers it was as with the children in school when one of them is to be punished, they all look as virtuous and obedient as if they were spotless angels. They are actually relieved by the visitation of the penalty."

Maurizius seated himself again on the iron bed and rested his elbows on his knees and his head in his hands in such a way as to cover his forehead and eyes. Thus he remained sitting cowering and doubled up. Herr von Andergast, leaning against the window with his arms crossed, observed him with a cold curiosity behind which a feeling not dissimilar to fear was concealed. The repetition, accurate almost to a word, of a speech made almost half a generation ago, filled him with astonishment; but the curious thing was that nothing about it seemed familiar, or known to him, the author of it, although he could judge with a fair degree of certainty that Maurizius had not altered or distorted it; it was rather that it seemed to him like something strange, something unpleasant and distasteful, exaggerated, full of phrases and rhetoric and forced contrasts. As he gazed down upon the cowering convict, his dislike of his own oratory, which he had just heard out of this man's mouth, grew into physical disgust, so that he had finally to struggle against the inclination to vomit; he had to grit his teeth convulsively. It was as if his words crawled along the wall like worms, slimy, colourless, hateful, ugly. If all achievement was so fleeting, so temporary, so questionable, how could one bear to be tested? If a truth for which one had once been willing to vouch before God and man could after a time become a piece of buffoonery, how did matters stand with "truth" in general? Or was it only that something in him had decayed, that the framework of his ego had broken down? How dangerous, how suspicious, how equivocal it was then for him to be here, to have this whole conversation! It was like a cunning attempt to stab himself from behind. He pulled his watch out, opened the lid: five minutes past four. But the idea of taking his hat and saying goodbye with professional dignity and going home without having carried out his purpose seemed utterly silly to him.

He stood there with his arms crossed, waiting.

7.

"You are quite right," said Maurizius finally from beneath his upraised arms, from which the sleeves of his canvas jacket had slipped back. "It was a good idea of yours to remind me that I too was once sixteen. I have not thought of that for a long time. You are doubtless right too about one's being the product of one's generation; this is clear to me now for the first time, when I think of what Leonhart Maurizius was like at sixteen. All of the things in which one believes one differs from him are as slight as the differences between the leaves of the same tree. Each generation is a species of its own and is represented by a different tree. I should like to know what the sixteen-year-olds of today are like. Do you know any? Well, you probably won't want to tell me about them. It is a tragic age. It is the great divide of life. Often one's whole future depends upon a single event at this time of life. Years pass, one has forgotten it, suddenly it turns up and one sees that one has been directed into a specific channel by such an event. In the second form in the Gymnasium I agreed with some of the fellows to go with them to a brothel. I had been a virgin up to that time, scarcely knew what a woman was, whereas the others had had their experiences, some of them spoke of love and women like worn-out rakes. I went with them because I was ashamed to show my innocence; consequently I acted as if I were particularly audacious and enterprising. At the house a girl led me to her room; I followed like a lamb to the slaughter; when we were alone I fell down on my knees before her and begged her not to hurt me; first she laughed herself half to death; then she seemed to take pity on me, pulled me into her lap, was very affectionate and began to cry. That cut into my heart, I asked her how she had come to this place; she told me her story, one of the sentimental romances such as almost all prostitutes serve to all greenhorns and sometimes to other confiding customers, and which are apparently invented and spread by the dozen because they so often produce an effect. I believed every word, was hot with indignation and pity, and she talked herself so into her fiction that she fairly melted with emotion. Not only did I give her all of the money which I had with me, but I also swore to free her from this terrible life and to arrange for her an existence worthy of a human being. I succeeded in getting a considerable sum of money from my father, a hundred and twenty or a hundred and thirty marks, if I remember correctly; with that I bought the girl off and rented a room in the suburbs, to which I took her. I visited her every day; I devoted every free hour to her; I placed all my pocket money at her disposal, chose suitable books for her, mostly very literary, read aloud to her, talked to her about what she had read herself and imagined in my idiocy that I could educate her, ennoble her and return her to society purified. She was really a nice youngster, rather pretty, very young and certainly not bad. There was no sensual relation between us and I was so strict about this that I avoided touching her hand, not indeed because I was indifferent to her—oh, no, I was sure I loved her—but I wanted to convince her that it was a 'pure love.' I talked to her constantly about 'pure love'; she listened patiently; I thought it was a revelation to her, whereas it need scarcely be mentioned that she was making fun of the silly boy and was bored to death. I still see the dark basement room; one could see the legs of the passers-by from the window; next door there was a carpenter's shop and one heard the swishing of his plane. She would sit on a sofa in the corner, looking at me with vapid astonishment, the meaning of which I did not understand, or she would laugh shyly and I would not interpret the laugh because I was full of nothing but my own excited illusion. Well, to come to the end, one day I discovered that she was carrying on her old profession quite unconcernedly and while I was weaving my dreams of rescuing her, she was receiving men night after night. It took a long time before I recovered from the blow. Perhaps as a matter of fact one never recovers from such a thing. All right, that was the sixteen-year-old. The romantic Maurizius. Not yet the Satan whom you depicted ten years later. A romanticist pure and without a flaw. Serious and suffering. But this is so, there was a theatrical panoply stretched over my youth. Those born about eighteen-eighty were in a hard position when young. From one's home and school, one was given everything that was necessary for the bourgeois and the so-called higher life, one's fundamental principles and ideals, the monthly income—and the person who had not that was of no account—and one's culture. But it was all shabby and full of holes; only the income, that was something solid; the rest was dross and cheap imitation, from the Christmas and wedding presents to the enthusiasm for antiquity and the Renaissance, from the regulated students' drinking-bouts and the patriotic celebrations up to 'throne and altar.' I did not feel this; I was no rebel; I enjoyed life too much; I took no interest in the general welfare; but somehow or other, one does feel it, since one is a past and belongs to it all. Only in those years everything egoistical was sporadic and whoever did not decidedly break with his surroundings and tradition—and there were such also—was gradually swamped and disposed of, and had to get on as best he could with his black moods. Of course, life was frightfully flat, and one was swayed by a terrible tension, it was as if one had one's soul immured and the only compensation one had received was a little shabby career and the few friends one clung to with all one's might. Grains of nobler substance were so fortuitously strewn into one's own nature, without any connection; this was then 'romanticism,' a category apart, a religion almost, and one could be 'romantic' and have very little conscience. I still remember that at nineteen I came home from a performance of Tristan, a happy, new-born person, and then I stole twenty marks from my father's bureau-drawer. Both were compatible. Always both were compatible. To swear to a girl a sacred oath that one would marry her and shortly afterwards leave her contemptibly to her fate, and in an exalted mood to read and assimilate the life and works of Buddha. To do a poor tailor out of his earnings and to stand enthralled before a Raphael Madonna. One could be tremendously moved at the theatre over Hauptmann's Weavers and read with satisfaction that the strikers in the Ruhr were being fired upon. Both. Always the two were possible. Romanticism. Romanticism without any foundation or any goal. There you have another portrait. A self-portrait. Do you think it is more flattering than yours? Its only redeeming feature is in its admitting two possibilities each time. Yours is cruelly implacable because it admits only one."

Faced with this passionately probing urge to confess which set the whole content of a life into motion as a dam breaks and the waters rush over the banks, Herr von Andergast was suddenly overcome with a feeling of cowardly nervousness, the fear of a truth which one has persuaded oneself that one is seeking and which one secretly hopes not to find. These states of mind are not very unusual. They are an epitome of an epoch in which "both are possible," as the convict Maurizius had formulated it; he was mistaken only in that he claimed it exclusively for his epoch and generation. Or was it only an outcome of the worlds of stratified sarcasm which Herr von Andergast sensed with so much discomfort? Scarcely. There cowered a desperate man panting to express himself, longing with feverish eagerness to be listened to, ready to pour himself out, to expand, to bear witness, to know, to tell, to shake off this formless crushing loneliness and to become amalgamated again with the firm contour of reality. Herr von Andergast said evasively, at random, when a new silence fell: "Quite right. And there was only one possibility left me." Maurizius lifted his head and stared at him with a disconsolate expression. "And what if your presupposition had been false?" he asked, his voice coming up from the depths with impatient eagerness. Herr von Andergast replied brusquely: "That is unthinkable." "Unthinkable? That's a good one. I only ask: Suppose! You can't even think of it? And suppose it were nevertheless false." "Does it seem thinkable to you?" "Perhaps." "Why did you remain silent then? During the preliminary investigation; during the trial; in the penitentiary; eighteen and a half years?" "Shall I tell you why?" Again that eager impatience coming up from below. "Yes, please." "Because I did not wish to commit murder." "What . . . What was that? Because you . . . I do not understand." "God forbid that you should understand." With a slight sarcastic smile.

Herr von Andergast, fairly at sea, mechanically pulled out his watch and opened the lid. Two minutes of five.

8.

Suddenly Maurizius sprang up. "Nonsense," he exclaimed, "what twaddle I am talking! Forget my damned chatter. I only wanted to sound you out. It is a thought with which I have sometimes played. I must not think aloud. I hope that you are not taking it seriously." He stood there with his shoulders flattened. Herr von Andergast, as if seeking to quiet the excited man, remarked quietly that no new records would be taken; he knew how to differentiate clearly between a confession, even the shadow of a confession, and the conventional tricks to prevent serious investigation. This is a deliberate offence, calculated to irritate Maurizius, to cause him to protest. But Maurizius emits a gasp of relief. "Keep silent," he says to himself, clenching the fists of his loosely hanging hands, "what is there really left to do but keep silent? The sole object of the whole procedure is to destroy a man's dignity. One can only help oneself by silence. Obstinacy hardens one, crushes one; one keeps silent from obstinacy and the only thing with which one can save a little bit of human pride is obstinacy." His glance becomes fixed and travels back into a distant past; it seems that his mind is dominated by pictures of widely separated events, which flash upon it in such a way as to connect a word, a dream, a picture of yesterday with those of twenty years ago. Herr von Andergast again very calmly states that he has never seen anyone cling permanently to his obstinacy, when his head, his life, his happiness was at stake; that was just the point of the legal process which Maurizius had so contemptuously criticized, that it freed the accused from his vanity, so that he would stand there naked as it were, naked in front of the deed, naked in front of the judge. A malignant laugh snarled from Maurizius' nose. "Wonderful," he exclaimed, "what wonderful hair-splitting! Naked in front of the watchman of justice, naked before the police commissioner, naked before the clerk. But that isn't it; the being naked; that's beside the point; it isn't that at all." He stands in a corner of the wall agitated with restless gestures. This restlessness is the only thing which reminds one of the days before he was a prisoner. An opening and a convulsive closing of his hands seems to grasp all that he has been obliged to bear, all that was unforgettably debasing from the moment of seizure to the judgment. The crude barracks tone of subaltern officials, or, worse still, their coarse familiarity. To fall into such hands means to lose all title to respect. Refinement calls forth sarcasm, intellectual superiority is answered with hate. Achievement, merit, no longer count, what you were until yesterday is stamped out. Finally they themselves are privileged to snub one of them who generally has the privilege of snubbing them, and they do it with malicious pleasure. He denies his guilt? A cunning trick. Suspicion is suspicion. Suspicion is as good as proof. Herein, if possible, they surpass their superiors, since there is added to all the rest the fact that they are convinced that the rich and the cultivated, in spite of all the proclamations about equality before the law, are secretly involved in a plot against the poor and ignorant, and so they try to vent their rancour, protected by the same law. When he had been arrested in the hotel in Hamburg, the policeman had ordered him to get up, had not permitted him to dress, but had made him stand in his shirt till he had searched all his clothing and examined all his papers and letters. For many years this man's bulldog face had been one of the frightful pictures with which his fantasy punished him, the contemptuous expression with which he had rummaged through his fine linen, the nod of suppressed envy and satisfied vengeance, this petty bourgeois nod of affirmation, illuminating a whole world, when he examined the gold cigarette case and the toilet utensils. Then the first night in prison with an old procurer and a syphilitic thief, the food, the pulpy beets sullenly pushed towards him, the stench, the dirt, this sudden degradation to the very depths, the green police wagon, the ride on the train with the two policemen, who were already playing with catch questions. Then being put under custody for investigation, the judge who conducted the investigation, who already knew everything, the deed and the circumstances and the motives, and was armed against every objection and received the most plausible explanations with the smile of one who knows better; investigation after investigation set for morning, noon and night. This man pushed the torture of questioning until Leonhart's brain beat in his head like a sore wound, even laying illegitimate pitfalls for him. Then the attempt to scare him by severity, to wear out his resistance by exaggerated clemency, first threats, then promises, the use of fellow prisoners to spy and eavesdrop, the whole mechanism of subterranean justice, the witnesses intimidated, the unceasing building up of a great web, the pattern of which was prescribed and which had to be turned out because the judge was ordered to proceed thus and was there for that purpose. One yearns so then for the final end of all this, even during the worst tension of the trial, one yearns with an exhausted heart, one does not want to struggle any more, one has given up, one is silent. One has become indifferent to everything. Therefore, the penitentiary into which one disappears is like a tomb in which one rests peacefully, at least for the first weeks. No more questions, no more hostile witnesses to puzzle one, no more lawyers persuading one, no more rumours, no more fears, no more formal oaths, no more signing, signing papers under the stress of torture, but the balm of peace.

"It is perhaps the most astonishing pyramidal system of human energies directed towards a definite goal which can be conceived of," said Maurizius quietly, almost sadly. "I admit that readily. Yes, I admit that. It's enormously clever. When one has reached the top, the delinquent has been squeezed to death at the bottom. I don't want to deny that there are also well-meaning, compassionate people with decent feelings in this army of hunters and their assistants. It would be unthinkable that there should not be, above all here in this prison there were some whose goodness and friendliness were of great assistance to me. There was, for example, a certain Mathisson, who was discharged six years ago because he gave a deathly sick man a letter from his betrothed, who used to comfort me and who always said: 'Patience, Doctor'—he always called me Doctor—'only don't lose confidence. Your day of justice will come.' He really helped me, even though I did not share his faith. No, there was no basis for doing that. Well, above all there was one . . . but I can't talk about him. . . . And how scarce they are, and how afraid they are, how carefully they must conceal their humane inclinations! For to show love, or even compassion, is to offend against discipline and since such a tendency soon gets gossiped about, one naturally has to be very careful. And when one considers that all these wardens—and not only these, the same holds true higher up, I dare not say how high—if one realizes that these people make one pay for everything that secretly embitters them, for all that they have not attained, for the misery in their homes, for their bad pay, for their social oppression, and sometimes for their shipwrecked lives; if one remembers that the subaltern souls among them are mostly people to whom it is a pleasure to torment others and make them suffer, and that they can't help this, that they are intoxicated with power and that this consoles them, for their lives are as dark as the prisons which they guard—then one must ask whether human beings are fitted to judge human beings, to punish human beings. What is the actual significance, as things now stand, of punishment? Who dares punish? Who has the right? One pronounces it; another repeats it; the machine seizes one; one gets under the wheels: punishment. It is a monstrous sham. A cursed pretence." He breathed deeply like a child after sobbing. "But I am making a nuisance of myself," he continued in a dissatisfied tone, as if he were annoyed at his own talkativeness, "only it is so seldom that one can talk to someone higher up. The top stands in the light and does not know what is below." A livid glance, in which attack, sharp restraint and wild defiance are mingled, is aimed at Herr von Andergast. Curiously enough, the latter accepts the convict's informal manner of addressing him without any title. It does not perhaps seem important to him to insist upon this proof of respect. It almost seems as if he had forgotten his office and the barrier of dignity between them. Unwilling and oppressed, he listens to the man's words. There are moments when he—like Maurizius—feels that his presence here, facing the man, their opposition, seems like the adjustment of a long accumulated, explosive tension. He has the sensation of doubting himself, of wondering whether he will be able to hold his own. Maurizius *vs.* Andergast: perhaps a final reckoning even? Well, we shall see.

He strides through the cell to the door and back again, close by Maurizius. He says: "All that, of course, is very bad. But you are generalizing too much. Admitting these abuses, they grow out of the world; the world is, as it is, rigid and not good. I don't want to gloss things over. Let us finally get at the gist of the matter. You won't take me for so stupid as to expect me to believe the reason you assign for your eighteen years of consistent silence. Or do you? You are trying to avoid the subject. Nevertheless you have given yourself away. You say it was because you did not wish to commit murder. For that reason. It is an astonishing argument in the mouth of a condemned murderer. Never mind. That was only a marginal gloss. For whom was the remark intended? It seems to me you have proposed an enigma easy to solve. Well then, Anna Jahn was to be spared. Spared in what respect? Why spared? Don't retract, don't do that, perhaps God Himself has brought it out of you. Yes, God Himself. Do not be afraid. Just talk out. . . ." Herr von Andergast cannot help feeling a little uncomfortable at the rhetoric of his appeal. Maurizius has joined him in his walk up and down with the slow movement of his head as of a dog which does not want to lose sight of his master for a second. He listens, opens his mouth a little; his small teeth peer forth; he listens again and drops his eyelids. "Now you think that you have caught me," he murmurs angrily, and immediately afterwards, in a changed voice, gently, humbly: "Is it very presumptuous of me to ask for another cigarette?" Herr von Andergast hastens to offer him his open case and gives him a light. Maurizius pulls the smoke deep into his lungs and expels it through his nose. Herr von Andergast sits down at the table and crosses his legs. He looks just the way he looked during those prescribed evening talks with Etzel, the kindly friend who is prepared to discuss interesting problems. Only his glance roves imperceptibly, his forehead is flushed. Again they look at one another in silence. Herr von Andergast in the midst of this silence wonders whether Sophia is there yet. It worries him to picture how she will look when she appears before him to demand her son. He would do the most difficult thing in the world if he could escape from this. Fortunately his task here is adequately difficult.

9.

"Didn't you ever set down your thoughts?" he begins with a question. His patience and composure, the result of concentrated self-control, gradually affect Maurizius like some soothing medicament. "It never interested me," he replied. "Why? For whom? When I was permitted to do written work towards the end of nineteen-eleven, I preferred to devote myself to my own special studies, but since I lacked material, I was obliged to turn to generalities. I had been turned in upon myself until it had made me quite blind. One ought to make that comprehensible to someone sometime . . . but one can't. One can't do it. The body becomes a screw and bores into some frightful mass. What did I want to say? . . . Yes, for many months I wrote at something, a history of the cult of the Madonna, based upon her representation in pictures. I came to some peculiar results in doing this, in regard to my own life too. While I was writing, I translated it simultaneously into Italian and Spanish; I had always been very fond of both languages. For a time, I even played with the idea of publication, thought such a thing possible, believed it might help me. Inwardly, I was long past this kind of trifling when a new director came, Captain Gutkind—the name was misleading. He forbade me to write, confiscated my books, and I was obliged to give up my manuscript. He was not well disposed to me, that captain, I was a veritable thorn in his flesh; why, I have never been able to make out. I did not first beg and negotiate; I simply destroyed the manuscript. Since then I have not had any desire for things of that sort." "Nothing of this incident came to my ears," said Herr von Andergast with contracted brows. "I believe that indeed. What does become known? Even a man like you would be rather horrified if he knew all of the things which do not become known. That captain, with his talent for tormenting one, almost made an end of me; what would have prevented him if he had not been taken off by a stroke before? Nothing else in the world could have moved him. It simply was not written in the stars that I should be his victim. Well, after that I pulled seaweed again, pasted boxes, made cocoanut cording, wove mattresses and sewed sixteen buttons on military coats the whole year." "I would greatly value some kind of autobiography if you could decide to write one. I promise myself a great deal from it. It might under certain circumstances be useful for the purpose I hinted at in the beginning of our conversation. I would give the manager orders, you could count upon all kinds of ameliorations. . . ." Maurizius' face showed he was looking for the trap behind the offer. He shook his head. "My life is a burned-out tree," he replied, "what point would there be in counting the annular rings in the ashes, or in writing lamentations about how high the blossoming crown once reached? No." "Don't misunderstand me, I don't want to bring any pressure to bear," Herr von Andergast assured him with a seriousness which to a certain extent indicated a new interpretation of the situation, of which he was first obliged to give an account to himself in his own thoughts. "It is no longer even confession which I care about, feeling as I do about these things at the moment. . . ." "But rather?" Herr von Andergast, pushing his head down between his shoulders, makes a gesture with his arms as if regardless of consequences he wishes to express all the uncertainty into which he has been plunged. Nothing could have made a more thorough impression on Maurizius than this silent declaration of renunciation. If it had not really been a sort of capitulation, unpremeditated and compelled by the moment, by a hopeless wandering about in a circle, it would have been the chess move of a genius.

Maurizius' face grew greyer than it generally was. He looked as if he could not decide within himself about something which tormented him endlessly, something which he wanted to say and do and could not say nor do. For days and years this had been the first visit to his cell from the "outside," for days and years the first man who had spoken to him in his own language. Millions of contrary sensations break in upon him in a few seconds. Impossible to retain a single one, every impulse is brushed away by a stronger, darker, wilder, more fearful one. Like one who was dropped ages ago on a desert rocky island, longing and yearning for communication, he is capable of forgetting that he who finally approaches him as his equal is also he who condemned him and exposed him, and so he trembles and fevers for mere physical proximity, for words and communication. To communicate, to have communication—it is almost the same thing; perhaps the exchange will help him to struggle up out of the frightful mental illness which being-alone-with-himself has become. Do sit down, he hears said, and he sits down, obediently, quickly, as if flung down. His eyes full of irrational sadness have a phosphorescence about them which indicates a decay of the soul. Three or four months more and the last internal spark will be extinguished, the unparalleled energy with which he has fought up to the present will be expended. He must cling to the person who speaks to him like a human being, who gives him once more the conception of human beings, who places him again in the frame of the world—then he can last for another year; so he must trap him, open a door of communication; and the pitiful cunning which he employs scarcely covers over his mad longing. Then the name of Anna Jahn is uttered. Maurizius doubtless knew that Anna Jahn had married? Does he answer? He has already replied, when he seems still to be thinking about it. He heard of it eight years ago. To the question whether the news was unexpected to him, whether it had altered his feelings, he replied with a laugh. Or if not a laugh, then merely an attempt at pretending he had forgotten, which attempt miscarried. Certainly the name has never been uttered in that room before; the cell becomes double its size, the table twice as high; his head swells and he feels as if he were having one of those gases pumped into him which exaggerate all dimensions. What does one know of these . . . these feelings? Oh, one is to ascribe a certain amount of penetration to the man who is questioning. Penetration! Rot! No penetration can reach so far. Words are mere words, a person betrays himself whether he wishes to answer or not. He had received the news from his father. It was in a letter. There were other things in the letter which the censorship had not permitted to pass. Probably also things about Anna Jahn. Since he at first regarded the report as a lie, he did not feel any desire to know the rest. Only gradually had he become accustomed to the thought and admitted the possibility to himself. Why not? Why should she not marry? What obligation was she under to remain single? Should she have become a nun? Well, perhaps; perhaps a convent would have been the proper place. His father, of course, in his ungrounded hatred, had eagerly picked up every calumny which had been spread abroad against her. A long time ago—perhaps it was fourteen or fifteen years ago—during one of his visits, he had hinted at something very base, namely that she and Waremme were said to have . . . but he does not wish to repeat it; the old man was careful never again to mention it, aside from the fact that from that time on, private conversations were very strictly supervised. But from that time on the old man, when he made his half-yearly visits, scarcely knew what to talk about, but merely stood there in his pitiful sadness, staring helplessly at his son. He no longer had the courage to mention his crazy idea. To judge hearsay, the Duvernon marriage had turned out quite happily, Herr von Andergast remarked dryly. "Duvernon? Oh, so that's the man's name? Quite possible." "There are said to be children. Two girls." The hand with which Maurizius was holding his chin trembled. "Children? Really, children? Is that possible? Children? She said once that she never wanted to have any children." "At that time she was still half a child herself." "From that standpoint she had no age. She never said anything which was not in her nature." "But she was the person who took the most conscientious interest in your illegitimate child." Maurizius presses his fingers to his eyes. His lips turn completely white. "Hildegard . . . yes," he whispers. "Is the relationship not kept up any longer? I mean between Anna and your daughter?" "That I do not know." "What? . . . You do not know? . . . Were you not . . ." "No," screams Maurizius. "Nothing! I was told nothing. I know nothing of my child." Herr von Andergast shows neither surprise nor indignation at this outburst of despair, which suddenly dies down again. He inquires sympathetically about the further details and finds that Maurizius was obliged to promise Anna Jahn, through Dr. Volland, whom she had selected as go-between, never to interest himself further in Hildegard; he must be dead to the child; under this condition Anna was willing to superintend its future education with the greatest possible care. Herr von Andergast thinks this overcoming of his own feelings, which has insured the mental peace of the youngster, was praiseworthy and has no doubt that Anna Duvernon will feel bound to carry out the duty which she undertook, as meticulously as would Anna Jahn herself. Maurizius turns his head as if he were being choked. Yes, yes. Possibly. But he does not know. He should know. He ought to have some sign. Does he even know whether the girl is alive? How much has died and gone to rot outside in the meantime! Herr von Andergast is surprised at the passion-attachment of the convict sentenced to life imprisonment, to a creature whom he has not seen since its infancy and whom he may never have seen at all. It seems to be a case of fantasy-worship, an anchor thrown out into eternity. In unconcerned tones, as one chats with an acquaintance over a cup of coffee, Herr von Andergast remarks that Anna Jahn must in her youth—for of her later life little is known—have been a woman very difficult to understand; for example, the care and pains which she had always taken in regard to this child, the offspring of an illicit relation between her brother-in-law and a strange woman, had always been inexplicable to him. Maurizius wants to reply, then presses his lips together and remains silent, shyly glancing at the man opposite. Then: "Not so inexplicable if one considers what she had already experienced and what happened when she came to us. No one has any idea of that." "Of course," admits Herr von Andergast, "what we found out was as perfunctory as the report of an accident in a news item. The realities lie in the background."

For a long time Maurizius looks down in silence. His head jerks nervously backwards, as if he were seeking to ward off something unpleasant which was trying to approach him. However, it is only a shadow. He associates with shadows, he questions shadows, he struggles with shadows. Finally he lifts his eyes, looks the solicitor-general searchingly in the face, and says, in a voice proceeding from a parched mouth, "I will try to tell it. I believe it will be quite good if I once tell it. Up to a certain point I can risk it. Partly in order to hear it myself. To see what is left of it. But not today. I am too exhausted. I have no longer control of myself. Tomorrow. Quite early will be best."

Herr von Andergast nods and gets up. At the door of the cell he makes the sign and the guard opens it. It is half past seven when he gets to the inn at Kressa and orders a room for the night. Sophia must wait, he thinks, with a mixture of triumph and fear, sitting at the window of his room in the inn, staring up at the grey prison citadel. But it is a fleeting thought, no longer of much importance. All thoughts are only fleeting and unimportant which do not touch the circle in which the convict Maurizius dwells.

CHAPTER X

I.

ETZEL of course understood at once that he had put himself in a situation which threatened to be dangerous. It is well that I should finally see his eyes, he thought, while moving as a precautionary measure into a somewhat remote corner of the room. They are not pleasant, those eyes; he has very good reason for hiding them; of what do they remind me? Frogs' eyes or something horrid, disgusting! He was white with tension as to what would come next. That he did not have the advantage was evident. He had opened his visor but his opponent had not done so. That they should go together to the meeting at Stettin Station was probably out of the question now. Now they both had something else to think of.

Warschauer put his glasses slowly back upon his nose. "Curious," he murmured in a drawling voice and with an expression as if he were boring a tunnel with his eyes into a past which had been completely blotted out. At the same time he scrutinized the boy constantly. "I have brought sausage and sprats," said Etzel, with a not entirely successful attempt to appear unconcerned, pointing to the package which still lay on the window sill. "There is still bread in the table drawer, and butter too, I think; don't you want to eat?" Warschauer cleared his throat. "Shut the window, Mohl," he said in a schoolmaster's tone, with a curious pounding voice, "it's getting cool." Etzel did as he was bidden; a moth fluttered against his face while he was closing the window; high above the roofs in the red dusk there were lights like searchlights. Meantime, he had recovered his courage; he took the package of food, cut the string, got two plates and a loaf of bread from the drawer, and busied himself putting a rather dirty blue checked table-cloth on the table, rattled the knives and forks and set out the percolator. Warschauer watched him awhile in silence; then he went to the alcove, leaving the sliding door open, and washed his hands with the usual ceremoniousness. When he returned the following took place.

He sat down and began to eat, seemingly without pleasure, absorbed in himself. Etzel, who assumed a more and more cheerful expression, as if he had long ago forgotten the mysterious little exchange of words, lit the percolator and measured the ground coffee onto a little board with a spoon. While doing this he counted aloud: one, two, three. While he was counting thus his heart was heavy with the thought that up to now he had not the slightest proof that this professor and Gregor Waremme were one and the same person. He had relied solely upon the statement of old Maurizius, but did this suffice? Of course, his instinct had told him that he was on the right track when he had merely seen Warschauer, but he had no certainty about it. The professor's obstinate silence filled him with an uncertain dread, which he must not allow him to notice. He felt certain that everything depended upon the first question and answer, and while looking at the alcohol-flame he determined upon his attack. He for his part did not dare break the silence, and he avoided looking anxious or curious, and only gazed attentively now into the flame, then into the coffee-pot. The figure of the professor compelled respect, even a sort of foreboding shyness, a figure which in the mind of this youth formed a unified picture, a personality like a finished composition, compared with the fortuitous and uncertain reality. And of this personality the boy sensed the depth and breadth. Finally Warschauer laid his knife and fork aside, stuck his finger several times into his mouth, which Etzel thought disgusting, and then said imperiously, almost commandingly: "Well then, what's up? How long shall I wait for explanations, my dear Mister Mohl, or Mister Nobody, or whatever your name may be? Why did you run after me? Who has sent you? What's behind the whole business? Good enough; here I am: George Warschauer, *alias* Gregor Waremme; what do you want, young man?"

So there was no more doubt about that, thank God! But when the name was mentioned, Etzel jumped as at a shot and took a few seconds to recover. "Right away, professor," he replied obligingly, with a smart laugh of harmless importance. "Just a little patience, the water is already boiling." Meantime he could still consider what to say. Warschauer was drumming a dull tattoo on the table with his short-nailed fingers. Etzel worked on calmly; finally he finished, poured the steaming beverage into a cup and pushed it over to Warschauer. Then he leaned his elbows on the table, blinked a little, still hesitated and commenced talking of old Maurizius. "An unhappy old man, professor. Have you any idea how old he is? Seventy-four. Incredible that such a man should still be alive. He maintains he will not die until his son Leonhart is freed from the penitentiary. Although there is not the slightest prospect of this. Sentenced to life imprisonment. Why should they let him go? But he has gotten it into his head and won't give it up for the world." He began to spread himself and explained very plausibly and with characteristic details that he had known the old man for years, his grandparents had lived in a house adjoining his for a time, and he, who was generally so shy, had often visited them and had talked for hours about nothing but his son, and the terrible fate which had overtaken him.

He had gradually become fond of Etzel and confided everything to him, all his hopes, the legal steps he had taken, the whole story and the course of the trial. "You must know him, professor," he interjected in flattering tones, "he said that he had been to see you once." Warschauer looked up in surprise. "Yes, he had spent a lot of time and money to find out your present name and where you were living and simply came here. Simply got into a train one day to come here to speak to you. But I believe that he did not say a word; the silly old fellow simply turned on his heel and went away again. Don't you remember?" It seemed as if memory were beginning to stir in Warschauer. A rather queer-looking old man, he admitted, a peasant or provincial sort of fellow, had once been there, he remembered; he had stood at the door, staring like some animal, had asked whether there was a room for rent and had disappeared again. It might have been about a year ago. "So that was the . . . hem . . . the father of Maurizius. How curious! But"— and he cleared his throat several times—"what did he want? Why did he come?" "On account of certain letters—" whispered Etzel, in the same confidential tone, bending further over the table. Warschauer, sipping his coffee noisily, held the cup in his hand and asked with astonishment: "Letters? What sort of letters?" "He says that you must have letters which Leonhart wrote you at that time before the misfortune. Other letters too, which he wrote to Fräulein Jahn. He swears that you have them. He would give half his fortune if he could get them. And since he did not dare that time, and is too old and sick to come again . . . in short I felt badly to see him pining away so, and I could not stay there any longer anyhow. I had always wanted to go to Berlin, so I told him I would try it, perhaps he would give me the letters." Warschauer shook his head. "I don't know of any letters," he remarked brusquely. "Pure imagination. You have taken your trouble for nothing, young Mohl." The words sounded sarcastic, but had a ring of complete honesty. Etzel had not expected to hear anything else, but he looked disappointed and said shyly: "Really not? Do look carefully, professor. For my sake. You really cannot imagine how that old man worships his son. He does not regard him as a criminal but almost as a saint. He simply worships him. He collects the silliest little details from former days. He has kept his childhood toys. Crazy, I tell you. Perhaps you will look around among your papers." There was a fleeting glance back of the dark glasses. The glance fell, travelled across the floor, returned, crept up the boy's body to his face and there met a totally different glance, bright, strong, bronze-like. "I don't own any letters," he exclaimed angrily and ground his teeth. "I own nothing written by . . . by Leonhart Maurizius, no letters to me, none to . . . Fräulein Jahn. That's all there is about it."

Etzel got up, looking a little surprised. He pressed his hand to his mouth, a boyish gesture which he could not overcome. He stood a slender little exclamation point, in front of Warschauer, who sat crouching in his chair in a long grey overcoat, a massive and formless figure. "Weren't you friends with him, professor?" he inquired with innocent curiosity. "I thought you had been a friend of his. . . ." Warschauer contracted his brows contemptuously and replied evasively, in sleepy, unwilling tones: "Friend . . . perhaps . . . it's possible . . . there were many at that time . . . it's possible." Etzel came a step closer. "And tell me, professor," he continued eagerly, asking as if it were a spontaneous question, "do you really believe that he committed the murder? I mean," he hastily amended, since the monstrosity of having put such a question to the state's witness, Waremme, frightened him, "I mean, is he guilty, even if . . . even if he did fire the shot?"

Warschauer did not reply, but looked at him with an indescribably dead, cold, frozen glance. It seemed as if he had not heard the question, or as if he had at once forgotten it. Etzel could not help shuddering slightly.

2.

Presumably Warschauer-Waremme had seen through Etzel's little tricks and subterfuges far sooner than Etzel had dreamed of. Up to this time he had only had a very unclear conception of the man's penetrating mind and his really tremendous experience. He sensed him, he felt his humble calm, which suggested boiling forces underneath and sometimes made Etzel fear a devastating outbreak, reminding one of a country-side visited by a cloudburst; he felt the stealthy, unsociable, suspicious qualities like those of a sick, driven, but still immensely powerful beast of prey, but he did not fully grasp it. So for a time he did not perceive that Warschauer had accepted the explanation that he had only come on account of the letters with a skepticism which was fortunately mixed with too much indifference for him to subject the young man to an inquisition which would in any case have been very unpleasant. He saw that the excuse bore no relation to the purpose, first weeks of beating around the bush, cunning artifices at Frau Bobike's, language lessons, secretarial assistance and then this: it was silly nonsense. Always, whenever he wasted a fleeting thought on the subject, he would dismiss it grinningly as ridiculous nonsense. For the boy himself, his bearing, his way of talking, his good manners, which he could not suppress in spite of occasional fits of crudeness and slovenliness; this or that indication of coming from a well-situated family, the texture of his stockings and his linen, the cut of his clothes, no it was too ridiculous, simply impertinent, thought Warschauer, without more anger than at the scratching of a mouse. A few days later it happened that he drew the boy towards him, pressed him between his knees and looked penetratingly and intently into his face. Then he took both of Etzel's hands separately and looked at them, the fingers, the nails and the palms, carefully. "You have a delicate skin, my boy, you have been cared for since a baby, according to all of the rules of modern hygiene, eh? A fine young man, not badly bred, delicate temples, delicate joints and a quick head. I like you, Mohl, I like you damned well." Then, chuckling unpleasantly, he released Etzel, who watched him with eyes which expressed the utmost surprise. He suddenly seemed to himself the size of his own thumb. Well, you are a fine devil, he thought to himself and turned away in discouragement. Warschauer suggested that they should go to a pastry shop and drink chocolate.

He obviously did not draw any deductions from having recognized Etzel's manœuvres to approach him for what they were. Perhaps it even amused him to see how far he would carry them and to what they might yet lead. He was of the opinion that people showed their motives and purposes of their own accord, if one only gave them time. They simply unrolled like thread from a spool. He was so certain. He was so beyond reach that he could afford this cynicism which looked like modesty and humility to others. When they were seated in a dark corner of the pastry shop on Rheinsberger-strasse, Warschauer, with that sweetish benevolence which always made Etzel feel as if he were being pinched in the lobe of the ear with nails, said: "You can ask me anything you like, Mohl. I will gladly give you any information. In this way you will find out more which is useful than by playing the Indian on the warpath and scenting my tracks. That's no business for you. You must learn something from me." Etzel turned scarlet up to his hair. "Nothing else interests me, you know," continued Warschauer, licking his lips, to which the chocolate was sticking, "nothing else interests me or touches me. All this beating around the bush, watching and lying in wait, affects me ilke so many flea-bites, I don't even look in that direction; but if I make one move in that direction, then, boy, beware, for one squeeze and the flea is dead."

"I like you, little Mohl." Think of yourself on the edge of a desert in a heavy but silent night, with a burning candle set beside you, and you have, admitted the grotesqueness of the simile, the approximate meaning of these words. The situation is as sombre as the mental state of this man, whose relation to the world is in the last stages of disintegration. "It does not interest me, it does not touch me." That is the key. The elimination of himself. One gets the impression of a person living in glass walls and walking around inside of glass walls, who is too contemptuous and disgusted to lift his eyes or to glance about. He could see everything, to the left and right, behind and before, he has the most penetrating glance, but it does not amuse him in the least. He is so disillusioned that he would not lift his finger to improve the apparently sad conditions in which he lives. The conversations which take place between people, on any subject whatsoever, are as unimportant as the buzzing of insects; they serve to make one believe in deeds which will not be performed and to cover others which will be denied if one confronts the speakers with those conversations. All of the great words, the sonorous panaceas, such as religion, fatherland, humanity, ethics, love of one's neighbour, and so forth, he regards as so many advertisements in a quack drug store. Except stupidity and greed he does not recognize any qualities which function, and which it would be worth one's while to examine, everything which is attributed to other defects is really only the consequence of that almighty pair. He has no opportunity to proclaim his opinions, and if the occasion presented itself, he would avoid it like the plague. Why should he communicate his thoughts? One might as well suggest to him that he should turn somersaults on Potsdamerplatz. Even if he felt the necessity of expressing himself in conversation, he would not have anyone to listen to him, for he is so lonely that by comparison with him convict 357 in the penitentiary at Kressa leads a sociable existence, for he can talk to the guards and associate with his fellow convicts; but this loneliness is chosen and voluntary. Nevertheless a striking resemblance in fate which might cause a mind of lesser calibre to ponder about occult connections. Warschauer is very far from doing such a thing. He has not had any desire to look about him for years, or to trace his path backwards. Not as if he had lost the past from his memory—how would that be possible?—but he carries it with him and it is superfluous for him to think about it. It is not for him, as for most people, the weather-beaten inscription on a tombstone, but the blood which runs in his veins and which overflows into the sea of death.

He does not take what he likes about the boy into the realm of consideration. It is not his youth alone, for he does not need it, does not look for it, does not value it. He regards it as a condition of vain struggles and presumptuous dreams. Part of it comes from his having killed the memory of his youth in himself; he hates himself when he thinks of himself at that time. Yes, he's very young, is young Mohl, but there is something attractive and matter-of-fact about his sixteen or seventeen years, no hysterical intoxication, no vapours of puberty, no slimy snail-shell romanticism. Is that the new spirit? Are there such now? Gay, cool, alert youngsters, who notice at once everywhere when a nail has fallen from the wall or a jar of preserves is missing in the closet? Scarcely. The full-grown specimen at most heralds a type which has already decayed. But there is a charm, a definite charm, which operates like a delicate poison and is as seductive as a rare perfume. Sympathy? No, it has little to do with that. It is rather connected with the desire to possess it. But how? To have, to have what? At times it seems gratifying to one's skin, like fur against one's naked body. Warm and piquant. It contains the nonsensical and the ridiculous within itself. But that is not all. If one analyses it carefully, it calls forth a feeling of tenderness and hatred, of groundless jealousy, of a desire to span an abyss at the bottom of which lies a shattered world. Since he has promised the boy that he will learn something from him, he will try to reconstruct this world not in order to tell a story of sour grapes, nor to erect a fictitious structure—quite the contrary. The youth seems to him like a son whom he has failed to beget, a boy sprung from some kind of protoplasmic miracle, who shines forth in a horrible wilderness. The eagerness to know which pervades the boy's personality, directed towards a goal which he, Warschauer, would rather not have investigated, perhaps puts the means into his hands.

He discovers that there is something fascinating about a pair of eyes which really look at you. What an abstruse idea, that of the unbegotten son! Really, the thought of a devil, or of a madman, in view of the fact that the mere physical presence of the boy gives him the same hermaphroditic sensation as touching a peach which has lain in the sun.

3.

Eagerness for knowledge. A weak description. One did not have to be a reader of souls to understand that it was more than a passing interest, more than affection for one capable of designation by name. Well, the thing to do was to wait, he decided, and did not at first involve himself. That evening he had simply sent Etzel away and the latter had been rather intimidated or had at least appeared to be. Days passed before he dared to hint at the subject again. Meantime he redoubled his eagerness to be of use, spent the afternoons and evenings in Warschauer's room, crept into a corner when other pupils came for their lessons, began to make a list of the books, put the drawers full of linen in order, sewed loose buttons on the professor's clothes, carried the manuscript to the director of the museum, memorized words and rules and made himself as inconspicuous as possible. Late one afternoon he arrived with a bunch of lilies-of-the-valley which he had bought on the way and gave them to the professor with an obstinate smile. The latter behaved in a strikingly exaggerated and hypocritical manner. He clasped his hands and exclaimed in the tones of a singing dervish: "How wonderful, little Mohl, how wonderful! Lilies-of-the-valley, what a glory for my humble domicile! What a delicate attention! There again one sees the product of delicate nurture and æsthetic endowment. Not under any circumstances could a person of the stamp of Paalzow's boy think of such a thing. Fascinating! Unfortunately, we are not provided with a worthy container, and must therefore rest content with a vulgar drinking-glass. Yet, 'tis the giver that ennobles the lowly vessel." He went on in this way for a time: Etzel became so nervous that he could have jumped at his throat. Suddenly Warschauer noticed that water was dripping from the boy. He had walked in the rain without an umbrella, his hat and coat were wringing wet and his stockings sticking to his legs. Then the carrying on really began. The professor wailed as if he had a seriously wounded man on his hands. He insisted that Etzel should take off his shoes and stockings, hung his overcoat and jacket up to dry, got a woolen blanket from the alcove and wrapped him up in it, made him lie down on the sofa, which Etzel only did after a good deal of angry resistance, and set to work to make tea in order to warm him up. His dismay, his busyness, his wailing, his exclamations, and the way in which he rubbed his hands were so obviously make-believe that finally Etzel could not stand it any longer and screamed at him with a white face. "Just stop that. You are only doing it to make fun of me. Because you don't want to talk to me about real things. But I have had enough of this. I am going home." He threw his legs off the sofa and sat up. Warschauer was just reaching up for the box of China tea on the wooden shelf. He turned around slowly. "About what real things, my dear young friend?" he inquired in honey-sweet tones, with pretended surprise. "Well, I have already asked you once," exclaimed Etzel with irritation, "you did not answer me—" "What? What's this about?" demanded Warschauer, still pretending that he did not know what the talk was about. "I asked you whether you believe that he is guilty—Maurizius?"

Warschauer behaved as if he were greatly surprised. With the box of tea in one hand and the lid in the other, he walked up to the sofa with stiff knees. "Since you are so well informed about the facts, little Mohl, you must know that I swore to it at the time." The voice no longer sounded oily, but dry. "Yes, yes, that I know," replied Etzel, devouring the black glasses with his eyes. "But one can be mistaken. Is it absolutely, absolutely, absolutely impossible that you were mistaken?" "The devil!" murmured Warschauer. It was the threefold repetition which called forth the exclamation. "Such a mistake would still have to be based on an actual fact, young Mohl," he said, and placed the box of tea almost soundlessly on the table. "Certainly," admitted Etzel, "he may for example have fired the shot and not have struck." Warschauer grinned. "So, so. Have shot and not . . . Extraordinary. A theory worth considering." Etzel's eyes gleamed angrily. "I'll tell you something. You cannot impress me with your sarcasm. It is as if someone does not want to fight honestly, but places himself in safety and sticks his tongue out. You ought to be ashamed." "I understand," said Warschauer calmly, and looked attentively for a time at the excited boy. "I'll talk to you frankly, Mohl," he then said. "Even if I had made a mistake, it ought not to have been a mistake." "What does that mean? Please explain." . . . Warschauer walked around the room twice, with his hands upon his back and his coat tails swinging. "In order to explain that, Mohl . . . it was a rhetorical figure. No possibility of a mistake." He stood near the sofa again. "How do you feel? Hot? If only you don't get a fever. . . ." "In order to explain that," Etzel repeated his first words like a child, when one keeps back a promised story. "What impatience! Calm your wild impulses, my little friend," bellowed Warschauer sarcastically, resuming his walk with a hollow back and coat tails swinging, which made his walk look like the strut of a rooster. "First, you are going to speak frankly, then it is a rhetorical figure," said Etzel angrily, "who can know what you are about?" Warschauer sighed. "My dear good Mohl, the whole business is so far away, the whole tragic farce . . . so far off . . . it has sunk under the horizon . . . merely shadows, only phantoms . . . it is best to wrap it in silence." He walked around the table, took up the box of tea, placed the lid upon it and struck it with his flat hand, a categorical sign of silence.

Etzel was in despair. The miserable old man; just now he began so well; what can I do, how shall I manage? Externally he remained quiet; he saw that he dared not go any further today. But everything in him revolted against this lame dawdling along step by step as if one had one's feet stuck in a swamp and the other man standing at the edge moved constantly away, pretending all the while to help one. He saw too that he would not get anywhere with the tactics which he had been using up to the present, and that he must change. Compared with this man, Trismegistus is a comfortable warm stove, he thought bitterly, and suddenly his father appeared before him, sitting half turned away, his legs crossed one over the other, an immovable monument. It was a shy memory, which assumed the form of a picture and then disintegrated again. He had no time, no room in his brain for other considerations than the one: what shall I do, how shall I do it? While he was brooding and pondering until his head was sore, his instinct had already pointed out the right way, instinct and interest. As the personality of Warschauer became constantly more puzzling and more incomprehensible, all that was disquieting about the man grew, he could not cease observing him, studying him, eavesdropping upon him, and he felt a burning desire to penetrate into his unknown life, where Georg Warschauer ceased and Gregor Waremme began. For of Waremme he knew practically nothing. Waremme stood behind a cloud. Waremme was the master who hid himself, Warschauer the unimportant assistant who received orders. The two figures were sharply separated from one another, far more sharply for example than E. Andergast and E. Mohl. Of these two Mohl was the more important, although later; E. Andergast could never have met Warschauer, that had been E. Mohl's task, and Mohl was now obliged to stalk Waremme. Poor Mohl, thought

Etzel, you alone, against the two, Warschauer and Waremme. With such a play of thoughts he would sometimes drive away attacks of discouragement. As for Warschauer, he accepted this half concealed, half naïvely impatient interest of Etzel's in a friendly fashion and merely waited for the proper impact to satisfy it. As I have already mentioned, such a demand, in so far as it concerned himself, he was perfectly willing to comply with. Two days after the last conversation it happened that Etzel pulled out from a pile of dusty old pamphlets one on which was written in a bold, unmistakably youthful hand the name *Georg Warschauer* and the month and year: *April, 1896*. Warschauer, who happened to look over, noticed his surprised face, came over, glanced at the name and said: "That's all right, that's my name, my real name. That was my name to start with." Etzel's eyes grew big. Funny, he thought, feeling as if he had been tricked; so it's only imaginary that Warschauer is a remnant of Waremme; before Waremme there was already a Warschauer; Waremme is merely an episode. . . . And he whispered the name gently to himself. "Georg Warschauer, the son of Jewish parents from Thorn, to tell you the facts, friend Mohl. And it's a long story."

He did not, however, seem to have any wish to talk then; apparently his confined premises or the early afternoon hour disturbed him, but it seemed to Etzel as if he were near to doing so and only needed to loosen up internally a little more. "Let's take a short stroll, little Mohl," he said, "the weather is fine, let us go and see a little life." Suits me," replied Etzel, "but the stroll won't last long, we'll end by going to a pastry shop." "Yes, yes, I know one that's not so dull as the one over in the Rheinsbergerstrasse; it's not far, either, next to the Zehdenicker Casino. There's music there at five. Today is Saturday, isn't it? There will be a jazz band today." Etzel consented, although he was not in the mood for jazz; but, knowing

Warschauer's liking for it and not wanting to put him in a bad humour, he went along. They sat for an hour and a half in this dreadful din, table close to table, lower middle class women, people from the suburbs, petty officials, store clerks and professional dancers in tawdry elegance, painted, and disgustingly made up. Warschauer was delighted; the whirling, sliding, pushing, twining motions of the dancers, the heated faces in the atmosphere of heavy dusk, and particularly the blaring, squeaking and whining of the instruments excited and delighted him. Once he seized Etzel's hand and whispered: "Boy, such a saxophone is priceless. It's worth a three-volume history of civilization. Look at the man beating the drum. Doesn't he look like a veritable Torquemada? Cruel, sinister, fanatical. A magnificent specimen, he certainly pulled the legs off of June bugs and set fire to cats' tails when he was a youngster." "Very possibly. But what delights you so about it?" asked Etzel coolly. Warschauer patted his hand. "Biological interest, purely from the standpoint of investigation," he assured him with raised eyebrows. "Do you know that young lady over there?" he interrupted himself, as he stuck his chin in the direction of a thin unlovely girl who had risen from an adjoining table and was staring impudently at Etzel. It was Melitta Schneevogt. She lifted a finger threateningly as if to say: now, I've caught you, you hypocrite. Etzel gave her a friendly nod. He noticed that her hair was bobbed; when he had seen her last it had still been long. "There is something going on there; she ought to be watched," went through his head, but he forgot it at once.

It was already dusk when they left, a fire alarm sounded near Senefelderplatz; soon they saw the red-brown flames shooting up through the cañons of the streets. People began to run; mounted policemen galloped by. A furniture factory was on fire. They walked for a time through the adjoining streets, hearing the fire department signals through the crackling and roaring of the flames; then the throng became dangerous; at Schröderstrasse they came to a park which was almost empty. They sat down on a bench; the purple glow of the fire shone through the tops of the lime-trees; a dog slunk by noiselessly, turned around, stopped in front of them, sniffed expectantly and disappeared again. Warschauer said: "Well, I'll explain that matter of the name to you. . . ."

4.

"True, the name," exclaimed Etzel as if he had not thought of it any more all this time. He sat down alongside Warschauer in order to hear better and—since it was growing dark—to see better. "The name, of course, is the least of it," continued Warschauer, "it's merely a key but to a particular door. Have you associated with Jews, Mohl?" "I should say so. There are a lot of Jews at home." "Had you any Jewish companions?" "Yes." "Did you get on well with them?" "Quite well." "So you don't object to them on principle?" Etzel shook his head. He was familiar with the opposition on principle, but he did not share it. "No instructions from your parents, no prohibitions, nor anything of the sort?" . . . "No . . . no." "You seem to hesitate. There *was* something?" "At times, but I paid no attention. If they were nice chaps I didn't let that bother me." "Fine. That's what I wanted to know."

He was silent a few seconds and poked about in the sand with his stick. "Can you conceive that a person should deceive himself about his birth? A curious complication. Not to want to be what one is, denying the roots from which one has sprung—it means wearing one's own skin like a borrowed coat. I was the child of Jewish parents who were living in the second generation of bourgeois freedom. My father had not yet arrived at the consciousness that the condition of apparent equality was actually only one of toleration. People like my father, otherwise a splendid man, were religiously and socially up in the air. They no longer had the old faith, they refused to accept a new one, that is to say Christianity, partly for good reasons, partly for bad. The Jew wants to be a Jew. What is a Jew? No one can explain this with complete satisfaction. My father was proud of being emancipated. Emancipation is a cunning device, it removes the pretext for complaint from the suppressed. Society excludes him; the State excludes him; the physical ghetto has become a mental and moral one; one sticks out one's chest and calls it emancipation. Have you ever thought about this, young Mohl, or have you by chance ever met a person who had occasion to think about certain . . . well, let us call them discords? No? You have had more important things to do, I understand; but perhaps nevertheless what is going on here in this country has reached your ears. I am not talking about the fact that they would prefer to take back their niggardly franchise; that would at least be honest, it would perhaps be more praiseworthy than destroying—yes, let me give you an example—than demolishing gravestones in cemeteries, don't you think so? What do you think of that, my dearest Mohl, demolishing gravestones . . . , desecrating graveyards . . . that is new in the history of culture, eh, what? *Dernier cri.* I think that compared to that all the poisoning of wells and the alleged ritual murders of Christian children by the Jews, although bloody and brainless, were, if one thinks broadly, things that one could excuse on the grounds of delusion and passion; what do you think? You are silent, little Mohl. I respect your silence. You see this thing about gravestones is a symbol, a peculiar and infernal symbol. Have you ever observed how the last sparks of a piece of burnt paper scatter before it turns black? So it is here. The last sparks of decency, self-respect, dignity, humanity, or whatever other humbug word they use, become scattered, and everything turns black. But I am digressing. However, I once coined the phrase: *to digress is to exhaust a subject.* Nor do I wish to dwell on my family recollections any longer. Just be patient, I am coming along, that is—to myself. Before that, one more axiom, my dear Mohl, and one of general application: In every life there is a moment when a person can make a decision according to the polar oppositions of his nature. According to which, Shakespeare might equally well have become a highwayman like Robin Hood instead of a dramatist; Lenin the chief of police under the czarist régime, as well as the destroyer of that régime. Possibly I might, if I had received a certain impetus—which for inexplicable reasons I did not—I might have become a Jewish leader, a Luther among the Jews. Instead of which—well, that's just what I am talking about. Our external behaviour is dependent upon a profound dualism, is as inbred in us as the instinct towards right and left. Don't ever let anyone tell you, Mohl, that a person might not under certain circumstances have behaved differently from the way he did behave. It is not true. The question is only how far one must go back to find the point where his freedom of will was still intact. Yet I can serve you with personal experiences of a sort . . . Am I not boring you? Really not? Fine. The thing which made me suffer like a dog when I was a child was the cowardice of my race. That they were satisfied with their slavelike existence and consoled themselves with a mythical, artificial feeling of being a chosen race, yes, that made me suffer. Or that they played the gentleman in the pens which were graciously allotted to them, or rather mimicked the mastership of their masters. I hated them all. I hated their idiom, their humour, their manner of thought, their business spirit, their specific melancholy, their presumption, their satire upon themselves. I would bite my pillow with rage at night when I thought of any slander or rebuff which I, or my father, or indeed any Jew had met with. I trembled with rage and shame in school when the word Jew was merely pronounced even in an ordinary statement; can you understand that? Everything was contained in the way in which it was pronounced, the prejudice, the falsification of history, the innate hatred which had not lost any of its coarseness or venom in the course of the centuries. For I knew all about it." Warschauer struck the pavement with his cane. "When I was nine years old I knew all about it, at fifteen I had thoroughly studied the subject and was up to any discussion. But discussions do not alter facts, not even the most infamous, not in our world any longer; and of all facts, there was one that was utterly unbearable to me and that was this: that I should be excluded from any sphere of life or activity. What, I? I with my gifts, with my intelligence, with the fire I had within me, could I not under any circumstances become, let us say for example, a cabinet minister? No, under no circumstances, nor yet the president of a scientific academy. And that was already aiming very high, my dear"—he laughed loudly—"those were already pretentious fantasies, my ambition did not dare to reach so high as a professorship. Under no circumstances would I obtain the recognition which a man of the most mediocre mentality could demand as a matter of course so long as he did not bear the sign of the vehmic court. The thought drove me mad. I could study, I could teach according to my methods, I could be creative, no one would hinder me more than one is generally hindered, and in the end they would not deny me their recognition, and if I accomplished something very remarkable, they would come to the point of admiring me; but . . . in their innermost souls, they would not believe me; at the bottom, they would deny my achievements and only under the most extreme pressure would they bestow upon me the honours which they lavished upon their own kind." He took his slouch hat off, but replaced it at once. "But all that was only the mental aspect. It's impossible to give you the essence of it all, the feeling; it is denied to me to be, to share, to exist. For

I could only live—at that time at any rate—I could only exist if I had the world, the complete fullness of the world, without any deductions or limitations, the whole wonderful breadth of mental life. Therefore, the objection which you have probably been making silently to yourself that any single one of all of these reasons would have sufficed to make me declare myself solidly on the side of my race collapses, that objection has no validity. As I have said, I do not love the Jews. Because I do not love them I felt myself released from a sense of solidarity with them. They could not offer me any substitute for that which I was denied. I was not a renegade in leaving them, I was obeying a necessity of my being. To say that I did not love them was only one half the truth. The whole truth is that I loved the others, those on the other side. This is not infrequently the case; the repudiated loses his soul, wastes it upon those who repudiate him. A very Jewish situation. That from which he is excluded is the promised land; that which he hasn't is his dearest possession. Paradise lost ever and again. Also a Jewish situation. The fall from grace. There I hated, here I loved. I loved their language—their language? my language just as my eyes are my own—loved their faces, their heroes, their countryside, their cities. I loved all this more deeply than they love it themselves, loved it and understood it better. That is not boasting, my son, that is—fate. Moreover, I have given the proof. Now to go back. The thing began with the construction of legends. When my mother died, a simple old woman, who had still held to the Jewish customs—I pretended that she had been a Christian, the wife of a retired military man—I persuaded myself of this so thoroughly that it became a fact to me, provided with the most convincing details, like a model Russian short story. But this only produced a mongrel blood and I wanted to be thoroughbred; by inventing a secret affair with a Silesian property owner, I, on my own authority, eliminated the rôle my Jewish father—who had meantime died—had played in my birth. That was all the enterprise needed. Nature had favoured me, I was blond, a genuine Germanic blond"—he laughed unpleasantly again. "The shape of my face, you cannot deny it, is not Oriental; already as a boy I looked like our peasant type at home. Aside from that, the will forms the face. In the first form of the Gymnasium I was already using the name Waremme. I got it by adoption. My adopted father was a Catholic, an author, a writer of tracts, an agent in obscure dealings and an anti-Semitic agitator; he was simply mad about me, he regarded me as a genius. Perhaps he was not so wrong. Perhaps not at that time. In any case, I knew how to make people believe in me. Not by any tricks—don't think that; I simply held the world in my hand and moulded it like a piece of wax. I never courted people. But up to a certain notch in my life, I had complete power over all who entered my circle; I learned to dominate people, a pleasure that has no equal, an art which demands to be exercised. The change of name took place under the protection of a clerical gentleman and with the assistance of a skilled lawyer. Baptism and entering the church were of course connected with it. Then I had plain sailing ahead of me. Did you say something, Mohl? I thought that you had said something. Plain sailing, that's it. Invisible hands had paved my way. The years at the university, Breslau, Jena, Freiburg—always going from east to west—a series of triumphal stations. Yes, from east to west, always farther, from the depths to the heights, then to the depths again, to the very depths: from east to west like the sun. But I am digressing again. I lived a carefree life. My father had left me practically nothing; but plentiful means came to me; the best introductions opened all doors to me; I became a member of exclusive societies; I talked to dreaded dignitaries as to my cousins. And I did not idle away my time, Mohl, not in the least, for rabid industry is the inheritance of my race; I did not know what to do with all the strength which I had in me; strength came to me from hidden sources, out of the unused stock of generations. I did not hate the sun, no, not in the least; the philosopher Waremme lent wings to the poet Waremme; then the poet to the discoverer of spiritual treasures; then came the intermediary between human beings; the leader; after that the statesman; and then the real goal appeared, creative politics. I felt a calling for that; the idea of a transformed Europe, a continental unity under a German-Roman hegemony filled me with an enthusiasm, oh, what dreams! What wild dreams! I naturally did not want to bind myself to any office; I refused the most tempting offers; it was all too little for me; I was afraid that my star might set if I used it as a lamp, but then in the midst of my soaring flight, came the fall. In the proudest heights the most horrible fall. But the catastrophe had a peculiar logic about it, a mysterious logic; I had not wished to see it, I believed that I could brazen it out . . . but, oh, hell, Mohl, you let me sit here gossiping, staring at me as a hungry man stares at bread and butter. I believe it's damned late; come, come, let's go."

5.

It was not very late, only ten o'clock. They walked back in silence. On Usedomstrasse, Warschauer wanted to say goodbye to the boy, but Etzel asked to be allowed to come up. He was not tired, so little tired that he was afraid of bed. Warschauer laughed more below the diaphragm than on his face. "You have lost the game, dear Mohl," he grumbled. "No more stories for today. Warschauer & Company are closing up shop." He put his key in the front door. Etzel felt that he must not let go now, otherwise everything would be over, what had thawed out would be frozen up again by tomorrow. He thought with terror of his lessening funds; in spite of the most economical care they were going down from day to day; what would happen when he had exhausted them? He could not seek refuge with Warschauer, who had nothing himself; besides that would mean surrendering to him unconditionally. Time was passing; the old man in Hanau looks as distracted as if death were already snatching at him; for the man in the penitentiary, week after week is passing; Trismegistus is sitting with his legs crossed, half turned aside and unconcerned with justice; somewhere in the unknown his mother is looking for him; Etzel cannot stand it any longer, cannot stand it; it is only with a great effort that he collects himself and conceals his feelings—that is the point—to remain cool and to keep his head. He realizes now in what direction this Warschauer-Waremme is pulling him, into what a false world he is being sucked, into the immeasurable darkness of this powerful soul; he had expected that it would all be different, simpler—difficult of course, but difficult as a problem in arithmetic is difficult, a tangle to be unravelled with patience and cunning, not difficult in such a way that a life with its whole burden of problems would lie upon his chest, a mysterious, strange, dark character about whom everything must first be unravelled. He had not expected to begin every day afresh with a minimum of information and a maximum of renunciation of his own wishes, for nothing seems to him to be quite clear about Waremme, nothing makes him love him, nothing makes him feel kindly towards him. What he most wishes is to see him bound before him and to be able to compel him with a red-hot iron in his hand to admit: yes or no; nothing further—simply yes or no. Oh, to pry out everything, bit by bit, to piece everything together bit by bit, and not to know whether one will get that yes or no. He shivers; he is cold; he is feverish; he is hot and cold alternatively every five minutes; but he says to himself, if you give in to yourself, you are a scamp or a dunce, so hold on.

He went up. Warschauer had consented to his staying for half an hour. He had not reckoned with the staying powers and tenacity of his "famulus," and above all, he had failed to take into account his own desire to pour out his story, which had been excited, and which now compelled him to go on automatically; suffice to say it was three o'clock in the morning when Etzel left the house, as I shall state in advance. When he got down to the street, the sky over towards Exerzierplatz was beginning to glow, and he was at first unable to place one foot in front of the other; he lay down at full length upon the stone steps in front of a gin-shop which had just been closed, pressed his eyelids shut and, placing his palms against his shoulders, drew as deep a breath as he could. He was trembling all the while. But I am getting ahead of my story.

There was noise in the narrow corridor above as they climbed the steps. Unpleasant, quarrelsome voices came from the Paalzow flat. Paalzow's boy was having a row with his mother about money, and a baby was crying pitifully. In Warschauer's room the air was like rancid fat; the professor could not find the matches at once and swore softly; finally the gas-jet was lighted, then they saw an army of big black bugs which crept out from under the alcove door, crawling disgustingly about the shelf where the food stood. "Pretty sight," said Etzel, and stood awhile lost in thought. Then he dipped a handkerchief in alcohol, threw it over the vermin where they were thickest and after a few hundred were stunned, he grabbed a broom and calmly brushed them out of the door. "Coffee?" he asked, and Warschauer nodded. The percolator was set in operation for the hundredth time that day. Warschauer walked up and down with the steps of a drum major, his hands under his coat-tails and his forehead unusually dark. A gramophone in the third storey ground out a popular street song and Etzel hummed the text: *Miss Lily, sleepy, cozy.* "I beg you, stop that nasty indecent song, Mohl," said Warschauer with a clerical manner, looking angrily at him. "All right," replied Etzel, "the next time I'll sing it through. But one good turn is worth another, they say, so tell me, professor; no, I won't keep quiet, I don't care how angry you look, now it must . . . or you should not have begun. He who says A must say B, no matter what you do. Now you have served the gravy and don't intend to have any roast? Listen to me, I have staked something, it is a question of . . . for heaven's sake, believe me or not, but don't keep me wriggling so, that's simply mean of you, mean, do you know it?" He was standing in front of Warschauer with clenched fists and gleaming eyes as if he wanted to knock him over. "Tut, tut, tut, what a muddle this cipher of a Leonhart Maurizius has made of your otherwise merry little head! So you want to know? How can I serve you? Only not too much at once, my boy. If you sound me, I am capable of giving you something which will take your breath away. I had a good time with you, my boy, you will have a bad time with me. Dear little unsuspecting boy, playing about bravely in tepid waters, tickling the fin of a shark; come here, come here, Mohl, come here to me this instant, I wish to stroke your skin a little, . . . Come right over here . . ." Again the image, again the voice of the clay figure, sleepy and sensual. "No," whispered Etzel, taking refuge back of a pile of books. "You coward," mocked Warschauer. "Don't you realize that you have a man of differentiated tendencies before you? A grain coarser and . . . I warn you. You are no judge of the quality of metals. Thank God. If that were not the case you would already be rotten. I warn you against the sanctimonious God of the Greek cult, against the priests of the new rhythm, the esoterics and the Order of the Illuminati who worship the hermaphroditic god in their Black Masses. These people will hunt you incessantly; this cult has won an army of adherents for the simple reason that they wish to couple Mars with Eros in order after the former's cruel fall to strengthen him by a secret conspiracy. Suppressed instincts are running rampant. You don't understand me? All the better. From me at any rate, you have nothing to fear. The bridge between us in this respect has no more solidity than a rainbow. Still puzzled and suspicious. At last you are beginning to get an inkling, thank Heaven." He walked quickly towards Etzel, took his head between his hands and, looking penetratingly at him, kissed him on his forehead. Etzel did not move. It was the cannibalistic side of the man tempered by a kind of intellectual superiority. Nevertheless, a cold shiver ran down Etzel's spine. "Well?" he murmured obstinately. Warschauer grinned. "I call that exploiting a situation ruthlessly," he said mockingly, "you have only the one thing in your head . . ." "Well?" insisted Etzel childishly eager. "Yes," said Warschauer calmly, "we were obliged to destroy one another, I him and he me."

He walked up and down contemplatively, his left hand on the back of his neck, swinging the right like a soldier. The water glass on the table rattled with his reverberating tread. He really looks frightfully funny, fat and sombre, thought Etzel, listening intently, all of his senses alert. At first he only threw out casual remarks. Some things sounded like rhetoric, as for example, that in Maurizius he had met a nature antipodal to his own. But as he became more precise, he threw an illuminating searchlight upon their relations. There had actually been a collision, but the strength had been chiefly on the side of the impinging body, the other had only been shaken out of its passivity. He had therefore had no choice, he had been obliged to join in the motion. "There was nothing else for me to do, I had to get in front of him, on top of him, I had to make him harmless." "Why that," said Etzel in astonishment, "since you have just said that he was a cipher?" Without interrupting his walk, Warschauer stretched his right arm in the air. "That, of course, but a representative cipher. A cipher situated where it helped to construct a tremendous number. All public life is made of such ciphers. In any case, he was a cipher with a following worth considering, moreover a gifted cipher, a brilliant cipher, which one could be certain would some day go up in the air like a balloon. But that was not the decisive point. What clinched the matter was . . . just note this. Here stood Waremme, Gregor Waremme, a new man. I had conquered the world, one redoubt after another. I had settled myself in a happy position; I had attuned my feelings accordingly; had achieved a task in the people. I needed—and please note—only to give them faith in me, to make them believe in me, a task, the consequences of which I felt for ten years in every nerve in my body. I have been told, of Salvini—an actor genius of whom you have perhaps heard—that after every big performance he had a collapse. One of my friends, a theatrical manager, told me that once, after the fifth act of Othello, Salvini had fallen unconscious behind the stage and a physician had been obliged to work over him for an hour and a half before calling him back to life. Speaking from experience, there are actors of that kind—and others. Some die a heartrending death upon the stage, and when the curtain falls they burst into obscene jokes. You are looking at me again with such naïve surprise, little Mohl; the parable of the actor obviously makes you suspicious. But I was an actor, I had to act and if I did not play with the most perfect art, with the most complete devotion, I could pack up and get out. *Actor*: don't object to the word! Do not take it in a plebeian sense; do not forget that it is a hundred years since Goethe wrote Wilhelm Meister and the poem about Mieding's death, and more than a hundred and fifty years since Lichtenberg's letters about Garrick. Since then the actor has sunk to be an employee in an industrial concern and a papier-mâché hero of the lower middle class. That, however, is beside the point. I remember that I once discussed the point a whole night through with Maurizius. He did not understand me. He was stupid enough on that point to drive one mad. Naturally, I was an actor, just by nature. And he was not, oh, God, he was not! That I was one—ruined me; that he was not—ruined him. . . ."

"What do you mean by that," asked Etzel, breathless with curiosity. "Explain to me above all why you were an actor." Unintentionally, he took a few steps behind the pacing Warschauer, who seemed to be walking on stilts, which made the pair look like a ridiculous caricature of the long and short of it. "Every unusual effort of the character, or the mind, is based upon a sublimation of the art of transformation," said Warschauer didactically. "Just bear in mind what branches of knowledge I had to master, the most heterogeneous subjects, philosophy, theology, economics, history, languages, government—all from the inside, from the point of view of their fundamental conception. Remember that from the beginning I had decided not to use any of them as a milch-cow, nor as the means to a title or position, for the well-considered reason which I have already suggested to you—that I wanted to rise higher. Consequently, I had to shift and veer, not only to bring myself constantly forward in the most advantageous way, but also I had to instruct and arouse my admirers, supporters, messengers and proselyters, calculating their talents and abilities precisely, to be able to instruct, distribute, inspire them. Then I was constantly involved in a complicated network of interests like the provost of a religious order; for according to my conception at that time, something tremendous was at stake; a strong party was counting upon me; the emperor's attention had been drawn to me; the Vatican was sending its silent emissaries to me; and remember that, last but not least, I had to be careful to eradicate my former traces; that I constantly had, so to speak, to contend against some last dark metaphysical remnant of a bad conscience which cast a shadow, even in my own mind, upon my purely humanitarian disinterestedness, making it appear a product of effort, if not of torment. Just add all this together and then deny if you can that it was anything less than dancing upon a needle point. He, he on the other hand . . . not an inkling! Living in a cozy nest. Not the least idea. Had simply sprung up spontaneously. The lily of the field. No effort whatsoever. Leonhart the effortless. Did he have to play a part? Was there a rôle for him? What did he know of the play in which he appeared, since he did not 'appear' but simply 'let himself go'? Let himself go, the effortless! Let himself go! Had his place at the table d'hôte, his ticket always waiting for him at the box office. Learning? A department-store where one provides oneself with one's materials. With expensive articles, of course, which do not easily show that they are mass production. The people who know are scarce and one must have hard luck not to be able to fool them. Art? A noble occupation. Labour? Is known to be ennobling. Only pleasure demands the sweat of one's brow. The gods have so ordained. And for love, they demand the sacrifice of a heart which has nothing . . . to give. A cipher within a cipher." He laughed bitterly and with curious reverberation. "Nevertheless, I cannot understand," Etzel ventured to object, leaning deep in thought against the folding doors. "Just because that is your opinion of him I cannot get it into my head that any friction should have arisen between you and him. How was it possible? The effortless—yes. But why just he? It might just as well have been, so it seems to me, a hundred others. There must have been—now I'll tell you something, professor, only you must not go for me . . ." "Well"—"I mean there must have been . . . may I say it?" "Don't be afraid, little Mohl, what must there have—" "It must have been Fräulein Jahn's fault. *Fault*—that sounds so stupid . . . *cause* is what I mean." Warschauer smiled his incomprehensible smile. "Oh, is that so?" said he in travesty of the Americanism. "I wonder. Clever boy. Never in my life did I see such a clever boy!"

And Waremme resumed his strutting up and down the room.

CHAPTER XI

I.

A LONG silence. Warschauer seemed to be consulting with himself. Presumably he was thunderstruck by the boy's boldness. What could he surmise behind it? His experienced glance could not fail to perceive the peculiar innocence with which the boy had now, for the second time, pronounced that name. Fundamentally unsuspicious in spite of all his assumed knowledge of facts and his curious dryness. As one might refer to an interesting figure in a play, whose fame one may be presumed to be familiar with. Or like a detective who at first diverts the attention of his victim by all kinds of digressions in order then, with studied coldness, to hurl the most striking evidence in his face. Silly and ridiculous! As if he, Warschauer, had anything to fear. He hadn't the slightest thing to fear. That he had settled in Berlin to lead an existence of almost shadowy secrecy was his own free decision; he was not being pursued; he had no reason to fear any investigation; there was nothing against him. He had obtained the right to resume his original name "over there." What had determined him to do this was very closely connected with the catastrophe which he called his "European failure"; but that had only been the preliminary to a far greater "failure." He could divide his previous life, from this point of view, into four clearly separate periods, he explained eagerly: the Jewish, the Christian-German, the overseas-international and the present one, for which he had not yet found a suitable title. Perhaps his agreeable friend Mohl would think of one. Something like "the reversion." "The regenerative reversion." It was extremely remarkable. He would recommend himself to various modern writers as the model for a Proteus. He could even give them information about the present state of the world, with which they could make their fortune. He himself had given up in this respect. It did not pay. He could not even decide to write one of the usual autobiographies. Twenty-five thousand printed publications appeared in Germany every year; it was damnably silly to add Number Twenty-five Thousand and One. Moreover, he would be boycotted; he would be regarded as a crazy man who wished to outdo the Terror of the Apocalypse.

He rambled along for a time in this tone, while Etzel impatiently stood first on one foot, then on the other; then he took the clothes brush from a nail and began to brush his coat with studious care. While doing this, he cast sidelong angry glances at the boy over the rims of his dark glasses, then he suddenly changed the subject and began to indulge in sneers with regard to his reference to Anna Jahn. "That was simply a shot in the back, fortunately from an unloaded revolver, my boy," he said sarcastically. "It was tactless and indiscreet. It isn't decent to blurt out things in that way." "Well, I simply thought that in that case, since you had the advantage," said Etzel not in the least frightened, "in that case you were victorious all the way along the line." Warschauer, standing somewhat bent over, made a face like a balky steer, wary and intractable. "From what do you deduce that?" he asked. "From various things." "For example." "Well, for example, from Fräulein Jahn's having still been at your house . . . or with you two years afterwards." Warschauer's brows contracted as if he were calculating. "Two years? No, you are mistaken. It wasn't even one. Wait . . . from the beginning of nineteen-seven till November." The correction was made in a tone of friendliness which warned Etzel to be on his guard. But Etzel paid no more attention to danger; he allowed himself to be carried along from one piece of audacity to another, as if intoxicated. Nothing matters any more now, he thought, as he answered pertly: "Yes, but I know that she did not return from where she was with you until much later, and there was nothing left of all the money which she had inherited from her sister. She was as poor as a beggar. I happen to know that quite accurately," he lied brazenly, "for I happen to know the lady who took her in, in her terrible plight. So I am nevertheless right when I maintain that in this case you thoroughly got the better of Leonhart Maurizius. He got nowhere and you disappeared with the loot."

The effect of this attack upon Warschauer was very remarkable. At first he looked as if he wanted to fly at Etzel, the putty colour of his face turned a blue-green and a red spot appeared in the middle of his forehead, and, most curious of all, the tips of his ears trembled, for his ears were not round at the top but pointed like those of fauns in ancient sculptures. For the second time since Etzel had known him, he took his glasses off, and for the second time Etzel saw the watery lightless eyes. A deep sigh lifted his breast and Etzel wondered tensely what the old man would do now. For him Warschauer, with his forty-seven or forty-eight years, was an old man, but he had never before made the impression of "being old" so strongly as in those fearful ten or twelve seconds. Warschauer's mouth opened and clapped to again, his watery eyes travelled about almost as if seeking an object with which to strike, then quite suddenly his features relaxed, he walked a few steps towards Etzel, stood still, shook his head as if he were disconcerted, dropped into a desk chair and sank into deep thought. About ten minutes passed thus. "Come here, Mohl," he suddenly said quietly. Etzel obeyed silently. Warschauer put on his glasses again and took the boy's two hands which he held tightly. "When I was still a student," he began in a lugubrious voice, "I had to prepare a young Count Rochow for an examination. One day I told him to tell me all that he knew about the Greek Helena. He said—I remember almost every word, because it was such an unparalleled hodge-podge of all the versions which he had read—Helen, the daughter of Nemesis and Zeus, first had a love affair with a swan, then married Menelaus, was seduced by Paris and after the fall of Troy went with him to Egypt where it turned out that she was the wrong Helen. The true Helen had remained with Achilles, was attacked by Orestes and Pylades, but was rescued by Apollo. All *ad hoc* knowledge is like this, my young friend; the result is a Helen who, God forbid, is at the same time a daughter of Nemesis and Leda. Human history, my child, if one wants to rely upon it, is like angling for fish in a burning crater. Anyone who gets seriously interested will at best merely learn something about fire and lava. He will not catch fish. And first of all, just learn one thing: it is always different. It is even mysterious to the person who has the experience. How could anyone then who merely knows about it presume to say it was thus and so? But I don't want to take you to task too seriously, little boy. I am sorry for you." He let Etzel's hands drop and got up without noticing the boy's somewhat disconcerted face.

2.

He went to the window, opened it, and murmured, "The sky over there is still red," closed the window again and continued: "What do you really think when you speak of Anna Jahn, little Mohl? Are you not at all fearful of the depths of your own ignorance? It has the effect upon me of a baby chattering about the nebula in Andromeda. You must excuse me, but there are dimensions and propositions involved here about which you cannot have any opinion. I do not believe either that I can be of any use to you in this respect. I would be so gladly; why should one not give a gifted boy some hints about psychological labyrinths which may sometime be useful to him? But with all your maturity, Mohl, it is astonishing what problems you treat without embarrassment . . . Don't get angry at me again, I mean it perfectly seriously and it is not only your being so unsuspecting which moves me. I wish that I were capable of reconciling your touching conceptions with the truth, particularly for my own sake, for how must I appear—a blackguard and a scamp, like repulsive old Wurm in Schiller's Intrigue and Love! But I scarcely know; I don't know, one would have to be a Tolstoy in order to depict . . . Perhaps it would interest you to know that I had already met Anna Jahn before she knew her future brother-in-law . . . oh, you know that anyway. She was the first woman who . . . well, well, how shall I express it, she was a phenomenon who made one pause. I still well remember the evening I saw her for the first time; it was at a little party at Frau von Hardenberg's, she was standing next to a Chinese vase a yard and a half high, and her head was resting lightly on her arm. She was seventeen years old, but Nature had nothing more to do, everything was so perfectly finished, so mysteriously complete. My impression was: That person is so proud that under certain circumstances she might bleed to death from pride. Well, what was the nature of the pride in her? Pride? One utters a word like that and forgets that it has a thousand meanings, from the most superficial to the most profound. I have only met one person with whom pride became fate, and that was she. I was . . . tremendously fascinated at any rate and this had its consequences. The teachings of East Indian Sikhs say: 'If a man is separated from his soul and the yearning of his soul, he does not remain standing in the road, but hastens his wanderings.' I think that you understand. It was fatality. Among humans the most composite elements—contrary to what holds in chemistry—are the most capable of reactions. She was the incarnation of the world into which I had to the very roots of my nerves to transform myself. I first understood the meaning of my existence through hers. That was how it was. We understood each other very well. That is, she listened to me very well. I have never, not in my whole life, not even in you, little

Mohl, seen so attentive, so eager, so breathless a face turned towards mine. In my youth I could take people by storm in conversation, I could kindle their enthusiasm endlessly, I could— What could I not do? . . . I could give them their own souls over again. There was no difference between men and women. There was no longer any resistance, they would see with my eyes, feel what I made them feel. Their hearts would become brave, they would understand the parables of the Holy Scripture, for the higher world is only accessible through parables. To me communication was my other nature, my real nature like the beat of my pulse; where I could communicate myself I already identified myself, it was the most sublime form of love towards men and towards women, a tireless siege to drive the others out of themselves, to free them from all barriers and reserves. I myself had none, neither barriers nor reserves, that was just it; you must understand that after all this. As regards women, I could not do without them. They had an easy time with me. I was simply tinder. I never weighed what was at stake for me. I was not saving with my person, I can indeed easily say that I was as wasteful as a person who has fifty lives. Some of my friends were amused at me, they said that I beheld a Helen in every woman. Nonsense. One must have knelt before many altars to know how unattainable gods or goddesses are, especially when one has sacrificed in vain. When the real Helen came, it appeared, oh, my prophetic Rochow, that this time she was really the daughter of Nemesis."

He walked up and down for a time in silence. Etzel's glance was fastened upon three disgusting black beetles walking behind one another over the board floor. But he did not see them, he was only listening. "What took place between us," continued Warschauer, "is of no further importance, not in this connection. The pragmatic does not play any rôle. One thereby loses the broad point of view and reduces an experience to a novel." A wretched pretext, thought Etzel; now he is keeping silent about the most important part of it, and actually Warschauer stammered uncertainly for some minutes. "Decisive about it was this, I fought for her, but she . . . she fought for . . . yes, for what? For a picture of herself worlds removed. If only she had fought for herself, yes, then . . . but for reputation, what one owed to one's honour and that one must guard oneself . . . godless, godless, godless, the morality of refined circles, a godless morality of conservation. I threw my time at her feet, as wastefully as a fool; a woman does not understand what that means, a man's time; she swallows it like lemonade, swallows as much of it as one gives her and if she wants to go to try on a hat, she on her side has no time left for you. She had talents, she might have become something, but she had no reverence, or faith, except that she went to confession every Sunday; but a human mission meant nothing to her. She should have been torn open, she was as tight as a young nut. I—well, I was no saint, no worshipper from afar, . . . What was I to do?" He struck himself on the breast threateningly with the flat of his hand. "What was I to do? I knew perfectly well that breaking the vessel would not open her soul to me, but there is in such cases a desire for revenge. I overpowered her and it was I who was beaten. Perhaps I was crazy. I did the stupidest thing. I lied to her, telling her that I was the son of a reigning prince. At the same time I multiplied my energies tenfold and worked like a Chinese coolie. But this kind of passion was mysterious to her. She was after all a German girl, you understand. It was too much for her, she was enveloped in her conventions as in an iron corset. She had a feeling that I was queer. She felt the strange blood, it repulsed her, she was entranced, and a little afraid. The more light I poured over her, the gloomier her spirits grew. Unravel me that. Not to be carried away, for God's sake, not to bow down, to tolerate, yes. She did not know that she could bind me if she would let herself go, that I would take root if she prepared the ground for me, but she could not understand that, the German Helena; this went beyond her horizon. There was an open break. She wandered from city to city until her sister sent for her. And what happened? There, there was a mission to her liking waiting for her. A motherless child to care for, a lyrical weakling to prop up, who did not demand a soul revealed, for his own was as open as the door of a tavern; he needed a little of the halo of the martyr, a little aunt-like sympathy, a little admiration; one could play the governess, the unapproachable, the intermediary, the rôle was perfectly in keeping, one was adored and one risked nothing. Without doubt they would have been decently and peacefully happy together, it would have been one of those marriages in which the husband has the position of a lackey and the wife—God knows how it happens—is a virgin at forty, even though she have borne half a dozen children. Undoubtedly it would have been so had Maurizius still been free. But as it was they were hurried into the stifling bourgeois tragedy where the suppressions, repressions and complexes flourish like contagious skin diseases, the struggle between love and duty, consideration and sacred ties, fear of gossip and calumny, a cowardly playing with fire, rivalry between sisters and a secret correspondence, forbidden paths and a bad conscience. The whole phrasemongering tempest of denaturalized conflicts fought itself out and the pitiful end would have descended like a hammerstroke even if I had not intervened. And should I not have interfered? They were so pitiful all three, they flapped like birds around a disturbed nest in their blind confusion, and the whole sad comedy simply screamed for a *deus ex machina* to take things in hand; they could not get straightened without me, they had no will left; only instinct, only fear. My Galatea, my Helena, seduced by a fool! If at least he had been a Paris, but not the ghost of one! I found her again besmirched, dragged in the mire; her whole being implored to be saved. What was she without me? But she would not have it so; and when I fished her out of the pool she was a corpse. I mean that she no longer had a soul. She walked the earth, to be sure, ate and drank what was necessary, bought herself clothes, visited museums and read books, and she was . . . a corpse. I am not Christ, I could not resurrect Jairus' daughter from the dead. On the contrary, I was a broken man at that time, dropped as if at some secret command. No dog any longer wanted to take a crust of bread from me; my most eager patrons no longer recognized me; people were no longer at home to me; one did not remember having exchanged ideas and worked out plans with me; letters came back unopened; my supply of funds gave out. There was nothing left for me to do except to break tent and, like crazy Johanna with the corpse of her husband, to quit the country with my soulless half-dead body. Further towards the west."

He walked to the window and drummed so loudly on the window-pane that Etzel, tormented by the nervous tension, involuntarily pressed his hands to his ears. After a while he ventured over and pulled him by his jacket. "For heaven's sake stop that," he said in low tones. Warschauer let his arm sink, but did not turn around. "And how was it when you took things in hand?" whispered Etzel. "That's the most interesting of all. . . ." Warschauer made a gesture of dismissal. "Maybe; at the moment it does not interest me," he replied brusquely. "Do you see that figure over there at the window? Of course not, you can't see so far, you poor salamander. A naked woman. She is washing her feet. Really beautiful. Peaceful and beautiful. Perhaps she is young and pretty; I can't see; she is sitting in the shadow, but if she's young and pretty let us be grateful to her for her carelessness. Life does not pass us over entirely. But I fear it is an illusion and that she is a dirty old jade." "Dear God, what nasty things you sometimes say! What concern of ours is that strange woman?" said Etzel. "Yes, yes, what concern of ours is that strange woman?" repeated Warschauer in a curiously depressed voice. Etzel looked up in surprise and then dropped his eyes in shame. Then Warschauer laughed harshly and his voice sounded broken. "I stood once thus at a window," he began to narrate without any transition, leaning his forehead against the pane of glass, "one night in a little French city, in a little empty inn late in the autumn, stood at the window looking out and in the window opposite I saw a girl playing a violin. One did not hear anything, one only saw the fervent feeling with which she moved the bow up and down and her delicate figure shimmering through the white curtains, and back of me, as you are now standing back of me, little Mohl, back of me, stood . . . Anna. The trunks were packed, we were to leave the next day, she for Paris, I for Cherbourg. We had reached the end."

After a pause, he spoke of the last ten thousand francs which he had lost at baccarat. There were then four thousand still left, the remainder of Anna's fortune; they divided it and the female shadow who had accompanied him up to this last collapse, perhaps only because she had never found an abiding place anywhere in the world, freed herself from him with the same lethargy with which she had gone along beside him. Paris? All right, Paris. And then? She did not know. A faded leaf in the wind. For a year he—at that time he was still Gregor Waremme and surrounded by the atmosphere of his dead fame—had ceased to lead any mental life. He had not wanted to admit his desperate disappointment, he had simply gone on playing the rôle, an actor without an audience, playing to empty benches. But the play had become a game of chance, it was only a change of masks. He said that the gambler was a bastard of the imagination, only he who had contempt for possessions could play for high stakes. He had not yet really faced within himself the frightful *débâcle* of his life, he dreamed of riches, regarded his exile as temporary, the loss of respect was a question of time. His goal was to make six or seven hundred thousand marks out of the hundred thousand which Anna had inherited; this seemed easy to him; with this sum he could then build a golden bridge for his return. It was now his business to force fortune, playing in a sullen, sour temper, day after day, night after night. When everything was spent, he came to his senses. "I understood, like a man walking out of an opium den on an ice-cold morning, that there was no foothold left for me in Europe. But the idea of crossing the ocean was at first only a dream. There, too, I dreamed at first only of some chance good fortune and that my native land would then apologize for the injustice done me and receive me again with open arms. So profound was my infatuation. But during the night which I have mentioned, I had a true picture of my past life; it stared at me like a monster from the underworld. I finally knew that there was no return. There was for me either a bullet through my head, or . . . burning my ships behind me, not looking back, losing myself, an unknown person in an unknown world. This is what happened. But, my good Mohl, there came years. . . . I fear that it is not in my power to give you any conception of them. . . ." He stalked back into the room, crossed to the opposite wall and crouched down upon a low pile of books, his forehead sinking far forward. His shock of white hair gleamed like ice upon his skull. Etzel made himself as small as possible and kept quite still. He would have liked to creep into the stove just to listen to Warschauer without being seen by him any more.

3.

It was not a narrative with a fixed outline. There was no story with tense crises. The account had not even a proper beginning, no pauses, no climax. Only from time to time pictures flamed forth like flashes of light over dismal and uniform waves of water. Etzel knew these flashes of light from the North Sea, where he had spent a few weeks of the holidays with his father, three years ago, at the Sydows'. Yes, Warschauer's manner of speech seemed to him like dismal and uniform waves of water; he had lost the effervescence, the passionate exaggeration of his words, and it all seemed truer. It was the difference between a speaker who constantly screams and makes faces, so that one can't listen properly, and one who sits motionless, whom one can scarcely see, and who simply talks and talks. . . . What Etzel heard drew him down like an inexorable screw—he even had the physical sensation of being pulled down; about it all he felt a tremendous logic which paralysed his heart. Apparently, there was no direct connection with his problem, but that did not disturb him, he would reconstruct the connection later on, for it seemed to him somehow as if all of this was only a variation of one thing, of the one "business," as if sometime, somehow, the settlement must come.

Waremme left Europe at that time with a complete consciousness of the finality of the step. An emigrant in the boldest sense of the word, an emigrant who no longer has a home. He had accepted the situation at the time. He had to forget, he had to begin afresh. Nevertheless, the essential difficulty of his position had not been quite clear to him as yet in the beginning. To turn one's back upon Europe does not yet mean to be able to live without it. He began to understand what Europe actually was for a person of his sort. Not merely his own personal past, but the past of three hundred million people. It was both what he knew of them and what he had in his blood. It was not merely the country which had brought him forth, but the picture and conformation of all of the country between the North Sea and the Mediterranean, its atmosphere, its history, its transformation. Not only this and that city in which he had lived, but hundreds of cities and in these cities the cathedrals, the palaces and fortresses, the works of art and the libraries, the traces of great men. Was there an incident in his own life unconnected with the generations of memories which had been born with him? Europe was not merely the sum total of the ties of his own individual existence, friendship and love, hatred and unhappiness, success and disappointment; it was, venerable and intangible, the existence of a unity of two thousand years, Pericles and Nostradamus, Theodoric and Voltaire, Ovid and Erasmus, Archimedes and Gauss, Calderón and Dürer, Phidias and Mozart, Petrarch and Napoleon, Galileo and Nietzsche, an immeasurable army of geniuses and an equally immeasurable army of demons. All this light driven into darkness and shining forth from it again, a sordid morass producing a golden vessel, the catastrophes and inspirations, the revolutions and periods of darkness, the moralities and the fashions, all that great common stream with its chains, its stages, and its pinnacles, making up one spirit. That was Europe, that was his Europe. How could he separate himself from this Europe? It was in him. He carried it over the ocean with him. It was operative in him when he merely breathed. He had accordingly, so it seemed to him, a task. As a missionary goes out to the heathen, so he went "across"—so it seemed to him—in order to proclaim the spirit of Europe.

"You can imagine, Mohl, what a magnificent conception I had of myself in this rôle. Columbus the Second. The apostle Paul of civilization and culture. With my head full of such high-faluting ideas, I could to a certain extent settle down there. What one can learn from books about a country and its inhabitants I knew. I regarded my theoretical knowledge as a useful foundation, in addition to which I knew the language as well as my own; cultivated Englishmen had often expressed their astonishment at my perfect English. I had always had a gift for languages. But I had no connections. I did not know a soul. I had no introductions of any sort. I did not even have a title. I wanted to become associated with a university; but it was impossible for obvious reasons; I could not refer to my former activities; I was afraid of inquiries; I had no academic degree; the contempt which I had formerly had for the approval of the masses wreaked its revenge; my applications were fruitless. Fortunately—for as matters stood then, I should have been a pitiful figure in any academic chair—something like a teacher in an Indian village school. After a few weeks I was entirely destitute. That did not worry me much. No one can starve over there. The whole country is so to speak a huge scheme of insurance against starvation. The public charities are so gigantic that beggars are almost as scarce as kings. And they have democracy. What lies between living and not starving is another matter. Conceive of a tremendous hospital, furnished with every modern comfort, filled with the incurable sick, not one of whom ever dies, and you will have what lies 'between.' Deaths would damage the reputation of the establishment. Well, you have convinced yourself during our acquaintance, I hope, that I am a person without any material needs. While I was living in the greatest social glamour—except when I wanted to attain certain ends—I did not use more for my personal needs than a poor student. That is one of the qualities by which, under certain circumstances, one can do more than a genius. The drunkard and sensualist has faith only in the abstainer. I easily succeeded in earning my bread by giving language lessons. But I was limited thereby to the lowest classes. I did not have the money to dress decently or elegantly, nor did I have the inclination; gradually a certain obstinacy came over me, as if my shabby appearance were a kind of self-protection; you will soon understand why I wanted this self-protection. The internal reasons were more important. Insignificant people barely tolerated me still. The insignificant do not require any pattern of intercouse, for they still detect something unstable in other persons, since they themselves are unstable—on the brink, I mean. For the little people over there still have some shreds of Europe about them, some little lost frippery, some tiny reminiscence of Europe. The secure ones, as soon as they merely commenced to be secure, to share in the security, were suspicious of me. I used words which they never used; I made allusions to things which they had never heard of. The sentences in which I spoke to them had a construction; there was a main clause and a subordinate clause. Never did the word dollar cross my lips. On the other hand, I liked to express myself in comparisons. And that was intellect, something extremely suspicious, something crushing, and the higher up one went socially, the more crushing it was. Naturally I became constantly more careful, constantly more modest. But the neatly devised, carefully planned avoidance and elimination of intellect which I pursued was still a kind of intellect. What could I do about it? I had not yet grasped a thing about the country. I merely saw one thing, that when a person showed a modicum of mind, no matter who he was, others made a wide circle to avoid him, and he could only make up for his *faux pas* if he eventually did something like saving a child from the torrents of the Mississippi. No, they did not love the spirit; they loved the thing, the object; they loved performance, eulogy, a fact, but spirit is to them mysterious beyond all measure. They have something in its place, the smile. I had to learn to smile. In San Francisco there was a barber shop whose owner had the sublime idea, after the earthquake had destroyed the city, of putting up a placard on the door of his shop, reading: *Whoever comes in here smiling is shaved free of charge.* When I was told that, I slowly began to understand. A country of children. So I learned to smile. From that you may realize, my good Mohl, that I was confronted with an entirely new problem in adjustment, for me, a master of mimicry, far more difficult than anything that I had done previously. Formerly I had been obliged to accomplish everything in the spirit and through the spirit; now I could only keep up if I dulled my spirit to the last degree; if I so to speak purged myself daily of my spirit. But those are *aperçus,* the children of experience, with those I can as little make you understand the nature of the thing as if I should assure you that yesterday's soup was too salty. I did not stay long in New York. There one is still on the edge of Europe; temptation is too strong. Of my confused wanderings there is not much to be said. I went to Kansas City with the family of a clergyman, from there south, and thence to the Middle West. One must adjust oneself to wandering if one does not know how to climb; to stay put means to go under; Jack tosses you to John, John to Bill and when Bill finds out that you are no longer any good, he leaves you on the junk-heap—all in a quite friendly fashion, of course. Keep smiling. When I got to Chicago, where I stayed ten and a half years, I fell sick; I was in the hospital eight months. During my recovery I made friends with a young negro, Joshua Cooper, an athlete, a pure soul. When he laughed at you, you always felt as if it were Christmas. He was a clerk in a negro bank; through him I got to know other negroes, I taught them, or their sons. That did for me in white society. My paths became darker; I allowed myself to be driven; I lost contact with the surface and reached the bottom. I met many Chinamen; I didn't do more than meet them; one does not get at them. Not there where they have no roots. They live like worms in wood, over there. Most of them lead the most mysterious lives possible to human creatures. It is unusual if one of them is what he appears to be; the cook is not a cook, nor the coal heaver a coal heaver. Many of them are in the service of an organization, so strict and powerful that compared to it the order of the Jesuits is as innocent as a girls' finishing school. I had seen a good deal of a tea-dealer called Sun Chwong Chu; when I went to see him one day—I had a message for him—the yellow servant led me to a cellar where four of his friends were standing in silence around his corpse. An hour before he had fallen over without a sound, his face was as swollen as a sponge. A murder without a murderer, dictated eight thousand miles away. You are probably thinking: What nonsense, my good Mohl! But one must have had the experience, in that country, the horrible has not yet been weakened by the stops and asterisks of culture. This city . . . when I open an atlas sometimes and look at it, situated in a certain geographic latitude and longitude, on the south shore of a certain lake, tremendous like everything in that country, its whitish water like thinned milk, when I look at it—merely look at the speck which stands for it—I am filled with shuddering astonishment. So it really exists, I say to myself; when I was living there its reality was not quite so incontestable. If the human soul could grasp what penetrates into it as quickly as the eye sees and the intellect understands, no one could live through what happens in a year, no one, not even the most hardened, and I, by God, am hard enough. Various things go through my mind, but if I wish to retain them, they have no more substance than a feverish dream. . . . There are a few things that happened which I should like to talk about, because . . . how do the lines run in Shakespeare?

> "Heaven's face doth glow;
> Yea, this solidity and compound mass,
> With wistful visage, as against the doom,
> Is thought-sick at the act.

Thought-sick? Well, I don't know. One is turned inside out, over and over. It is frightfully interesting. A picture-book, as rare as it is nerve-racking. But first comes something pretty. A prelude. One morning I was walking through the streets full of warehouses, my ears mutilated by the noise of machines and people rushing, tearing, shrieking, when I heard a remarkable sound. The song of a bird, think I in astonishment, the sound of a bird in this hell of filth and iron; whence the birds, how is it that I can hear them? I walk up to a sort of partition and ask the negro, who grinningly directs me forward; in front of me there is a wall of cages, thirty thousand canary birds, which have just been unpacked, singing out of thirty thousand tiny throats, an orchestra, a tremendous concert ridiculously and charmingly drowning out the noise of cranes and motors, the screams of locomotives and people. I stand there, not knowing whether to laugh or to cry; it is so mad, so holy and so fairylike. Well, let us turn the pages, a summer afternoon, heat which parches one's lungs, the mazes of the stockyards; the sky a curious reddish yellow, the air sticky and thick enough to cut. Passages miles long, wooden tunnels, labyrinths of tunnels crossing the streets, the death-bridge for the animals which are to be slaughtered. A dull bellowing, oxen and calves in endless trains, a quiet fateful stamping. At a particular place the hammer falls upon them, in a minute hundreds die and fall into the pit. It is oppressive to be there, so close to countless creatures about to die; I see them stepping forward, shoving and shoved, the necks of the rear ones resting upon the flanks of those in front, from morning till night, day in, day out, year after year, with big brown eyes full of foreboding and wonder, their distressed lowing resounds through the air; perhaps the invisible stars are shaken by it; the pillars tremble with the heavy bodies; the sweetish smell of blood rises from the tremendous halls and warehouses, a constant cloud of blood hangs over the whole city; the people's clothes smell of blood, their beds, their churches, their rooms, their food, their wines, their kisses. It is all so tremendous, so unbearably immense, the individual scarcely has a name any longer, the separate thing nothing, nothing to differentiate it. Numbered streets, why not numbered people, perhaps numbered according to the dollars they earn with the blood of cattle, with the soul of the world? Another page. An autumn night, a mad storm and rain. There is a street, Halsted Street—I lived near it—it's thirty miles long, hopelessly long, as long as all the misery and wretchedness which it harbours; they call it the longest street in the world, and it is that, the new road to Golgotha. There are houses there which seem to consist only of refuse and garbage—one has to burn the garbage in front of the doors in order not to be stifled in it; there are dark dirty corners with ruined barracks in which a hundred families live in a dozen holes so that the life which is crammed into them spills out of the window and on hot nights men, women and babies lie about on iron balconies on top of one another like sardines. There are bazaars where all kinds of trash are sold which this tangled mass of wormlike humanity imagines it needs for its nightmare existence. There is a swarm of cement-coloured children with greedy, criminal eyes and rust and smoke and dirt and mountains of shreds of paper and broken-down automobiles and commercial signs in every language in the world, and the stench of benzine and the stench of sweat and the fumes of blood. Well, to come to the point. I went out that night I have mentioned; new tenants had moved in next to me, an Irish family of five; all the money that they had saved had been stolen from them at the station and their despair set the whole house in commotion; their sobbing and complaining irritated me. I had an appointment at midnight with Joshua Cooper, who was going to Louisiana for a few months; he had asked me to meet him at a bar on Twenty-second Street, also a sweet neighbourhood. From far away I already heard wild screams, at first I thought it was the rain beating on the corrugated sheet-iron roofs, then I saw a gang of fellows running and twenty feet ahead of them a colossal negro. Beyond a shadow of doubt, it is my Joshua. He is almost naked, they have torn his clothes off; he is actually flying; his good black face distorted with the fear of death—such an expression I have never seen before or since on any human being—he rushes along, swinging his legs in tremendous strides, his arms stretched forward, and on his forehead, exactly in the middle, there gapes a small wound from which a thin stream of blood runs down over his nose, mouth and chin. The second of his dashing by teaches me what is in store for him; it is all over with him. Already his pursuers are catching up. Twelve or fifteen youths. Yelling like animals, mad with rage. I am nailed to the spot. The storm carries away my umbrella; I don't even notice it, my hat is gone; I am standing at a corner of a house; I don't notice it. I have already said I am a hard devil, but at that time . . . run, my good friend, run, Joshua, I stammered aloud to myself; these twelve or fifteen fellows . . . there was nothing of the human being left about them—beasts? Why, every beast has the soul of a Quaker compared to theirs. They were people to whom robbing and murder was a business, they were people who silence you by a blow in the face and think less of it than others of breaking a window; Acherontic figures, the two-legged beasts of the suburbs; we haven't that kind in this country, the most depraved here reminds one still that a mother has borne him; their most infamous trick consists in devising crimes which they then ascribe to the negroes; this, of course, proceeds from some intellectual centre—as formerly in Russia, when the Jews were massacred—and is called lynch law. No, not if I get to be as old as Methuselah, shall I ever forget my Joshua fleeing before those howling brutes, with the swiftness of a ghost, the stream of blood running over his innocent black face and his arms stretched out in front of him. I never saw him again, I never heard of him again. God knows where his carcass is rotting."

4.

Warschauer got up heavily, walked over to Etzel, who was sitting on the edge of the sofa, and tapped him on the forehead with his finger, once, twice, until the boy raised his eyes to him. The picture of the negro running through the stormy night with the blood trickling over his face was almost beyond endurance, he felt cold to the very bowels, involuntarily he made a parrying gesture. "Well, little boy," said Warschauer, sitting down beside him and placing his hand upon his shoulder, "have you enough of it?" Etzel shook his head. "I shan't have enough until—" He stopped with his brows contracted. "Well—until . . ." "Until I know everything about you, everything, everything!" Warschauer shook his head with ironic concern. "Everything is quite a lot; everything, everything—is your usual presumptuousness, Mohl. But you are in luck, I am in full swing. If you will give me your hand a little, your delicate aristocratic little hand, and let me hold it between my paws, I'll be a nice uncle and will go on spinning my yarn." Almost greedily he snatched at the hand, Etzel unwillingly putting up with a tenderness which was repulsive to him, only because it was demanded as a payment. The gas flame sputtered and a fat black fly buzzed about among the papers on the desk.

The monotonous droning, reminding one of the dull chant of a Sunday school superintendent, began again. Etzel succeeded in freeing his hand from the mushy warm one enclosing it, but was careful to avoid any other motion. "It would be a false conception, little Mohl, if you thought of me over there as a sort of Isaiah foretelling the destruction of the world with raging and flaming prophecies. Not a trace of it. In the first place, downfall is out of the question over there, a conception discovered by a few professors with belletristic interests in order to produce a sensation about the catalepsy of soul which has overtaken Europe; in the second place the seeing eye acts as a regulator to the suffering heart. Since most people are struck with blindness, they suffer all the more. The person who sees becomes cold—a cruel truth, but if it were not so, how could we, you and I, get up every morning out of bed, put on our shoes and stockings, read the newspapers again, and go to Frau Bobike's? How would that be possible? And as for me, I suffer exclusively from myself. To suffer from others is a swindle. Let a person only suffer enough for himself and he need not fear that he will ossify. We know far more of one another than . . . we know. I had a burden to carry. I had things behind me. You know, at least, part of it. I had to take care to remove Waremme's sting, you understand; that gradually became a cardinal point. I had to calculate, to settle the accounts. The Jew exists to settle accounts. That is what God has intended him for. Warschauer. Warschauer *versus* Waremme, you understand. The one side and the other: two parties. Europe and the past; America and the future: more and more this became the leit-motif. And don't imagine that I shall ever waste another word about that damned Maurizius affair; that is over, I tell you; I don't intend to waste another thought upon it; you may do what you like." He remained threateningly silent for a few minutes; seeing that Etzel kept quiet, he continued: "That was the story of my friend Joshua. From my point of view he was a martyr. Today martyrs do not arouse very much attention any more, there are too many. I myself don't take any stock in martyrs. They are an obstacle; they keep things back. One must shape one's fate. Any idiot can succumb and sacrifice himself. The East has given us this faith in martyrs, this adoration of martyrs. There, for example, is the Russian soul, covering millions of square miles of earth and celebrating orgies of martyrdom. That's a bad state, dear Mohl. They lack effort, quite simply those modest small efforts which go to make up a sum. I went about over there in ignorance for a long time until a man opened my eyes. You shall now hear about this man, for he is the reason that I got where I now am. He was to a certain extent the first link in a long chain. His name was La Due, Hamilton La Due. A moderately well-to-do salesman, forty or forty-two years old. He had been born in the West, on the coast of the Pacific, where fresh gay unprejudiced child-like people live. His knowledge was about that of a German non-commissioned officer of recruits; his personal charm something which one does not find in this part of the world. Not that he was in the least handsome or elegant, none of these; but sympathy and kindness and guilelessness poured from him like steam from a kettle. He had a lot of acquaintances in the city, but of what he did—besides supporting himself, I mean—no one had any real conception. I assume that he sought an escape by simply plunging into something different with the stealthy exuberance of a child playing a forbidden game. I got to know him one day when I was inquiring at a juvenile correctional institution about a young girl who had been there for some time because she had taken to drink. I was standing below on the steps when a green police-automobile, as big as a moving van, drove up and out of this huge vehicle, entirely alone, there jumped a little boy of perhaps twelve; sullen and morose, he sprang up the staircase, two steps at a time, just like a habitué of the place. He was just about to disappear through the entrance—the policemen could scarcely follow him—when my La Due came out, seized him quickly by the collar and asked what was the matter. Well, and what was it? He had stolen a penholder and an eraser in school. A criminal, and one who had been previously convicted, too. Just think of it, a penholder and an eraser. La Due at once went with him into the office and then came back, leading the boy by the hand. He had stood bail for him. He told me about it laughingly. I have never yet met anyone so easy to talk to. 'Come along with me,' he suggested, 'I have something to do in the district prison.' He deposited the boy in some shop or other and then took me with him to Maxwell Street. On the way he forced a cake of chocolate upon me, apparently because it was very unpleasant to him to be in anyone's society without being able to give him something. He always had his pockets full, he was constantly distributing cigarettes, boxes of figs, little volumes of poetry, a stick of sealing wax, little paper favours, whatever he happened to have with him. All the while he was laughing and stammering, gazing about curiously with his opossum face, calling 'Hello, Frank,' across the street, or slapping Henry encouragingly on the shoulder as he went by. In Maxwell Street a Jew who had recently emigrated from Kiev had been arrested on the charge of falsifying records, but he protested his innocence and La Due had interested a lawyer in him; he was to meet the lawyer there. When we arrived, the lawyer was not yet there; we waited awhile in the so-called board-room, where there was a pestilential smell. La Due tripped gaily about, singing; he looked as if it were his birthday. A frightful noise caused us to go up to the first floor; they had arrested six negroes and negresses, I no longer remember why—they were figures from the inferno, there were two prostitutes among them, and a leprous old man dancing about on one leg with rage. La Due took part in the negotiations, at the end of five minutes he had calmed the brawling, squabbling group; one of the furies, the witch-like one, thickly rouged, with a goitre, even joked with him, moving her little Japanese parasol, which she always kept open above her head, to and fro with horrible coquetry. It was a scene which turned my skin to goose-flesh. I stepped into the street for a moment, the confused tangle of people and motor-trucks, the whirling eddies of dust, the screaming colours of the advertisements, the lead-coloured sky, it was a moment when one no longer understands one's own existence. Perhaps you are on the moon, I thought, perhaps this is a city in the moon and these are its inhabitants, these ghosts and furies are living in deserts of craters and lava. And then suddenly there stood La Due before me, with his beaming birthday-face; he had divided a large California orange, the size of a cocoanut, in two, and handed me half of it. He had bought a whole basket full at once and the gang of arrested negroes had at once seized upon it, which the attendants had allowed with a shrug of their shoulders. Finally, the lawyer came, we were taken to see the imprisoned Jew; he was cowering in a cage; the whole prison consisted of iron cages like the one in which the Jew was cowering. When he saw us he began to sob aloud. La Due sat down beside him on his wooden bed, stroked him tenderly on the head and told him to tell us how it had all happened. The man became like another person, in a dialect which could scarcely be understood he pictured his misfortune, it really seemed that he had been the victim of some treachery; in any case, La Due was able to calm him about his prospects. The curious thing was only how he had heard of him, and of the hundreds and hundreds of others for whom he was constantly on the go. That remained a riddle to me. Gradually I became fairly familiar with his life, since he took German lessons from me; I don't know today whether he wanted to help me, or whether he really was so eager to learn. He had no assistants, he went on his hunting in the slums alone, not advised or sent by anyone. The thing was obviously based upon a kind of snowball system. For example, after he had helped the Jew in Maxwell Street, six other Jewish immigrants at once appealed to him. Jews were particularly dear to his heart, Jews and negroes. What he accomplished he did himself, according to his own lights, from person to person. He had no welfare people around him nor backing him up. He did not swim in the great stream of philanthropy. He was completely indifferent to where the millions for philanthropy came from and for what they were used. Perhaps he was scarcely conscious that his own activities belonged in quite a different category of human service. He never allowed himself to pass a judgment, he was too respectful for that and thought too little of himself. I said to him once that the whole of social work was a thimbleful of milk in a quart of ink. He looked at me sadly. 'Really, do you think so, is that so?' he asked, as he shook his head inconsolably. I am sure that he did not admire the people who undertook social work on a big scale, but there was one, a woman, the Samaritan of Hull House, the founder of the juvenile court, whom he worshipped on bended knees. One merely had to mention her name and his eyes became moist. One day he came to me in an unusual state of excitement and told me what had occurred the night before. A fourteen-year-old boy had come to Hull House in a state of great fright and anxiety, had asked to speak to Miss Blank, and, when he was told that Miss Blank had gone to bed he had thrown himself on the floor, thrashing about in despair. Miss Blank must come, Miss Blank must come. So Miss Blank was sent for; she knows the boy; he is one of her protégés. Alone with her, he falls on his knees, implores her to save him; the police are after him, he has killed his father. For what reason? For months, night after night, with the frightful dullness of a piece of machinery, his father had cruelly misused his mother; the boy had not been able to look on any longer and had stuck a kitchen-knife into him from behind. I should like to have been present at what took place then, it must have been something quite unprecedented. La Due had gotten to Hull House, where he often looked in for tips at midnight; he had gotten the account fresh from the mouth of Miss Blank and he later took the boy, who had become quite submissive, to the police station. He pictured the incident with his western impetuosity. Miss Blank had listened to the boy and then begun gently, but decidedly, to persuade him to give himself up and admit the deed. He refused passionately. He had not done anything wrong, he had dispatched a common brute, nothing else; the world was a better place to live in with that brute no longer in it; the deed deserved praise, not punishment, not imprisonment, no, no, no. His eyes glowed, the whole boy was aglow. To live was his right, to have done away with that monster was his right; father or no father, that did not concern him and anyone who is interested in that has no heart in his body and no sense in his head; no such person could know how that brute had tormented his poor wife, and so on. Miss Blank knew the boy's obstinacy; he was one of her most gifted protégés, but tremendously wild and uncontrolled. With the utmost exertion she slowly convinces him that he has no right to take anyone else's life. I am only repeating, for it is not at all my point of view—why should one not cut such an ulcer from the body of the human race? However, what I think about it is incidental. She persuades him that for his own sake, for his own honour and pride he must take his punishment; the deed cannot be concealed; how shameful if they must search for him, arrest him, if instead of his giving himself up like a man and a hero, he should look like a coward and a liar! And how could she then ever believe in him again? That is the chief purport of her talk, that then she could no longer believe in him; that makes the deepest impression. Finally she softens him, he falls on her neck weeping, his obstinacy is broken. It has taken hours and hours, with arguments and counter-arguments, with examples and confessions, with hesitations and spasmodic reserves, with pleas and arguments and appeals on both sides. I am only telling you this to show you what kind of people they are over there, how strong and unyielding, how readily they are accessible to one another, how tightly intertwined. What La Due later did for the boy was less decisive, although not less important. Thanks to his tireless efforts, the boy's punishment was a light one, La Due having interested the newspapers in him and paid one of the best lawyers out of his own pocket. The better I got to know him the more he cast off his modest exterior. I saw a human being who, for all his insignificant exterior, represented a unity, the crystal formed from the raw material. There were probably countless persons like him, and the more I looked into this tremendous complex the more I became convinced that he actually was only one of countless men like himself whom I had accidentally found. This shook my European pride profoundly, just as an Alexandrine Greek would perhaps have been disconcerted if he had accidentally met a gentle Nazarene in Gaul. But a Nazarene. . . . La Due had no message, he was no evangelist, he had simple childlike friendliness, nothing else. He had no moral principles, no Puritanism, none of the 'He that is not with me is against me.' He probably did not think about matters at all. He accepted everything as it was, the frightful and the pleasant. He never grumbled; he never scolded; he never showed any irritation; he was never out of humour. If he was dog-tired and someone asked him a direction he would, if possible, take the person to his destination and moreover entertain him with his cheerful chatter. When Ethel Green, the distinguished film star, was shot by a jealous lover, he could not control his distress, there was not a jot of difference between him and any shop-girl. Yes, he even made a pilgrimage to her coffin, as did a hundred thousand others. For he was just exactly like many other people and nevertheless he seemed a magical man among the masses, magical like the focus of a crystal lens. In that tremendous nation, with its tremendous cities, tremendous mountains and torrents and prairies, its tremendous riches and tremendous poverty, its tremendous factories and tremendous fear of anarchy and revolution, there in the midst of all that we find harmless, little La Due . . . how shall I put it, as a new kind of human being. I could not cease wondering. Through him I learned to understand that the whole is still an unleavened mass. 'Oh, we are so young,' he would say constantly, with his naïve enthusiasm, 'we are so frightfully, wonderfully young.' And that is it, that is the fact. The period of preparation. A baking-oven of the nations. Everything is still mixing and growing. Nothing has gotten cold yet. South and North, East and West all pushing towards the centre. A white world and a black world pushing up against each other; the negro, a creditor with ancient scores to collect, ceaselessly pushing on, taking parts of cities, overflooding provinces, with Asia behind him as a sinister threat, and then, the actual fated opponent Russia, preparing for a world duel, Russia on the other side of the planet. . . . What was there for me to do over there with my imaginary intellectual mission? What should I, laden with things of the mind, do over there? There was material, material, material, after a hundred years one might begin to talk of a soul. In contrast to this glowing crater,

INTERREGNUM

Europe was a cabinet of antiquities. I had gone far enough west in every sense to be able to turn around with a good conscience. Without my doing anything external or internal about it, I felt that I was driven back to where I had come from. The rebirth of George Warschauer was inevitable. I had become constantly more familiar with the life of the millions of Jewish emigrants; Hamilton La Due had been at home in the world of the ghetto for many years; his best friends were among the Russian Jews. 'Those are wonderful people,' he would exclaim upon every occasion when he could praise them, 'wonderful people,' and he would tell story after story of their pride and devotion and gratitude. There is a historical and psychological process going on there, a fusion of elements which, on account of the differences of blood, is producing something like a new kind of soul. I took part in this sombre life. Broken by European catastrophes, having landed over there, these Jews have, under a cloak of eastern heaviness, a breath-taking speed. I associated with Chassidic scholars; I dug my way through our old writings and I saw what I had missed. I could no longer make up for it. From a certain day on I felt myself old. I had not put anything in the granary; to the times which I saw coming I had nothing to give. So it was necessary that I should seek safety. That was it, to find a little place between the two raging furnaces on the right and on the left. It would not be a Tusculum; it would be at best a hidden observer's post with some slight embers remaining aglow from the great oriflamme of extinguished ages. Which storm will blow out this tragic remnant, the storm from the right, or the storm from the left? Which do you think, Mohl? For in the decades since my flight from myself and my search through the world, that sleepy moujik has stretched his frame; there has been an uprising of the people everywhere between the Vistula and Lake Baikal. One can be prepared for something, the good people here who are sunk in inactive wishing and desiring up to their waists haven't the slightest inkling of what is ahead of them; they dream of inheriting the knout and of taking possession of this inheritance, meantime they are musically delighted by the elegiac songs of olden days on their gramophones. . . . Do you know this, Mohl? The boat song of the Volga, an incomparable alarum, and they edify themselves with it as if it were a pious hymn . . . Have you never heard it?"

He stood up, spread out his arms and walked up and down with a thundering step singing with a frighteningly powerful voice: *"Ei ukhnem . . . ei ukhnem . . . yeshcho . . . razik . . . yeshcho darar . . . ei ukhnem. . . ."*

5.

Etzel had likewise gotten up and stood as if extinguished. His one cheek, upon which his hand had rested, was flaming-red, the other was white. He had pushed the joint of his finger into his mouth and was biting it raw. His feverish eyes showed fear and a tremendous helplessness. Dear God, he thought, with his heart standing still; one feels as if one had been in swaddling clothes up to now. One must hold one's ears shut, one cannot listen any longer, one must turn one's eyes away, that fat man with his powerful body will tramp one dead, everything is over life-size, a Polyphemus throwing boulders of rock about. How can I get hold of him, how can I get him back to the one thing I have come for, for which I have taken all this upon me, all this of which in my pitiful ignorance I hadn't the least notion? . . . Etzel felt as if he were racing behind an express train with a wheelbarrow.

His hopes have shrivelled down to nothing. How is his own poor speech to have any effect against this cataract of words, what can he do, in his ignorance and only sixteen years old, when opposed to this world-embracing brain? What does he care about the prisoner in the penitentiary; what do the six-thousand-odd days and nights of imprisonment for a crime of which he was not guilty, mean to him? And yet another day and yet another night, but how does that concern him? He has experienced something else, he knows of other horrors, to him all this is like water running off an oilskin; what does he care about the misfortune of one, the guilt of another? He has constructed a system of justice in which the single individual does not count, *ad usum Delphini,* presumably. He had been so near, one question more perhaps, and the secret would have been discovered, just a second, he should have begged: How was it when you took matters in hand? Instead of that he had dragged him along with his damned Waremme-Warschauer problem and he had been victimized and made a fool of and was biting his finger raw. He summoned all his courage, and when Warschauer ceased his song, he placed himself in front of him and said: "In this way we have gotten entirely away from Maurizius." "Yes, we have, you wretched toad," replied Warschauer furiously, "just spare me your nastiness, will you?" "Yes, I'm quite willing to believe that you don't want to hear any more about it," continued Etzel bitterly, "but the toad must croak even if it runs the danger of being devoured by the eagle." Warschauer bowed sarcastically. "You're very quick-witted, a very quick-witted toad," he remarked mockingly. Etzel's face was burning, a challenging laugh escaped his lips. "The thing doesn't give you any peace yourself," he said. "Your oath, professor, think of your oath. It may be that you have forgotten about it, only I don't believe that *it* has forgotten, you know, there, inside of you," he stuck his finger out towards Warschauer's breast. The latter retreated a step in silence. "Yes," insisted Etzel with a tumultuous onset of audacity. "That inside of you, you cannot cheat *it;* that is what has driven you around the world so; for that you have to pay, you and the man in the penitentiary and the old man and I, one grain of guilt and a bushel of suffering, yes, yes, yes. . . ." He was suddenly as if beside himself.

Warschauer pressed his lips together, went silently to the door and opened it wide. "Young Mohl," he said coldly, "you may, you can regard yourself as put out. Get along." Etzel hesitated, turning white. Warschauer looked into the dark court. *"Ei ukhnem,"* he began to sing again as if he were already alone, but interrupted himself at once to say commandingly to the boy, "Well, are you going?" "I haven't any door-key, I can't get out," said Etzel obstinately. Warschauer took the key out of his pocket and held it out to him. Etzel took it and walked slowly across the threshold. Warschauer banged the door after him. While Etzel felt his way down the stairs, he again heard through the closed door the *"Ei ukhnem,"* like a sarcastic refrain. Tears of anger and helplessness clouded his vision.

The front door was open. In the hallway Paalzow's boy was leaning against the wall, holding a whispered conversation with a nasty-looking customer. When he perceived Etzel he made a spiral motion of his body in his direction and stared at him in an ugly fashion with his hands in his trousers pockets. Etzel paid no attention to him and walked on. "I'd like to meet you sometime in the moonlight," Paalzow's boy called to him threateningly. "Really? And why do you need moonlight for the purpose?" Etzel replied over his shoulder. Then it was that his strength suddenly left him and that he lay down in front of the gin-shop. Perhaps a kind of fear of ghosts contributed too, it was the first time so far as he remembered that he had had such a feeling, but at every street corner he thought that the huge negro with his arms outstretched and the thread of blood running down his face was dashing towards him. He did not, however, feel any better when he had lain down upon the bricks, his nerves were tense to the breaking point, he saw wooden bridges with endless trains of oxen moving over them and it seemed to him as if he heard the *Ei ukhnem* painfully roaring from their thousand throats. He saw the Jew sobbing in his iron cage and the eleven-year-old murderer sticking the kitchen-knife into his father's back. He saw Hamilton La Due kissing the suppurating wound of a leper and the Chinaman lying in the cellar surrounded by his friends. And constantly meddling all the time, with the other pictures, was the negro with the thread of blood running down his face, fleeing from his pursuers in mad fear. "Oh, God, mother," he sighed like a little boy, when he finally got up and staggered towards the Anklamerstrasse. In addition to everything else he was, of course, extremely tired. When he put his watch on the table next to his bed, it was twenty minutes of five and day was breaking at the windows. He did not have to make any light. Accustomed as he was to spread insect powder over the red cotton pillows and the coarse linen sheets spotted with his blood, he did so now again. He fell asleep at once, and slept as if drunk. A glowing wheel with saw-like edges whirled madly against his breast, it was an impression from earliest childhood which sometimes returned; he knew in his sleep that he was having a fever, bedbugs as big as the roaches in Warschauer's room crept over his neck and face; Frau Schneevogt came and put the breakfast tray on the table; he was aware of it in his sleep, and, sleepless in the depths of his soul, he slept on. Shortly afterwards, so it seemed, the woman came in with lunch; grumblingly, she took the untouched breakfast out again, he saw and heard her in his waking-sleeping condition; he felt the fiery saw again and thought: If it cuts me, God will be doing me an injustice; I must first speak to my mother and the other thing . . . another day gone by. . . . Finally he opened his eyes and his head was clear, his shirt was hot and wet and sticking to his body, his legs were so heavy that he could not move them. I'm sick, he thought, that's the last straw. I've plagued myself with that nasty devil for six weeks and don't know any more than I did before, nothing, not a thing. What will happen if I get sick? That simply can't be; it's wasting too much time. Why did Anna Jahn go to France with him? That did not come about by fair play, he simply glossed over that; that's the most mysterious part of the story. What shall I do? I had better wait now until he comes here, not budge, he will be sorry and come, then I shall have the drop on him. He had a vision; his seething brain produced a remarkable clairvoyance, for everything came to pass later on; he saw Warschauer here in the room, walking up and down like a drum-major and then . . . did he talk of the "thing" then? His clairvoyance did not reach so far, his wishes did not dare to pretend the truth to this extent. . . . Why am I so cold? It's lucky that it's already June, so that I need not have a fire.

The harsh voice of Melitta penetrated from the next room. He listened. They must not notice that I am sick, he thought; if they do they may send me to the hospital, where they'll ask for papers, and that would be a filthy mess. What's the matter with me anyway? A sore throat; I can't swallow decently; it will all be over by tomorrow. And in order to make an unsuspicious impression in case one of the Schneevogt ladies should come in, he took a volume of Ghisels' from the shelf, which he had put up on the wall, and opened it. Then he heard the hard voice of Melitta from the next room saying desperately: "Such injustice cries to heaven. A thing like that makes one want to spit upon the whole gang of humans. A person'd better take a cord and hang 'emselves." The wall was so thin and the door closed so badly that he could hear every word and also the anxious attempts of mother Schneevogt to calm her. The door bell interrupted them; both women left the room and everything was quite still. She said the right thing, thought Etzel, as—with wide eyes and an oppressive feeling of a debt unpaid—he stared up at the ceiling; how can one stand it? And everyone lives on, even those who say they can't, and I, too. What about justice? Is there really such a thing as justice? Don't we merely imagine it, as pious persons imagine a paradise? Perhaps our intelligence is not capable of recognizing justice, perhaps it lies beyond the possibility of our understanding. But then everything that one does would be so temporary and everything that one attains would be so senseless. There must, there must, there must be some squaring of accounts; it's now eighteen years and nine months, dear God, there must, there must. Yes, what must there be, Etzel? You are erecting an adamant *must* in your sixteen-year-old rebellious soul, but by what power in heaven or on earth is it approved? He closed his eyes and saw Joshua Cooper with the blood running down his face from forehead to chin, an emblem of hopelessness. A cold shiver ran down his spine, he snatched at the book, which was still open in his hand, and on the page to which he had just turned, he read the following lines: "On the fullest glass there can still float the petal of the rose and on the petal of this blossom there is room for ten thousand angels."

What words! Like a star! He knew them, but he had never been able to understand them before; now after all that he had experienced they shone forth like starlight. To the man who had written this he must go that very same hour. There could be no further hesitation, nor delay; if there is anyone in the world who can answer the question, it is the man who wrote those words. Fever, what of fever, one can't pay any attention to that! It is four o'clock in the afternoon, it will take an hour to get to the West End; the time will not be unfavourable for finding a person at home. Perhaps he would be fortunate enough to find Ghisels at home and willing to receive him. In spite of the heaviness of his limbs and the soreness of his throat, Etzel crept out of bed, washed his face and chest and, slipping into his clothes, left the house.

6.

He went up in the lift to the fourth floor of a detached apartment house and rang the bell at one of the two doors of an apartment. After a fairly long wait, a young man with a nice face and horn-rimmed spectacles appeared. He had left open the doors of the room from which he had emerged, and one could hear voices talking eagerly. In the little hall five or six hats and sticks were hanging up, also a woman's coat. Ah, thought Etzel, and his heart fell into his boots, you're having bad luck, brother Etzel. The young man inquired what he wanted. With a shyness which he simply could not overcome, Etzel replied that he would like to speak to Herr Ghisels—Herr Ghisels, the "Herr" sounded so silly and stiff that his tongue could hardly pronounce it. The young man smiled, with a smile which said, So would many people, and asked for his name. Etzel replied that his name was Andergast, Etzel Andergast, that he had written to Herr Melchior Ghisels about six months ago, and received an answer from him; perhaps Herr Ghisels would remember this. It was the first time in a long while that he had used his own name; he had, of course, never intended to appear in this sacred spot with a mask over his face. But it was nevertheless a curious feeling suddenly to be himself again, not as if he were returning to something familiar, but rather as if he had put on a brand-new suit and did not feel quite comfortable in it, as if it were somewhat constricting. The pleasing young man wanted to know whether he had come about anything in particular. Etzel shook his head. "No, not just that," he replied; he would be satisfied if he could merely see Herr Ghisels, to spend half an hour near him, in the same room with him, would suffice. You are lying, it would not suffice, contradicted an inner voice. The young man smiled again, and looked at the remarkable visitor, not without interest. "Just come in here," he said, "while I ask Herr Ghisels." Etzel entered the narrow antechamber while the young man disappeared. As his knees were trembling and he was a little dizzy, he sat down on a chair; everything about him was silent, he was divided between respectful expectation, fear of being repulsed, and fear of the great moment. If an author—I mean one who like Ghisels brings new ideas into the world and shows the world new paths—could measure what prompts the soul of a boy whom he has touched and who does not take the step of calling upon him without serious internal conflicts, he would summon up all his ingenuity—and his whole heart as well—in order to be prepared for such a meeting. But only a few, the very rarest, are true to themselves in this way; perhaps too it is beyond the power of the human soul always to be what one is in one's creative hours. Perhaps a part of the fear which Etzel felt came from this, the most spiritual fear that there is: How will my picture of him accord with reality? How shall I feel when I have left this house, when I have seen him, heard his voice, listened to his words? What will he say or do; how will he talk or look, and what must take place in order that he shall remain what he is to me? The temptation not to wait for the young man's return, but simply to get up and leave, grew stronger every minute; nothing could happen then, then one would have retained one's God. It lasted so frightfully long. He listened. He heard a monotonous voice narrating. His hearing was so sharpened through fever and excitement that he understood certain distinct words through the two intervening doors. Someone was reading aloud. It was clear that the young man could not announce the inopportune visitor until the reading was over. The electric bell at the front door sounded shrilly. In the rooms inside one did not seem to hear it. The bell resounded again. Etzel considered whether he should open the door but decided that he had not the right to do so. Then through a different door from the one through which the young man had disappeared, there came a woman of thirty-eight or forty. Her bearing and manner told Etzel that she was the mistress of the house. Her face showed traces of great beauty, but looked tired and faded. Etzel had never thought about there being a "woman" here; it surprised him and increased his uneasiness. The woman paused in surprise when she saw the young man and asked: "Didn't the bell just ring?" "Yes, twice, madam," replied Etzel, feeling as if he ought to excuse himself for sitting there so stupidly. The woman opened the door. Outside stood another woman, still very young, bloomingly young, very pretty, with shining eyes and a bright saucy mouth. What ensued was extraordinary. The two women measured one another in silent hostility. The young woman outside seemed disagreeably moved at seeing the other one before her. The impression one received was that the younger woman had definitely counted on not finding her. The mistress of the house drew herself up a little, shrugged her shoulders and laughed a short cooing contemptuous laugh and banged the door. The brutality of the gesture for a person of her shy, melancholy nature had a terrifying quality. Then she stood there with bent head, one side of the blue silk shawl which she wore around her shoulders had slipped off without her noticing it. It was as if she had for a few minutes forgotten everything around her. An indescribably profound grief portrayed itself upon her features. She looked like a stone figure expressing complete absorption in grief. Suddenly she started and walked into the apartment with heavy steps. She did not even glance at Etzel again. He sat huddled in his chair feeling as if he had accidentally picked up an object belonging to someone else. And he had a still more painful impression that Fate did not respect even this door, that here also the tempests of life raged, that not even the exalted man who had written, "On the fullest glass there still may float the petal of the rose and on the leaf of this blossom there is room for ten thousand angels," was spared the perplexities of life, and that waves of passion and of sadness rolled over him too. Now everything was to a certain extent exposed before Etzel's eyes, the holy of holies had become a human abode; and just as one walks with less assurance over a bridge when one knows one of its pillars to be decayed, even though motor trucks cross it, his spirits had now been damped and the ground had become uncertain. Meantime the young man reappeared and asked him courteously to come in.

7.

Melchior Ghisels' house was a refuge for the mentally harassed, for struggling, striving, helpless, shipwrecked, confused men and women. People came to him as to a great physician; often his room was not empty from noon to midnight, people of every age, men and women, writers and artists, actors and students, emigrants and politicians, flocked to him, so that his wife and his most intimate friends were sometimes obliged to protect him from the throng of visitors. He had been in seriously bad health for several years and was no longer equal to the strain. They all hung upon his every word, told him their most intimate concerns, placed their conflicts of conscience and their professional cares before him, wanted him to criticize their works, engaged him in far-reaching discussions on problems of art, religion or philosophy; and there was scarcely one of them who did not end by bowing before a word of authority from his mouth. There were persons in this throng with whom he was by no means on a confidential footing, and of whom he was not even fond, but whose mental needs and financial difficulties occupied him intensely for weeks and months. Then these people disappeared without a trace, and he generally heard nothing further from them. This did not disappoint him nor did he feel betrayed or cheated when a man withdrew himself from his influence or repaid him with ingratitude. This too enriched him. Not in the sense of experience, but in an increase of his extraordinarily profound intuition of life, which made him mild and indulgent, and above all, so understanding that he sometimes became incomprehensible through self-contradiction. He did not take anything about another person lightly, not even the pretentious vacuity of the dilettante; even his sarcasm was conscientious, if one may express oneself thus. What he himself said had, on the other hand, a lightness which is peculiar to the person who completely masters all his resources; to converse with him was a delight because it was so easy. What he communicated seemed to be only what he wished to be free from, thus releasing the recipient from any obligation; by simple acceptance one seemed to be as active, as communicative, as creative, as intellectual and full of knowledge as himself. Everything about him was organized and concentrated, and proceeded from a central point, and that despairing void between the mind and the soul, which is the reason why—out of the legions of gifted persons—not one single great man arises, did not exist. Thus he had the capacity to find an interpretation of his own for all events, and all personalities, for all of the work and all of the destinies which he assimilated within himself, making it fruitful beyond the realm of the merely mental.

That Etzel still half a boy, immature, without experience of the world, with the awakening of his consciousness of life should be drawn as if by a magnet to such a man, the impress of whose personality had reached him only through his books, shows a magnetism, whether one calls it instinct or strength of soul, which the boy also possessed. Of course, the same profound instinct had made him more hesitant and fearful at every step which brought him closer to the object of his fervent esteem. The incident of the two women then became an external symbol for his gnawing doubt as to whether there existed anywhere in this world a creature, even the most tried and exalted, from whom one could learn that which, if it could not be determined and disposed of, made life without value for him altogether.

He entered a large room furnished with beautiful old furniture and found himself at once in the presence of Melchior Ghisels, a man of about fifty, of more than average size, with a well proportioned body, movements and gestures which were naturally free and elegant, a clean-shaven face, a strong, energetically curved nose and deep-set eyes which had a quiet, penetrating, thoughtful, kindly expression. His mouth was small and incomparably expressive; his lips, when silent, pressed tightly, almost painfully tightly, upon each other; whereas, when he spoke, they looked as if Nature —which often produces hypertrophy in these necessary organs—had created them to form words, pregnant, ominous words, characteristic only of this mouth. The effect of the fleshy protruding ears upon this noble head was bizarre, almost unnatural; but just as the mouth was made for speaking, so these red shell-ears seemed to be wide shells made for hearing well and much and accurately.

Asked to take a place, Etzel seated himself silently and modestly somewhat outside the circle of the other visitors. The faces at which he looked without embarrassment almost all pleased him; not one was callous, or vulgar. There were four young men, a white-haired gentleman, and a young girl, who also, curiously enough, had white hair. Ghisels had contented himself with mentioning the name of the new arrival; he omitted all other ceremony. At times he glanced at him with a penetrating glance of slight surprise, raising his black bushy eyebrows slightly. The conversation which had been going on continued; Etzel heard only Melchior Ghisels' voice. He did not hear what the others were saying, nor did he understand the meaning of Ghisels' words; he only had a vague impression of neat formulation of a flow without effort, of the charm of form; he only listened to the words, listened with such thirsty intensity that when the voice ceased, he started imperceptibly and then waited with urgent attention until the sonorous sounds, which covered all the other voices as if with dark wings, rose again. It was an extraordinary pleasure, an extraordinary release. During the weeks of confused conversation with Warschauer-Waremme he had unconsciously become accustomed to his voice, as one becomes accustomed to a daily torture; finally it had become the only voice which he heard; for he had scarcely spoken to anyone else; he had forgotten how a voice which comes from the soul sounds, what truth and quiet pulsation it has. It was the difference between the sound of a gold piece and that of a leaden coin when one clinks them on the pavement to test their genuineness.

"Are you not well?" asked Ghisels suddenly, turning towards Etzel. "You look very white. May I not offer you some refreshment? Anything at all, just tell me." Etzel shook his head, thanked him; the words tumbled over one another; he smiled; the smile seemed to please Ghisels, for he placed his hand for a moment upon his shoulder. Etzel understood that he meant that he was to be patient a moment, that he would not be sent away without having been listened to. As a matter of fact, the gathering broke up soon after this, the white-haired girl and the young man with the horn-rimmed spectacles remained a few minutes longer and Ghisels talked with them a little while longer in a facetious vein. When they had finally left, the mistress of the house came in and gently persuaded Ghisels to lie down on the sofa. He really looked extremely tired; the woman waited until he had lain down; then she wrapped his legs in a camel's-hair rug and asked whether she should open the window. She spoke in a curious way; she scarcely opened her lips or separated her teeth, it was all so tense, she seemed so accustomed to suffering, even in her walk and her glance. Again Etzel had the sensation of cloudy sadness and of a foundation which was not firm. "I am afraid that I am molesting you?" stammered Etzel. "Don't let that trouble you, no," replied Ghisels, and to his wife: "Yes, dearest, open the window; it is such a beautiful evening." The woman opened the window and silently left the room. "Just look," said Ghisels, pointing towards the western sky. Etzel looked. As if this house were the first, or the last, of the whole city, the tops of the pines stretched away beneath the windows towards the horizon like an even carpet of green. Over this hung a claret-coloured sky, the whole of which was broken up at regular intervals with patches of purple and gold clouds like glowing girders. While Etzel was seeking with a concentration of adamant to collect his thoughts and hesitating how to express them, Ghisels turned his eyes towards this display of tragic and magnificent colour.

In a few words Etzel touches upon his relation to Ghisels' work. In order not to seem presumptuous, he only hints that his attitude towards the principal problems of life has been decisively influenced by Ghisels' writings. But he has not contented himself with reflection, he has gone a step further. This is the meaning which he thinks he has discovered in the writings: that one must go a step further. Melchior Ghisels becomes noticeably more attentive. The matter is this: His father is a high legal official. Between his father and himself a secret antagonism has developed—during the last year it has become acute. He has felt constantly less in harmony with his father's general point of view, his interpretation of life and his static attitude towards the world, although he is otherwise a man of great capacity. Yes, he is an outstanding figure, incorruptible, honest and cultivated. Of course he, Etzel, has from his earliest childhood heard much of his father's public influence. Bad things, often very bad things. These things gradually made him unbearably uneasy. Everything seemed turned topsy-turvy, his whole home life together with all the rest. His father's attitude towards the law and towards justice was dominated by something which he could designate only with the word "desiccated." A dead tradition. A law without any soul. He suddenly spoke fluently and with fervour. There were discussions; these discussions had led to a break; he had fled to his relatives; he had been obliged to free himself from the pressure of a relationship in which sincerity no longer dwelt; so long as he eats his father's bread he is, as it were, in his father's service; for the present he only needs the opportunity to collect himself and come to his senses and look about. One reads and one hears so much that is puzzling and tormenting, on the subject of law and justice; he has the impression of a mental epidemic, of a mental pall, and if one does not clear up this subject for oneself and get straightened out in this regard towards the world, it is simply impossible for a young man to erect a foundation for his life, and therefore he has decided to ask Herr Ghisels for his advice and opinion.

Extraordinary boy! Even here, before one who is to a certain extent his master, he kept silent about the real, the fateful fact, just as he had kept it from Camill Raff and Robert Thielemann. And just as he had used his relation with his mother as a screen in his conversation with Thielemann, so he now used his relation with his father. Was it a delicate sense of shame before his own "deed," which often acts as a deterrent in highly gifted natures, or fear that someone would tie his hands? Or was it doubt of himself, because of the fantastic colouring which his venture might wear in the eyes of the "experienced"? Although he had reached the point where he no longer attached the slightest importance to the experiences of the experienced, and had the conviction that a Melchior Ghisels could never make himself their advocate—he who had called experience a monument over a tomb. Or was he silent from a kind of superstition, as if his success depended upon silence, or was it the magic spell which the constantly recurring vision of the convict in the penitentiary cast over him? Whatever it was, one or all of these causes, it was stronger than his will and determination, stronger than the boundless confidence which he felt towards Melchior Ghisels. The latter had listened to him with growing interest. "You are very young?" he inquired, for Etzel seemed to him even younger than he was. "I shall soon be seventeen," replied Etzel. Ghisels nodded. "A large number of your contemporaries are still living by borrowings from their own future," he said, resting the back of his neck against his folded hands. "I am the last person to criticize that. As to the present day, we are all badly off. But borrowing upon the future has dangers which one cannot foresee. It always reminds me a little of the Indian child marriages. Those children are ruins at twenty." He paused and went on hesitatingly. "You seem to me breathless over some incisive experience. . . ." Etzel turned scarlet. Good heavens, he thought in fright and astonishment, that man does really see into one. But Ghisels made a gesture as if to beg the boy not to regard his remark as importunate or coercive. "Just forget that, don't pay any attention to it, as if it had not been said. I see that there is something there which must be respected. What brings you to me is nothing new to me—unfortunately. It is a crisis which has gone beyond making harmless circles in a pool. A few years ago one could still console oneself with the opinion that it was this or that isolated case, one could adjust oneself to that—one can get used to the isolated instance, but today we are threatened with the collapse of the whole structure which we have been building for two thousand years. There is an ingrained sick desire to break things down, in the most sensitive human beings. If this cannot be stopped—and I fear it is already too late—it must lead within the next fifty years to a frightful collapse, far worse than any wars or revolutions up to the present. Curiously, the disturbance often proceeds from those who live in the delusion that they are called upon to safeguard what are termed our most sacred possessions. This is evidently the case with your differences with your father. I have often discussed the matter with my friends. Most of them blame politics, that is, what is called politics today, a corroding acid which devours all human relationships. I have observed it much. I have another comparison for it: an oven in which the heart of our youth is burned to cinders." Etzel with his hands flat between his knees leaned forward and replied eagerly: "I understand, you are speaking less of politics than of the social discipline in general. . . ." Ghisels smiled. "Yes, or of the false, or lacking, discipline, which rests upon force. . . ." "Certainly, I have always felt that, and therefore I could never adjust myself. They always try to sound out one's point of view. Then, the person who has the desired point of view may act contemptibly. I don't know whether one may speak with the editorial *we*. I should not like to do so. I once saw a modern play in which a Gymnasium student said *we* on the stage for a whole evening: *we* demand this, *we* think that, *we* are taking this or that path. . . . It was quite ludicrous. . . ." "Yes," replied Ghisels with good-natured sarcasm, "the impression became current that it was a prime accomplishment to be twenty years old. A state of affairs in which we of forty and fifty are not entirely guiltless. And yet there is a unified spirit, since there is a unified despair. But you wanted to say something different. . . ." "No, no, only what you have just said," replied Etzel in a passionate glow, his features becoming so animated that he looked quite pink and no longer felt either fever or pain. "I only wanted to say just that. We must despair if justice is made a wanton. Why, everything rests upon justice, doesn't it? One reads in old books that soldiers wept if the flag of their regiment was disgraced. What shall we do if the only flag we still look up to is disgraced day after day and moreover by the standard bearers themselves? Justice, it seems to me, is the beating heart of the world. Is that so, or is it not?" "It is so, dear friend," corroborated Ghisels. "Justice and love were originally sisters. In our civilization they are no longer even distant relatives. One may give many explanations without explaining anything. We no longer have a people, a people constituting the body politic; consequently, that which we call democracy is founded upon an amorphous mass and cannot dispose itself and elevate itself intelligently and strangles all ideality. Perhaps we need a Cæsar. But where shall he come from? And we must fear the chaos which would produce him. What the best people do in the best case is to provide a commentary for an earthquake. The rest is . . . so." He blew over the back of his hand as if blowing away a feather. "I should only like to tell you one thing," he continued. "Think about it a little; perhaps it will help you on a step, for we can only move forward very, very slowly, and step by step; between each step and the next, there lies all of the weakness, all of the omissions, all of the delusion, even the noble delusion, of which we are guilty. It is not a means of salvation, not a tremendous truth which I have in mind, but perhaps, as I have said, it is a hint, a useful suggestion. . . . What I mean is this: good and evil are not determined by the intercourse of people with one another, but entirely by a man's relations with himself. Do you understand?" "Yes, I understand," said Etzel dropping his eyes. "But, do not regard me as ununderstanding. . . . I must say this . . . it is an example . . . if my friend or the father of my friend . . . or anyone close to me . . . or even someone not close to me, if he is imprisoned unjustly, and I . . . what shall I do . . . how does my relation to myself help me in such a case? Surely there is only one thing which I must demand: right and justice! Shall I leave him in torment? Shall I forget him? Shall I say, how does that concern me? What then is justice if I do not see it through, I, myself, I, Etzel Andergast . . ."

He had gotten up involuntarily and was looking Ghisels in the face as if he were demanding right and justice of him and indeed this very moment. Ghisels too rose from his recumbent posture to a sitting one. For a time he returned the boy's glance steadfastly, then he looked out towards the fading sky, and said gently, as he stretched out both arms: "I have nothing to reply to that except: Forgive me, I am but a feeble man." For a moment he looked as infinitely tormented as the painting of the Crucified by Matthias Grunewald. Etzel's head sank as if he had received a blow. He at once understood the magnificence of the answer and the tremendous resignation which it contained. And there was something else which he understood in his heart, which had become heavy indeed: The ten thousand angels upon the rose-leaf were a metaphor, a poem, a mysterious and beautiful symbol, nothing further, oh, nothing more than that.

The door of the adjoining room opened and in the lighted rectangle the black figure of the mistress of the house appeared, saying in her broken toneless voice: "You must come to dinner, now, Ghisels," Melchior Ghisels got up, painfully as only the suffering move; he took Etzel's hand and pressed it with almost anxious warmth. Etzel almost kissed it. On the street below a cab was driving by, he signalled it and fell into it half fainting, as it stopped in front of the house.

CHAPTER XII

I.

When Herr von Andergast, after a sleepless night, for which perhaps only the miserable bed at the inn was responsible—although the Spartan solicitor-general was not in the habit of paying any attention to such discomforts—entered the cell at seven o'clock in the morning, Maurizius was sitting at the table reading. The convict put the book aside, got up and watched with a peculiar fixedness as the warden shut the door again, not without an expression of curious astonishment on his alcoholic bloated face. "Good morning," said Herr von Andergast, in pleasant tones, whose artificiality could not, however, deceive the ear of the prisoner. "Good morning," was his precise military answer. "Have you gotten a little rest?" A bow was the reply. "May I ask what you are reading?" Herr von Andergast took the book up, it was the chronicle of the city of Rothenburg by Sebastian Dehner. "Ah, does that interest you? Superfluous question, since you are reading it." "One gets a good picture of how the people lived, or rather how they were prevented from living." "Hem, I don't know. The people in those days lived more vigorously than today." "More patiently, at any rate. When their houses were plundered and their cattle killed, they complained to the Kaiser, and if the Kaiser did not help them, they undertook pilgrimages of intercession. The people were always very patient, they are so still. All government is based upon that, upon the patience of the people; that is how governments manage to muddle along." Herr von Andergast frowned. "You are bitter," he said with an obvious desire to be indulgent, "but let us not waste our valuable time in polemics. You had the intention . . . I hope that you have not changed your mind. You see I have acted upon your . . . your suggestion and placed myself at your disposal for the day." The old rigidity came over Maurizius. With a fixed glance he answered: "I shall do what I have promised." He leaned against the wall. Herr von Andergast drew the chair towards the window and sat down upon it. He made a cordial gesture towards Maurizius to suggest that he should also sit down, the gesture he had made at the beginning of the conversation the day before. But Maurizius did not seem to notice it. He remained standing against the wall. His eyelids closed halfway, his little teeth bit at the beautifully curved upper lip, he passed his slender hand nervously over his forehead several times, and began to speak in a low voice, which dropped so low at times that it could be heard only with the utmost effort.

2.

He can tell the day on which he saw Anna for the first time quite accurately. It was Monday, the nineteenth of September, 1904. "I came home from the university, in the hall hung a lady's fur-lined coat from which there came the delicate odour of verbena . . . the smell still comes back to me sometimes in my dreams." He hesitated as if to sniff, so it seemed to Herr von Andergast. The entire beginning of the narrative was interrupted by frequent hesitations and pauses, obvious attempts to think back, almost to reach back, as one may strain to snatch rather fearfully into the water for some lost object. To recreate this even inadequately is, naturally, impossible. When he enters the room the sisters are seated opposite each other. His wife says smilingly, "This is Anna." He cannot conceal his surprise. He has heard much about Anna's beauty; his expectations in this respect are high and he is prepared for her arrival; nevertheless the sight of her surprises him. She is more beautiful than he has expected. In any case, she is different from what he expected. Her presence is restraining. Above all the idea of her being in the same house is not pleasant. Aside from the disturbance to one's peace and comfort which a house-guest means, this eighteen- or nineteen-year-old girl has something about her which compels one's constant attention. What it is one cannot at first define, one merely feels it. In the course of the next few days he notices, and cannot keep from telling his wife critically, that Anna has unpleasant manners. He describes several occasions when she annoyed him by her haughtiness. It even looked as if she sought such opportunities. She treats me as if I had stolen the silver spoons, he says to Elli. The latter tries to excuse her sister. She regards herself entirely as her protector. But it does not escape him that the two do not understand each other. Elli admires Anna's universally admired beauty, she tries to give her advice and assistance, for Anna is worried about her means of livelihood; her difficult position forces Elli to be kind to her, but a difference in age of twenty years cannot be bridged; a sister cannot demand submission, nor is Anna in the least inclined to be submissive. He observes. He remains in the background. He takes a certain pleasure in criticizing things which he dislikes about his sister-in-law. Her habit of going to confession every Sunday annoys him particularly. When, one day, he becomes irritated to the point of making a sarcastic remark on the subject, she replies that a godless man should not discuss the sacraments. The same evening he reads her and Elli a short essay on Dürer's landscapes, which he has just finished. The work seems to make an impression upon Anna. He asks whether she calls the man who has written that godless and, if so, what a godless person is. She remains silent, she seems to be thinking. She has a constant enigmatical smile upon her lips. When one has been much in her society, it becomes an unpleasant, stereotyped smile. It is a ready answer for all sorts of things: compliments, advice, service, contradiction and demands. It wavers between contradiction and challenge. Maurizius spends an unusual amount of time in analysing this smile. He calls it a specifically virginal smile, demure and lacking in respect. There is a peculiar kind of audacity which one finds and tolerates only in girls of eighteen. If one could have taken the smile from her lips, as the label from a box, one would perhaps have uncovered a blemish—the defect in the enamel, he calls it thoughtfully. But don't let us spend any more time on it. He is evidently taking pains to make the figure of Anna—about which Herr von Andergast cannot find anything captivating—quite clear, and at once mentions a characteristic incident. One morning Elli says to him: "Just think, Anna does not want to live with us." "Ah, we are probably not distinguished enough," he replies, "although old Jahn in Cologne did not live in a palace either." "That's not it," replies Elli with embarrassment. "It does not suit her to have her room next to our bedroom. I have already, because she expressly asked me to, put the clothes closet against her door and had the space between stuffed with mattresses, but that's not enough; it is unpleasant to her." "Such prudery is disgusting," declares Maurizius. Elli tries to calm his irritation; Anna has grown up in a convent, one must bear that in mind and overlook her consequent exaggerations. "Yes, it is the Catholic about her," he admits with dislike and, with his experience of a man of the world, he pronounces commonplaces about the corrupt fantasies and the havoc which they play behind demurely lowered eyes. However, Anna's eyes are not demurely lowered. On the contrary, her glance takes in people and things with severe candour, "above the smile which I have mentioned," as if the most intimate concerns were not unknown to her. One does not understand her at all. Her whole personality does not fit in anywhere, not into the bourgeois world, not into the great world, not into the Bohemian, certainly not into the demi-monde. She is not amusing; she does not know how to conduct a conversation; she has not read much; she does not cut any figure in society.

Only beautiful? One gets tired of that. It becomes a bore. And yet, and yet . . . a deep well . . . deep, bottomless waters. One of her most unsociable characteristics is that she will not stand any risqué stories whatsoever. This abhorrence, which she frankly acknowledges, leads one day to an open quarrel with Elli and later on to a discussion with him, Leonhart. Elli had one day invited a few people to lunch, among them a Herr von Buchenau, who later became one of Waremme's intimates, a rich sportsman and collector, no longer a young man, very intellectual, very cynical, and popular as a teller of bold anecdotes. With these he keeps everyone breathless, the stories become constantly more obscene, while he is recounting a scarcely veiled indecency—he is accustomed to hardened listeners and does not stop at anything—Anna suddenly gets up, as if she has only just understood the whole conversation and, casting such a look at the surprised Buchenau that his words stick in his throat, she leaves the room and does not return. The next day Elli takes her to task, telling her that grown people do not pass their time in telling pious anecdotes, that she would not allow her guests to be affronted and so forth, and finally appeals to Leonhart for his opinion. Anna merely looks straight ahead with her mysterious clear eyes; she is seeking Maurizius' face, but she looks towards his knees with a curious sleepy smile. He is careful not to say anything, the scene is distasteful to him, for the first time he cannot find his sister-in-law in the wrong. Elli calls over her shoulder to her sister: "I believe that you are so pleased with yourself that you no longer notice when you offend." Whereupon Anna replies: "Oh, no, you—" "I remember," said Maurizius, "that the three words penetrated me through and through. They sounded, I still remember the sound exactly, as if a blind person could not conceal his astonishment at being accused of being cross-eyed. Perhaps you are surprised that I can repeat all this so accurately; I can vouch that no word has been altered or invented. Every syllable is engraved upon my brain, I could draw every expression, only the sequence sometimes gets twisted, otherwise everything is as if it had been yesterday."

He walked a few steps away from the wall, but turned back again at once, as if it contained an invisible sentry box which protected him against some danger known to him alone. Herr von Andergast, with his hands folded over his crossed legs, his head slightly turned towards the window, was disturbed by the dull sound of hammering which came up from the prison yard and compelled him to redouble his attention in order not to lose anything which the dull voice by the wall said. From one point of view he was familiar with these events; at least they awakened familiar associates; from another angle they were entirely new. It was about as if one were to read a book, the contents of which one has up to now known only by detailed accounts either from the newspapers or from reading a book about the book. One convinces oneself in this manner with a certain fright that even the most accurate accounts have almost no resemblance to the life in the book, the life of experience and its direct precipitate. Remarkably enough he noticed that this experience oppressed him and increased the tormenting mental uncertainty and irresoluteness from which he had been suffering for several days.

3.

Maurizius, with the same dull fixed glance, comes to the point where he begins to tell about his first confidential talk with his young sister-in-law. He seems to feel that what was discussed between him and Anna on this occasion was not of great importance. Only what it led to was important. Every tiny incident naturally becomes a ring in this chain. That she had heard of his gay, adventurous past as a seducer is quite evident. To feel regret for this does not occur to him. According to the point of view which he had then, this reputation would rather serve to make a man interesting than contemptible. She has not much faith in his improvement by his marriage with Elli; she still regards him as not to be trusted. Very well, no one has ordained her as a judge; her morality is not his; one will try to get on without her approval and without her sympathy. After all, who is she? An exacting young lady living on the credit which comes from having a very beautiful face. In spite of this her noticeable contempt galls him. He cannot get used to it, it robs him of sleep; it embitters his leisure hours; he constantly sees the slightly contracted brows over the clear, cool, brown eyes. He passes over all of this quite briefly. None of it was an iota different from thousands of other similar cases. Just as he up to a certain point in his life—so he states—lived the average life of the average man. Suddenly, at a certain point, "fate" takes hold of one. It rolls towards him like a tremendous stone ball. Three minutes before, and one had not even had an inkling of this monster "fate." "Don't you think," he asks into the air, "that our so-called 'fate' generally springs up outside ourselves in a cruelly sly way and in a certain way rolls on outside of us? One dances along idiotically and only when one no longer knows which way to turn, does one realize with fright: 'Oh, that is *fate,* this is what has happened to me.'" He feels as if he has been struck in the face when during the course of the conversation Anna says to him: "You sold yourself." At first he stands as if struck dumb; he feels himself insulted and misunderstood; she seems to regret the ugly words; when he defends himself with all of his powers of persuasion against the ugly reproach, she listens to him not without emotion. When she leaves she gives him her hand. Her silence contains half a request, half an assurance. Has he convinced her? It is not certain. He does not feel at all easy about the matter. He realizes, with despair and with the suddenness of lightning, that she is right. An awakening fraught with consequences. From that moment on he is forced to cloak one lie with another, to heap one lie upon another until he finally chokes. The affair of the anonymous letter which he has written himself is the beginning of a progress towards an abyss. Here he digressed again in his sombre observations and spent much time upon the difference between a verbal lie and a factual one; it was the same difference which might exist under certain circumstances between a harmless germ and an infectious organism. If a man marries an unloved woman a curse rests upon this marriage which he can never escape from; it leads inevitably to self-destruction, especially when, as in this case, it entails the destruction of the other person. The more elevated the pretexts which he has used, the more hopeless the event will prove. He had thought that he was acting with unusual wisdom when he had made Elli his wife, and he did not have even the most superficial knowledge of her personality. If it was shrewd calculation, then it was a contemptible action, no matter what noble reasons or pretexts he had had in mind. If it was silly temerity and frivolous fatalism, then he had still less reason for being surprised at the suffering which it brought upon him. No, there was nothing to be surprised at. If a person transgresses and accepts the soul of another person, secretly keeping his own soul, but behaving as if it were a fair exchange, he commits a crime, perhaps the greatest of all crimes. The fault is not an iota less egregious because one excuses oneself by saying: I did not know it. In such a case one should know. Here above all the sentence "ignorance of the law does not protect one from punishment" holds. The law, what law? The law within oneself. One must know that.

He cowered down, but only for half a minute. While Herr von Andergast was thinking over the moral self-laceration of the convict with some remains of sober distrust —and what an abysmal meaning the word *convict* suddenly assumed!—the latter went on. "A few days after this discussion with Anna the letter from the Swiss lawyer had come, telling me of the birth of my daughter Hildegard and of the demands which my former beloved made upon me." He knows that she is deathly ill; he knows that she lacks the bare necessities of life. He sees himself in a morass of difficulties and does not know what to do. His first thought is Anna. He confesses that, aside from his helplessness, there was an irresistible, even morbid charm, about involving Anna in this whole matter. He has reached a tolerably good understanding with her; she has told him all sorts of things about her life, nothing of importance, of course, nothing which would allow him to see inside her; in this respect she is completely inaccessible. But she has discussed plans for the future with him, she even begins at times to take an interest in his work, astonishing him at times by the steel-like precision of her remarks; all of this encourages him to take a step which he does not ponder carefully; it is—simply a gamble like a stake at roulette. She listens to him; she does not say anything; she goes away and he becomes even more uneasy; has he again forfeited her respect and sympathy? Two hours later she telephones him to meet her on the promenade, declares that she is ready to go to Switzerland to get the child and to take it to the home of her friend, Mrs. Caspot, in London. She does not leave him any time to ask questions, to inquire about details, she has decided that this is to be done; he is merely to provide the money for the journey and for the salary of the trained nurse who is to accompany her. He is dumbfounded. He would never have supposed her capable of such enterprise. Under the cloak of coldness, under her proud suspicious *noli me tangere* there are buried maternal instincts and forces of pity; perhaps—too—she is glad of the opportunity to make him forget the wrong she has done him. Fantasies, nothing more. She wanted to get away, that was all. The trips to Switzerland and England, to come out with it at once, are attempts at escape. Only attempts, of course, but means of gaining time and of hoping for some helpful uncertainty. Certainly, she also later developed an extraordinary passion for the child, Hildegard; during the worst of the black times which followed she never gave up her care for the child, as if that were something for her to hold on to, a last neutral interest free from torment or fever; but at the time that she made the decision she was simply driven by fear. The change did not escape him. She is distracted, she laughs when there is nothing to laugh at, in the midst of her preparations for her trip—the train is leaving in half an hour—she remembers that she has left her wrist-watch in the university library and almost has an attack of hysterical crying. He calms her with the greatest difficulty, implores her to tell him what she is so disturbed about, she seems frightened and refuses; finally, in a voice as if she were making a tremendous confession, she says it is due to the attacks. She has been spared for a year, now she feels that they are going to start again, the constant pressure in her brain proves this. This is true and not true. He will come to know these attacks, but she is not so much afraid of these; there is something else which oppresses her soul but which she does not speak of, she cannot bring it over her lips. He does not discover what it is, not for a long, long time; when he does discover it, he can no longer fight against it; he is already in the fiery furnace. "At that time I could still perhaps have struggled. If someone had said to me: If you love life, go away with her, hide yourself with her, do not even appear again in your country, in your city, in your home; disappear, be dead to the world which you have known up to now, perhaps I should have done it. For at that time she was already to me . . . at that time she, dear God in heaven, she . . . No, there are no words for that. Perhaps I could have persuaded her, who knows, perhaps, but that did not happen because such things never do happen, such promptings would spare one life and death too. But life must be lived, that is it. . . ." He broke off, walked to the table, took up a stone pitcher and poured out a glass of water which he drank greedily. With his two arms resting on the table and his head leaning far forward, he remained standing in silence for a while.

"Well . . . Waremme," said Herr von Andergast quietly.

"Yes, Waremme."

4.

After a pause Herr von Andergast, who was apparently afraid that Maurizius for some reason or other, either because his internal emotions were too strong, or perhaps because the pictures had faded from his memory, had lost the desire to make further revelations, wishing to help him over his hesitation by the most eager and sensitive questions, asked: "So he had unexpectedly appeared upon the scene of action, if I understand correctly?" "You understand correctly." "And Anna Jahn already knew this when you told her of the affair with the child?" "Yes, she already knew then that he had traced her." "What—traced her? So he, as it were, pursued her?" "If he did not pursue her he was nevertheless looking for her. That she was staying with us was easy to find out." "Certainly. But what reason had she to hide from him, even to fear him?" Maurizius was silent. Herr von Andergast continued: "All right. I assume she had a reason, the very best reason; I will assume that, although I have no conception of what it could be; why did she not then seize the opportunity which you offered her? Why did she come back? A plausible excuse to have stayed abroad might easily have been found. She need only have written you, for example, that the child was sick, or that Mrs. Caspot was away, or unreliable. You certainly would not have objected if she had protracted her absence indefinitely. In this way she could have gained time, much time, and in the most inconspicuous fashion." "Very clever. But she could not do this." "Why not?" "Because, because . . . she was a helpless victim." Herr von Andergast looked incredulous. "A helpless victim? His victim? Oh, come, now. That only happens in trashy novels. Such a one was making a sensation at that time, you may perhaps remember; Trilby was the name of it. Sad stuff it was; there was a certain Svengali, a conjurer. Those are simply wild West stories, you know. I at least have never been able to convince myself that such things happen in real life. A helpless victim . . . Explain yourself more clearly." Maurizius shook his head without looking up. "One can't explain anything in such a case. A trashy story? Perhaps. Yes, I saw the play Trilby once. Such rubbish often has a lot of truth in it on its contemporaries." "How did you get to know Waremme? Not through the Jahn woman, so far as I can judge from the records. . . ." "No, not through Anna. A few days before her return I met Herr von Buchenau on the street, he stopped me and said: 'Dr. Maurizius, you must come and have tea with us today; you'll meet a fellow—I tell you—such an experience as you've never had, a polyglot, a new Winckelmann, a poet, a mind created by the grace of God.' Just those were his words. Since I knew that Buchenau was a skeptic, as cold as a fish, whom no one had ever seen enthusiastic, I became curious and I went. And really it was an experience such as I had never had." "Of his relation to the Jahn woman you knew nothing at that time?" "No. The next Sunday—it was the twenty-seventh of November—I saw him with Anna on the parade. He greeted me very cordially, both stood still and I went along with them." "Was it from that time on that you three began to associate as friends?" "Yes." "So the Jahn woman's apprehension in the beginning—to use the least objectionable word—must have been gradually allayed? It must have been a mood, hysteria?" "Oh, good God!" murmured Maurizius. Herr von Andergast looked at him tensely. Maurizius stuck his index finger into his collar as if he could not breathe. "Or, had you the impression that something, something decisive had taken place between them?" "Certainly," replied

Maurizius, in a lifeless voice. "Certainly. Something frightfully decisive." He supported himself against the top of the table. Herr von Andergast waited. Remarkably enough, he felt his heart beating fast. "Something," continued Maurizius, "something—that"— Suddenly his voice became cold and firm. "She had been raped by him." Herr von Andergast sprang up. "Come on, man," he exclaimed, losing his self-control for the first time, "that . . . that is . . . mad; you are hallucinating. . . ." "She had been raped by him at seventeen," said Maurizius stonily, holding on to the table so convulsively that the knuckles of his fingers turned white.

From the court below there sounded a shrill order. The hammering, which had ceased during the last half-hour, began again. Under a pale-blue morning sky a flock of swallows flew by. Herr von Andergast sat down again. He was looking for words. "This is probably a case," he said hesitatingly, "of one of the usual mistakes in terminology. Experience shows that rape, or violation, is very unusual. The mental state of the victim afterwards is, as a rule, conducive to a state of mind which colours the earlier occurrence and gives rise to the accusation." This legal digression drew a wan smile from Maurizius. "You are mistaken," he replied, "it was a perfect case." Then, after a sigh, "It is so curious, the whole thing—" "Why curious, what do you mean by that?" "I mean this: the papers dealing with the case probably comprise a history of several volumes and the man who is the responsible editor as it were, is constantly forced to show his ignorance of every fact that is not entirely superficial. You are certainly in this position; you cannot deny that. Forgive me, I don't wish to offend you; but perhaps you can deduce for yourself what is the true state of our legal procedure. The scales of justice—my God—it is not a delicate instrument, but a very coarse lever, which only operates when a hundredweight of something pulls the scale down. Forgive me, it has simply occurred to me." Herr von Andergast decided to ignore the outburst. "I only don't understand how you could have found out about it," he said; "that the woman herself should have . . . But that is difficult to assume, one needs no special knowledge of this difficult character for that. . . . Perhaps there were others who knew? Perhaps later at the end of the case, perhaps someone tried to make you believe this monstrous story in order . . . so that—well, so that you might conquer certain hesitations. What? Just recollect a little." Maurizius shook his head, again the tired smile showed itself. "I found it out from Waremme himself," he said. Herr von Andergast started. "Wha-at? From Waremme himself? You must be speaking of the very last phases of the story, and the confession was intended to mean: you are really not losing such a lot after all, the statue was dragged through the mud long ago. . . ." "A wrong guess. It was not a confession." "What then?" "I did not find it out in the end, but in the second month of our acquaintance, the beginning of January." "Well, I simply don't understand anything more about it," slipped from Herr von Andergast. Maurizius threw him an unusually malicious glance. "That I am quite willing to believe," he said, and, taking up the water-pitcher, he poured himself out another glass and drank it at a gulp.

"One can't make much of any of that unless one takes into account the influence which Waremme had upon me at that time," he went on, and walked over to the iron bed and dropped down upon the foot of it with signs of exhaustion. "I was completely his slave. I saw with his eyes; I spoke in his words, my judgment was his; I carried myself like him, copied him in everything. My background compared to his was a little pile of chaff. I had merely dabbled in everything, and accumulated, or learned in order to earn my bread. This made me a sorry wretch next to him. Everyone was on his knees before him. So long as one was in the same room with him, one was completely fascinated, completely defenceless. To such a superior brain, one involuntarily ascribes a supremacy in moral matters also. I don't know how this happens, but it is so. For people who have built up their lives upon culture and knowledge, morality is only a protuberance upon the body of the intellectual sun, if I may express myself in this way. In those years this was particularly the case. That is why we young people lived in such . . . such an insubstantial ether, such a caricature of the infinite. Only much later, only since living in this place, have I come to see this clearly. In Waremme I saw, or I thought I saw, where one could get if one . . . well, I should have said if one was a somebody, but he never made you feel that you were so insignificant, such a gambling, cheating, ambitious nonentity. He did not humiliate you; he was too good a companion for that; with all of his glow and intensity, he carried you along with the same passion when he ordered caviar and champagne as when he provided poetry and ideas; he was always inexhaustible. One could spend night after night in his society and not get tired, there was no thought of sleep. Such a person is incomprehensible; I am convinced that such a man only appears every hundred years, just like a Kepler or a Schiller; I am also convinced that he was the devil. Yes, simply the devil. Better reason than I, for this conviction, no one can have. Evil, you know, real evil, is extremely rare in this world, rarer than a Kepler or a Schiller; much rarer. Well, I don't want to bore you. You will say that I am stringing a lot of mystical stuff; the devil has been the excuse of all of the damned for long enough. At the time I am speaking of, Privy Councillor Bringsmann was still alive, the literary historian, a man whom we all revered; the best society met at his house every Friday, and one could spend very instructive and delightful hours there. The Privy Councillor was a great admirer of Waremme; he was made enormously much of there; they could not do enough for him. On the first Friday of the New Year—it was Epiphany—there were particularly many people there and Waremme had promised the Privy Councillor to read aloud the writings of Gorgias, which he had just finished translating. Almost all of the professors and their wives were there—it was a distinguished audience. When I entered the large drawing-room with Elli and Anna, the reading had already begun and all the chairs were occupied. Of the reading itself there is not much to tell, only I noticed that Waremme stopped for a moment or two when we came in and threw us an angry glance; evidently because we were late. He was a tremendous pedant about such things; that is to say, in those days I regarded it as pedantry and a desire to dominate; but there was also a tremendous amount of vanity about it, and one was always made to feel it if one had hurt this vanity. I don't remember whether my wife or Anna was at fault in regard to this delay, Anna, in any case, was so nervous about it that she stepped on the seam of her dress coming up the steps, thus causing a further delay because she was obliged to fasten the hem with pins. She turned deathly pale with excitement, and her hands trembled. Waremme was overwhelmed with praise and applause; everybody crowded around him, he seemed much elated and more talkative and stimulating than usual. I noticed however that he sedulously cut me as well as Anna—with Elli he was never on good terms—and I thought 'That is carrying one's revenge for an insignificant slight too far.' Among the guests was a Heidelberg professor who had recently published a work about the legends in Shakespeare. Waremme knew the book and had been annoyed, when he had read it, about some opinions which showed a lack of understanding. We had discussed the matter only a few days before; he had been especially irritated at some disparaging remarks about Measure for Measure, for he had a particularly high opinion of this play. He did not miss the opportunity of a discussion with the author and finally drove him so hard that the poor man had nothing further to say and would have been glad to beg for mercy. The debate had aroused general attention, all the rest of the conversation had ceased. Intoxicated with his success and with the glances of admiration, and by a secret purpose which I only half and half perceived later, he delighted the gathering with one of his famous *tours de force*. After a charming, short introduction, he recited from memory the whole ending of the second act, that wonderful conversation between Angelo and Isabella, in which he promises her the life of her brother if she will yield her body to him. I cannot forget with what expression he did this, with what force he recited and how he increased the tension, like a great actor, and yet not like an actor, rather like someone to whom it is an experience at the moment. 'Sir, believe this, I had rather give my body than my soul.' And how Angelo answers: 'I talk not of your soul. Our compelled sins stand more for number than accompt.' And how she says that women are like mirrors into which they look and break, which are as easy broke as they make forms. And then her passionate disgust: 'Ha, little honour to be much believed, and most pernicious purpose!—Seeming, seeming!—I will proclaim thee, Angelo.' And Angelo answers: 'Who will believe thee, Isabel? My unsoiled name, the austereness of my life, my vouch against you, and my place in the state, will so your accusation overweigh, that you shall stifle in your own report, and smell of calumny.' And when he came to the passage—however does it go?—for twenty years, since that day I haven't heard or read those words, but time cannot erase them, with such passionate and burning defiance that it caused us all to shiver: 'I have begun; and now I give my sensual race the rein: fit thy consent to my sharp appetite, lay by all nicety and prolixious blushes that banish what they sue for, redeem thy brother by yielding up thy body to my will.' Then suddenly some ladies in the back of the room screamed;

there was a clash of plates and of metal; a panic started; I pushed through the crowd and saw that Anna had fallen to the floor, and in falling had knocked over one of the service tables so that she was lying among broken china and spilled tea and pastry, with her limbs convulsed and her eyes rolling. That was the first of her attacks which I witnessed, the second took place in her apartment six or seven months later, after the scene with Elli. We took her into the bedroom of the hostess; Waremme too tried to help; it was several hours before she had recovered sufficiently to be taken home. That evening Waremme asked me to go to a wine-cellar with him; it did not take long to persuade me; it seemed to me that there was something to explain which he alone could explain, for I had felt some strange connection between the recitation and what had happened to Anna. He ordered a bottle of champagne and emptied it alone; then a second, at the same time smoking one cigarette after another, paying no attention to my disturbed face nor to the conjectures which I stammered from time to time. It was already midnight—we were the last guests at the place—when he suddenly struck his forehead with his fist exclaiming: 'What a barbarian I am, what a hopeless idiot not to have thought of it! It must have seemed to her like a frightful blow from behind; where in heaven's name were my senses that such a thing could happen to me?' My eyes grew big. I had an inkling. I knew that Anna had a morbid antipathy for the theatre, even for anything connected with it, but that Waremme should recite a wonderful dramatic scene before a friendly group could not possibly lead to such a catastrophe. I remarked something of the sort to Waremme; he seized me by the wrist across the table, turning white as chalk, and said: 'By God, no, but there is a frightful similarity. Life has played the frightful joke upon her of putting an Angelo in her path who was not satisfied with impertinent demands, but at once translated his wish into action, you understand?' *Did* I understand? I understood so well that from that moment on I understood only *that;* it was the only thing my brain contained, unthinkable as it was. I had the feeling . . . But what is the use of thinking of feelings; the world suddenly seemed to me like a huge cesspool. Waremme looked like a ghost, he said that I was to go home with him, that he could not talk here, nor could he be alone. The affair had upset him so; everything had been started up again; he must talk to a friend; he had kept it to himself so long that it was tearing his soul. And more of the same sort. So I accompanied him to his apartment, he brought out cognac and drank a quarter of a bottle, describing the details as he walked up and down, but talking only of Angelo and Isabella. I knew of the amateur performance in Cologne at which Anna had been prominent, but I did not know that Waremme had been their dramatic coach; he mentioned this only in passing, as if it were of no importance. They had rehearsed an old French pastoral with ancient music. Anna had taken the part of an aristocratic lady, dressed as a Pierrot. After the performance, this man . . . this mysterious Angelo, had himself announced in her dressing-room on an important message which could not be postponed. She received him. It was fairly late. Anna had, according to her custom, taken quite a long time to change her clothes; the employees of the theatre had left; the ladies and gentlemen who had taken part in the performance had left; the servant-girl who was to take Anna home was waiting at the stage door. Anna was therefore alone with this Angelo, who was, of course, not a complete stranger to her—as I could deduce from everything—in this empty building, alone between an empty court and an empty corridor; it struck me how masterly—in spite of being passionately wrought up—his description of the location and the situation was, almost literary in its finesse. Why the visitor had chosen this time for such a terrific blow I do not know, it was all so curiously equivocal. Well, enough said, he brought the news that her brother Eric had been killed in a skirmish in South Africa; the telegram had arrived that day. She had loved this brother beyond anyone else. Perhaps he was the only person whom she had ever really loved. It was a very deep and a somewhat dark relationship. One can imagine how such unexpected news affected her. Whether he, this Angelo, had been especially entrusted with this message—Waremme did not say, only that he had tried to calm and console her. The matter does not stop with consolation, he throws the mask off, so to speak; he becomes violent; such a tempting opportunity will not occur soon again; he completely disregards her refusal; her resistance merely spurs him on and thus she becomes his victim. While Waremme was talking, I felt as if I must go out and search the world over for that beast in order to strike it dead; but during his narrative he worked himself into such grief that he had scarcely finished when he threw himself into an armchair and broke out in a frightful attack of weeping. After he calmed himself, he left the room and I heard him moving about in his bathroom. He had taken a shower and after a quarter of an hour he returned in elegant pajamas. Curious. And curious too the way in which he suddenly shows himself calm and superior and draws my attention to the fact that the slightest lack of tact on my part towards Anna may seriously injure her health. Besides himself, I was the only person who knew the sad secret. This was a mutual bond and obligation. Anna had in a moment of despair confided in him; at a time when she considered that life was already over for her, he had succeeded in comforting her, in dissipating certain moral prejudices and tendencies; the miscreant meantime had disappeared, there were a hundred reasons which would prevent him from reappearing on the scene. Objectively viewed, it was not very different from a person being knocked over by a wild horse and carried bleeding from the scene of action; subjectively, of course—here he seemed overcome again and his voice trembled—subjectively, if one thought of the wound, to a person of great delicacy, imagination and feeling, one could not dismiss the matter so lightly. To him at any rate the matter was a tragedy which weighed upon his soul and only because he felt himself so greatly her friend, only because he knew that friendship was the only soil in which the injured roots could find fresh nourishment, did he cling to her. This sounded curiously like a warning, or as if there were some purpose behind it. Finally, he put his arm affectionately about me and said that he was not mad enough to ask for an oath of silence; he thought too highly of my common sense and delicacy; one's word of honour and things of that sort meant nothing to him. The necessity was dictated by the situation, which made a coarse touch a crime; the fragility of this wonderful woman demanded consideration. If only on her account, we must regard ourselves as allies united to protect her. I gave him my hand, I was incapable of speaking; I don't remember how I got into the street or home, my brain felt burned out."

5.

Maurizius walked slowly through the cell, twice, with his dragging step, before he sat down again and continued: "When I ask myself today, after more than twenty years, having had time—ample time—to consider the whole matter from every point of view, what the real, the profound motives were which moved Waremme to make this disclosure, I cannot find any satisfactory answer. Perhaps he wanted to prepare me, to forestall some hint or gossip. But what had he to be afraid of? From Anna he had nothing to fear; of the mysterious Angelo it is scarcely necessary to say that he was a mere bogy. No one else knew. No one else in the world had an inkling; no one had any suspicion in that direction. Why prepare me? What had he to fear from me? I was rendered helpless by consideration for my sister-in-law's reputation and person. I might have killed him in anger; but he could not be protected against that by his careful calculations. He must have felt fairly safe, or he would not have ventured upon such an audacious game with me. It was none of those things, perhaps rather he wanted to scare me off. He had long ago noticed that my relation to Anna was becoming constantly more intimate and affectionate; he wanted to stop this thing, to make me understand that she was not to be touched, not to be pursued, that there were barriers here which not even he could break down; how much less could I hope to pass them? Even he ventured no more than service and friendship; in this case there is no chance for anything else, for anyone who is not a scoundrel without a conscience. It would have accorded well with his character to spoil the game even for a rival whom he did not take seriously, by these indirect means. I am saying this from what I came to understand later; at that time I was dazzled—although steeped in suspicion. I was obliged to think constantly of his mysterious gift of persuasion; I felt as if he had only been trying to assume some tremendous pose; and, whenever his great outburst of grief and emotion recurred to my mind, I felt the same mastery about it as about the recitation of the scene from Shakespeare. Both probably came from the same source; it was a waste of time to look for the plan or purpose behind it. It was perhaps his unbridled instinct for self-enjoyment and self-importance; a certain claptrap attitude towards life was second nature to him; he would under certain circumstances have rushed into danger for it. Perhaps the whole thing was a creation of his imagination, a mystification, a Waremme myth, this was a possibility too. Of course, the last assumption was mistaken. Up to that time I had thought that he loved me, certainly that he preferred me to others—I had sufficient grounds for thinking so—now suddenly it seemed to me that he hated me, hated me with a groundless secret hate which would make him capable of anything, because he was always capable of anything, either good or evil, in justice I must admit that, of good certainly, he was capable of good. But why in the world did he hate me? I don't know even yet, for jealousy alone will not explain it; he was too despotic a person for that, far too much convinced of his importance and superiority. So I could not find either prop or support anywhere; I wandered around senselessly for days; I should have loved to hide; I was so afraid of seeing Anna again; I felt that I must keep her from seeing a certain picture in my eyes which was driving me mad. I behaved like a person whose most precious possession, a Leonardo, or a Rubens, had been soiled by vandals, as if I had been her owner and had held acknowledged rights to her virginity, as if this thing should not have happened to her because I was in the world. I was torn, simply torn in two; I hated my work, I couldn't find any peace anywhere, I couldn't utter five consecutive sentences to anyone, and my life with Elli became a torment in spite of all the goodness and understanding which she had at first shown. A few weeks later, things changed. They could not go on as they had been going, I had to be able to breathe; I had to talk to Anna even if the greatest misfortune ensued. I had never been capable of hiding anything. Everyone could read on my face what was going on inside of me. It was hard for me to keep a secret; this sometimes made serious difficulties for me; but it was not easy for me; it tormented and oppressed me and I was frequently indiscreet from pure egoism, and would betray a confidence which had been made me. For this reason I was regarded as unreliable, and quite rightly so. In this case I had already been silent beyond my strength and I said to myself: This thing which keeps you silent is delusion; it is your duty to Anna and to yourself to slough off these paralysing chains. So I asked to speak to her one day and she let me enter her room. She had sensed for a long time what was wrong with me. I had often thought that I felt that something was working upon her and that she was struggling with the desire to confess it. But people of her sort do not confess, certainly not of their own accord; they prefer any sort of torture. Whenever her figure and personality came very vividly to my mind, I never doubted that something frightful had crossed her path, which had marked her forever. And when I was so near to her that I felt that I need only lean over and take her and open her up, she would suddenly go out like a candle and become quite cold and quite conventional. Many weeks later she told me that she had never even in confession alluded to the crime which had been committed against her. I call it crime, she made veiled allusions to it or did not mention it at all. On that day then, when we were alone in her room, and I had assured myself that we could not be disturbed or overheard, I collected all my courage—cowards always make straight for their goal—and began to ask her directly whether this and that had really taken place. I naturally used indefinite hints, which did not lack for definiteness, however. She started and looked into space. Her face took on an expression of sombre obstinacy. Once I saw her looking towards the door, as if she were considering whether she had not better leave the room. I snatched at her hand and she folded her arms across her breast and pressed her lips together. I said: 'Listen, Anna, between us that cannot alter anything.' She was silent. I said: 'You must understand that I did nothing to discover this, but since I do know it, I can perhaps help you to overcome it.' She still remained silent. I don't remember all of the things I said; I believe that I even spoke of calling the guilty man to account. She was silent and kept silent. I felt as if I were sitting opposite a dumb woman. Finally I said: 'Anna, if you care as much for me as for that pincushion over there on the table, tell me what to do for you, or at least what attitude to take, whether you will allow me to speak to you about it, anything, anything, only don't sit there like the Sphinx and let me play Œdipus.' She was silent. I snatched for my hat and was about to dash off. Then she made a slight gesture with her arm; insignificant as it was, it was full of request and entreaty. Then I said with folded hands: 'Anna, is it true? Don't say anything but yes or no.' She said, 'Yes,' quite lifelessly. Then I said: 'Fine, now everything is all right; now you have shown me that I am at least worthy of an answer; now only tell me one thing more; is it a burden, is it a grief; I mean, does it darken your life?' She nodded. That moved me unutterably, that nod. I asked further: 'Have you the feeling that you cannot get over it?' Again that nod. I knelt down before her and took her hand, which she permitted me this time to hold without resistance. 'And is it he,' I continued to ask, 'is it this person who throws this cloud over you?' She replied; 'Yes.' 'And can I do anything to free you, from him or from any threat or pressure which he exercises upon you?' She whispered thoughtfully, with a quivering mouth: 'Perhaps.' 'Then tell me who he is; I ask, tell me his name!' Then she got up and took a step back. 'Oh,' came in a long murmur, 'don't you know?' And she laughed with a curious arrogance or contempt. 'You don't know? . . . Why, what do you want of me?' Her glance had become hard and angry. Now it was my turn to be silent. What did this mean? Just imagine how dumbfounded I was, how bewitched, that in spite of my suspicion, which, of course, only developed when I had not seen Waremme for a few days, not even now to have the courage within me to accuse him! Anna, upset and disturbed as she was, to find that Waremme had made me his confidant, nevertheless felt relieved with regard to me; that I now realized clearly. But she naturally could not have dreamed of the sentimental web of lies which he had spread over his ecstatic revelations, for no matter how well one knows another person, all of his subterfuges and lies never fully enter one's consciousness; they remain mere knowledge. At the moment when she turned away from me with such offensive brusqueness, exclaiming only half aloud, 'Go, do get out of here, it's terrible that you are still here,' the revelation came and I almost screamed: 'So it was he after all!' She said nothing. She walked to the window and again laughed that low laugh which sounded so arrogant and desperate. 'It's all right, now,' I said, feeling that I was turning white to my very neck, 'there is nothing more to be considered; I see clearly; now I can act; you will have nothing further to fear from him!' With that I left. From the nearest coffee-house I called up Waremme's apartment to ask whether he was at home. I was told that he had gone to Bingen and would not be back until the next day. Oh, my fury and my impatience! That same evening Anna sent me a note on which was written: 'Don't do anything; you will merely injure yourself.' No, my dear, I thought, there is not going to be any more dodging. Now, this time, matters will be settled one way or the other. What I had in mind I no longer know; however, I was reckoning without my man. Just listen to how shamefully, how shabbily matters turned out. In the first place, Waremme postponed his return two days. I was not at that time a man who was strengthened by waiting. Meantime, Pauline Caspot wrote that Hildegard was ill with scarlet fever. In frightful anxiety I implored Anna to go to Hertford. She said that she couldn't; she hadn't the strength. There were all kinds of negotiations afoot with a Frankfurt pianist; she was to take some sort of examination. Elli was insisting with hostile obstinacy that she should take up some regular occupation; first she was to paint, then she was to become a piano teacher, then study languages, or, she was to become a milliner. It was simply hellish, a perpetual torment. The conversation with Anna was Tuesday; on Friday Waremme returned. As I was going by the casino towards eleven o'clock, he was standing at the door, talking to several men. He hurried towards me, with his arms extended as if he had not seen me for years and had longed for me as for a brother. I, dizzy with excitement, said: 'I must talk to you, Waremme.' He looks at me sharply, his chest becomes tense and his back hollow, and he says: 'I understand. You have abused my confidence; you have not been able to hold your tongue; all right, let's go to my place.' He calls a cab and we drive to his apartment. 'How can I be of service to you, sir?' he says coldly and sarcastically as we enter his rooms. 'I ought simply to shoot you down, Waremme,' was my reply, 'but perhaps it's a pity to waste the bullet. Furthermore, I want to avoid a scandal, so I leave it to your ingenuity to suggest another solution, a satisfaction for Anna's honour.' You can see from these high-faluting phrases that my decision was already wavering. He answered by shrugging his shoulders, and said with dignity: 'I can't make a word out of what you are saying; talk like a sensible man. How much further are you going to go with this comedy?' 'Am I still to believe that Angelo and Waremme are two different persons? At least confess and let us settle the matter decently between men—or do you prefer a horse-whip?' He turns white, runs his hand over the back of his head and looks at me with pitying astonishment, which irritates me completely. 'Between men, no,' says he. 'First behave like a man and not like a silly boy, please, please,' and he waves me back with both hands as I make to attack him. 'If you want to behave like a college boy this conversation is superfluous. Listen to me calmly, afterwards—for all I care—send me your witnesses. I am quite at your disposal.' And now came the most indescribable and incomprehensible thing, an oratorical performance such as I have never seen again. It made even your plea to the jury seem like helpless stammering. What emboldened me to accuse him? On what did the accusation rest? Upon a complaint of Anna's? No? Merely upon a hint? A hint given in words? No? A silent admission? Merely upon that? I regarded that as a sufficient excuse to attack him, to go for *him,* Gregor Waremme, as if he were a stable boy? There was nothing which he wished so little to do as to speak disparagingly of Anna; her desire for truth was as incontestable as her sincerity; but had I no eyes in my head, that I did not see the condition which she was in? If not, would I kindly inform myself; any psychiatric dilettante could give me the information about the circumstances pertaining to such a situation. 'Or have you never, sir, heard of psychomotor disturbances which may attain the stage of a katatonic stupor and which can be suddenly interrupted after months by some strong emotion, frequently fatal to surrounding persons? Have you never heard of mistakes of memory, disturbances of imagination in which, in all innocence, one person is mistaken for another, the situation being completely similar? Just make a few inquiries, take a course at our clinic. Unfortunately,' he continued with the most painful emotion, 'these phenomena are not new to me in Anna.' For years he has devoted himself to fighting against them; by years of a carefully tested mental therapy he has succeeded in bringing about an improvement, at times even in eliminating them entirely, but he has not been prepared for the brutal unexpected intervention of a third person. He had so earnestly and by all that was sacred implored me to use the most delicate consideration; why hadn't he kept quiet; why hadn't he drunk himself insensible that cursed evening; but how could he ever have supposed that I, a friend, an understanding spirit, a person with perceptions, could have laid crude fingers upon that trembling plant? That sublime creature, he exclaimed with tears, so noble, so sensitive, equally beautiful without and within, only with this one vulnerable, suffering spot. Can one not feel this; isn't a Maurizius enough of an artist, enough of a poet to hear what is behind these words, to see what lies behind appearances? 'For God's saké, Waremme, forgive me, forget what I've said, advise me.' I don't remember exactly what followed, whether the reconciliation took place that day or the next. This in any case was the result. That day he still did everything to convince me of his innocence, or should I say to overpower me and rape me into this conviction by an unprecedented storm of temperament and words, for his whole nature was that of a ravisher. Six weeks later, at our second great discussion, he no longer regarded it as necessary to pretend the frightful lie, or what is worse, the half-lie of fabricating a nervous disease; for I had become wax in his hands. He had sucked all will-power and decision out of me like a vampire and I accepted as fate what he had prepared for me. But I haven't yet gotten so far. This was Friday, the tenth of February, I believe: all of these dates have sunk into my mind like milestones. On Sunday Anna had come to us for lunch. After lunch Elli had had a quarrel with her; I no longer remember the reason; only, I remember that Elli was in the wrong and that Anna defended herself with unusually calm and telling arguments. She was as calm as a lake in the mountains just before it freezes. Her voice tormented me, her whole personality tormented me, that—what shall I call it? one is forced always to use the same expression—that mysterious transparency which did not allow anything to be seen. I went down into the garden and ran up the paths and down, then when I saw her on the balcony, I motioned to her from under the window; she considered awhile, smiled at me and came down. On the steps she slipped and I sprang towards her and was in time to catch her in my arms. I mention this only because it is one of the three occasions I held her in my arms; I shall say no more of this. We walked for a while, I talking choppily of all sorts of things and she silent, as was her way, but I all at once had the feeling that she expected to hear something particular from me. Finally it was as if she had asked me aloud. Then in my simply mad desire to be honest and frank towards her—little as lying generally troubled me, I could not lie towards her—I said, for I could not do anything else: 'I have talked to Waremme, the suspicion which you have aroused in me is unfounded; I was misled; I would give the rest of my life if you would tell me who it was, for it could not have been he, that's impossible, isn't it, Anna?' Her face turned as white as porcelain, the charming calm expression changed to one of hatred and perturbation; she stood still, whispering aloud: 'How repulsive you are to me! Oh, God, how unspeakably repulsive, you and your wife and all of you!' I was frightened to the very soul. In my stupidity I did not understand in what a light I had shown myself, and you see on that day all those horrors began, compared to which everything which preceded it had been child's play, and which one can never surmount, or forget, if one has once experienced them."

6.

He got up and went to the iron stove and placed his hands flat upon the top as if he were cold and the stove heated. Herr von Andergast took his cigarette-case out of his pocket, opened it and saw that it was empty. He sent for the warden and ordered him to get some cigarettes. It took a quarter of an hour for the man to get back. During this time, Herr von Andergast stood at the window and looked into the court where the sixth group of men were ending their sad walk. I shall order my motor for two o'clock, he decided, I must ask Herr Pauli downstairs to telephone to the office so that they may know where I am; if Sophia has meantime sent word that she is there I will arrange an appointment for an early evening hour; perhaps she has heard from the boy during the last few days; that's possible, although highly improbable, and if she has heard, the nastiest point of the meeting would be eliminated; perhaps it need not even take place. But these thoughts connected with his home and his professional duties were merely a semi-voluntary withdrawal into a different sphere of thought and resembled the moisture of his breath upon the window-pane. When the warden had brought the cigarettes and departed after a military bow and click of the heels, Herr von Andergast offered the convict one, but Maurizius, who had now taken his hands from the cold stove, bowed stiffly and said: "Later on, if you will have the goodness." Herr von Andergast himself had no desire to smoke. "The time which you had in mind when you were speaking stretches from the middle of February to . . . to October," he said, summing the matter up with a dryness which was painful to him for a moment, in an attempt to get the convict to resume his communication. In trying to be easy, although it scarcely paid any longer to try to operate with ease, Herr von Andergast ran his hand through his grey beard from his Adam's apple upwards, his violet-blue eyes meantime wandering through the cell, his glance resting hastily upon everything except the figure of its occupant.

Maurizius lifted the cover off the stove, stared into the dark hole and closed it up again. "It was simply a perfect process of pulverizing," he began again, "in which everyone was at the same time both wheel and victim. Two or three operated together constantly to crush the third or the fourth. A fine piece of machinery. Anna between me and Waremme, Elli between me and Anna, Anna between Elli and me, I between Anna and Waremme, and Elli among all three of us. That went on day in, day out, week in, week out, until the horrible end. If you would give me a cigarette now I should be thankful." He smoked in silence for a while. At times he raised his eyes uncertainly. He seemed to be pondering whether it were possible to make what he was commencing to narrate at all comprehensible. It probably even now seemed to him something hopelessly mixed up. "At first I could not make out where I was at with Anna," he continued; "until March she only came to see us two or three times, and always chose the hours when I was away. From Elli I heard that she was in the best of humour, that she had ordered various new dresses, and was going to balls and teas, allegedly with friends, but as a matter of fact she met Waremme at all these places. And the more she avoided our house the more eagerly Waremme sought my society, as if he placed the greatest value upon it. At the end of March I published my work upon the influence of religion upon the reproductive arts, from the Nazarenes to Uhde; he wrote an interview for one of the Frankfurt papers comparing me with Justi, and —exaggerating a good deal—even with Rohde and Burckhardt. I felt honoured and flattered even though I was conscious and admitted that his share in the ideas which I had developed was not insignificant. But suddenly there began to be some talk about a plagiarism which I was said to have committed, and when I investigated the rumour I was told that Waremme himself had spread it everywhere. I took him to task and he laughed: 'Silly boy, don't bother about such nonsense, plagiarism simply doesn't exist for distinguished minds.' That same evening, as we got up from the gaming table in the casino, he pulled me aside and said with an expression of amusement: 'Do you know who brought up that silly talk about plagiarism? You will never guess. Your sister-in-law, Anna. She found a few sentences in one of my early writings which exactly correspond with your wonderful criticism of Feuerbach; I had already at that time written about the eclectic neoclassicism of the painter.' This seemed very odd to me. The next day I asked Anna whether this was so. She did not know a syllable about it. She took no interest in the story, but told me in her frozen manner that Waremme had become engaged the week before to Lili Quästor, and that the girl had poisoned herself the previous night. I had heard of the engagement three days before, although it was not official, but since Waremme had not said anything about it I had not dared to believe it. 'You look as if you were responsible for her death, Anna,' said I, horrified. She looked at me with one of her penetrating glances and replied, 'So I am, you have hit the nail on the head.' To which I replied, 'Anna, think of what you are saying.' Then it came out that she had written a letter to the girl in which she had told her of her previous incontestable rights. I said, 'You must have dreamed that, Anna,' and denied passionately that she was capable of doing anything of the sort; then it came out that Waremme had forced her to write the letter. The engagement had been too precipitate; the girl had bored him; the advantages which he had hoped for had been proven upon closer examination to be illusory; whether he had seduced her was never known; in short, he wanted to get out of the affair, and Anna was just good enough to do it for him. Perhaps too it was a way of producing an effect upon her. He knew the persons whom he used in his game of chess, but this Lili Quästor was one who could not be played with. To such a man calculation and compulsion are merely conceptions like empty shells. What happened later, up to the murder, was also calculated, and yet not entirely that either, because there was a burning cyclone in that situation, a destructive element which no one could reckon with, not even the devil with all his arithmetic, because he too throws his share into the big lottery. This burning wind, which I now began to feel, first blew Anna closer than ever to me; every glance, every syllable said: 'Free me from this incubus.' She had moments of such fear that she felt, as she once said, as if she wanted to slip into my breast pocket for protection; but she could only tolerate me when I was gentle and serene; the slightest gesture of approach frightened her beyond measure; when I spoke of running away she would hold her opened right hand with the tips of her fingers extended upwards towards me, as if Elli's picture were written upon it. Adultery was to her the sin of sins. At that time I came to look into her fairly well, during that time between the end of March and the eighteenth of May; from that day on everything changed. I forgot to mention—probably because there is a good reason for letting it sleep in oblivion—for it constituted the depths of my weakness and my dishonourable subservience—that Waremme meantime had given me to understand openly and clearly that the whole tale of the unknown Angelo in Cologne had been an invention to which he had been driven by necessity in order not to endanger our friendship. He confessed this to me on an excursion to Biebrich, as we were sitting on a tree trunk in the woods one night, waiting for the moon to rise. I have spoken of my weakness and cowardice in my relations to him, but that night he was as honest and sincere as so demoniacal and complicated a nature could be. He was unusually impressionable, his surroundings affected him enormously, a landscape or the darkness of a forest could move him greatly. I saw him once in a severe thunderstorm in such a condition that I was really sorry for him. This fear of storms —or whatever it was—he once profoundly explained to me, he had transmitted to Anna also. During a thunderstorm she was simply a flapping little bird. So, as we were sitting cowering on the trunk of the tree, neither seeing the other's face, he came forth bluntly with the statement that he had not had any other choice than to appease me with the sickening tale of this so-called Angelo, for he could not have borne to have me hate him and regard him as an enemy. Now that, through a variety of experience, I had come to know his nature, he no longer feared such a defection; I was aware as well as he that we were chained to one another, not only by the wonderful creature who was the sublimest thing on earth to both of us, but also by the most powerful intellectual bond which could unite two men in a serious historical crisis. Not so fast, don't be so bombastic, was my thought; nevertheless I listened with breathless attention, for who could resist the Orpheus-like charm of his conversation? Then, frankly, I was simply worn out with all this endless business of yes or no, it was so or it wasn't, and nothing surprised me any more. Thus he came to talk about his love for Anna. That wrenched me out of my apathy: he said things which made me shudder. I can't repeat his words; I no longer remember them; I only know that they fell upon me like a shower of hot nails; I don't recall what pictures or comparisons he used; I only know that while he was talking I said to myself uneasily a few times: Do you come into the case at all by comparison? He admitted that he had taken her forcibly there in the dressing-room of the theatre, but he said that if he had not done so he would have gone and hanged himself an hour later. I believed it of him. 'Although she fought me like an outraged angel,' he added, 'her innermost soul was already mine, as it is still mine today, and she knew that and knows that.' He wasn't a robber, nor a sensualist à la Karamazov; it was blasphemy to speak of a crime when two lives were being destroyed if their union was prevented. When the moon finally rose over the tree tops we walked the whole way to the station in silence; only once, when we got near our destination, he put his hand on my shoulder and said: 'I am sorry for you, Maurizius; you are done for if you don't drop her; it will be your ruin.' I still feel how my heart rose into my throat as I replied: 'That's idle talk, Waremme; I know that I am on an inclined plane; but if God would spoil this business for you I should feel better.' He shrugged his shoulders and replied: 'God does not do anyone the favour of interfering with the fate which He has in store for him; I too am only an instrument.' You will admit that this was no usual conversation; indeed it had something cataclysmic about it. Moreover, it was the last talk which has remained accurately word for word in my mind; the rest have melted into mist, probably because the whole structure was breaking up and the conversations of individuals no longer mattered much."

7.

He interrupted himself and walked with a curious crooked gait across the cell to a corner in the wall, and when he began to talk again it seemed as if he were talking internally and had completely forgotten the presence of the chief prosecuting attorney. Sometimes a sentence would come forth in a dismal fashion; others remained fragmentary. At times he would interrupt himself and gesticulate in silence; for example, he stood for a time with his hand clasping his forehead and shook his head for a quarter of a minute. There was something mysterious about all of this, and touching, in its way. He seemed to have difficulty in keeping events apart; particularly in the period during which Elli had a fatal and decisive influence upon events, his memory was less clear than with regard to other matters. He kept harking back to the eighteenth of May, which he had already mentioned; it seemed to be an important date in his relations with Anna. Herr von Andergast remembers that the telling inscription upon the photograph which Elli had found in her sister's desk had been marked with this date. He avoids with almost anxious shyness anything which might throw an unfavourable light upon Anna when talking of the meetings and conversations which took place between them. Herr von Andergast cannot help wondering at his discretion, which seems to him like a petrified superstition. He has the impression that on this eighteenth of May, Anna for the first and only time gave some unmistakable proof of her affection for him, for which he was able only now and again to snatch a scanty and uncertain corroboration. Perhaps it was a fleeting caress, perhaps in some lost second he had succeeded in begging a kiss and in the sick tension of his feelings he overestimates the charity and draws deductions from it upon which his delusion finally breaks. But from his confused hints one can deduce that Anna on this occasion threw off more of her reserve than previously, particularly on the subject of her relations with Waremme. Much in regard to his bearing towards her only becomes comprehensible to him through Anna's assurance that since the disgraceful attack in Cologne there has been no manner of physical relation between them, not the slightest demonstration, or the least hint which would give him any hope of her surrender. This must have driven this supremely vain, jealous, sensual, possessed and obstinate man quite beside himself. That she cannot free herself from him she does not deny; that her body is chained and her spirit powerless against his, but always directed against him, she admits desperately. She shows him the letters which he has written her in the course of a year and a half, more than four hundred letters, twelve, fifteen, twenty pages long: outpourings, entreaties, dreams, poems, which petrify her and make her turn pale when she merely speaks of them. That then was the famous eighteenth of May. A few days later, Anna, completely up a tree, tells him that Waremme has proposed marriage to her. Incredible as it sounds, the divorced man, the father of two children, who are being kicked about somewhere in the world, without any evident means of support, the man who jeers at bourgeois legitimacy, the gambler, the political adventurer and visionary—for he is constantly showing himself to be that more and more—wants to unite this overwrought creature with his restless uncertain life, devoid of all foundation, in order to destroy her completely. Maurizius is filled with repulsion, but he does not dare show it. A pious old Catholic lady, so he hears, a Baroness von Löwen, is going to give her a considerable dowry, but she is previously to withdraw into an Ursuline convent for six months. Constantly more incomprehensible, constantly madder. No, he, Maurizius, cannot rebel; sticky gossip is spreading its poison through the streets, but he cannot spread his arms out to save her, for he does not know whether she wants to be saved; he doesn't even know whether she loves him, or only puts up with him or even hates him, and he knows as little whether she loves, fears, dreads, or hates Waremme. One knows nothing about her; one does not know her; one would have to cut open her breast and examine her heart. This kind of woman, so it seems to him today, when the flood of life has been a transparent sheet of ice for nearly two decades of merciless criticism, has no real kernel to her nature, she is destructive, banefully solitary and self-centred, limited in herself and to her own fate; he walks about gesticulating: "Vessels to which we give the content, perhaps even the soul, certainly their motion and destination. Perhaps they only become our victims because they are so narcistically bound up in themselves, and what is narcissism? It is something which has no body and they make us responsible, make us pay to the day of judgment for wanting to embrace something which has no body, a mere counterfeit of a human. Thus one becomes the victim oneself and is made the fool of Frau Holle in the Snow, in our old fairy tale."

It sounded like a frightful day of judgment. "And it was the same with Elli," continued Maurizius, with his eyes shut, as if talking in his sleep, "I suddenly discovered what it is to be sisters, and the deep secrets which Nature thus constructs. Just because there was as much difference between them as if they had sprung from different worlds, did so many resemblances and similarities come to light. Similarities, to me they were similar as coal and diamonds are similar. One must bear in mind that Elli . . . that selfish selflessness, or whatever you want to call it, was true of her too. I don't want to whitewash myself, there's nothing more to save about me; I am eliminating myself; but suddenly it was no longer a human being whom I had before me. A she-wolf, a bloodthirsty she-wolf was what Elli was when she turned against her sister. And a heartless usurer insisting upon interest and compound interest upon her loans when she turned against me. The structure suddenly burst asunder. A wonderful thing that which we call bearing in a person—the scaffolding, there was no bearing, no carriage left. Merely a raging. A woman with the most delicate nervous system, the most developed mentality, good, distinguished, high-minded. And that . . . I was reproached for . . . a certain thing was used against me . . . namely, that we continued in spite of these horrible quarrels to live together. . . . Well, yes, a man will lower himself as far as a woman will let him fall. I repeat, and this is not intended as a justification; my whole misfortune is concentrated upon this one point: one can so to speak transact unclean business with sensuality, conclude a base exchange for one's dreams and ideals. As often as I have thought about the matter, I have always come to the conclusion that with the exception of one in a thousand, men do nothing else, and thus they corrupt the whole world. I was certainly not that one exception, not I. And Elli played *á banque* when she stole my dreams from before my eyes. She did not know that stolen dreams become a pestilence to the thief. But what am I talking about? It was in the end only a question of flesh and blood that we were living together with that misery in our hearts. But the awakening then . . . the vengeance, the rage; you are still yourself and beside her, that she was cheated, the years by which she was older than I became her Erinys; she and I holding on to one another plunged headlong into the deepest pit of evil and savagery. When she made a spy of herself and questioned people about me and fought with me over that shabby bit of money, and screamed her misery out of the window so that it might as well have been printed in the papers every day, and swept through the house night after night like a will-o'-the-wisp and could not understand, oh, *would* not want to understand that I was a poor devil like herself, one to whom God had given his fate to drink to the dregs. . . . Then there came a day when I said to myself: 'It would be better, woman, if you did not exist, better that you should disappear from this frightful scene.' Sir, I tell you that it seemed to me a good deed to destroy her, for, so I said to myself, such a life is a burden and a torment for the person who lives it, and a burden and torment to those who must share it with her. Should there not be a way out; should one not be permitted to make peace? With this criminal wish upon my conscience I am, of course, not guiltless. No, indeed. Don't think that. . . . I am not guiltless, still less am I innocent—which is something quite different. There is a place where a person's life is over, the idea is past, and what follows then is like the afterbirth after a confinement. . . . But one must not venture too far; I know, I know. In one of my worst periods, I said to Anna: 'If the worst comes to the worst, I'll shoot you and then myself and then we'll have peace.' That was already the day towards the end of September when that nasty business of Waremme's with the students came to light, which knocked the bottom out of things. Anna almost died over it; and at that time I already owed all that money; my wife did not help me; she was on her knees to that interest-sweating capital of hers, praying to it. She was bewitched, but the question is whether she was still a living human being with the living ideas of a human being in her breast, or a sorry corpse which merely twitches its muscles like the dead body of a frog. But that's beside the point so far as my guilt is concerned; I for my part was through; I was only sorry on Anna's account; but she did not wish to die; I have often racked my brains why she protested with such mad horror against death; perhaps it was the pious child in her, the belief in the sinfulness of suicide. I have heard too that extraordinarily beautiful people can free themselves much less from the fear of death than others, as if their beauty placed some duty upon them, which one of our sort knows nothing about; that was probably the reason too why she was so afraid of my return. Since I had made that remark about the shooting she trembled when she saw me, she probably scared Elli with it too and drove her out of the house; in her feverish anxiety she screamed to her: 'Your husband is coming, he wants to kill me!' It must have been something of the sort. She must have run through the house like a hunted doe . . . with the fear of death in all her limbs . . . it must have been like that. . . ."

He pressed the thumb and middle finger of his right hand to both his temples. Herr von Andergast got up, slowly as if his limbs had turned to lead. "So," he murmured, "well . . . so. . . ." Then, after a pause during which he lost his breath, with apparently professional dryness, speaking with the mechanical knowledge of the proceedings of the process: "And her . . . her playing the piano previously was only because in her senseless fear she no longer knew what she was doing; is that what you mean?" "Quite possible," replied Maurizius with reserve. "And then?" continued Herr von Andergast with a simply superhuman attempt to appear indifferent, or at most superficially interested. He even pulled his watch out of his pocket, did not, however, open the lid, but slipped it slowly back. "Then," echoed Maurizius, casting a malicious obstinate glance at the man asking the question, "then . . . why, you will have to go by the records. They can give you better information about it." But after a sinister silence, during which the feminine little teeth bit nervously at his nether lip, there burst from him: "Everything was in league against her. . . . There was no further escape . . . all of her tormentors . . . were close upon her . . . the measure was full . . . no one had any insight, no one had any pity . . . why had she still to send for Waremme? . . . for he only needed to turn the switch from a distance . . . I, my God . . . too late . . . too late!"

He stopped, deathly white with terror, swayed, and caught himself against the wall. Herr von Andergast walked towards him with the same leaden stupor and caught his glance. They looked each other steadily in the eyes for fully twenty seconds.

Maurizius lifted his hand; shyly, defensively. Herr von Andergast saw that the finger nails had been bitten. It was evidently a result of his loneliness and his lonely brooding. "From whom did she get the revolver?" he whispered hoarsely. Maurizius started. "Why, do you think I saw anything?" he exclaimed wildly: "I saw nothing, nothing, absolutely nothing . . . that's just it . . . nothing. . . ." Herr von Andergast sank his head resignedly. "That's just it . . . nothing, nothing," repeated Maurizius with a gesture of hopelessness. "And you? You yourself? Did you or did you not have a revolver?" continued Herr von Andergast unswervingly in his dry voice. Maurizius laughed shortly. "It is another era," he replied enigmatically, "I am no longer twenty-six; I am forty-five." As he said this, his eyelids suddenly twitched as they had done in the courtroom nineteen years ago. Again their eyes penetrated into one another. "Very well, I shall note these things," continued Herr von Andergast with the curious feeling that something in his spine was breaking.

Maurizius stands by listlessly, while Andergast takes his

hat and gives the sign to the warden and leaves the cell. A second jailor appears with a leaden dish. It is lunch for convict number 357. A thick cabbage soup with a few shreds of meat floating in it like dark tree-roots on a yellow pool.

CHAPTER XIII

I.

CONVERSATIONS between two people who have something decisive to settle with each other seldom take the course which the participants imagine or plan for, least of all when they tend towards a so-called reckoning. Sophia von Andergast, in any case, had distinct expectations of the meeting with her divorced husband. That the meeting was somewhat different from what she had looked forward to, in her passionate excitement, simply lay in the fact that the man with whom she found herself face to face was no longer the person whom she had known. The impatience with which she arrived at the house of the general's widow was so driving that she stared at the old lady with a complete loss of composure when the latter told her that the solicitor-general had gone away, and that she had not been able to learn when he would return. Not until the following noon did they learn, on telephoning to his office, that he would be back in town towards evening. Sophia had spent a sleepless night and towards four in the morning had left her bed and gone into the garden. When the old lady had her called for breakfast at eight o'clock, they searched the whole house for her and finally found her dozing on a bench in the pavilion, her arms crossed over the side of the bench, her head between her elbows. It was with difficulty that she was persuaded to take a cup of tea and to the reproaches of the old lady, who became almost convulsively talkative, she replied only with a stereotyped forced smile. Altogether the general's widow missed the openness and affection which she felt she had the right to demand; she was obliged to hold herself in check and to say to herself constantly: She is not merely an unhappy woman. She is the mother of my

Etzel. I did not invite her here in order to have a pleasant time with her, but because something is finally to take place; there can't be the slightest idea of pleasure about it. In spite of her usual urbanity, she was a little obstinate and egotistic and wanted, quite modestly, and in spite of their mutual cares, that Sophia should woo her consideration a little. But Sophia showed merely a uniform politeness, which angered the old lady, who eagerly accumulated everything which she disliked about the new arrival, a certain bareness of words and reserve, a firm and determined appearance and, last but not least, her extreme care about her appearance: even in her morning dress she looked as if she were stepping out of a bandbox. The general's widow said to herself, She takes excellent care of herself; that does not tally with such worry and suffering—as if worry and suffering were only corroborated by carelessness. But it was rather naïveté than pettiness which caused the old lady to criticize these things. She had probably pictured to herself the touching figure of a *mère prodigue,* a Niobe bowed with grief, instead of which she found herself dealing with a lady who was not easy to fathom, a woman of curiously reserved mind, silent, flexible, cool, whose features had remained surprisingly youthful. One would take her for thirty-two at the utmost, whereas the widow had calculated that she must already be thirty-eight years old. But all of these disparaging criticisms were only idle bubbles in the old lady's head; at the bottom there was something deeper, there was jealousy. That Sophia looked so unexpectedly young, that she had such charming manners, such perfect teeth, such a slender figure, that Etzel's heart would fly joyfully towards her—if she knew her Etzel—this hurt her and gave her some bad hours.

She had decided to talk as little as possible about Etzel, in the beginning at any rate. This determination was founded upon an impulse of jealousy, although she herself believed that it was intended to save Sophia and to torment her as little as possible. But after lunch, when she had gone into the drawing-room with her guest, her tongue ran away with her; on the one hand, it did not seem decent to her to keep what she knew from Sophia; on the other hand, she was somewhat elated by her knowledge and impatient to display it, as a proof of her care and thoroughness, so to speak. For she had sought out Dr. Camill Raff on her own responsibility; shortly before his removal to the place to which he had been transferred, she had had a detailed conversation with him about Etzel. She had learned important things from this talk, and if she combined these with what she had herself experienced with the boy, above all with his last visit and his vehement demand for money, a good deal of light was thrown upon the path which he might have taken, although it was not for this reason less worrying and unusual. If only he had given some sign of life, she would not have betrayed him, she would have respected and kept his secret; certainly she would have done so if his heart was set upon it, but simply to disappear thus . . . to leave the people at home eating their hearts out with worry and anxiety . . . The widow spoke considerately of "the people," but she meant herself alone. Sophia had listened silently and with keen attention. She was silent now too when the old lady had finished talking. Only a spark in the big brown eyes betrayed that she was taking part in the conversation internally. The widow hesitated a minute; it was the same sparkle, the same bronze gleam which "he" had; there was no doubt; he had that from her; suddenly the stupid jealousy disappeared, and she felt hearty sympathy for the woman. Sophia breathed a sigh: So that's what he's like. She had never been what is called a passionate mother, that is to say she had never made a show of her love, and at the time when she had still been with him, she had put great value upon a light touch in their intercourse. Always ready to laugh and play with him, she had carefully avoided weighing him down with the selfish tenderness which would have engaged him prematurely in a confused world of feelings. Perhaps Herr von Andergast had only tried in his way—and what a cold, bloodless intellectual way it was!—to complete what she had begun out of the fullness of a rich nature. Nor had he completed anything; when the illumination of the heart is lacking, pedagogical principles are what remain, and these had gone woefully astray. When Sophia had been forced to separate herself from her boy, no one had heard a complaint from her, much less any show of despair; people had even discussed this openly and said that she was incapable of any profound feeling. Now it was a peculiarity of hers that she could live cherishing a picture in her heart as if it were a human being made of flesh and blood; certainly she had up to the present day the feeling of an active association; during all of these years she felt as if she were educating the boy from a distance to be her ally. Miraculous forces were at work here which had nothing in common with the pursuit of a set purpose. Therefore the exclamation of relief: So that is what he is like. Therefore, the gleam like Etzel's in her eye.

2.

Towards evening she went out and drove into the city. Wandering slowly through the streets, she was constantly divided between what was homelike and what was hostile; one recollection was clear and melodious; another was dismal and tormenting. The newly painted old houses in the neighbourhood impressed her as being deceitful, but in front of the Römer she stood still, gazing up as one looks up at a revered face. Looking constantly at the ground, as if following a track, she reached the Kettenhofweg and stood before the Andergast house. Her eyes wandered over the windows of the second story, they were all dark. This darkness announced absence, the absence of the two human beings who, to her mind, were as far apart as horror and felicity, and whom she was forced to picture as close together as father and son. If she could go up now and face that man whom she had come to call to account, what words would she use? What sentence would she pass if it were possible now, now at this moment of fulfilment, when she realizes her despoiled life in one single breath, how would he stand before her if she screamed into his face: where is my child, give my son back to me? But this moment of eloquence is always only a moment of fantasy. It crumbles to dust against reality. For on the other side there is also a human being, the most matter of course in the world when one *thinks* of him, the most unexpected, puzzling and paralysing when he *appears*.

But in that "moment of fulfilment" all that she has experienced in ten years disappears like a drop of water in the ocean. How she wandered from hotel to hotel, from city to city. She had no human being to go to, no place to take refuge in, no one to talk to, no home, no help. Coldly and silently she had accepted the instructions of the man up there, had signed the contract; her future had been dictated by him; she had no more rights, merely as much freedom as he gave her, as much money as was left from her inheritance from her parents. She had been ill, she had been ill frequently and had never called in or sought a physician. During the war she had lived in Switzerland, torn up by the surrounding conflagrations, in cheap boarding-houses among banal people, and had succeeded in not drawing any attention to herself, or in creating unpleasant interest. She had studied botany and mineralogy, she had injured her eyes with art embroidery, she had walked much, often beyond her physical strength, and had found it difficult to become accustomed to her loneliness, although she could not live among people. In spite of the most diverse intellectual interests and an unbroken desire for life, her heart so to speak was empty; the existence that she led was utterly joyless; she could laugh and amuse herself, but only among indifferent people; as soon as anyone, man or woman, began a more confidential intercourse, her whole personality changed and she quietly dissolved the relationship. She could not really believe in anything any more; her relation to the outer world was in every sense destroyed; in recent years she had only had a relation of friendship with two people, a Swiss painter, who had buried himself in a Swiss châlet, and an old scholar, M. André Lévy, a professor at the Sorbonne, a famous bacteriologist whom she had met in Geneva and at whose house in Paris she had spent much time. I have spoken of her uninterrupted desire for life; nevertheless she was relieved every evening when the day was over and every morning when the night had gone by; for especially among the unhappy there is a sense of obligation from day to day which is stronger than that towards life itself.

Just twenty-four hours after that "moment of fulfilment," she entered the Andergast house. The general's widow had arranged the meeting with Wolf von Andergast by telephone. To return to the house where one has experienced the irrevocable is less a test of memory for the heart than for the eye. Most people, it seems, even when their feelings have become dulled or have died entirely, have a certain repository for them from which they can at any time pull them forth, if they require them for ghostly stage properties, whereas apartments and objects fade gradually from them so that seeing them again makes us for the first time aware of their former and present individuality. It is as if one had only for a time covered a frightening picture with one's hand in order to lessen the effect of the fright. Of course, this was not the case with Sophia; her soul, as we have said, had kept its fervour undiminished through ten years, nevertheless the evidence of the objects with which she was suddenly surrounded weighed her down; above all, they destroyed the effect of the passage of time, making the idea of growing older, and having grown older, an incomprehensible deception of nature, for everything is just as it always and ever was, ten years or a week, the difference is imaginary. There is the tread of the third step on the second turn, which already creaked then when one stepped upon it; there is the place above the window on the staircase where the red-brown paint had faded into yellow. She had clung tremblingly to this brass knob on a certain day after she had learned that her beloved had shot himself in the temple, and she was uncertain whether she had the strength to go to the house where his body lay. How often had she seen the porcelain name plate with the name, "Dr. Malapert, Oculist," written with a flourish; how hopelessly often she had pressed the button in the second storey, and with what reluctance she had waited for the door of her own apartment to open! Now she is standing there again, pressing the button again; the door is opened for her to enter; there the mirror still hangs, giving back her picture as if it had not missed a single day. There on the hook hangs a stiff hat, the symbol of something revoltingly uniform and formal, under it the coat, to which the revolting odour of cigarettes still clings; on the wall opposite the picture of the old emperor with his parted beard and affable expression. Here is the door out of which she went the last night after the last tearless good-bye to the sleepy boy—weeping was no business for her—and finally the other door, covered with a portière, which she had never opened without the wish that it were already over and she were out of the room again.

3.

At seven o'clock Herr von Andergast said to Rie: "There will be a lady here at half past seven, it is not necessary to announce her." Rie nodded knowingly. The widow's Nanny had not failed to tell her who the guest was whom they would receive. She regarded herself as the victim of nebulous secret plots. She gave the cook wrong instructions and in her nervousness let a jar of marmalade fall on the tiled kitchen floor; then she stood there thinking sadly: Everything's going to smash. "Do you remember last autumn," she said, "the same thing happened and our boy knelt down and wanted to lick up the sweet stuff?" The cook pretended to remember, she had even been surprised because the boy was not usually so greedy. "Would to God he had been," said Rie, "then we would still have him with us, a greedy person is attached to his home." At that moment the bell rang, the chambermaid opened the door, Rie stepped noiselessly into the hall and saw a medium-sized woman, not exactly slender, walking with firm steps towards the study, and her hostile thought was, She still seems to know her way about here—as if this circumstance were a proof of corruption. She had never before had such a tremendous desire to listen at a door; only her innate sense of decency kept her back. For a while she stood on the spot listening, then as everything was quite still, she went back to her room disappointed.

At half past five Herr von Andergast had come home and had ordered tea, but had not touched the cup; he had walked noiselessly up and down the room the whole time. It was impossible for him to get the voice of convict Maurizius out of his ears. Whatever he did, or thought, it followed him like the persistent cooing of an invisible dove. At times the fragment of a sentence would stand out from this unmodulated purring; then he would start, cease walking, turn his head to one side, frown, and murmur aloud to himself. He had lighted more than a dozen cigarettes, one after another, but had thrown them all into the ash-tray after two or three puffs. Sometimes he would press his hands to his forehead, in the way he had seen Maurizius do, and his face would take on an expression of frozen brooding. A flood of questions stormed his brain; it was like a whirl of snowflakes and he could not pause over any of them. From time to time he would pull out his watch and assure himself uneasily that time was passing, as if everything depended upon his formulating something before the moment when he would cease to be alone should come. But the feverish whirl of his thoughts did not lessen while the hands of the clock ticked on. Only the cooing, that ceaseless cooing. Finally out of the chaos the following tangible question arose: Why did he not say it at the time? Why, when—since his admissions had such an unmistakable imprint of truth about them—why, why had he kept silent for nineteen years? He might just as well have decided, three, five, twelve, sixteen years ago as now? What had prevented him? Shame, obstinacy, consideration are not feelings which stand a test, in which each separate year becomes an eternity, in which the idea of sacrifice, which evidently plays a rôle as the fruit of an unprecedented passion, must suffer part of the general internal decay. While he was thinking "general internal decay," Herr von Andergast felt hot and cold around his breast; so he was nevertheless infected by the atmosphere around this shadow-man; he had understood the nineteen years of death, perhaps he had even been moved by them more lastingly than he had assumed. What had prevented him, what was it? he continued to ruminate; a presentiment of understanding seized him. Perhaps the matter goes very deep, was his consideration, perhaps he was conscious that the truth was true for him only, but not for me, not for us; for me and for us it only became mature at the moment when he was ready to pronounce it, almost against his will. What if, the thought suddenly shook him, the truth were only a result of the passage of time? Suppose I, three, five, twelve, sixteen years ago was so bound by time, so dulled that I would not have been capable of accepting the truth, this same truth which now seems to me so credible and so simple. Perhaps truth matures only in time. And through time . . . The thought was so disconcerting, it threw such a deadly grey light upon everything which he had called verdict and sentence, up to now, that for a few seconds he felt as if the firm kernel of his personality were disintegrating. In his trouble, in order to save himself from self-dissection, he snatched at the recorded details of the "case" which had already occupied him like a puzzle during the whole of the drive from Kressa. He wanted to see how far Maurizius' representation accorded with the dates which had been established in the documents, he had already turned to these considerations and dropped them again. He had scarcely begun to study them again when there was a soft knock at the door and Sophia entered.

Herr von Andergast remained standing behind his desk as if it were the wall of a fortress. It was one of those situations in which even a formal greeting is absurd. He had not seen this woman for almost ten years. It had not once occurred to him, during these ten years, to examine his feelings towards her. A matter which had been settled had no more claim upon the regulated proceedings of the day. The ability to dispose of things—to close an incident—was as prominent in his private as in his public life. There was a set time for paying off arrears in both spheres of life and, if the time had passed, the matter was dismissed. The woman had closed the door behind her and was standing five steps away from him, but he did not see her, that is, he did not want to see her; he was not at all curious. His somewhat inflamed eyelids were sunk, the powerful body swayed a little. He waited. I am adequately prepared; how can I be of service to you? his icy distant manner implied. But there was a transparent paleness about the nose. Sophia walked over to the leather chair which was standing somewhat in the shadow of the bookcase and sat down silently. She looked at the man with her dark eyes. The corners of her mouth quivered bitterly and threateningly. It seemed as if she wanted to compel him to speak to her first. She knew his obstinacy and felt, as in former times, contempt towards an attitude which she knew was only the barren fulfilment of a line of conduct. But she soon realized her mistake; with her sharpened instinct it was soon evident to her that a change had taken place in this man; it seemed as if nothing were left of his stony immovability and his assumption of complete power except expression, glance and gesture, the empty rind of a fruit. This perception did not make her any milder, nothing could conciliate her, but neither did it arouse any satisfaction in her. It did not interest her. He was not in her eyes a person about whom one thinks. The place which he had once occupied in her life—almost exclusively in a destructive sense—no longer existed. In a burst of accumulated decision she had taken the trip; her former lawyer, with whom she at times corresponded about business matters, had informed her of Etzel's flight. The two letters which she had addressed to Herr von Andergast in March and April, in which she had demanded that the present state of affairs be changed, since the alleged free renunciation had been forced upon her and was consequently an untenable and unworthy regulation, had also been written with his knowledge. No answer had been vouchsafed either letter, and when she had written this to her legal friend, she had added: "It was an unpardonable error to appeal to one who does not understand the human language." The news and the fact that they had not been able to find the boy had driven her beside herself and made her indifferent towards the consequences of a step which, regarded sensibly, was of little practical use. She wanted to act, at least she wanted to show that her former intimidating fear no longer existed. Now she sat here in silence, stifled as it were, just exactly as she had sat when the admission of guilt had been forced from her after Georg Hofer's suicide, and the senseless document had been presented to her for her signature by the man who, under the mask of the judge, unscrupulously exploited her guilt and indulged his revenge.

There ensued a dialogue which can scarcely be rendered here. It was weighed down by its own weight; it departed from all conventional formalities; it lost itself in depths where two souls stood opposite each other, disembodied as it were, in their constitutional hostility; it was full of hints and innuendo, silences and trite abbreviations. Often one answered the speech of the other only by a silence which was clearer than any argument; broken fragments of thought were communicated; a shrug of the shoulder contained a story; the air of the room was laden with vibrations which affected the nerves of the two participants. Herr von Andergast began by saying that unfortunately he had not had the good fortune to be informed about the object of this visit, although he could guess its purpose—a colourless manner of expressing himself; the voice in which he spoke was the same which he used in addressing a litigant during a consultation. After mature consideration of the admissibility or inadmissibility of such an interview, he had decided in favour of the former. Nevertheless—and there followed a shrug of the shoulders as if this were the end of his wisdom. Sophia flew into the air. What an impertinent paper majesty, she thought, with rage. Then she smiled and sat down again. The occasion to which he had alluded, he continued a shade more politely, thinking that he had emphasized his point of view with sufficient clearness in the introduction, could not, however, move him to any explanation or discussion; he did not recognize now, any more than previously, any demands of this sort. "Ah, really," came like the cry of a bird from Sophia's chair. Unpleasantly struck, Herr von Andergast looked in that direction. "That is so," he corroborated coldly. Sophia leaned back and crossed her arms over her breast. "Vain hope," she said indifferently, "there will be no demands made, so that there will not be anything for you to dispute." Herr von Andergast lifted his eyebrows questioningly. Then I understand still less the wish for this meeting, the restrained irritation of his expression seemed to say. The first *"du"* from the woman's mouth had been a shock to him, although it was impossible to see how it could be permanently avoided. He took up the seal which lay next to the inkwell, weighed it in his hand and looked at it attentively. His thoughts moved in two concentric circles. The one embraced everything relative to the convict Maurizius and filled a part of his brain which had been worn sore; he had the feeling that he had left the cell too soon, thus losing the most important revelations. I must make up for that, he said to himself, there are things which must still be cleared up. Internally, he reconstructed the scene of the murder; he reconsidered again and again the circumstance of the revolver, which had disappeared; he calculated how much time Waremme must have taken to go from the casino to the garden gate, and found a suspicious difference of one and a half to two minutes. He remembered that night had fallen, that it was a foggy October evening, and reproached the prosecution with having attached too much importance to the accidental witness; the same old mistake, as he resignedly admitted. He measured in his mind the distance from the gate to the entrance of the house where Anna Jahn had stood, thirty-five yards, bearing in mind that Waremme had to run past Maurizius, if the latter did not really fire the shot, and had probably turned around then and faced Maurizius with the revolver which he had picked up from the ground, in his hand. All this he pondered, deciding that he must go to see the convict again and that quickly, in order to get him to give some supplementary explanations. All the while he concealed from himself that it was the personality of Maurizius himself which attracted him and held him breathless in a way no one had ever done before. At the same time, he anxiously evaded the only possible deduction from the whole situation, namely, that Waremme must have perjured himself. To say this clearly to himself was beyond his power; but it took an enormous effort of will to keep it from coming to his consciousness.

Thus all these tormenting visions remained in the one circle impinging from time to time upon the other in which Sophia was visible, and in which, in spite of his decision not to think of the boy in connection with her, Etzel invisibly stood. Although he produced the impression that he had not really looked at Sophia at all, his furtive observing glance had already taken her in a long time ago. The red-brown hair still had the same slightly golden tinge; the sweet oval of her cheeks had not essentially changed; her eyebrows were still so characteristically arched, giving her face the expression of that constant short-sighted curiosity which had so often made him impatient; her throat had hardly any lines. Her bearing indicated nothing of her hard fate, nothing of her illnesses, nothing of the path of expiation which she had trodden. There was no regret, no humility, no gesture of pleading, nothing oppressed, no trace of being in need, or of being deserted, none of those things which one expected and would gladly have seen, but rather freedom, gravity and caution. How could that be? There was something wrong here. Was this the result of the inflicted punishment? This calm face, this superior silence, this self-sufficient smile—so it seemed to him, actually it was a painful smile, just as the whole inner life of the woman was expressed in certain soulful lines around the mouth. Far more frightening was her resemblance to Etzel, the mere way in which she sat there, the suspicious tense glance, secretive and constantly on the defensive, the mixture of childishness and irritating maturity in the features, the eagerness for knowledge and . . . craftiness even, it was extraordinary and remarkable, ghostlike almost. This was something for which he had not been prepared, it would perhaps oblige him to revise his tactics, to be stricter and to make regulations to prevent the dreaded and evidently dangerous similarity between these two similar characters from developing.

And Sophia?

4.

The matter with her stood simply thus: alarmed, she had naturally thought at a distance of some disastrous quarrel between father and son. She had supposed that this had been called forth on the one side by the despotism of Herr von Andergast, the coldness of his disposition and his habit of keeping people who were dependent upon him in severe check, forcing them to silent obedience, on the other hand by the natural revolt of a young spirit thirsting to express itself and control its own actions, and snatching therefore at the first pretext at hand in order to throw off an unbearable yoke. She had painted stormy scenes, an open rupture, she had supposed that the flight had been unplanned, unthought out, an act of despair, that after adventurous wandering around in the world, it must lead either to a return and punishment or to collapse. The information of the general's widow had shown her the matter in a different light and corroborated her confidence in those mysterious communications of the soul which had merely been obscured by those other anxious and frightening pictures. But she had still had doubts. The meeting with her husband had quieted these. As sensitive as a seismograph to the internal emotions of others, she recognized the indications of a catastrophe in Herr von Andergast's unrest, in the sudden kindling and subsiding of his glance, in his shy vigilance combined with an absent-mindedness bordering upon distraction. What had occurred was something far more fraught with meaning than a simple running away of a half-grown boy who had rebelled against the paternal rule. Even if it had occurred on her account—for one could imagine that the crime committed against his mother had not remained unknown to the boy, and he had left his father for the reason with the secret hope of going to her—even then she would not have felt the satisfaction which she now enjoyed. This "meaning" was of a higher kind; the requital was more telling. Who would have dared to hope just such a thing as this, or to prophesy it? She smiled. It was a smile not of triumph, rather of surprise, as if she could not quite believe this wonderful thing. Then she said fearlessly: "The demands which I could make no longer have any content, only you do not know it." "How is that?" asked Herr von Andergast with a feeble attempt to appear interested, replacing the signet in its place. "That is, you know it well, only you keep yourself from realizing it, artificially," continued Sophia. "How could a person not know if he has been struck to the very quick and the principles of his life turned upside down?" "May I permit myself to say that your remarks are utterly incomprehensible?" "Certainly. My ambition in that regard is slight. But the matter is not particularly obscure." "I am all attention—" "You do not imagine that this is merely a temporary disturbance between your son and yourself? The boy will return when he has carried out his purpose, or when he is convinced that he cannot attain it. He will come back, without a doubt, but not to you. Never again to you." Herr von Andergast laughed dryly, but with some uneasiness. "I should think there might be measures and arrangements," he replied. "Compulsory measures and compulsory arrangements." "Yes, but that is not the way to win back a soul." "I do not place any value upon the soul." "I know that. So you will try to exorcise the soul. You have obtained brilliant results in this way—" "I shall do what duty demands." "Of course. Duty is a stern master. And what does duty command you to do? Imprisonment?" "I refuse to discuss the matter in this form." "The form, my God," said Sophia pityingly, "I can't discuss the matter with you as if I were an automaton in your office, considering what is at stake." "Namely?" "I have not come to demand anything, but rather to prevent something." "And what is that?" "If you did not understand so well, you would not ask so badly." "You seem to fear, after all, that I am not so powerless in regard to future developments as you wished in the beginning to make me believe?" "Who would doubt the keenness of your vision? Your acumen is the best thing about you. Powerless? No. I do not regard you as powerless. You will never be that. Unfortunately. You are to be pitied for that reason. When one is powerless, one often discovers one's real force. You have spent yours on a dead object. Do not drive it to the point of absurdity. You have utterly lost the boy."

For a moment it seemed as if Herr von Andergast wanted to throw off the armour which made him immune, the violet-blue eyes glowed unpleasantly; the transparent pallor around his nose spread over his face. But he remained silent. The woman is forgetting herself; the woman is decidedly becoming too personal, he thought angrily. But he remained silent. He walked over to the brown tile stove and leaned against it with the gesture of a man who with silent contempt repudiates the idea that his person may be made the object of psychological subtleties. Sophia's voice remained in the same key in which the conversation had been conducted up to the present: "One day his eyes were bound to open. It had to become plain to him who his father is. For he is my son. That he is my son is undeniable. Or is it not? Of course, I did not have a proper conception of him. Curious admission for a mother, is it not? But I have not waited in vain all these years, done nothing but wait. Your calculation was false. Even if you do not care anything about the soul, as you say, the soul has proved to you that one cannot do violence to it. The antagonist in the spirit. It's admirable with what a conscious aim you brought him up to this. Your mother told me . . . if one keeps everything together, a clear picture ensues. You probably don't remember that I could never believe in Maurizius' guilt. You, of course, did not deign to take any notice of what an eighteen-year-old creature thinks and feels . . . that, *mon Dieu, cela ne tire pas, à conséquence*. We came to know each other thoroughly on the day on which the judgment was confirmed and you told me about it with beaming countenance. A shudder ran right through me. I can still hear the tones in which you uttered the words, valid and legal, as though they were a message from heaven. When I announced our engagement to my father—he was taking a cure in Nauheim, three weeks before his death—he wrote me a letter concerned only with the innocence of Maurizius, and with you as the person who conducted the prosecution. He, the legal scholar, was deeply concerned, for the law was not to him a matter settled according to the tablets of Moses. He was greatly troubled about our engagement. Curious. Nothing is lost in the world, the scattered grain of wheat fell into the heart of my child, and grew into a tree from which he plucked the fruit of knowledge. In your eyes right and the law are institutions which are proof against human criticism. I dreamed once that a tremendous crowd of people grovelled on their knees before you, begging you to revoke a decree, but you stood like a pillar of stone. A frightful delusion to imagine that one could be unfailing, an unfailing judge. Not to have been able to make mistakes, what a curse! You took my child from me, yes, my child; a mother *possesses*, perhaps of all people in the world she alone *possesses*, but I am not complaining, and I am not complaining about you. How do they say it in your legal language, I am recapitulating; you stole him from me—but let me finish talking, the word exactly expresses the fact—at an age when you could hope to model him entirely according to your ideas, in your likeness; he was wax in your strong hand. You based your behaviour upon right and law, regarding them as dependable satellites, and truly they have served you well. Then the human being who was lawfully seized grows up, and what happens? He disturbs your foundations, and tears up your delusion; justice and law desert you. No dialectics can question this. I need only look at you to see that this is so. Up to an hour ago I had no conception of this, no conception that . . ." She sprang up and took two steps towards Herr von Andergast, and with her right hand clenched on the open palm of her left hand, she asked with a curiously joyous voice, in which no excitement could be heard: "Shall

I tell you what has happened besides this?" Herr von Andergast lifted his arm with his finger outstretched commandingly. The gesture at this moment had the ghostlike effect of a legal gesture. "I will forgo that," he said hastily, "we do not have to settle that with each other, I must beg to be excused from any further discussion." Sophia replied sarcastically: "I understand you are depriving me of the floor, but you are only depriving yourself." She took one more step and smiled curiously, passionately, almost convulsively, whispering with her face turned upwards: "But where is he, where is he? He must come soon. I should like finally to see him. . . ." Herr von Andergast bent his head. For a time he was utterly still, until the word perjury penetrated to his ear, making him wince.

5.

Sophia had turned away and walked up and down the narrow room between the desk and the bookcase, as one sometimes does when one is inwardly very tense. She appeared to be looking with curiosity at various objects, the barometer near the window, a bronze figure in a corner of the room, the back of a book. At the same time, she began to speak in her previous light conversational tone and with her quick play of features, and whenever she stood still or turned around, there was a threatening upward tilt of her nose. What she said made the impression that she wished by her ruthless uncovering of the past to hint at her equally ruthless decision with regard to the manner in which she intended to shape her future. The unusual boldness of a woman who is capable of thinking, and has learned to think, and is not afraid of any consequences of her thinking, became more apparent than heretofore. It was as surprisingly new to Herr von Andergast as if the stove behind him had turned into a human being and was taking part in the conversation. There arose again before him that frightful notion of "too late," which, since Etzel's flight, had dragged through the nights, making them exhaustingly long. It grinned at him from every wall, at home, in the office, in the street, everywhere, everywhere, too late, too late, too late. . . .

She did not hesitate to speak of her offence coolly. "When I was unfaithful to you that time," she said. She designated the adultery as an unsuccessful attempt at flight from a dungeon. "I was a free person up to my twentieth year," she said. "From the day of my marriage I was condemned to supervision." With a slight shudder, she remarks: "One becomes a mother as lightning might strike. According to right and the law." Then: "What did my life consist in? What did my marriage consist in? A husband made up of sexuality and profession, sex at night, profession by day, an increasingly turbid mixture of the two as custom made him more sure of himself. He did not have enough humanity about him, even to consider why the languishing thing at his side was silent and more and more silent, at best said yes or no, and was polite and obedient, and dressed well and for the rest went to the dogs. He was the master, the husband, the father, the breadwinner. All very thoroughly, all very conscientiously, according to justice and the law. What more does one's heart desire? Yes, but the heart, even if it needs not to be ashamed to love, refuses to love. Contrary to justice and the law. And in its hunger and helplessness feels that it must love, anyone at any price, if only to test itself to know that it is not in the world for nothing, merely for the kitchen, the cellar, the bedroom and the nursery; and so it gives itself to whoever snatches for it, if only it be someone halfway acceptable. Also against justice and the law. Love . . . all right, let's call it love. Many a passion springs only from the fear of emptiness. And those are the maddest. Georg Hofer was no hero. A gifted everyday person, decent, generous. If he had been more he would have scorned your prejudices and not have sworn the oath which was to save me and cost him his life. Perjury! This nightmare drove him to his death. No, he was not a strong man, he was entirely permeated with the conceptions of honour of his class and quite convinced by your justice and your law, which always seemed to me like the skull and bones painted on bottles containing poison, as a warning. When you compelled him to take that oath, you already had my confession, and you knew that you would destroy him with it—according to justice and the law—and you forced me to confess with the lie that by doing so I would free him from the oath! Perjury . . . a useful instrument, this way or that, sometimes one uses and ignores it; sometimes one damns and persecutes; the end justifies the means. Why, you live in a world of perjury. But the one, however, with which you caught him and me is a black spot in your life which you cannot extirpate, even if you live like a repentant monk for the rest of your life; you cannot get rid of that, you cannot cover it over. I have often asked myself how one can get along with such a situation; probably by not looking at it; you have so much power and endurance in averting your eyes."

"Yes, perjury," said Herr von Andergast tonelessly, his yellow face standing out in the darkness from over his bent body. "Yes, he must have sworn a false oath." Sophia looked towards him in astonishment. Naturally she did not know what internal disturbance had produced this exclamation. She stood still, looking penetratingly at him. Then he said brokenly: "It is not a good thing to bring up those old stories. It is not a good thing to do, Sophia. There are particular reasons for that just now. You are a woman, who perhaps understands more than others, but that . . . no. You women, recently, have been making an appeal for which we are not prepared. There are differentiations to which you attain because you have the time, a great deal of time, and know nothing of an imperative *must* and *has to be*. If I were what I *could* be, I should, in a higher sense of the word justice, be in the right against you. But"—he interrupted himself with a profound sigh—"consider that today almost every man approaching fifty is broken in his attitude towards life. I am unfortunately no exception to the rule." Sophia stood with her eyelids and their long lashes sunk. "Take your hands off the boy," she replied. He, again his whole stiffness returning: "I cannot see with what justice—" Sophia interrupted him with an impatient gesture: "Justice, justice . . . I have paid the price." "Nothing has been handed to me, either." As she was silent, he looked at her and suddenly knew the price which she had paid. There are women, who after a lifetime of voluntary deprivation, dictated by an all-consuming goal, attain a second virginity. He looked at her, she smiled, a narrow smile full of silent force. Suddenly she bowed to him, proudly aloof, and walked towards the door, pulling her glove over her left hand as she went. Herr von Andergast dropped into the chair in front of his desk, leaned his elbows on the edge of the table and pressed his hands over his face. He sat thus for two hours and did not hear Rie's frequent and constantly more timid knocks. Finally, towards eleven o'clock, she anxiously decided to open the door and to whisper through the crack that his cold supper was waiting for him. She was, moreover, to a certain extent reconciled to the woman's visit, for when Sophia, on leaving the room, had seen Rie standing in the hall, she had walked up to her and silently pressed her hand.

6.

At seven o'clock in the morning, Herr von Andergast was already on his way back to Kressa. What did he wish to do there? What did he expect? What drew him thither so impatiently, that his car seemed to move as slowly as a post-coach and he observed every obstacle on the road with bitterness? More interrogations and questions, there was no sense to that. The police court details with which he had still deceived himself the day before had ceased to have any meaning. They could add nothing to the picture, they could take nothing from it. Wherein then did this urge consist? He avoided this matter in his own mind. To examine this kind of unrest, as if one—why, it was laughable!—as if one were obliged to see a friend before making decisions which could not be postponed, would have led to precarious paths. Friend . . . the convict in a penitentiary? Friend? Perhaps he was not well, that his mind should produce such strange vagaries. Overwork. The strain and repercussion of unpleasant experiences, first with his wife and then the trouble with the boy. Hastening to deny that either had much weight, deciding not to think of it, not to suffer from it, denying any responsibility, he was perhaps loading down the importance of the Maurizius incident by means of sophistries, so he said to himself, from internal motives of counter-demonstration. A refinement of self-observation which did honour to his intellect. At the same time that which drove him to return to the convict was the same thing which made him long for the boy, not, however, in such an offended and darkened manner, as if the best within him had been misjudged, but more shyly, as if one must propitiate Fate, but the barriers were so strong that one could not break them through. These entirely joyless men of this stamp and generation, familiar with friendship only from the reminiscences of their boyhood, only become aware of their complete isolation at a very advanced period of their lives. It sometimes happens then—as with some women during the climacteric—that they seek to obtain what they have lost, by resorting to actions quite contrary to their character up to the present. Before his mind's eye there floated the idea of talking things out, coming to an understanding—still more—although there was no prospect of this, as he knew only too well—making himself understood, all the time fighting against the compulsion, shrugging his shoulders at himself, thinking of pretexts to make this renewed visit plausible. This, however, could not prevent his constantly hearing the soft voice in his ear, seeing before him the broken gestures, the fluttering glance of the prisoner, the charming curved mouth, reminding one of Napoleon's mouth, the little feminine teeth, the chalk-white hair. And besides all this, there was the feeling, which he had already had the first time he stood facing him, that here was a man entrusted with the task of telling the world secrets of which it had not had any inkling previously.

Shortly before reaching Kressa, the drive was interrupted by rain and the chauffeur was obliged to put up the top. Then, in the office, he was obliged to wait a quarter of an hour while the supervisor was informed, for the latter was making a report. When Pauli came, he said that prisoner 357 had been taken ill during the night, they had allowed him to remain in his cell, as he had wished, instead of moving him to the hospital. It was, according to the physician, only a slight indisposition, indigestion, or something of the sort; after taking bicarbonate of soda the patient felt quite all right; the baron could quite well talk to him. The man with the excited eyes, who was writing, got up and eagerly handed over the notification of illness. Ten minutes later,—the prison clock was striking nine,—the warden unlocked the cell.

Maurizius lay on his iron bed, covered up to his chest with a heavy grey blanket. His face was chalk-coloured, his eyes looked like two black coals in their dark-ringed sockets. At the sight of the solicitor-general, he sat up suddenly with an expression which seemed to say: What! Again! Not yet enough? Over his rough shirt he wore his denim coat, the buttons of which were open at the neck. Herr von Andergast walked up to him, looked down upon him from his imposing height, a frown of dismay upon his forehead —and suddenly he stretched out both hands to him. While waiting for the gesture to be returned—which it was not—

his teeth gleamed through his lips, which looked puffed and swollen. One would have supposed that the white face of the prisoner could not get any whiter, nevertheless it did. What does that mean, his angry, frightened glance seemed to ask, what's back of that? The distrust characteristic of years in a penitentiary. Herr von Andergast dropped his arms. For a while he stood sunk in thought. Then he walked over to the window, looked out at the rain falling like a dull fine cobweb, then took the wooden chair, placed it next to the bed and dropped heavily into it. Pressing the finger tips of his two hands against one another, he said thoughtfully: "I want this time to give up any unpleasant inquiries, or investigations. So do not be uneasy. I am sorry that your health seems to have suffered from the strain yesterday." Maurizius placed his head, which he had thus far held up with strained attention, back upon his coarse pillow. "Pshaw, health!" he remarked indifferently, that was all. Herr von Andergast bowed. "One question," he continued, in the completely altered tone which he had taken towards the prisoner today, a tone from which sounded unmistakably, "I am speaking from man to man, from equal to equal," and which made Maurizius listen as if he were trying to hear a voice not easy to distinguish in a crowd. "One single question. If you think it well not to answer, I shall understand your silence. For it could only have one interpretation." Maurizius looked into the air. "Please go on," he whispered. "Would you accept your dismissal if you were pardoned, without undertaking any further steps? Your word would suffice me."

An electric thrill runs through Maurizius' outstretched body. He presses his parched lips together and is unable to speak. A wild dance of mingled scenes tears through his brain. He would like to scream something. He cannot scream. He would like to cover his face with his hands. He is unable to. His back feels like a lump of lead and his heart seems like a limping motor about to stop. Herr von

Andergast understands. With curious shyness he places his hand upon Maurizius' arm. He says: "I am offering you what it is possible to offer. You still have a future before you. You must not throw it away on account of a phantom." Maurizius' face becomes convulsed. "A phantom? Phantom, you say? A future without this . . . this phantom? Future . . . with what is inside there"—he points to his eyes—"and there"—he slaps his breast with the palm of his hand . . . "future!" Herr von Andergast talks to him as if he were an obstinate child: "You must adjust yourself. Life is a powerful force. A stream which filters dirt and poison. Just think of freedom." That's banal, hopelessly banal, he thinks, full of anger at his stale, trite words. Again a tremor runs through the worn body of the convict. "Freedom . . . oh, yes, my God . . . freedom . . ." His eyes become wet. "Now, you see," said Herr von Andergast, touched. He suddenly feels like a benefactor, a real friend. This moves him, he forgets that these alms are not even a present, he does not feel the mockery and sarcasm. Maurizius lies there in silence. Five minutes pass and he does not move. Finally his lips tremble and he begins to speak.

7.

"You don't know. No one in the world can have the remotest conception of it. Everybody's imagination stops at that point like a balky cow. Nothing that one says, or that is known outside, is adequate. Some people think that they have realized it because they have steeped themselves in certain pictures which affect the fantasy. They have not even comprehended a speck of it. Others again say it is not so bad, that every individual adjusts himself to conditions, that habit is everything, that conditions are getting better every year, that legislation is yielding to the spirit of the times, and more of the sort. They lack any conception. All of the injustice and suffering of the world are based upon the fact that experience cannot be transmitted. At most communicated. Between what is meted out and what is unbearable, there lies the whole path of experience which none can tread but alone. Just as one must always die alone, and no one knows anything about death. Not so bad . . . no. For a long time one thinks, not so bad. If one were not mentally, morally, spiritually, socially done for as a human being, as a son and father and husband, the rest would really not be so bad. Quiet, as I have already said to you, quiet and peace. No more ambition, no cares about money, no excitement, no scenes, no newspapers; just order, peace and quiet. Nothing more comes to one through the walls. Freedom, one has had enough of that. It has landed one where one is. One says to oneself: 'You don't need freedom, it merely makes you wayward, as one becomes a drunkard if one has too much wine.' For a long time it is thus. You have certainly heard of the Spanish water-cure. The person is put under a dripping spigot and at regular intervals drops of water fall upon a certain part of the body. At first it is only unpleasant, then it becomes painful, then a frightful torment, finally every drop feels like a hammer beating upon one's head until skin and flesh and bones become one tremendous wound. When I came to this house I thought: 'Not so bad.' Day after day passed, week after week, month after month and I still thought: 'Not so bad.' There were even moments and hours when the condition of being endlessly shut in gave me a feeling of internal security, as if nothing further could ever happen to me. You must consider what was behind me. The rigidity of one's thoughts must first break down. Well, then the fog lifted. One day the director said to me: 'You have been in this place fifteen months.' Let me remark in passing that I was never addressed as *'du,'* always as *'Sie,'* at a time when the others were spoken to as *'du,'* for I was an intellectual, a former doctor of philosophy. Well, that went through me like a flame, that fact of fifteen months. Fifteen months, I thought, where have they gone to, where are they? What have I seen or known of them? Ordinarily that is a period of life which one notices, in a good as well as in a bad sense, outside one feels the passage of time in one's bones and one's finger tips. . . . I said: 'Director, is it really fifteen months?' He laughed and said: 'Lucky man for whom no hour strikes.' That was the beginning. The beginning, namely, of the fear that one's senses will lose their grasp upon living time. This fear became so frightful that I prevented myself from falling asleep at night in order to hold on to the time, to be aware of the time, as men at the races keep their eyes fastened upon the colours of the jockeys in order not to miss the moment at which the winner passes the goal. But that is a false comparison. 'I don't want to compare; anything,' I said, 'would be wrong and crooked because the comparison would be in terms of your world outside.' This anxiety about time ate into my nerves, just as if I had had something to lose. Almighty Heaven! What was there for me to lose or to miss . . . with a lifelong sentence? Just pronounce that to yourself: lifelong! What is there to lose then? But the human brain is a crazy institution. This torture drew its fellow close in its turn. With the anxiety about time, the torment about what was going on simultaneuosly began. That was if possible worse. For example, I am standing in the workshop, my hands going through the same perpetual mechanical function, then it comes over me: now at this minute the letter carrier Lindenschmitt is going down the Promenadengasse and ringing at the Villa Kosegarten; now at this minute Professor Stein and Professor Wendland are meeting at the corner of the university building and putting their heads together because they are carrying on their usual intrigue against Professor Strassmeyer. I see them. I see the letter carrier Lindenschmitt, with his drunkard's nose, snatching at the leather bag, and pulling out the letters. And I see the maid in the

Villa Kosegarten first sticking her head out of the window, and shaking her dust cloth before she pushes the button which opens the iron gate. I see it because I have seen it a hundred thousand times and because it's difficult for anything to have changed about that. This varies with every hour, in every city where I have been, at the station, in the hotels; I see what was going on in the art collections at that time, the people I was in the habit of meeting there, who were always to be found there, and who must be there now too. I see the first wagons rolling through the sleepy streets in the morning, and in the evening the first gas-jets flame up at the street corner; I see a bronze statue in the museum at Kassel which I was always fond of and I think: Curious. Curious that it stands there and I know that it stands there; it is as if I could touch it; but I might as well imagine touching Orion; it is and is not; it is there and it is not there. And so it is with everything, with the trees which I know, with little boys whom I know and who in a miraculous, dreamy way grow bigger, with objects which belonged to me and about which I ask myself where they are now, where they are at this moment, for they must be somewhere. . . . This stayed with me and did not leave me and, like my anxiety about time, it caused the time to pass more and more slowly; I felt every day more and more; I always felt the present day, you understand; and when all of the separate days were over and collected together, it seemed as if some tremendous beast of prey had devoured them all at one bite. Then just as anxiety, time produced this, the horrible feeling about all that was going on simultaneously caused everything to stretch forward into space endlessly. I could not believe there were walls here; I would walk towards a wall as if it must open like a curtain on the stage. Space, space, space everywhere; that I was locked up seemed a silly joke. But all this was a silly trifle to what came later on. . . ."

He turns his head sidewise several times; then he crosses his hands over the top and continues. "Of course, this torment about the time was the source of everything else, especially the one . . . well, how shall I explain it . . . the *if* torture, the *if* and *if I had* torment. *If* in this or that situation *I had* done thus and so, *if* in this or that conversation *I had* replied this or that, then everything would have turned out differently. If on the twenty-fourth of October, *I had* used the slow train instead of the express, how everything would have turned out differently; and then, to imagine how it would have gone off. All of the past was rearranged and recomposed as if in a delirium. I saw all of the nonsense and the stupidities, all the precipitations, and realized that one cannot force time back in order to change matters. It would have taken so little to change it, it was so simple, this broke one's heart and upset one's mind. And repentance and regret and insight, which came too late; in that person you confided too much; and that person you believed in too fully; there your suspicion was misplaced; to him you should not have told so much about yourself. And all of the things that one thinks of having forgotten . . . forgot to write that important letter to Elli which would have prevented the whole misunderstanding; forgot to tell Anna what would perhaps have saved her and me and my wife, that it was my sacred intention to emigrate alone if everything went wrong, making sure only of Hildegard. Twenty times a day one feels as if one could make up for it, and set matters straight and then one realizes how impossible this is, impossible for once and for all, and then comes a wild revolt against that impossibility. That is the hardest thing to become accustomed to, the fettered will; no, that's stupidly expressed, the fact that one no longer has any will. The organ of will inside of one lamed. For example: the teeth exist for biting, fine; one bites a piece of bread and a tooth falls out of one's mouth and only when all of your teeth are gone have you gotten accustomed to it. That's how that is. Consequently, mere existence and knowledge of oneself come to have something curiously abstract about them, so that one begins to distrust every impulse of life. One gets dizzy when walking, a shudder comes over one when one is forced to climb down the steps; every window seems like a precipice which one does not dare to approach; to get out of bed seems very dangerous; eating and drinking seem like curious anachronisms; to talk to others is like talking to oneself; one cannot laugh or cry; that has remained 'outside.' One still wants and wants and wants, but there is nothing to desire. That drives one mad. The most exciting part of it is that the words with which one expresses one's will decay just like the will itself. Everything is so limited, the up and down; the range is so limited, no wish, no urging, merely the most common needs venture to make themselves felt; inside of one the brain spins and whirls to the point of despair. It is like walking in the woods and having the paths close in behind one. That's how speech drops away, what is precious about it is no longer there, its delicacy fades, the higher conceptions melt into something ordinary and vile. Sometimes memories arise like fiery dragons; one holds one's breath and it is nothing more than some simple meeting with a friend, or that some gentle hand has given one a flower. But it is all immeasurably far away; one is surprised; one could sob with amazement that one has had such an experience. Two or three times a year I started out of my sleep, screaming: 'I, I with a question mark.' But that's a curious matter about the *I;* listen carefully to the people who have been in this house for years, when they speak, and you will notice that before every I which they utter they pause a little while, as persons whose eyes are bandaged are afraid of stumbling. That always moved me deeply. Indeed the people here, that's a very special subject. I don't know how I can make you understand it, or even explain it; I see no end to the subject; when I merely begin everything swims before my eyes. I haven't the talent of a Virgil, and a Dante has never looked at them, it seems to me. I don't want to bore you, either; I hope that I am not boring you? That is well. Before that I want to tell you something about the hopes and expectations, because I was speaking of one's memories, which gradually become as flimsy and as tiny as microbes, with the exception of one or another which stands out like a beacon light, and although there is nothing to it, overpowers one, although one can't tell why. . . . But what one expects, what one's curiosity attaches to, is something so low and so pitiful that one is ashamed. What kind of an expression the warden will have when he unlocks the door; whether the clergyman will rant during the sermon the way he did the last time; whether a new prisoner will be brought in today; whether one will succeed in getting cigarettes; whether the mouse will appear again today which ran up the director's trousers, to the general amusement of everyone yesterday. . . . Yes, about the people. During the first few years, it was a relief to me to be occupied with the others in the workshop. Seventeen months I slept with a group of men in a dormitory. But during that time I was still stunned; I did not see their faces, I could not tell one from another, I was surrounded by yellow shadows; as long as we were compelled to silence I did not notice that they were hostile to me, and when they were permitted to speak, I did not listen to them and did not notice. They regarded me as proud and reserved. He imagines he's better than we, they jeered, calling me schoolmaster and Professor Fritz, but, of course, one knows all of that. But once there was a conspiracy, and another time they smuggled in some gin and there was a debauch of drunkenness, and I pretended to know nothing about it and did not give anyone away—although the director and the supervisor thought that they would have an easy time with me—and after that they respected me in their fashion. That then remained the tradition. The tradition about a convict is very strong in such a place. Nevertheless, I did not at that time know anything about anyone. No one interested me, I did not ask about anyone, or anything, really the shoes were the only thing which I knew about any of them; at night, that was the most remarkable thing, at that time I had no sooner fallen on my bed than I was sleeping like a log. You can find a lot of people to corroborate that. There are many people, who like myself, come from the intellectual world into a penitentiary, and who lie there like logs at night for years. Evidently, Nature comes to one's assistance; she does not wish everything to be destroyed in one at once, and closes the last door which she has against the rage of man. But once at night, I woke up and something was creeping and crawling and fingering at my body. I can't tell you the sensation it gave me, I felt a beard and hairy arms and sweaty hands. I start up, trying to push the fellow off; he spits his stinking breath in my face and grunts: 'Hold your trap, you dog.' Then I commence to struggle with him and beside me and beneath me—for my bed was one of the upper ones—I hear chuckling and whispering. The fellow gets one hand on my throat, the other on my genitals, I push my knee into his stomach and my fingers into his eyes, he curses frightfully; all around the giggling and whispering continues; finally I get the better of him and throw him noisily from the bed to the floor. The warden appears and everything is already deathly still. The next day I put in a request for a separate cell, without any allusion to the incident. The director we had at that time was not hostile to me—it was the same who had told me about the fifteen months—when I said to him that if I did not get a separate cell quickly, I should go to pieces, he looked at me penetratingly, as if I were concealing something from him and then replied: 'Very well, it will be arranged.' It took three weeks before I got it. We were greatly overcrowded at that time, meantime I had to defend myself from several dangerous attacks by this fellow; but that too passed and then I got my cell. And then began something new, a new period in a way."

8.

Maurizius becomes silent. His blue-white forehead quivers feebly over the bones, like the skin of milk, his Adam's apple rises and falls as he swallows. Herr von Andergast sits in his chair, as immovable as granite. He looks as if he were asleep. But he is so far removed from sleep that the break which the convict has made becomes an eternity.

"The newness at first consisted," Maurizius resumes, "in my having ceased to sleep. I pined and lost my strength. My inability to sleep was due to my constant boring into the past. No longer in the sense of *if* and *if I had,* as formerly. There were a lot of discussions with people, justifications, reproaches, settling of accounts, constant pondering day and night over the reason for certain words, events and actions, about the real true character of this or that person. I would wonder about the illusions I had had in regard to this person and that, the mistakes which I had made upon such and such an occasion, the injustice which had been done to me by this person and that, and the person would then stand there before me in the flesh. I would wrangle, remember forgotten facts, bring forward the keenest arguments, and this went on and on further and further, like a wheel whirling down an abyss. I would quarrel with a printer who had cheated me four years before, then I would take some fellow student to task—some insignificant fellow—on account of a slander. Once it was a heated discussion with a colleague on the faculty, whom I attacked on account of his dull classicism, another time it was a rencounter with the wife of a privy councillor who did not reply to my greeting, and I told her truths about her snobbery and worship of caste right to her face, as I would in reality, of course, never have dared to do. Or something else, I became sick at heart, six years after it had occurred, about the way my best childhood friend had betrayed me, and I talked to him about it, reproached him with everything and he saw how contemptible he had been and asked me to forgive him. On the other hand, I remembered how I myself had been untrue and unfaithful, there was a young woman in particular whom I could not forget—I had served her an ill turn and I used all my powers of persuasion and all of my spiritual strength to reconcile her. There was a certain planned sparing of myself in the way in which I occupied myself first with strangers, or with people who had become strangers to me, and I concentrated more and more on them when I felt that in this way I could avoid the others, those who were close to me. But it could not be permanently prevented. I still gained time by going over the hearing of the examining magistrate; this I could frequently reproduce question by question. This occupied hours and days, finally I was able to turn everything in my own favour by making the man so skeptical by my explanations and objections, that he admitted that the grounds for suspicion had broken down. I enjoyed this like a victory and was quite excited with delight. But in the midst of this pleasure, I recalled my behaviour towards my father, how ungrateful and unkind I had been and how grieved he must have been about it, and I made all kinds of confessions to him, and decided to write him a letter. I thought out a letter of many pages which could make him understand the compulsion of the position I was in . . . still making excuses for myself, still deceiving myself, still the same old person. But now Elli came between us and reproached me with what I had never dared to reproach myself, with the complete insincerity of my character, and I struggled with her to induce her to show some mercy, but I found no mercy; I begged for love, but I found no love; no repentance and no contrition were of any use. At least at first; later she became milder and I was able to tell her everything and to clear myself from the worst reproaches. Once she even cried and once an exciting drama took place between us. After a frightful scene she had cut her veins in her bath; I rushed to her; she was lying in her tub, already still; the water was quite red and between her legs my little daughter Hildegard was kneeling with a mirror in her hand and looking at me with wide eyes as though noticing now, for the first time, what sort of a person I was. No dreams, sir. I am not telling you any dreams. But what then, you will ask, what then, when for example, I faced Gregor Waremme with so much confirmation and evidence that he finally broke down and I felt: Now you are done for, you Satan. . . . What then, what then? It was perhaps an orgy of the witticisms which occur to one after the party, a pandemonium of what has not been said, and not been done, of what has been swallowed and suppressed, all that one has wished, everything that one has dreaded, the things one chokes and bleeds to death for, later on. It was reality and the appearance of reality inextricably mixed together, the laws governing past events linked with casuistical passion out of the course of events and turned the wrong way, like writing seen in a mirror. Although all this had lasted from about May to November, the most important person had not yet put in her appearance. I say appearance, for my thoughts had naturally often touched upon her; her name frequently occurred to me; it was like a beam which supported the whole structure, first my life of deceit and now my life of atonement; but I had succeeded in keeping it veiled. With incredible cunning I had been able to dodge the picture, I was so afraid of it, I so dreaded seeing it and holding on to it that I steeped myself in memories which were indifferent to me and exaggerated them until my brain resembled a burning merry-go-round. It was all in vain. As the nights grew longer, when winter came, then . . . suddenly it came over me within an hour. I don't intend to be ashamed of myself. I have made up my mind to tell everything. It is beyond anything which shame forbids me to say; it no longer has anything to do with that. Who knows whether anyone else will ever get into such a position that he no longer cares how his words react upon himself, or are judged by anyone else, only cares that for once they should come out of their subterranean chamber, out of the grave in which they are buried, and who knows whether I myself will ever be in such a mood again? It's by no means certain, I feel as though very soon things might lose their colour and I myself might not be so clear in my own mind about them. To recognize one's faults is a condition of illumination in which one no longer either loves or hates oneself. So this was how matters went with regard to Anna and her appearance before me. . . . First, it was Anna, the girl, the woman whom I had known, who to me . . . well, why should I go into that? I think that you understand. She came in a dress with ruching, or lace, with her beautiful hair-dress, with her blue or her green shawl; I knew everything about her so well; it was all so beautiful, so unique. Her eyes, her mouth, the colour of her hair, her lips, the angular turn of her hand at times, the way she took five quick steps, then suddenly two slow ones, the way she blinked her left eyelid a little when she smiled, and the way she lifted her chin when she asked you a question, and the way she would press her hand to her cheek when she was thoughtful. . . . And that was so unique, so individual, so characteristic of Anna. . . . And then I knew, never again. You can never see her again. You will never see her again. Never again. She is alive, she is walking around a room, she is talking to people, is pressing her hand against her cheek, is lifting her chin questioningly, she is wearing the dress with the ruching: and you will never see her again. Perhaps you know that poem of Poe's, The Raven; every stanza ends with the refrain: 'Nevermore, quoth the raven, nevermore.' I said it to myself every day: 'Quoth the raven, nevermore.' Now I was carrying an unquenchable hope around with me, that sometime everything would come to light and that I should be completely exonerated. But as soon as Anna's picture came to me, my hopes would at once disappear, and I knew with deadly clearness: Nevermore. Since my whole existence still flowed over towards her, the picture could not lie, and therefore the hope must be false. But I could get used to this so long as that was the situation, but . . . this yearning . . . oh, yearning cannot express it. Yearning; there is no word for what I felt. It is the torture of tortures, it is dying without death. One feels as if one could not stand it another day, not another fifteen minutes. The doors must spring open, now, this very second; the time which passes is not real; if you cannot get to her tomorrow, your brain will burst; the walls and bolts and gates do not exist and yet, great God, they are there!! In some city or other, in some house or other, she is living, breathing, thinking, sleeping, and here: no more. It is incomprehensible, sir. Of course, you will object there was your guilt. And truly, I had heaped up enough guilt. Man is cut off from man by guilt. And woman from man. The law has taken its course, even though it was for a mistaken guilt, but you are condemned for your own, and perhaps that was greater than you knew. But all of this was true only for a certain period. This ecstasy and enthusiasm of self-sacrifice can only last so long as one can hold on to the picture one yearns for. Suddenly the animal in you revolts against it. Waiting, waiting, you can't go on in this way. The animal gets the upper hand and one is no longer responsible for what happens. The picture one has been yearning for fades. Anna is no longer Anna. A loving awareness of her no longer exists. Your legal judgment separates man from woman, this arrangement turns nature into a beast. Despair produces the secret vice. This institution says: 'What can I do? I cannot help it.' Think of what happens among those who have no picture that they yearn for. They possess only what the memory of their senses has preserved, pictures of prostitutes, whom they tear to pieces. Jack the Rippers, all of them. I have seen men turned into brutes . . . oh! I too, in the end, had no more control.

The picture yearned for split to pieces like wood under a hammer. Shadows grew out of one's memory and conceptions, and shadows became bodies. Women, women, women, not one had a face, only breasts and stomachs and thighs, warm skin, tickling hair, a narcotic something that was just sex. This fell upon one like hot rain, and turned one's blood into slime, the palate into a piece of leather, one's hair into a sweat-cap. There was no peace left; it drove one about the cell by day and by night; if one lies down for a moment . . . what one sees makes all the indecencies which delight the sensualists look pale. Compared with this, the famous temptations of St. Anthony look like illustrations for a ladies' journal. He could get away from his fate, there was renunciation, but what person can maintain of himself that he has made the final renunciation? There is always something which he holds on to, in a word, he can—open the door. But here? Just think; I was not yet thirty. If they had only castrated me. Just think, not yet thirty and buried alive. Everything turns into the sexual act and arouses sexual madness; when two clouds in the sky approach one another; when the carpenter in the workshop mortises planks together; when the warden sticks the key into the lock; the blade of grass sticking out of a crevice; one's own tongue when one wets one's lips; the Latin capital H in the title of a book; the cork in the bottle. Then the thing is so horribly multiplied in such a place; one feels that everyone is being roasted on the same grill. The infection of five hundred other blood streams, intoxicated with the same drug, has a worse effect upon the mind than the worst dissipation. The loathing, the dark filthy loathing! One no longer has the least value in one's own eyes. All one's thoughts turn into sand and mud! The heart dries up and becomes a filthy pouch. Has anyone outside any conception of this? Impossible. Otherwise, no child that is born could ever play joyfully again; no young bride could lie down upon her wedding bed without freezing with horror and loathing. Naturally, these conditions, too, have their climax and their decline. With me it lasted, about . . . let me see, a year and a half. I don't know whether you have even an approximate idea what a year and a half means, first in general, then particularly in such a hell of ten square yards. Every statement about time is really a negation of time. Afterwards there comes a sort of festering dullness. One is so knocked to pieces that one feels as if one could take oneself apart like the figures in a box of bricks; here is the head; the feet are a mile away. This again lasted a few months. Then one begins to sleep again, a new kind of sleep which one has not known before. One . . . I am speaking, of course, of myself. The impersonal merely comes from the fact that one is an example, a number; sometimes I would ask myself whether there was any content between myself and my contour, it was a process of dissolution, something frightfully dead—crazy idea, wasn't it? The sleep which I mean was peculiar in this way, that there was no body to it, as if one had lost all volume, as if one were flowing, as if one had become a pudding, a mere carcass. One smells like a carcass to oneself, do you understand? And that penetrates into one's sleep. When I had overcome that—and is it not crazy that everything really passes, really p-a-s-s-e-s, is that not dreadful? Well, when I had gotten over that, I slowly understood that I had been in my cell for days and years alone. 'What,' I said to myself, 'alone?' It was almost as if I were awaking from death. Where are the people? I was afraid of the emptiness. I was afraid of the loneliness and of being alone. I began to talk to myself. I caught myself saying the same sentence to myself for an hour at a time. The mechanical occupations which they gave me did not help at all. I might just as well have stuck my fingers in my mouth one after another. At this time, I asked for books. I received the books; I was permitted to write. That helped. That helped me for eight months. During those eight months

I performed intellectual work. I had a curious experience. Apparently, it was the same work as formerly, outside in the world, I used the same words, wrote in the same style, worked with the same conceptions, drew the same deductions. But that was all on the surface. As a matter of fact, everything was mummified. It was as if an automaton had set to work who copied the real Leonhart Maurizius with painful accuracy. There was no spirit, or soul, in the work. When I read it and reread it, I could not find any objection to it; the construction was good, the thoughts were logical, sometimes even quite original, my memory functioned perfectly, and for a long time I did not know what made me so uncomfortable about it, until I realized that it was an imitation. Maurizius was playing Maurizius. A more mysterious thing you cannot imagine. Playing with the knowledge and the products of another existence, acting as if one still believed in them, taking their expressions and turns of thought, their chief theories and fundamental principles for true and living, although they really are a lot of corpses which only quiver artificially; treating them with a seriousness and a zeal which he knows in his innermost heart serves no purpose except to deceive himself. Nothing real left. It was all so stupidly sad that I was obliged to exert myself to grind out my daily task; in the end something was turned out, even if it was only a dead compound. Do you know that obstinate guilty boredom which seizes upon one when one produces something mechanically instead of carrying out a genuine impulse? It is like lying before God. One day, I could no longer do it. I remember it was Good Friday, nineteen-thirteen. I got up and threw my pen in the waste bucket. 'That's the end,' I said, 'the end,' and I felt so sick that I vomited. Then I walked around my cell for a few days as if I were looking for something. Then that talking to myself began again. Then I began to press my ear to the wall and to listen. I made signals, I pounded on the stone and listened. There were replies to the signs; but I did not know what they meant. I sang songs; the inspector came and forbade my singing. At night, I would hammer upon the iron bed with my fists, at times I would walk up and down in the darkness calling names, Christian, John, Max, always the same names and I would imagine people whose names were Christian, John and Max. The cell would become enormous like a great hall, and immediately afterwards as narrow as a sardine box; the ceiling would be immediately over my head and the floor several flights below, and I was left choking and dangling in the air. You see delusion has infinite possibilities; good sense has only one. I occupied myself in working out how many radii a circle has; how many stars can one conceive of there being in the sky; could one write all of Homer upon the inside surface of the door? Endlessly I tried to count the threads in the blanket, the fly specks on the windows and the grains of rice in the soup. And I added and calculated. I said the Lord's Prayer backwards and tried the same with The Lay of the Bell, by Schiller, for days, until I howled like a dog for fear of going mad. I heard rattling from everywhere and steps constantly. When winter came, towards the end of November—you must not be surprised that I always give the dates, I must proceed chronologically in order to keep track of events—that is towards the end of the year, I became very ill. In the hospital, I was in the room with six other men. Three of them belonged to my group; I knew them from our daily walks. They were all seriously ill. One of them, whom I did not know, had such a deep wound in his head that when it was dressed, one could look into his brain. We were forbidden to talk, but we managed nevertheless to exchange a few words. Here, of course, no one wore a mask. In the workshop, at religious services and during our walks, we were still obliged to wear masks at that time. Two of the men had life sentences, one had already been there twenty years and was counting on getting out in five years. He spoke of it constantly with glowing eyes as if five years were only like five days. One of them had been in a prison in Baden until recently, and during his last days there, he had witnessed an execution which took place before his window. It had made such a frightful impression upon him that he had convulsions constantly. I looked at these people. I looked at them as a man on a voyage of discovery, who comes upon an unknown island, looks at a new species of human beings. The thought which frightened me was: You have been seven years in this place and haven't the slightest ghost of an idea about one of them. And those are your fellows, that is, your world. From the other room, I would sometimes hear a delirious man raving. One man sobbed day and night. The doctor said that he was pretending. But shortly afterwards he was put in the insane asylum. My neighbour, a little red-haired man, whispered a lot to me about himself and our comrades. Then I saw that if I were to go on the way I was for another year, I, too, would have to go to the madhouse. I trembled at the idea. Why does one want to hold on to the future? Why does one want to live? It is a puzzle. Suddenly, you may believe it or not, my life had content again. When I ceased to destroy myself, there arose again, like a shy little blade of grass, something like a self in me."

9.

"How long were you in the hospital?" asked Herr von Andergast, in a broken voice. The answer to the question was less important to him than the sound of his own voice, for he was afraid he could not speak. "Nine weeks," replied Maurizius. "When I was well again and got back to my cell, I went to see the director and asked him to let me sweep the halls, or do some kitchen work two or three times a week. He refused; one always refuses on principle whatever a man asks. A month later, after the big revolt, when the cabinet minister had visited the place, it was granted." "I remember," nodded Herr von Andergast, placing his left hand, on which the diamond ring sparkled, over his eyes, "I remember that insurrection. A wretched business. . . ." "Yes, a wretched business, if you like. . . ." "You, of course, had nothing to do with it?" "No." "There were six people shot down, if I remember correctly." "Yes, you remember quite rightly. Six shot down, twenty-three wounded." "How did it happen?" Maurizius smiled; it was a wan smile. "Perhaps there were worms in the bread." It was as if he had said: "What's the use of explaining to him?" As a matter of fact the question, too, was a mere pretence. The fact of the matter is that the solicitor-general only pursues the accustomed forms—in matters of bearing, position, poise, prestige, information he asks for—with his mind in a mental vise, like a person who clings desperately to ultimate habits before chaos breaks loose. His condition can hardly be defined: he wants Maurizius to go on talking; he wants it at any price; at the same time he is afraid of him, afraid of what is yet to come, to such an extent indeed that he would like to hold his hands over his ears. He considers the possibility of directing the conversation on some neutral subject—by comparison with the present account, the discussion of the trial, the murder and everything connected with it seems neutral—at the same time, he is aware of the cowardice and weakness of this attempt to withdraw. He would like to go away; the moment he resolves to do so, he realizes the absurdity of the decision and the impossibility of carrying it out. An inexplicable desire holds him chained to the chair; an inexplicable depression makes him incapable of acting according to any plan; he looks at the face on the coarse pillow and cannot get away from it, he wants to look at his watch and cannot even put his hand in his vest pocket. "The guilty were most cruelly punished," murmured Maurizius. "Your interest in your fellow prisoners was probably strengthened by the event," Herr von Andergast remarks listlessly. Maurizius throws him a broken, almost paralysed glance.

"Yes, and by the worms in the bread and the stinking meat." "That does not happen," Herr von Andergast flares up, "that's carefully watched—" Maurizius shrugs his shoulders. "All right, take it in a metaphorical sense. There are worms in the bread," he answered angrily.

He broods for a time, then he begins to stammer in the way which was noticeable during the previous conversations. He returns to the inhuman punishments, the ice-cold showers, the beatings with leather straps, the strait-jacket, darkness behind bars. His pupils dilate, become movable, a deep black. He moves his head sideways in torment, then up and down, lifts it and lets it fall on the straw pillow. He utters a name Klakusch, the warden Klakusch. It seems connected with some decisive experience. But before that there was something else. It is not easy to keep track of his confused narrative, moving back and forth; it is evidently difficult for him not to mix up the periods, particularly after the continuous solitude in the cell had ceased and the empty space was once again filled with figures. Moving about the building more freely on two days a week, he meets his fellow prisoners. He becomes remarkably intimate with them, curiously enough with the worst of them, the so-called incorrigibles. A sinister charm attracts him to them, it is something he seems to pant for and languish for. Can darkness dazzle? Perhaps it gives him a passionate intellectual pleasure that everything which moved and lightened the world to which he once belonged has become smudged in this smoky abyss. The high attainments, the moral goals, art and philosophy, have all become unrecognizably charred stumps. Humanity is cut right through into an above and a below. Below the dictatorship of meanness is absolute. He has met two or three hundred people mysteriously alike in their degeneration; fellows who sit on the watch on the borders of society like tigers in a jungle. Evil is not thought out or devised, it merely is. The faces are seared by every conceivable crime. No foreheads. The chins seem to have been hacked off. All types for the criminal pathologist. It is questionable whether they possess that which one calls a soul. Destined to crime from the beginning, they measure the value of life by their greed, the goods of the world by the danger which winning or destroying them brings. Law? A scrap of paper. Duty to the state or society? Why, that's a joke for chickens to cackle over. Religion, ditto. A bourgeois life? An escape from the police. A penitentiary? A matter of course. Love? Are there not sluts enough in the world? Worry? Swill whiskey, you damned idiot! Parents, wife, children? The talk of greenhorns; deserves a good swift kick. Death, darkness, the end of things.

So one would think. Maurizius brings all this forward in such a way that one feels the counter current underneath, like an advocate for the defence, who is preparing his thesis by its antithesis. He is so full of knowledge and experience that have gone to the heart, that his discharge of emotion almost resembles an epileptic seizure. But his emotions have presumably saved him. That is probably what he meant to hint with his "shy little blade of grass" and the resurrection of a "self." During the second half of 1915, at a time when the war had already begun to pour its human dregs into penitentiaries, the warden Klakusch came into his life. He came from Kassel, had been transferred. He was a man with a yellow patriarchal beard, which covered his whole face and reached to his belt, a pressed-in nose and little red swimming eyes. He always wore his cap pulled deep over his forehead, looked disagreeable and would laugh in a nasty or gloating way at times, one could not guess why. He served in the corridor on which Maurizius' cell lay. "I disliked him at first," admitted Maurizius, "he would often stand staring for five minutes in silence in the doorway, then he would click his tongue and leave. That clicking of the tongue made me particularly nervous. One day he walked up to me and spoke to me. 'You are a cultivated man, I have been told. Something of a scholar. Just listen to me, can you tell me something, what really *is* a criminal?' I looked at him in surprise. 'Why, what do you mean?' I asked. 'Well, I only mean that there are so many; you know, it gives you all sorts of ideas, you know.' 'What kind of ideas?' I asked. 'Well, yes, just ideas,' says he, wiping his running eyes. 'There, for example, is number three hundred and sixteen, a boy who would not hurt a fly. Really a touchin' boy. Killed his girl because she maltreated him frightfully. When he gets out after the eight years that they've heaped on him, he's a goner. Anæmia or tuberculosis, you know our illnesses. And beside that. What is he to learn here with us? Have you ever looked at him? Funny that that should be a criminal.' He clicked his tongue and went away. He wasn't at all curious about my answer. I thought to myself: 'What kind of a person is he?' I wasn't through racking my brains about him for quite a while. He must have liked something about me from the beginning. At first I suspected that he wanted to pump me, or had attacks of talkativeness and was playing with me. But my doubts and distrust did not last long. There was something remarkable about the man. He pretended to be so simple, he seemed so harmless and when one had been with him awhile, one had the feeling that he knew about everything in the world and one merely needed to ask him about it. But he was only interested in the penitentiary; he talked of nothing but the convicts. He was seventy-four years old and had been working in prisons for thirty-five years. He had seen armies of criminals pass before him and was more familiar with the execution of justice and punishment than many high-placed officials. But he did not take any credit to himself, he did not take credit to himself for anything, not for the way in which he did his duty in that difficult capacity, nor for his experience, and he did not seem to have an inkling of the unsoundable depths of knowledge he had within him. But one cannot give any conception of him even if one wrote a book about him. 'I'd like to know why you're always so sad,' he said to me one day. 'I always say to the boys: everything's regulated for you, you have a good bed, sufficient nourishment, have a roof over your heads—what more do you want? No worries, no business, don't have to struggle—what more do you want?' I replied: 'My dear man, that consolation does not come from your heart.' He arose stiffly and said: 'No, it really doesn't. You are right.' 'Well, then what's to be done?' I ask. And he: 'What's to be done? If one knew that. But realize this, the judge can't do any differently. The mistake is this: When a judge condemns he, as a human being, is condemning a human being and that should not be.' 'Really,' I ask in astonishment, 'do you think that that must not be?' 'It must not be,' he repeated in a tone which I have never been able to forget; 'a human being should not condemn a human being.' 'And what about punishment?' I objected. 'Isn't punishment necessary? It has been since the world began.' He leaned over to me and whispered: 'Then we must destroy the world and create people who think differently. That has been hammered into us since childhood, but it has nothing to do with real human beings. It's a lie, that's what it is. A lie. He who punishes lies away his own sin. There you have it. But don't repeat that or the superintendent will send me to the devil.' Now that seemed very curious to me. Soon I waited impatiently every day for the hour when he came. He told me everything that happened in the house. Once he was unusually excited, which he showed by frequently clicking his tongue. 'They have just brought in two little boys,' he said, 'they have condemned them to four and five years for a street robbery. Vagrants. They hadn't had anything to eat for two days and two nights, were walking along the street in the rain; in a village they find a drunkard lying in a ditch and take all his money, seventy-five cents. Nine years of penitentiary for seventy-five cents.' He took me by the shoulder and shook me, as if I had condemned them, as if I could help it. I said: 'You see what a world we live in, Klakusch.' He looked at me with a contracted brow and said: 'I want to ask you something, in regard to a person and to his action; is a person an action?' 'No,' was my answer, 'the deed is not the person, and therein lies the whole mistake.' Then he left me, and as he went out he murmured: 'So it isn't, it isn't, the deed is not the person.' Suddenly he turned around again and said: 'Yesterday I had a discussion with two hundred and ninety. He sits and sits and thinks and thinks. Real penitentiary case. Committed incest. His woman played around constantly with other men, he let her go along, did not dare to protest, he was too fond of her. Finally his desire gave him no peace any longer, there was a pretty daughter in the house, a light-headed little thing, took after her mother; she seems to have seduced him; the wife finds it out and, in order to get rid of him, she denounces him to the police. The way things go with such people. I ask him: Was it you who did it? He doesn't understand. I strike him on the chest: You, I say. Yes, I, he said frightened. Well, then you are guilty, say I. And he: But there is no judge for such a thing as that. How's that? I ask. I don't recognize the judge, he says. Such a stupid wretch.' 'Perhaps not so stupid, Klakusch,' I interrupted. 'Perhaps,' he admitted, 'perhaps, and do you know something else? He became good by having become bad; I have seen that happen often. There is no getting to the bottom of these people; one can study them a hundred years and not know them. Some come in and instead of repenting, they say: 'I was out of luck.' As if it were a lottery and everyone paid for his card, as if there were only cheats and murderers in the world and he who is not caught wins the haul. But that isn't a moral feeling, is it? Where is there moral feeling, anyway, will you tell me that?' He looked at me craftily, but I could not tell him. Then he suddenly said to me solemnly: 'But I can tell you something; I can tell you what a criminal is.' 'Well?' said I eagerly. 'A criminal is one who ruins himself, that's what he is. The human being who ruins himself is a criminal.' 'That is true, Klakusch, that is frightfully true.' He nodded in a friendly way and patted me on the head. A few days later he came with the news which he already announced before he had closed the door. Number four hundred and twelve had made his confession. It was already known in the whole institution. He had been obstinately silent for three and a half years; it had been impossible to get a syllable out of him; he had only walked around and walked around, malignantly, with his teeth gritted, scratched his fingers raw against the walls and raged against God and man. This morning at five o'clock he had suddenly asked for the rector, and when he had come, he had screamed his whole guilt in his face, with a frothing mouth, and had fallen down in a corner of the cell and hadn't yapped again; he was still lying here. It seemed to me as if he was still standing before me in the flesh. When he pictured such an event, one would see everything to the smallest detail. And not only that, it remained graved in your memory; it became a vision. He told me, for example, that one winter night, many years ago, a man who had been set free came to him and begged him with uplifted hands to take him into his room, or to hide him somewhere in the penitentiary; he did not know where to go; he hadn't a cent of money; he could not be responsible for himself, it was heart-breaking, a broken desperate man. He, Klakusch, had talked to him the whole night, and had straightened him out to a certain extent; he had given him a little money and sent him away with the advice: At least, don't do anyone any harm. He had told it so that I had not been able to eat a bite all day; I can still hear how he talked to him: Boy, little boy, and: Don't sink so deep into your trouble, and this: Don't do anyone any harm. Once we spoke of that miscreant who had been in the place for four years, the man who had strangled a woman. He told me that at the penitentiary conference they had been quite at their wits' end; they did not know what to do with him; he was so refractory. I said such a person wasn't a human being, it was a mistake to treat him like one. Klakusch replied that it certainly looked so; if one promised him a double portion of dripping on his bread for murdering his brother, he would probably not hesitate a moment. 'Well, then,' I said. 'Maybe so,' he said, 'but so much is certain: in his mother's womb he was not yet bad.' And as I kept silent he added: 'If he was not yet bad in his mother's womb, he is just such a human being as you or I and the Regierungspräsident. The reproach which I bring against him does not yet mean that I am just towards him.' 'What do you mean, Klakusch, *just?*' I asked him. He said: 'No one should really use that word.' 'Why, Klakusch?' He said: 'It is a word like a fish, it slips away from one when one seizes it.' Then: 'If one had the the voice, what could one not attain? But the voice is lacking.' A few days later I had some words in the hall with a convict, who was very repulsive to me, a sly, sombre fellow, who was disgusting to me for the nature of his crime, too; as an assistant teacher he had seduced a lot of little boys to all sorts of nastiness. I told Klakusch about my row with the man; he listened quietly, then he said: 'I would like to give you some good advice; it won't cost you much to follow it: just try being nice. Just try it some time; try being nice; you won't believe what it will do. Just a little niceness, you know, it's like the magic weed which opens brass locks. Just you notice sometime and try it.' I, like an obedient pupil, really tried it. And I saw that he was right. Frequently enough a friendly smile would alter the sourest expression on the spot. I had the most remarkable experiences. These people no longer regard it as possible that anyone should be disposed towards them as one is towards any chance acquaintance outside, I don't mean to say being polite or agreeable, for that's not it, that would even make them suspicious in many cases. The point is to show them some respect, the most ordinary consideration, that they have forgotten and they look at one with astonished eyes and don't know how to behave at first when they meet it again. It even happened that one of them turned around and began to cry like a little boy. You will perhaps regard this as sentimentality, in which case it would be better if I did not talk about it; then I would have been wiser to have kept quiet from the beginning. With me it resulted in my becoming more intimate with Klakusch daily; when he had a day off, I missed him so that I was anxious and uncomfortable without him; he, too, became constantly fonder of me, although he seldom permitted this to be noticed. Once he said that he had never had a son, if he thought of one he would wish him to be like me. 'Doesn't it make any difference to you that I am a convict, condemned for life?' 'No,' he replied, 'in this case it does not matter at all.' Then I decided to ask him another question, only I did not know how to go about it, I was even afraid. And then that was the end. It happened four years ago. He has been dead four years."

10.

"I don't understand," said Herr von Andergast hesitatingly. "Is his death connected with that, with your question?"

"Just so. I will tell you that later. Then . . . enough. Since then I have often thought of what remarkable relationships a person can stumble into. Anyone standing outside would undoubtedly call such a relation as that between me and the warden Klakusch as romantically improbable. Perhaps he would even say that it had arisen in my imagination and had not existed in reality. And if a persistent skeptic goes for me hard, it is possible that I myself regard the whole thing as a dream. For that is the way with all experience, after a certain time it becomes a dream, the ego to whom it has happened is no longer the ego which remembers. There may perhaps at times have been dream-faces now and again when the old man stood there with his flax-coloured beard at twilight in my cell; at that time

I already had this cell and I felt as if I had a human soul in my breast again, because the old man had one. For that is what matters. When alone, a human being has no soul, that you may simply take my word for. And consequently, alone, he has no God. And when I think of the nights his voice was still in the room, I could continue to talk to him as I sometimes do even yet—for me no one dies—and many of his words which I have saved have sounded forth to me from night and non-existence. A brain like this"—he touched himself on the temple—"is like the gong of a Chinese temple: when one only touches it with one's finger it resounds as if a cathedral bell were ringing under water. But in order to allay your doubts about my romanticism and to give you a correct idea, you must not forget what a fertile ground such a penitentiary is, and that plants flourish there which you in the outer world have not yet classified. Things take place there about which one must assume that they come from some intermediate world. Everything is so narrow and so wide, so empty and so full, and that which one calls fate is so close to one. I just wanted to say that as a preliminary. I don't know whether it means anything to you. For several days—naturally, I mean during the hours we were together—I had been talking to Klakusch about the institution in general. During that year, after the revolution there had been many improvements, and things had been made easier; this had aroused certain hopes in me, but Klakusch thought that this was useless; if the flour was bad there was no use putting raisins in the dough. The evil must be looked for elsewhere, and —this the students did not see—it lay in the measuring rod. 'If a person had been guilty in some way, guilty a finger's breadth,' he said, 'any poor little ordinary human being, they would condemn him to a yard of punishment without any consideration of the person who was to be punished.' At first I did not understand him, finally I realized that he meant, not the external person that was sufficiently 'considered,' but the internal. The chief point was, he explained to me, how much responsibility for himself a person was able to stand; in this respect no two people were alike. I objected that we had gotten away from the real principle of punishment long ago, as well as from the principle of retaliation and the idea of deterring; the protection of society and the improvement of the criminal was the only concern that we had left. He said that the initiated simply laughed at the idea of either protection, or improvement; how was one to keep an insane person from lacerating his face with his own hands? The world of human beings was such an insane person; it pretends to protect what it constantly destroys by its lack of understanding. For this reason he said: 'Stop, world of humans, and attack the problem from a different angle!' We had this conversation one December afternoon; since morning the fall of snow had been darkening the cell and before he left Klakusch said: 'I don't enjoy things any more, my days are full and over, I know too much about things, nothing more can go into my head or my heart.' When he came again towards evening to empty the bucket—he always did it for me, though according to the regulations of the house, I should have done it myself—as he stood there before me, I summoned my courage and asked him: 'Tell me, Klakusch, do you think that there are innocent people sentenced in this house?' He seemed unprepared for the question and answered hesitatingly: 'That might well be.' I continued my questioning: 'How many innocent people who have been condemned have you known during your work, I mean, known as guiltless?' He considered awhile, then he counted on his fingers, murmuring the names in low tones. 'Eleven.' 'And did you at once believe in their innocence when you first came to know them?' 'No, not that,' he replied, 'not that; if one believed in their innocence and then had to watch them eating their hearts out, if one were certain, then, I say . . .' I urged him on: 'Then, what then,

Klakusch?' 'Well, then,' he said, 'then, speaking strictly, one could not continue to live.' It had already become dark in my cell, I could still just perceive his figure, so I ventured the question which I had on my heart and which I wanted to utter. 'Well, how do matters stand with me, Klakusch, do you consider me guilty or innocent?' And he: 'Must I answer?' 'I should be glad if you would answer me openly and candidly,' I said. He considered again, then he said: 'Right, tomorrow morning you shall have your answer.' And early the next day came the answer. He had hanged himself from the window-frame of his room."

Maurizius turns his face to the wall and lies there quite still. A quarter of an hour passes, there is complete silence in the cell. One cannot tell how long that mysterious silence would have lasted if there had not been a knock on the barred door. It is the penitentiary physician who is making his rounds. When informed of the presence of the high official, he asks permission to see the patient, he will not disturb them for long. A fat gentleman comes in with gold-rimmed spectacles on his little round lump of a nose, he greets the solicitor-general like a reserve officer, reaches for the convict's wrist in order to feel his pulse, rattles forth his satisfied condescension, then bows and leaves.

Herr von Andergast has risen. He feels as if he has sat for nineteen years upon that chair. During this time he has become old, tired, useless. His shy glance wanders over towards the convict who is lying there stiffly, his two hands clenched into fists upon his breast. One ought to say something, thinks Herr von Andergast. No, replied another voice within him categorically, one must not say one word. He snatches at the hat which he put on the table nineteen years ago and the brown leather gloves. He makes an effort to be silent. Herr von Andergast, baron and solicitor-general, with his hat and his brown leather gloves in his right hand, slips, like a thief, out of the cell of convict 357.

The motor is waiting. "Drive quickly," he calls to the chauffeur, and falls into a corner of the car staring out into the rain with wide-open eyes. He does not see, he does not look, he does not think, he does not feel.

Back at the office at three o'clock in the afternoon, he sends a telegram of two hundred words to the Minister of Justice in which he urges him to grant an immediate pardon to the prisoner Maurizius.

PART THREE

THE IRREVOCABILITY OF DEATH

CHAPTER XIV

I.

When Etzel got out of the motor he was dizzy. "Get hold of yourself, boy," he said to himself. The light from the lamp on the street corner poured over his face like liquid wax. Four flights of stairs, each consisting of twenty-three steps, makes two hundred and ninety steps. Damned hole! Pilsener beer bottles and buckets of white-wash for painting. On the top flight there was purple darkness. The door of the flat was open. Melitta stood in the hall, a ridiculous green shawl wound around her so tight that she looked like a bean-pole. "Was anyone here?" asked Etzel uneasily. The girl replied rudely: "Who in the world should have been here; who comes to see you anyway; was anyone ever here?" Etzel replied: "That's true; but it's possible that someone will come." "It will be the right one all right," replied the charming creature; "you seem to me in general to have distinguished acquaint-ances." Once in his room, Etzel dropped in a chair, stuck his hands into his trousers pockets and pressed the nape of his neck against the back of the chair. He wished that the gas light were already burning, but he was too tired to light it. This wish was performed sooner than he had dared to hope. Frau Schneevogt appeared and expressed her astonishment that he was sitting in the dark. He said coolly that he liked the dark. She declared him to be an eccentric young man and made a light. She asked whether she should bring him something to eat. Since he had not touched his lunch, she would warm it up for him. While she spoke, her face assumed an expression like an advertise-ment of rigid honesty. Etzel thanked her and said that he was not hungry. Frau Schneevogt observed anxiously that she did not like his appearance. "A little grippe," he said lightly, and he crossed his stretched-out legs in masculine fashion. She recommended him to go to bed, and promised to bring him some hot sugar water, an infallible remedy. Etzel thought resentfully: If you were only out of here, you horrible woman. She, however, was thirsting for an opportunity to talk, or at least to find some support. She inquired whether he had heard the quarrel which she had had that afternoon with her daughter. Later it had begun again and Herr Schneevogt himself had gotten frightfully excited. Etzel interposed that he had heard a noise and inferred that the family was having some difference of opinion. "If it were only that," sighed Frau Schneevogt. Since she showed such an urgent desire to initiate him into the difficulty, he gave up resistance. The thin perturbed hands seemed to gesticulate right before his eyes.

The matter was this. In the business where Melitta was employed—a large women's clothing shop—an employee who had recently been taken on had been crippled by an accident in the elevator, which was out of order. He had only been employed to help out, he was really a down-and-out actor and had not been registered with the workman's compensation, which had been overlooked. He demanded damages, the cost of his treatment; the firm denied their responsibility, maintained that he was responsible for the accident, and produced a series of other employees as witnesses. These people were prepared to say anything that one asked them to say; they were trembling for their miserable jobs. Only Melitta refused. And she was to be the chief witness; she had been in the packing room at the time of the accident. She not only refuses to speak for the firm, but decidedly takes the opposite stand, she is prepared to swear that the elevator was not operating properly for two days previously, that the man had not been careless, or as some people were said to have said, drunk, that he had simply been snatched up by the machine and in a half a second was hanging with mutilated arms and shoulders. The manager was beside himself at the girl's lack of loyalty, Frau Schneevogt complained. She and Herr Schneevogt naturally are beside themselves too. It has been hinted to Melitta that the department in which she is working is going to be given up very soon, but that they are considering taking her on as head of another department which they are about to open. "You understand," says Frau Schneevogt. Certainly, Etzel understands, in spite of his dull aching head he comprehends, a contemptible mixture of menace and bribing. "The silly goose," wails Frau Schneevogt, wringing her hands, "does not know on which side her bread is buttered. At this time, when a person can be in the street for months before getting a halfway decent position." Mother Schneevogt had gotten as far as this in her story when the door flew open and Melitta shot in. She went at her mother like a cat: "And if you stood on your head and waved your legs in the air till midnight, I'd never and never do it." Then she turned to Etzel with her hard dissonant voice: "There they are holding a bait before your nose to get you to do a dirty, mean trick, to do a poor devil who's a maimed creature for life, anyhow, out of a few cents, not even enough for those rich good-for-nothings to pay for their caviar at lunch." Should she allow herself to be wheedled? Mohl was to express his opinion: shall one keep quiet in such a case; or isn't it more honest to drop the whole lot and croak in the dirt? She threw herself on a chair, raised her sharp shoulders and broke into hysterical weeping. Well, that's fine, thought Etzel in dismay, a crazy woman, and he tried to get up. "Go out," said Melitta commandingly to her mother. "I've got something to talk to him about."

She waited until the door was closed and then whispered with a sinister face. "That fellow is done for if a lawyer doesn't help him to get his rights. I know one who is said to be a tough customer. J. Silberbaum, Lottumstrasse. Such a fellow, however, won't lift a finger without a cash advance. Lend me forty marks, Mohl, and I'll pay it back to you in instalments. I'm out of funds just now. If I had the money I should not have to ask you for it." Etzel concealed his embarrassment. All in all he still had eighty-six marks. Board and lodging were paid ahead for the month, but what assurance had he that he would be able to leave for home by the end of a week? Perhaps sooner, perhaps day after tomorrow . . . but that depended. It depended in the first place upon Waremme-Warschauer's coming, that he should to a certain extent humiliate himself, and then upon one's getting him . . . well, upon his baring his breast and uncovering his brain. That was what it depended upon. There was, of course, no certainty. If he was left in the lurch and had to wait in that tremendous city, so tremendously strange, what could he do with forty-six marks? And now this devilish fever: a million bricks shone before his eyes. These considerations shot through his head with lightning speed while Melitta, sitting on the chair, observed him nervously, without paying any attention to the fact that her short skirt had slipped up over her thighs. To say no when one was asked for help in such a matter was impossible. To close one's purse when it contained what would save someone else; impossible. To cheat oneself and excuse oneself by saying, I haven't it, or I need it myself, was not to be done. In that case, Etzel might just as well have remained at home with his Rie and let her make him apple-pancakes; what was the point of all that he was doing? . . . "All right," he said, "I'll lend you the money," and he fished the rather shabby wallet out of the lining of the pocket of his vest, into which he had himself cut a pocket which he had sewn in as best he could, and handed Melitta two twenty-mark bills. She had obviously not supposed that he would do it; she had thought to herself that the attempt would not do any harm, so she looked at him with some surprise. He and his circumstances appeared to her more mysterious, not to say more suspicious, than ever. "You really are a good boy," she remarked appreciatively, and with a remainder of suspicion: "is it Kosher money?" "Kosher, no, it's Christian money," he replied, "but from a damned decent source." "All right, fine, thanks very much," said Melitta, and stuck the money into her blouse as she got up. "Tomorrow morning I'll go to Silberbaum and I'll show you the receipt." "Not necessary." "Yes, it is. I might be cheating." "For that you would have struck someone else. Hope so at any rate." "Won't you tell me, Mohl, what your business really is?" "I'm looking for my uncle who ran away with the trustee's money." "Hem, not a very remunerative job, it seems to me." "Nor to me—the sheriff's winking at me." As we see, the illuminated dwarf had adjusted himself very well to the language of his surroundings. "Is that the reason that you asked for someone whom you're expecting?" inquired Melitta slyly. "Is it perhaps your uncle himself? Do you think that he will come of his own accord and place the money he owes on the table in the house?" She gave a lifeless laugh. "No, the one who is to come is someone else. I have a bone to pick with him too. He doesn't come from a bad family either. You saw him with me at the jazz concert the other day." "Ha, that fat old barrel." "Yes, the same. It would be a bad mess if he did not come. I have reasons for thinking that he will come, if not today, then tomorrow. He knows where I am living. He even took a note of it. He has no time during the day, so he must come at night. Just let him in as soon as he comes. Tell your mother too to send him in to me at once. Tell everyone in the whole house, tell them all that I'm here . . . do you understand? It is frightfully important, important as the elevated railway, do you understand?" "Boy," cried Melitta frightened, "either you are tipsy . . . or . . ." "It is only that I am a little—" stammered Etzel, "a little sleepy-headed, you know. Why does the gas make such a noise today?"

Melitta did not waste many more words; she helped him undress and when he was in bed, covered him up carefully. "No doctor," he murmured entreatingly, before falling into a feverish sleep, "please don't get a doctor." "Don't worry," said the girl soothingly, "we'll get on without one. One of our sort does not rush for a doctor." There is something back of that, she said to herself, that he should be so afraid of the doctor, but since he had done her such a service, she resolved to care for him herself as best she could. She had a little household medicine-chest, in which there was some aspirin; she dissolved two tablets in water, which she gave him with a spoon. Good-looking boy, she thought, observing his feverish face.

2.

He spent the night in a condition between unconsciousness and a tremendous rush of thoughts. Melitta had left the door into her room open and at times she came in with a candle to look after him. He could not stand the light and whimpered a little, putting his fingers over his eyes. The mechanical piano in the dancing-school across the court sounded like an army of horses thundering over a battlefield of sheet-iron. There was no end to this, no end at all. The young woman in front of Ghisels' door struck him in the face with an automobile horn. When he looked more carefully, it was not a motor horn, but a saxophone, and the young man with the horn-rimmed spectacles said: "That's an unsuitable occupation for a centaur, young lady." His grandmother appeared before him as a trapeze dancer on a balloon, and Frau Schneevogt threatened her with her fist and exclaimed bitterly: "If I had such an income, I could do that too." Andergast, name the year of the last Hohenstaufen; you're wrong, sit down. A woman swathed in black walked along a horribly dismal street on Trismegistus' arm; an explosion caused pieces of plaster to fly through the air; his father caught them in his hand, stuck them in his brief case as *corpora delicti,* and said to the mummified figure: "You are Anna Jahn, I arrest you in the name of the law." Then he was in an open lorry driving above the city and the railroad tracks ran up into the air like pillars; the lorry was empty except for a small wooden case, which, however, curiously enough, was transparent, and lying loose in the case, like apples, were a lot of human heads; he recognized the head of Paalzow's boy and of the negro Joshua Cooper. Then Camill Raff came and yelled to him: Let us fly, and seizing him by the wrist ran panting towards a gate which was about to be shut any second, then they were lost. . . .

Melitta was obliged to go to work the next morning; she entrusted her mother with the care of their sick lodger; but she too had her errands to do and thus Etzel was alone in the flat for most of the morning. The fever had left him, he felt as if he had been beaten, and lay motionless with half-closed eyes. Like all children and half-children, when they are sick, he flirted with the idea of death and pitied himself, because he was so neglected and deserted, with all his heart. Only the consideration that probably no one would discover his death, if he died miserably and anonymously here in a horrible tenement in the north of Berlin, robbed the idea of some of its sweet melancholy charm. Neither his grandmother, nor Robert Thielemann, nor good old Rie, nor he, Trismegistus, would know. This, indeed was disastrous, Trismegistus would have to know. It was perhaps the only way of getting at him. Mohl, Edgar, of unknown birth and unknown antecedents, the corpse is to be seen at the morgue in Plötzensee. After a while his identity is clearly established and oppressed mourners, worried by their conscience, make pilgrimages to his grave. *Hic jacet Etzel Andergast, alias Mohl,* a victim of his honest efforts, mourned for by those who share his opinions. He did not, of course, know that this stage of self-pity was already returning health. The sounds of the house above and below, the voices and steps which seemed to come from a hollow abyss, the rattle of window-panes, the barking of dogs, the cries of the street vendors, the whir of aeroplanes, he was back already in the midst of things, the nervous body of the world.

Etzel lifted his head and listened: the front door bell. After a pause it rang again; another pause and a longer ring for the third time. It is conceivable. He only has lessons till eleven, and generally does not go to Frau Bobike's before half past twelve. Etzel feels in the pit of his stomach that it is he. He smiles. A tense, puzzled, thievish smile. All of his determination, all his expectations and fears are expressed in this smile. Shall he get up and open the door? He has no night clothes. How mother Schneevogt would have stared if he had pajamas among his clothes! Before he can put on his trousers the person outside may be gone. He hears voices. Thank God, Frau Schneevogt has come. And his voice. No doubt of it. That bass voice, those chest tones, that trumpeted "Oh."

Warschauer-Waremme walked in. Back of him, full of excited curiosity, Frau Schneevogt. With arms uplifted in entreaty, Warschauer approaches the bed. "Why, Mohl, poor little Mohl, are you really sick, seriously ill? I thought, why doesn't Mohl come? What's gotten into him? He can't really be angry at his old friend, he won't have taken a momentary fit of nervousness seriously? What's the matter? Head? Stomach? Throat? Lungs? Can I do anything for you? Fever. Poor fellow! My good woman, that is a very excellent young man; I hope that you are looking after him, that he is not being neglected. . . ." An unchecked flow of words. He walked up and down the room acting dismay, pity, eagerness to help. Frau Schneevogt, who was endlessly impressed by him, was offended, and made it understood that both she and her daughter were doing everything that the patient required. "Excellent woman," said Warschauer, but thought that the air in the room was bad, and he opened the window. Then he walked up to Etzel again, put his hand on his forehead, then on his heart, muttered anxiously, clicked his tongue, and his black spectacles under the brim of his slouch hat —which he had not taken off—looked like the openings to two dark pipes. "Make him some bouillon, my good lady, if possible a little chicken broth, and get some simple laxative from the drug store, calomel or castor oil. Let him take that." "I'll do that, doctor," said Frau Schneevogt respectfully. Etzel was obliged to laugh. Warschauer too grinned benignly. "See there, see there," he rejoiced, "you're in good spirits. Your impish nature coming to the surface. *Vivos voco.* My dear young Mohl, I must say goodbye for the present; tiresome duties call me; this evening I'll come up again and keep you company for a while. Goodbye, my dear." He waved his right hand affectionately and turned to go. His grey coat tails flapped grotesquely behind him. Frau Schneevogt accompanied him into the hall with a servile smile.

Etzel looked angrily at the door through which he had disappeared. What a repulsive thing to do, he thought, I'd like to know what he means by it, whether he wants, as usual, to divert me and put me off, or does he intend some special stroke? Well, then this evening. . . . Now it's *either—or;* I wish it were already midnight, I wish it were already tomorrow. He made out a plan, but of what use was a plan if one had such an opponent to deal with? Before one has a leg placed, he crushes one's toes. The most promising way was probably to pretend to be sicker than he was; to pretend to be very ill. To carry the matter so far that the illness had reached a crisis and that an improvement could only begin after he was free from a certain mental and moral burden. A cunning trap. All of the passionate craftiness, of the Andergast obstinacy, of sixteen-year-old enthusiasm that was stored up in his mind and heart, was now busy in demoniacal preparation for the decisive hour. I do not, in this case, hesitate at the hackneyed word, the demoniacal is one of the motivating forces in those natures which are capable of behaving according to their lights out of innate honesty, even if they have a superficial varnish of intellectualism, or as Etzel was wont to do, misunderstood their profounder forces and sought refuge in the intellectual and the logical. This is nothing but a clever insurance against associating more intimately with the demon in question, whose appearance upon the scene is always disquieting.

3.

Towards half past seven Melitta came home and hurried to Etzel's room to inquire how he was. He said that he was better, which satisfied her; unfortunately she could not stay at home, she added; at half past eight there was to be a meeting of the employees of the store to discuss the question of the accident in the elevator. She would, however, certainly be back at ten o'clock to see how he was getting on. She had talked to the lawyer Silberbaum, had paid him the forty marks; the matter was in good hands. She showed him the attorney's receipt, but he did not even look at the rag of paper. "Mother is making you an omelette and you'll have some tea with it. Tomorrow morning you'll be over the filthy thing." She had suddenly something frank and companionable about her, which was an extraordinary contrast to her previous snappy challenging manner, which he, however, did not value very highly since he regarded it as too cheaply won. This led him into observations about this "cheapness" and he decided that one overestimated people if one criticized their naïveté on such occasions. People are not primitive enough, he reflected seriously, one ought to be more primitive, one is too much like a lead-pencil with too sharp a point which breaks off too easily when one has scarcely begun to write.

Since Frau Schneevogt was eager in her persuasions, he ate half of the omelette and had the tea put near his bed. Doubtless, the friendliness of his landlady had its material roots, but that did not disturb him at all; she was really too cheap, although the next day, when he was about to pay his bill, he found that one miscalculates most easily about the things which are most readily purchased. It was quarter of nine when he finally heard the door bell ring. "It's raining, my good Mohl," said Warschauer as he came in, "I am dripping." He took his hat off and shook it, took his coat off and shook that too, looked for a while for a hook to hang them on, and finally, after much sneezing and clearing his throat, placed them on the same chair on which Melitta had sat the night before. "Well, how goes it, how are you, my poor Lazarus?" he asked, and taking a chair by the arm, he lifted it over the table, put it next to the bed and sank down into it. "Hello, what's that?" he stopped and listened. It was the mechanical piano in the dancing-school which had begun its horrible grinding again. "Crazy. And can you sleep with that? My sympathy." He walked to the window, looked across and saw bent shadows gliding around against the brilliantly illuminated curtains of the windows. He gave a dull laugh. "A pretty camera obscura," he said, "an illustrated Charleston, one smells the sweat of pleasure about them and those sounds which pierce the ear are like the trumpets of Jericho. I like a thing like that. It puts one right into the midst of action." Etzel sighed. Warschauer returned to the bed and looked at him with fright. Here too the almost ludicrous exaggeration of which he had not yet rid himself showed forth. "Would you mind speaking a little less loudly, professor?" asked Etzel. "Certainly, of course, your nerves, of course," murmured Warschauer, looking as if he could not forgive himself his lack of consideration. "Indeed this must only be a flying visit," he continued with an eager gesture of the hand, "I would not be burdensome for anything in the world. Not for anything would I retard your convalescence. For you are convalescing, according to the satisfactory reports of the lady outside." "I don't know," murmured Etzel, "I feel pretty badly again. . . . But, you know, professor, it's so miserable to be alone in this room, with that horrible music over there, I can't sleep anyway. Do stay a little longer. . . ." "All right, all right, don't say another word, I'll stay as long as you like, Mohl. It would be a poor sort of friendship if I ran away. Shall I sit still? Shall I read to you? Shall we chat? You need not exert yourself at all. I will provide the entertainment."

What is he up to? Why is he suddenly pure honey again? Etzel wondered. For a second he perceived Warschauer's metallic, blazing glance through his dark glasses, and a cold shudder ran down his spine. The brief silence lasted no longer than the pause between the opening and the shutting of a door. "I don't care about being entertained," Etzel said then with the irritable self-pity of a feverish person, "nor have I supposed that I should lie here in silence listening to you while you talk of any old thing. It isn't a question of any old thing at all." "But of my sympathetic friend?" "Hem, of that, on account of which you kicked me out day before yesterday." "'Kicked out' is a hard word. Really, dear Mohl, that's too crass a designation for an angry expression of impatience. If I had meant anything unpleasant, would I be here? Could I sit by your bed then with an easy conscience?" "I really don't know why you waste your time on me, professor? What do you find in me? What can interest you in me? And if you do find something in me, why do you play with me like a cat with a mouse?" Warschauer suppressed a smile. He ground his jaw. "What do I see in you, little Mohl? Frankly, I have not thought about it. I have too much of the animal about me in that regard." Etzel frowned. "I don't believe you, professor. You know every moment what you are doing, and why you are doing it." "Ah, you regard me as an intriguer who looks far ahead?" "Perhaps not that. But you are far above me and you take a mean advantage of me." "That's impertinent, Mohl." "It's the truth." Warschauer said "hem" and then "hem" again, and pulled his glasses about. "You are exciting yourself unnecessarily, Mohl," he said. "You must not excite yourself. Have you a thermometer? Your eyes are suspiciously bright. Only be quiet, keep calm. I'll see what I can do for you. If it will make you easier. . . . I mean, about the definition of what attracts me to you. As a matter of fact, it's not simple. Your temperamental outbreak recently, which compelled me to an energetic, I admit somewhat too energetic, measure, corroborated certain of my assumptions. I play with you, Mohl? That's a bold twisting of fact. It seems to me rather that you have played with me, or tried to, at least. Your hand on your heart, how is it; how was it?"

Well, now we are in the middle of things, thought Etzel with a mixture of fear and relief and pressed his hands together underneath the bed clothes. "Not a bit of it," he replied somewhat awkwardly, "I told you at the very beginning what I want. It all began with my asking you whether you regard Maurizius as guilty. You evaded the question. Every time that I have spoken of it, you have either dodged or made fun of me. And the last time again." Warschauer distorted his face cynically. "And what could have induced me to express my real meaning to any little whipper-snapper who comes along? Since we are talking seriously about the matter, you see I am taking you quite in earnest, as if I were addressing a delegate from some society for the protection of human rights, so that you cannot any longer complain about me; since we are amiably discussing certain misunderstandings, tell me the motive of your demand. Is it that pitiful *petit bourgeois* story, the awkwardness of which would merely have filled a hard-boiled old fellow like myself with pity, if I had not gotten angry at it? You are blushing, Mohl, that's quite in order, it's very becoming to you, and suitable to your years, but if one wants to fool a Georg Warschauer, one must take a good deal more trouble about it, Mohl. One cannot tell such a person the first trashy story that occurs to one when one is only half awake. Do you understand?" "You are right," whispered Etzel, dropping his eyes, "but what should I have done?" "What should you have done? The same thing which I now expect you to do. There is one sort of person to whom one owes the truth under all circumstances, namely the person from whom one wishes the truth. Do you understand that?" "Yes, I understand that." "Well then. Clever boy."

Etzel started to speak several times, while Warschauer observed him with an immovable masklike face. The mechanical piano ground out a patriotic song. "I could not stand it, professor," he finally exclaimed in low tones, struggling for breath. "I read the petition for pardon which old Maurizius wrote. Then I had him tell me the whole story, I simply went to him. He gave me the reports, the newspaper clippings. But that wasn't necessary. He enlightened me as to a great many details, but from the first instant I was convinced that the verdict was false, that it was a gross miscarriage of justice. I was as certain of that as of the ten commandments, or that Martin Luther was not a swindler. I did not care about the old man, he really left me cold, as a matter of fact, I even hated him and his petition for pardon. What does he mean by that? To whine for a pardon, to be satisfied with a pardon when he himself is convinced of his son's innocence? I didn't want to say that to him—and what good would it have done?—but in my eyes he was merely an old fool; his protestations would not have made the slightest impression upon me, if I had not been convinced with my whole heart that the man was innocent. And if you ask me how I reached this assurance, I can only answer: 'I do not know.' I only know that I am so convinced that all of the courts of the world would not alter my mind. Perhaps you will understand better if I tell you that I grew up in a house in which a verdict is what a sacrament is in a church. Sometimes one has apparitions in the dark, hasn't one? A person can under certain circumstances reach the point where a process inspires him just like a thought; am I expressing myself clearly enough? Then it is stronger than any consideration, or any knowledge. When the inspiration had taken hold of me I could no longer remain; then it meant: *that* man must have justice done him, or I shall go to pieces. Do you understand now, professor? Now you have the truth."

He had spoken very slowly at the end, and had raised his folded hands over the bed cover. His forehead, with a few damp hairs across it, looked like a cut gem. Curiously enough, the expression around his mouth was a half obstinate, half sickly smile. His face had suddenly lost its boyish expression, for some minutes indeed there was mature suffering in his features, his glance was fixed with steely expectation upon the black glasses, back of which apparently there was no life, behind which nothing seemed to be going on. "I thought something of the sort," murmured Warschauer, "my deductions were in that direction. Saul went in search of donkeys and found a kingdom. Mohl set forth to seek justice and will have to be glad if he finds donkeys. Don't look at me so contemptuously, my dear Mohl, that is not cynicism, but experience. I suppose I may still continue to call you Mohl, although from your revelations I must assume that it is a mere *nom de guerre*. All right, let it go at that. I have become accustomed to the name as to a stimulant and have no further curiosity. Certainly, for your years, you have not carried yourself badly. That is . . . that is . . . my dear Mohl, that is good material, exceptional stuff, damn it, little Mohl; why did you have to run across me; what devil got hold of you and led you across my path?" Etzel looked astonished. "Ah, yes, a very logical devil," said he, shrugging his shoulders. Warschauer struck the palm of his hand horizontally through the air. "I am not talking of the fact that you had a purpose, but that it was a murderous attack upon me, yes, a murderous attack," he said with such an angry face that Etzel was frightened. "I can't understand you." "I am not supposing that you do understand, boy, you're too misguided by your purpose," was the brusque reply, "although up to this minute I had flattered myself . . . enough. I had settled the accounts. I had closed the books. I had no further use for any events, no more exertions. Then you broke in upon the peaceful idyl. At the beginning of the first book of Samuel, there is a sublime word about Saul, whom I just referred to in order to make a comparison: God gave him another heart." He looked darkly at his white jelly-like hands, which lay upon his knees. "None of that belongs to the subject, professor," said Etzel harshly. Warschauer sprang up, walked across the narrow room, turned around and sat down again. "All right, let us talk about justice," he replied with his chest curiously raised, which gave him a boastful and, at the same time, an offended appearance.

4.

Yes, there was something boastful and offended about him, which reminded one of a repulsed lover who felt that he has given sufficient proof of his excellent qualities. But when he began to speak, the fire of his mentality seemed to devour the loose, repulsive, dangerous, phantom elements as never before. "Justice, the great mother of all things, as some author once put it. Perhaps it was I. In former days I loved proud euphemisms. A clever prelate once said to me: 'Dispute not, lest you obtain your due.' Everyone must beware of that. One can demand anything of human society; it will make all kinds of concessions; but to demand justice is pure nonsense, for it has not the means of granting it. Nor is it organized for this. It is as if one wanted to initiate a baby into the mysteries of integral mathematics and in doing so had failed to give him the requisite milk. I crossed on the ship with a man who was going to the League of Nations, an orthodox puritan from Boston. He said to me with enthusiasm: 'The task is to bring about justice among the nations.' I laughed in his face. 'You have been asleep and gone by several stations.' I said to him, 'you should have gotten out at Ellis Island and seen the barracks for the immigrants, and a little trip to Mexico would not have done you any harm either; you are going in the wrong direction.' He stared at me with his mouth open, he did not understand a syllable. All those who seek justice are always going in the wrong direction, whatever way they go is always the wrong direction. I suspect that it is a form of self-seeking cerebral excitement, a forced intellectual growth. Michael Kohlhaas is the most detestable figure in the world; no one outside of Germany can understand such a Prussian train of thought. The woman brought before Solomon, who demands that the child they are quarrelling about be cut in two, is only the last logical step. Justice means cutting the child in two. Don't flare up, Mohl, it is as I am telling you; your humane considerations don't amount to as much as a little bottle of oil on Niagara Falls. Solomon was a wise man, but he reduced all apostles of justice to ridicule and made all pacifists absurd. Was there ever since the world began a just cause for war? Did ever a general fight a battle for love of justice? Was ever any one of the famous men who invaded and stole property, or anyone who slaughtered masses of the population, called to account unless the act was unsuccessful? I advise you to think some time about the relationship, I almost used the word affinity, between the conceptions of justice and revenge. When and where in history were kingdoms established, religions founded, cities built or civilization spread with the help of justice? Do you know of one case? I don't know of one. Where is the forum which shall pass upon the criminal extermination of ten million Indians? Or upon the poisoning by opium of a hundred million Chinese, or the enslaving of three hundred million Hindus? Who stopped the ships full of captive negroes which sailed in fleets to the North American continent between the sixteenth and the nineteenth centuries? Who raises a hand for the hundreds of thousands of people who perish in the copper mines in Brazil? What judge undertakes to punish the pogroms in the Ukraine? Do you want more examples? I am well stocked. You will object, for it is your moral panacea; one must improve things, one must change things. Trash and nonsense! One does not improve things; one does not change things. 'One' namely. 'The things'—that's another matter. But there it is a question of development, the whole way from the monkey to Pericles. The undertaking is too great, the make-up of the individual too small, my good Mohl. Presumption, what a presumption! You can use your gifts to better advantage, you representatives, you! For you certainly regard yourself as a representative. Of the spirit of the time? Of the generation? Do not deny it"—Etzel was not thinking of denying or even remarking anything, he was only listening with round wide-open eyes—"do not deny it, it is the fashion, it is the type. Every father's son of you, every runaway boy who wants to make the world happy must end by knuckling under and being glad to be allowed to sit at a desk and write a decree, at least preventing the manure in some neighbouring Augean stable from offending the nostrils of the public. They are quickly cured of the idea that they have in this way accomplished more than the scorned authors of their being. What is the use of crying for justice if the crass reality with which we are surrounded constantly and shamelessly reminds us that we live upon the fruits of injustice? Every bite of bread which I eat, every dollar that I earn, every pair of shoes that I wear is the result of a complicated system of irregularity and injustice. Every human existence and every human activity today presupposes a hecatomb of victims. You and people of your sort presuppose the existence of a desire for justice, the inherent idea of it, so to speak. That is a mistake. It is a wrong conclusion. Humanity as a whole does not care a hang for justice. Humanity is not constructed for dealing with justice. At times it intoxicates itself with the thought—namely, at times when butter is plentiful—but if dividends are at all threatened by it or the fall of the stock market, their enthusiasm falls and even the noisiest frogs climb off their perch and cease making a noise. I knew two bank directors from Leipzig, both at the same bank. The company failed, countless families lost their savings. The one, the decent chap, gave his whole fortune to the bankruptcy officials and faced his trial. And then he was locked up; he got three years in prison. The other, a scamp to the day of his death, was able to slip through all of the meshes of the law, made safely away with his booty and is today an admired nabob covered with decorations, the pride of his fatherland. The poor servant-girl who in despair chokes her newborn child does not get any mercy from the law, but the other day a highly placed nobleman in Mecklenburg poisoned his wife in order to inherit from her, and the solicitor hesitated six months before making the charge. Last year I was at a trial where a woman was condemned for harbouring her daughter with her fiancé at night. I shall never forget the terrible screams of this woman when the sentence was pronounced, such lamentation about a destroyed life, such despair about the condition of the world, I have never heard in any human voice. On the other hand, some silly jury somewhere exculpates a woman who has admittedly murdered her husband, because she wears elegant clothes and uses highfaluting language. If you can prove to me that in a single one of these cases a rooster crowed, a symbolic rooster, of course, as to whether justice was administered, as the expression goes, I'll give you a dollar. You had the misfortune of having an inspiration, dear Mohl, as you said yourself. You could have had seven, or even seventy thousand similar inspirations—why did you have to have just this one? You are attaching too much responsibility to a chance discovery. You are overreaching yourself. You are wasting your life, your mind, your strength and your time on a lost cause, an affair which is dead. Who is Maurizius, who cares about Maurizius? What is the difference whether he is sitting in a penitentiary or a flat, whether he is guilty or innocent? How does that line of Goethe go: At the day of judgment it's only a fart. To use the grand word justice in such a state of the world is, upon my soul, running a coffee-grinder by steam power."

All the colour had faded out of Etzel's face; his lips were quivering, his chin was shaking; shivers were convulsing him from head to foot and with glowing eyes he devoured the man before him. He no longer needed to pretend to be sick, for he was sick, sick in heart and soul, sick with scornful contempt, with furious disappointment and bitterness. He made a senseless gesture as if to hurl all that he felt at the man's face, as one picks up a stone to throw it at a person who has insulted one, then he stammered, tossing about on his bed. . . . "Why, that . . . that . . . that is incredible, no one can believe that . . . anything so contemptible . . . no, anything so rotten . . . that, one has to listen to that . . . they pretend to be human beings . . . that pretends to be a human being . . . let him get out . . . goodbye . . . get out. . . ." "Mohl!" exclaimed Warschauer, honestly frightened. He had evidently not expected this effect. "Water!" panted Etzel. "Yes, certainly, at once, my dear, precious boy," murmured Warschauer in dismay, and walked clumsily around the room looking for a bottle of water. Finally he found it, poured out a glass and brought it to the bed. Etzel gave a deep sigh and lay stiff upon his pillow. "Come, come, come," said Warschauer, "my dear good boy, what is the matter? Control yourself, little Mohl, look at me, look at your friend. . . ." "Hot," whispered Etzel, "feel sick. . . ." "Yes, certainly, my son, of course, you're hot . . . naturally, we'll put a compress on you . . . fever, of course." Really the boy's whole body felt like the tiles of an overheated stove. A mysterious phenomenon, for as a matter of fact, Etzel had no fever. Had he such tremendous control of his body that he could simply carry it along by the emotions of his soul, merely because the appearance of the thing was necessary in order to impress the other man? What was dissimulation, and what was a last heroic attempt and surrender? Like a crazy man running a match, he kept on towards the goal unconscious in the midst of ice-cold consciousness. Warschauer dipped a handkerchief in a pitcher of water, wrung it out so that only the dampness remained, returned to the bed and removed the boy's shirt. Etzel lay there stiff and still and did not budge. When he saw the boy's naked body before him, Warschauer fell into a trance of observation. Back of the dark glasses there was a mysterious glow like two tiny black flames. He opened his mouth. He looked like a bewitched man who has begun a prayer and does not know how to go on with it. "Boy," he whispered, "little boy, you . . . " Then Etzel seemed to wake up. Quickly he seized Warschauer's two arms with his two hands. He looked at him with an indescribable glance, bold, wild, imploring and commanding. He dropped the man's arms, got up on his knees and dug his fingers into the man's shoulders. Then he let his shoulders go, snatched at the glasses and tore them off his face. He held the glasses in his left hand like a trophy. Kneeling naked with the glasses in his hand, he said: "I want to know everything. Do you hear me? I want to know how it was with the *deus ex machina*. You may tell me. I am worth it. Come, professor, who shot? Did she shoot, did Anna Jahn shoot? Yes or no, yes or no?"

A dull animal-like glance from the watery eyes was the answer.

5.

A feeble smile flickered over Warschauer's chalky face. He no longer had the strength to repulse the boy, who was as if beside himself. He gently took the glasses out of his hand and put them on the chair. He stroked the shoulders, the back and the hips of the beautiful slender body, his teeth chattering. "Yes, yes, all right, she fired the shot," he said, with a kind of senile indulgence, "if you've set your heart on it, little Mohl, why should I keep silent about it? . . . Yes, she shot . . . what else was there left for her to do?" . . . Etzel clasped Warschauer's right hand in both of his. He slipped back upon the bed without letting the man's hand go. He was almost stunned with happiness. He stared with passionate longing into those watery eyes. He had the feeling that so long as he kept his eyes fixed upon him, the man could not run away. Warschauer sat down upon the edge of the bed and, grinding his jaw, and now and again protruding his lips in the same senile, almost babbling tones, he recounted the details of what had taken place. That she was beset. That she had completely lost her head. Three bloodhounds back of her, her brother-in-law, her sister and he, Waremme. That is how she regarded them, three bloodhounds. She did not know how to get in or out. He had given her the revolver that afternoon. He had said: 'One can never tell what may happen; it is a last resort.' He had not considered that in her despair she might kill herself. As a matter of fact she came near doing it. She admitted this to him later on. It was his magnetic will which saved her at the last moment. He had had a premonition of something of the sort. He had walked up and down in front of the windows for an hour and a half. He had not been at the casino at all. He had left there an hour earlier than usual. The witnesses had either been mistaken or had been misled by his assertions afterwards. He had walked up and down under the side windows of the house for an hour and a half; he kept his eye on the lighted windows and at times he could see her shadow. He had learnt by experience that when he concentrated his thoughts upon her, she would fall directly under his influence and her will would become subject to his. She must, however, have heard his footsteps in the dry underbrush through the half-open window. This roused her anxiety to a climax. She sits down at the piano, plays something or other, breaks off again, dashes down the steps, telephones to him, Waremme, to his house and to the casino. In vain. 'For heaven's sake, Elli,' she then screams up the steps in a paroxysm of terror, 'your husband is coming, come down or there will be an accident!' Thereupon Elli rushes down the steps and goes at her sister like a madwoman, seizes her by the throat and hisses at her: 'Disappear this instant, or I'll strangle you.' At that moment the garden door bangs to, Elli flies out and Anna with every drop of blood in her body standing still staggers after her. At that moment I walked out from behind the house towards the steps," concluded Warschauer, "at the moment the shot was fired. What happened further is not interesting. It accords fairly well with the facts, which have been sufficiently rehashed. I, of course, took the revolver and did away with it." "But first you went towards Maurizius with the revolver?" asked Etzel breathlessly. "Yes." "In order that it should look as though you had taken the revolver out of his hand?" "Yes, of course. An excellent remark." "But how is it possible that Anna Jahn allowed him to be arrested, to be condemned, how is it possible that for nineteen years she . . . I can't grasp it. . . . How could she do such a thing? How can a person?" Warschauer looked sidewise at the floor. "That . . . is a secret of her nature. I can only give inadequate explanations. I have already said: 'I was dealing with a corpse. A corpse which I had to galvanize in order that it should simulate life.' I never took my eyes from her. During the whole preliminary investigation, while she was in the south, I remained close to her." "But later, later, those many years later? Professor, professor, just think!" Warschauer let his eyes wander along the wall as if he wanted to count the blood marks caused by the bedbugs, suddenly he looked straight into Etzel's face and said with mysteriously contracted brows: "That goes very deep. One can scarcely sketch the structure of that soul. She had already made her decision on this point before she came under my influence. I shall now say something which no one in the world except you and I know. It may at first seem something very usual, but in view of the person in question, it is very unusual. It is that which made me the final arbiter. When I understood the situation, I felt as if a giant had seized me and broken my back. Namely, she loved the man, that was it. She loved him so, with such a furious passion that her mind became clouded and she became incurably ill. This was the profoundest thing to her, this love; it was the leap into Orcus. And he, he did not know it. He didn't even have a notion of it. He for his part merely loved her, the unfortunate man, but he begged and wooed her and whined, whereas she, she had already taken the plunge. That he did not know this—this she could not forgive. That she loved him so endlessly—she never forgave either him or herself for it. For that he had to suffer punishment. He must no longer be in the world. That she had shot her sister for his sake must never, under any circumstances, build a bridge from him to her. She had made this an iron law for herself and she immured herself in it. She created his death, she created his expiation, she was his most cruel persecutor, and in order to bear his life and his punishment with him, she transformed herself into a soulless fury. At the same time she had a bourgeois pride and a bourgeois cowardice along with it, which one will scarcely find again combined to such a degree in one person. For the period which permits such creatures to flower is a thing of the past. When she saw her name connected with the whole affair in the papers for the first time, although she was treated with the delicacy which a raw egg requires, it had the most extraordinary effect upon her; for hours and hours she kept on washing her hands and her sense of disgust rose to the point of convulsive shuddering. No, Mohl, you cannot understand that character, and I must say, Heaven forbid that you should. A savage pagan and a silly bigot, full of arrogance and a passion for self-destruction; chaste as an altar-piece and flaming with a mystic dark sensuality like a primeval forest; strict, but hungering for tenderness; surrounding herself with insurmountable barriers, hating anyone who attempted to break them down, hating him who respected them—and all this, above all, under an evil star. There are many people who live under an evil star. They lack light. They desire their dark fate and they pursue it for so long and challenge it until it comes forth and tramples upon them. They wish to be crushed by it. They will not bend; they will not yield themselves; they wish to be trampled upon. That was how it was with her. All right, so much is said. Only be patient, Mohl, I am coming to what you really want to hear from me. The oath. . . . I know, I know. . . ." He got up, collided against the chair; his glasses fell from it; he leaned over and picked them up; one lens was broken; he shook his head and put them in his pocket. Then he walked to the window, looked for a while out into the rain and turned around. "The oath was nothing more than a question of poise and a technical consequence. It is difficult to maintain one's carriage with a broken spine, but nevertheless, it had to be. I was standing on a heap of ruins and there was no doubt as to the last victim that was yet to fall. At least, not for me. It was not for me to measure the value of one human life against another; the question was: where in this complete darkness is there still a spark of future, what can be saved from the *débâcle?* Between Leonhart Maurizius and myself there was a duel to be fought, not a knightly duel, but a duel of fate. Fate against fate. If I remained the victor in this battle between us two, fate made the decision. Do not believe that one can do that with a strong conscience alone, the magic sign is necessary too, which one receives from invisible spirits. Conscience alone would perhaps not hold out, but the call has its effect, one scarcely knows whether it comes from heaven, or hell, even while one is listening. The evil star, that one does not see. Guilt . . . yes, certainly. Guilt is relative and unfathomable, a magic globe which reflects only the person who recites the Jewish-Christian abracadabra while he gazes. Today it looks like guilt. There are hours . . . sometimes at night . . . one weakens with the changes of the moon. If I had won a kingdom, the kingdom of this world as it once seemed as if I might, then there would be no guilt about me. It would have been compensated for. As it is, the game is lost. Are there really things between heaven and earth which scholastic wisdom does not even dream of? or, to enlarge the meaning, about which we cannot even dream? Sometimes there are nights . . . Mohl, Mohl, I fear that we are all pitiful creatures, all cut out of the same block, and all just good enough for the worms. A sad bit of knowledge. A sad ending."

He sat down upon the edge of the bed—Etzel meantime had covered himself up to his neck—took the boy's hand and said: "I haven't hesitated to tell you the truth since you set your whole soul upon it. Why shouldn't I do you that favour? It was no practical value for you, the perjury was superannuated long ago. God . . . yes, . . . really, in the final analysis I am indifferent to everything; nothing is of any importance to me any more in this life. If I examine myself carefully, I am quite indifferent to it. But I would like to keep the steering-wheel in my hand a little while longer. So don't give way to exaggerated hopes. Even if you were to bring my confession before a court, it would not do you any good." He smacked his lips gloatingly. "Your judicial mechanism is so rusty that people will be careful before digging a sacrosanct corpse out of the grave because a seventeen-year-old madcap makes a lot of noise. Moreover, I am still the man who makes his own laws, and does not ridiculously hazard all of his bourgeois prospects, shabby as they may be, for the sake of a late passion. For I have a passion for you, that I will frankly confess, my boy. It would be ungrateful towards my fate if I did not do so. You have taken my faded heart in both your hands and accidentally, and without my being able to prevent it, you have lifted it up into a wonderful light. For the sake of that you deserve a crown. No hard feelings, Mohl." He got up. "Moreover, I shall soon disappear from the present stage. Somewhere in Polish Silesia a daughter of mine is living, married to a civil service clerk; I haven't seen her for twenty-three years, I want to see how she is getting on. You know, towards the east, towards the east. Perhaps I shall find some resting place there. A sort of home for my old age. And you will understand that for this purpose I must take a halfway clean name with me. Those people have the right to ask that of me. But if you are able to find me up there a second time, you glowing little standard-bearer you, then I shall perhaps be ready to make a valid statement. Then, for everything is possible, I'd help you in the end to put the sick judicial system on its feet by giving up my unworthy self. *Pereat Warschauer, fiat mundus.* Just see to it that you are there half an hour before I shuffle off." With a dry laugh he picked up his coat and hat. "Well, it's gotten late once again. Goodbye, young Mohl. Tomorrow I'll inquire about you again. I hope you'll be well by then. How do I get home?" Etzel slipped into his night-shirt and replied: "One can go through the saloon downstairs; it's always open." His voice sounded so altered that Warschauer was surprised and turned around again. The same change showed in Etzel's face, a cold, clear decision. "Hem, really," observed Warschauer, and he left. Etzel heard him groping his way through Melitta's dark room, then two doors banged and everything was still.

He lay on his back and looked into the air. He felt as light as a down feather, as free from the earth. But the thoughts which went through his head were heavy and dark. Ten minutes perhaps had gone by and he had not yet been able to decide to turn off the gas, when the door creaked, then opened gently and Melitta, wrapped like a flag pole in her ridiculous green cloth, stood upon the threshold. She did not cross it, but stood there looking at Etzel with a tense, keen, searching expression. Etzel moved his head a little towards her and returned the look. "Did you hear?" he whispered. She nodded. "Everything, did you hear everything?" he repeated in a whisper; one could not quite understand why he did not speak aloud. She placed her finger on her mouth and replied: "Pretty much." "That is well," said Etzel, nothing further. "There is a storm coming," said the girl. At that moment the mechanical piano ceased to play for a moment and a low clap of thunder was actually audible across the roofs. Melitta closed the door again. Etzel got up in bed and turned off the gas. He wrapped himself up in his bed cover and said to himself: "Good night, E. Mohl," and at once fell into a sleep as deep and quiet as that of a little child. When he woke up in the morning he crushed a disgustingly bloated bedbug on his sleeve, breathed deeply and said: "Good morning, Etzel Andergast."

It was seven o'clock; he jumped out of bed and commenced to pack his belongings. Three hours later he was at the station.

CHAPTER XV

I.

THERE was a young public prosecutor in the office, who had been working in the prison service for a few months. He had undertaken the task of telling the convict Maurizius the conditions under which his dismissal was to be effected. "Do you accept?" inquired the attorney, not without some slight curiosity, with regard to the man, not to his answer. Maurizius, standing stiffly, breathed hard. "What conditions are in question?" "They are not expressly stated." "So some pretext or other could make me a prisoner again?" "I think it is a formality. If you behave as the situation requires. . . ." "You mean if I don't make any trouble for the courts." "I have no instructions in that regard." "What is the period of the conditions?" "A year and a half. Accurately stated one year and five months. Until the termination of the twentieth year of punishment." "So if I aroused the displeasure of the legal authorities, I might have to make up these seventeen months?" "Theoretically, yes. But as I have said, it is a formality." "And if I refuse now, shall I be released unconditionally in seventeen months?" "Doubtless," replied the young lawyer, embarrassed and somewhat annoyed. At the word "refuse," Superintendent Pauli looked up in surprise, and the inspector standing behind him shook his head suspiciously. "So they want to keep a handle against me," murmured Maurizius. "Do you accept or not?" asked the lawyer sharply, pointing to a document on the table, which was waiting to be signed. The excited scrivener could no longer bear to sit quietly in his chair. He got up and stared curiously at Maurizius. The latter did not move. His cheek bones became brick-red. A tremor ran over his shoulders. He opened his mouth, but could not speak. Everybody looked at him. Suddenly he made a gesture as if he were about to fall down. He had only wanted to walk up to the table, to the edge of which he held on. The clerk handed him a pen. Maurizius dipped it in the inkwell, looked at it a moment in a disturbed fashion and then wrote his name on the paper where the scrivener pointed with his finger. The sound of one gasp out of four mouths was heard through the room like a low wind. "To-morrow morning at eight you may leave," said the manager. "At seven o'clock the room supervisor will call for you to change your clothes." "May I be permitted to telegraph my father?" Maurizius brought the words out chokingly. The public prosecutor and the manager exchanged a glance of doubt. "We should prefer you not to," said the lawyer. "We want to avoid all unnecessary excitement." "But I won't know how to get on outside. . . ." The attorney smiled. "That comes of its own accord. When you are once at the station . . . why, good heavens!" "You could telegraph your father that you will be home tomorrow, in the course of the day," suggested Pauli with a wave of pity. "We only don't want him to come here, so that the hour of your release may not become known in that way. The papers would make a sensation of it." Maurizius replied: "In that case I shan't do it at all." The warden who took him back to his cell—the one who looked like a drunkard—asked graciously: "Well, how do you feel about it?" When Maurizius stared at him lifelessly, he cleared his throat and trotted off.

2.

At eight o'clock in the morning.—Still fifteen hours. How can one live through them? He looks at the walls, he looks at the black stove-pipe. He walks forward a few steps and says to himself that while he is doing so, time is passing. He passes his hands over the bristles of his beard and wonders whether he could still get himself shaved today. It would certainly be allowed. It would pass the time. He will consider it. This again passes time. He seizes the table and pulls it two yards to the left. He places a chair in front of it. Why he is doing this is unclear to him. He sits down, opens the chronicle of Rothenberg and reads: "April 4, 1659, the citizens fired on two window-panes of the old fort and then a regiment went forth with bugles and drums." He calculated: 1659, that is, two hundred and eighty-six years ago, now there are fourteen and three-quarter hours to be lived through. If one closes one's eyelids and presses one's thumbs tight against one's temples, a moment comes when one suddenly feels the quick passing of the hours; he has often experienced it. Today that method is an utter failure. What is patience? The receding of one's blood. To forget that one wills, that is patience. Unfortunate man —so you are willing again! He stands up, drags the table to the window, then the chair, sits down again and reads: "On the 29th of July a foreign girl, twenty years old, with her mother, was placed on the whipping post, led through the city by the hangman, and expelled from the land for having stolen one hundred marks, at her mother's instigation, from a man, H. Daniel Rücker, whom she had served three-quarters of a year. The daughter screamed and cried pitifully. She had wanted to return the wretched money to where it had come from—from the war. Rücker had served as field-clergyman, under Bernhard von Weimar." A distant time; the wheels had rolled on; the human misery had been sighed away.

He closes the book. He feels a sudden horror of looking into the past, of finding out about the past. All the past is like a prison; what is to come is endless space. But where does what is to come begin? When fourteen and a quarter hours have staggered by like heavily laden draught horses or now? With every single *now?* And this *now,* which lies between heart-beat and heart-beat, or between second and second, eighty-six thousand four hundred pauses of weariness and despair every day. Now there is a tomorrow again. He whispers the word tomorrow with hesitating lips. It is like the glowing point of white light when one rides through a tunnel; slowly, indescribably slowly it expands; the circle widens; the glow lessens; slowly, very slowly, in spite of the tremendous swiftness of the train. To tomorrow another morrow is chained, a third, a fourth, a fifth, every *now* becomes a *then,* every *is* becomes a *was.* Thirteen and a half hours. He walks around and walks around; twelve and a quarter hours. He counts his steps. In the grey twilight of the cell an image is suspended like a blossom hewn of purple stone. Morn. Crystal morn. That unlooked-for tomorrow, the thought of which made him quiver with irrational rapture, tremble with irrational fear. . . . Paths, streets, gaits. Walking forward. The sky: an unbroken arch. Towers, trees, gardens. A woman. . . . He clasped his hands together. A shudder ran through his whole body; a woman. . . .

Eleven and a half hours. He throws himself upon the iron bed and gives himself up to the tormenting sweetness of a dream which he dreams with open eyes.

3.

There is, so he fancies and dreams, a heart in the world which is longing for him. Hildegard, who has grown up among strangers, is waiting for the day which will unite her with her unknown father. Up to her fifteenth year his name was never mentioned before her. When she was twelve, she overheard a whispered conversation between her foster-mother and a worthy old gentleman who had taken an interest in the child and since then she divines everything. On her fifteenth birthday, her foster mother tells her carefully what it is necessary for her to know. She is at once convinced of his innocence. She does not talk about it; she is careful for her part never to mention him; but in her strong deep soul the belief grows constantly that some day he will stand justified before the world, as well as the still stronger conviction—in contrast to which everything else is insignificant—that he will come for her and take her away with him. She will make him happy. She will blot out the memory of all that he has suffered. It will be like effacing the writing from a slate with a wet sponge. The plans which she is making for her own life have no other content then to make amends to him for his suffering. She is waiting for him, she is longing for him with a child's whole longing. She is waiting for him to be rehabilitated. . . . His brain goes on incessantly spinning this dream, throwing all experience, probability and reality overboard, and what rises from the depths has all the simplicity of a child's fairy story, of a boy's wishes and a boy's dreams the night before Christmas. She is young, not a girl who hangs her head; it was a mistake for her to try to assume the rôle of a nurse, to give up the joys of love and marriage for his sake; she will choose a husband who is willing to share with her the task of offering the "resurrected" man a house and home. There will be children, sweet blond grandchildren, the house will be joyous, the evenings will pass cozily in their pleasant home.

But how will the first meeting be? The shadowy hypothesis of the dream picture assumes the clear outlines of an event which is actually taking place. With a sovereign nonchalance, his imagination recasts his first conception that Hildegard is not to marry until later, until she has been united to her father for a year. For some altogether excellent reason, which remains however quite unclear, she has decided to marry at once, and, as chance will have it—or is some mysterious and festive intention at work?—the wedding takes place a few days after his release. It seems almost as if his release were to be celebrated in this way. But he can no longer arrive at the church in time for the ceremony. When he enters the house where the young couple is expecting him, all of the guests are already assembled. His appearance causes a considerable sensation. Servants whisper and hurry hither and thither. His coat and hat are taken; he is shown the way; folding doors are opened into a drawing-room filled with ladies and gentlemen. Every face is turned toward him. Astonishment, awe, pity, respect are seen on all those faces. An orchestra which has been playing up to the moment ceases to play, and a silence ensues like the silence on the stage when someone who is believed to have been lost returns to his family and friends after many years of hardship. An old man with a yellow beard and very distinguished looking, slightly resembling the warden Klakusch, approaches him, bows down before him and shakes his hand. Maurizius is unable to utter a word; he is too profoundly moved. His glance travels around searchingly; where is she? Where is Hildegard? Then he hears a low cry from one end of the room; the whole bridal party is seized with joyous excitement; a path opens amid the guests and a white-clad figure, with a flowing veil and outstretched arms, flies joyfully towards him. He presses her to him, clasps the warm loving body to his heart, the happy face against his cheek . . . now everything may still turn out well. One can forget. One is transformed and renewed.

Minute upon minute falls silently into eternity, like detached stones into an abyss. They have been doing this thing now for eighteen years and seven months, and now they lie far down in unfathomable depths, a pile of débris. Day breaks.

4.

He says goodbye to the superintendent and inspector; they shake hands with him, wish him good luck; the iron door closes behind him and he stands alone in the sunlight. The street has a downward grade; his feet seek an even level; the adjustment requires a certain amount of effort.

After he has walked twenty steps he finds it difficult to convince himself that he need not turn about; that feeling is in his legs, that compulsion to turn about; he is obliged to struggle against it for days. That one *can* walk ahead, that one *should* walk ahead, is at first frightening. It feels like being tossed into the air and thrashing about desperately with one's arms and legs. Too much breath comes into one's lungs. Everything is a little heavy, the light, the sky, the unaccustomed clothes, the hard leather of his shoes. One walks with irregular puppet steps. After a short time he gets tired, stands still, looks around and feels helpless. People stare curiously. He smiles. They turn away without returning his smile. He must find some neutral expression to please them. Is this the right way to the station, please? The first street to the left; the second to the right. Thank you. But why return to the prison? Straight on, man, straight ahead! Children! There are children standing over there. He stands still likewise, turning white. They are very small, these children. Strikingly dwarfish. And there —two women. He is obliged to lean against a display window and, stretching his hands out backwards, he comes near breaking the glass. The owner comes out and snorts at him angrily. He apologizes much too humbly. For a moment he feels an insane desire to seize the women and touch their breasts; but he pulls himself together; his face becomes serious, almost sinister. From that moment on, this serious, almost sinister expression becomes his mask, and the more the impressions of the visible world beat in upon him, the more impenetrable it becomes. Thus he walks through the crowd; thus he stands on the station platform; thus he sits in a compartment of the train with a serious, almost sinister, unapproachable and immovable face, his eyes half closed, his lips pressed somewhat inward. Every time he sees a lady with a short skirt and light silk stockings, a pale flush spreads over his forehead, and his nostrils quiver. This is new to him. Everything has become different. Everything has changed. Do people still speak the same language? He listens. They are the same words, but it seems to him that they have a rhythm and tone which are unfamiliar to his ears. He begins to wonder and become uneasy; has the lapse of time which has deprived him of the connection between his pre-prison days and the present made too great a gap? Is it only the relation between his eyes and ears which is affected, or is his whole organism unable to bridge the chasm? A feeling of discomfort overcomes him and increases until he feels cold and desolate.

At Hanau he leaves the train. For a while he wanders around the streets. The cloudless sky glistens like a fluid mass of lead, it exhausts him extraordinarily to walk in the sun; the glare blinds his eyes. He stands in front of an optician's, hesitates, goes in and asks for a pair of glasses. He is shown six or eight pairs and chooses some dark ones. The rims are metal. The salesman recommends horn, they are fashionable and look more elegant. Very well, he nods, takes the horn glasses and puts them on at once. He feels safer in the glasses, more secure, his discomfort decreases. He looks in the mirror. For a long time he cannot avert his eyes from the pale face with the dark glasses.

A quarter of an hour later he stands in front of the house in the Marktgasse. He is looking for the flat. An old woman tells him to take the wooden stairs in the court. Fear and dread make hard work of climbing up the stairs. The word "father" is something which has faded away. It is a remnant of a previous world. He feels neither joy nor expectation, merely fear that he will be expected to show feelings which he does not possess. He asks himself whether this kind of feeling has not altogether died within him; but when he thinks of Hildegard he answers the question with a passionate negative. But perhaps "Hildegard" is only an idea. An empty form created by himself; a figure which does not exist in reality, but which he imagines with the illusion of possession? It is the first time that he feels such a doubt and he casts it from him as if he had polluted something sacred. Where does this confidence for which he hasn't the slightest foundation come from? Must he not, on the contrary, say to himself that everything will have been done to cut off the child from any external and internal tie with him, an easy thing to do when one considers the whole situation? The solution to this conundrum lies in the domain where human nature ceases to be rational, and where, surrounded by dark primeval forces, it takes flight into a life behind life.

He pulls the bell. A stony minute goes by. In the court below a cat miauls. Steps behind the door. A mumbled inquiry; the door is opened; father and son stand facing each other. The old man stares dazed. His face turns vermilion, he sways forward, his arms outstretched towards the door post. "I knew about it," he brings forth in rattling tones, ". . . read it in the papers. Did not think that you . . . already today . . ." The rest is drowned in a sob. It sounds like a hoarse tense cough; he does not cover his face, and tears trickle out of his astigmatic little eyes. Leonhart Maurizius remains curiously cold. His features maintain their strict, almost sinister expression. Why am I not touched? he thinks, as he leads the old man by the arm back into the room. He looks around. When he sees the sadness and poverty of the house, a curious fright takes possession of him. He had not yet thought about his future life. He had by no means regarded his father as rich, moreover he had heard in the penitentiary that not only the well-to-do, but those of moderate means as well, had become destitute on account of the depreciation of money; apparently this has been his father's fate also, otherwise he would never have been obliged to take refuge in such a hole. This caused considerations about his means of livelihood to come up in his mind fleetingly, changing his vague uneasiness into a perspiring anxiety. For this meant being dependent upon people, applying to people; it meant answering questions, accepting favours, little bits of favours after the outrageous largess to which he owed his liberty, this indescribably longed-for condition which he is constantly seeking to grasp and to realize, and about which he succeeds only in acquiring a dismal foreboding similar to the knowledge which a sleeper has of the room in which he sleeps. In a wave of generous enthusiasm he has given all of the money which he has saved from his earnings in the penitentiary, except fifty marks, to the fund for the benefit of prisoners. It was a small sum, but it would have helped him to make a beginning; here there seems to be real need.

This care is unfounded, as he discovers within the next fifteen minutes. For a long time the old man looks at him, lost in adoration. The leathery cheeks under the grey bristles of beard still quiver, he grasps his stiff left arm with his right hand, he is unable to speak. Leonhart's glance travels over towards the table where a quantity of papers are lying about, next to them an open newspaper, showing one of the inner pages, upon which is printed in large letters the telegram which announces his release to the world. Above it, in large sprawling letters, written with a blue pencil are the words: Praised be Jesus Christ. The blue pencil is still lying on the newspaper. This suddenly moves him, the pencil really more than the words, there is something curious about objects; they sometimes still reflect an animate personality, when just discarded. Now the old man recovers himself and pointing to the papers, says as dryly as possible: "That is yours, that is all yours." He has waited for this moment for years and years, and he now stands there like a bashful lover, devoured with impatience, who is putting a precious gift, which for him is the epitome and expression of his devotion, into the hands of his lady love. He at once falls into a hasty, almost humorous bustle of activity, turns the pages, explains, mentions figures; this is the bank account; here are the monthly statements and there the account of the interest. This is his will, everything ready, since noon today, in perfect order. Leonhart stares and stares. "And you?" he asks with an eloquent gesture that embraces the room. The old man laughs like someone caught playing a trick at cards. He clears his throat, coughs, spits, there is no end to his furtive bleating. Leonhart lowers his head. From outside, above the screeching of old women and the tooting of motor horns, comes the long sound of a bugle. He drops into a chair, visibly tired, and the question "Where is Hildegard; do you know?" comes to his lips. The old man hides his disappointment that Leonhart should show so little pleasure at his accumulated fortune—for it is a fortune—but since he can answer the question and Leonhart can thus perceive that he has thought of this too—that he has been active for him in every direction—he is again filled with pride, and, nodding importantly, gives the information: The girl was in a Belgian boarding school until June of the previous year; then, according to his investigations, she had gone to Paris and the south of France with several friends. She had unusual musical talent and was to be trained as a singer, since the middle of May she had been visiting a married niece of Mrs. Caspot in the country at Kaiserswerth on the Rhine; there she was to remain until the autumn and then go to a singing teacher in Florence. Kruse was the name of the family she was living with. Leonhart falls into silence. "I shall go there tomorrow," he said suddenly. "So soon?" asks the old man. "Do wait a little." "It must be tomorrow." He gets up; he is nervous and restless. The dim half-light in the room irritates him. He would like to go away. He hints that he would like to attend to his wardrobe, he has nothing to wear, not even a shirt, except what he has on his back. The old man laughs with amusement. It is already attended to. He went to a shop in Frankfurt the day before; he made purchases.

Everything has been attended to, everything is first rate. He stalks to the door opening into his bedroom, a real hole. There, lying on the bed and on the chairs are suits, coats, all sorts of underwear, shoes, cravats, hats. He stretches out his stiff arm triumphantly. It is the second great moment of happiness that day, which turns him into an all-providing deity. Now Leonhart seizes his hand and holds it in his own for a while. "Go and look at the things," the old man urges. "If anything doesn't fit, we will exchange it; if there is anything wanting we will buy it." He pulls his pipe out of his pocket and after several attempts succeeds in filling it. His legs tremble. "Just go and look," he says, poking the boy's ribs with his finger, "meantime I'll rest a little." As he drops heavily onto the sofa, Leonhart goes into the bedroom, more to please the old man than because it tempts him. But looking at all those things releases a tension in him, they are the means of creating a needed gulf between himself and the world. There are even silk shirts and silk stockings; he feels the material; his glance falls upon the closet, both doors of which are open; inside are hanging the suits which he wore nineteen years ago. There is his frock coat, his fur coat, a brown tweed, it is like a house where souvenirs have been preserved to remind one of a dead person; a chance chain of thoughts makes him suddenly see before him the lady with the white feather-hat whom he had noticed on the last day of his trial, and whose face had struck him because of a peculiar sensuous pain. Not once in nineteen years has he thought of her or seen her before him; now the picture is almost too vivid; what impresses him as sensuous pain about the face makes it peculiarly clear, he also perceives the little scar in her upper lid and the cameo around her neck. He feels as if he must go down into the street at once; if he leaves the house he must meet her; he goes back into the living-room, intending to tell his father that he will leave at once after all; but the old man is crouched peacefully in a corner of the sofa, his pipe, which has gone out, in his hand, his chin sunk upon his breast. The grey bristles of beard look like moss; the boil on his head resembles an electric bulb. Leonhart bends down to listen to the old man's breathing; something in the pose does not seem right to him. No, it is not sleep. The old man is dead.

5.

Compelled by this event to exert himself, Maurizius becomes painfully aware of his helplessness and of that which he regards as a barrier between himself and the people in the world about him. The talk with the doctor, the official report of the death, the removal of the corpse, the ceremony of the funeral, the arrangements for the grave, procuring money, and all the formalities connected with it, visits to the lawyer, consultations with the owner of the house, explanations, signatures—all this causes him much difficulty and suffering. Then, in addition, the newspaper men who have traced him, from whom he flees and hides. It is six days before he can leave. He spends the night in Cologne. At eleven o'clock in the morning he arrives in Kaiserswerth and asks for a family by the name of Kruse. He is directed to a country-house close to the bank of the Rhine. He drives there and rings the bell of a tall garden gate. An elderly woman appears: he would like to speak to Frau Kruse. On what business? A private, personal matter. Whom is she to announce? Art-dealer Markmann, from Frankfurt. He is so deathly white, so distraught, that the woman looks at him suspiciously. She disappears. He waits. His throat is as dry as sand, he is forced to swallow constantly. A tremendous great Dane trots idly across the lawn, stops, looks at him intently, growls and remains at attention. The woman comes back and regrets that the lady of the house has gone out—will he please communicate with her in writing? He replies that he must leave. She shrugs her shoulders. He asks with such foolish persistence that it is bound to arouse suspicion, whether the lady would be visible after lunch; the matter which had brought him here was important. An indefinite answer. When he has already decided to go he turns around, and against his will, although he realizes instantly it is a piece of stupidity, which reveals his intention he asks: "Does Fräulein Körner live here?" The woman becomes embarrassed, looks at him more penetratingly than ever and, replying that she could not say, slams the gate in his face. So there is no doubt that his visit is expected and measures have been taken against it. It seems to him that he is being observed from one of the windows of the house. He sees a curtain moving. He has had a dark premonition, which he has not wanted to admit, and from which he has kept his thoughts distant, as one chases flies from something sweet; now it slowly becomes a certainty; they want to keep him from his child. And if such a plan exists, if anyone has summoned up courage and callousness enough to plan such a thing, then he may expect that it will be carried out mercilessly. They are not going at the matter with mere fumblings and negotiations, but aim at the whole loaf, and the business thus despicably inaugurated at the gate does not permit him to hope for a more amicable sequel. What is he to do, what in God's name is he to do? Does Hildegard know that he has returned to the world? Does she know of his existence at all? Perhaps she regards him as dead. Perhaps she does not even know his name. What has justified him in thinking of her as a creature who belongs to him? Has he indeed any claims upon her, except those which he assumes in dreams far removed from reality? But suppose she does know of him and is prevented by force from seeing him. Such a regulation must in the long run become futile. What is he to do? What is he to do? He walks up and down along the lane of trees opposite the villa; wilder and more frightful thoughts than any which he has had up to the present mutilate his brain; he cannot get rid of them, cannot calm himself. After two hours he goes back to Düsseldorf. When he gets to his hotel he telephones. "Villa Kruse" answers. This is Victor Markmann, who wishes to speak to the lady of the house. She is at the telephone, what is it about? It is a question of a meeting with Fräulein Körner. Fräulein Körner is away on a trip. Away? Since when? Where has she gone? We cannot give any information about that. I have a message for her, an urgent message which cannot be delayed. From whom? From someone closely related to her. We do not know of anyone closely related to her and privileged to send her secret messages. Perhaps you will explain yourself more clearly. It is impossible here. I am sorry, but . . . tell me the name of the person. A pause. Finally, in half-choked tones: Maurizius. May I know your address? The Park Hotel. You will receive a letter in an hour. He waits in the hall. Exactly an hour later a letter is handed to him; it runs: "Having expected what has now transpired, we sent Hildegard out of the country to visit intimate friends three days ago. We could not have assumed the responsibility of subjecting her to a disturbance which would, in view of her very sensitive nature, have upset, if not have destroyed, her whole future life. The man under whose instructions you are applying to us must readily understand this and must regulate his conduct accordingly. It has always been the chief solicitude of those in charge of the dear child's education not to burden her with a knowledge which would have darkened her life at the very outset. This was one of the duties which we assumed when we took charge of her, and it must be carried out to the end. It is for everyone concerned simply a matter of course. Mr. and Mrs. Kruse." Maurizius clambers to his feet as if out of a pit, crumpling the paper in his fist, and falls fainting onto the floor. Some of the guests come to his assistance; as they are about to take him to his room, he recovers consciousness. The fact that consciousness is of no use, or pleasure, to him is another matter.

THE IRREVOCABILITY OF DEATH

6.

His determination to see Anna Jahn, now Mrs. Duvernon, and to bring about a meeting with her, could arise only in a mind which had been robbed of its normal relations to the outer world. It was a blind desire to cling to the past, a flickering hope of thus finding a way to Hildegard, a consolation, a reprieve against the gate slammed in his face, against a final denial, against the "Be off with you, branded creature!" It was the hope of finding a few human words, a heart which recollected, which was in some way responsive and receptive, and would show him a path to a brighter world. So mistaken was he still, so incurably romantic, to such an extent was he still floating in the rarefied atmosphere of compensation and brotherhood of souls. And this besides: Things cannot and may not be as they are and therefore they are not. He was still denying and refusing to see the existing facts, still running his head against a stone wall, contrary to all common sense. He was a victim to that all-combating sensuality which accepts no truth, recognizes no alterations and fabricates possibilities which no longer exist. Such persons must learn, learn with difficulty, and be beaten on the head by experience again and again. So, the next day, he travels to Echternach, near Treves, close to the border of Luxemburg, goes to a small inn and writes Anna Duvernon, under the name of Markmann, but in such a way that she must know who is writing, that he is here for a few hours and must speak to her; she is to set the time and place. The Duvernon brick factory was about fifteen minutes' walk from the town and the house very nearly, so he had been told. He sent the letter by a messenger, emphasizing that it was to be given to the lady herself. This was at three o'clock. At half past four a small motor drove up to the inn and from the window he saw a woman leave it and hurry in. He remained at the window, as if paralysed, and when there was a knock at the door his lips were unable to frame the words: Come in. His visitor was already in the room, breathing nervously, her face pallid, staring restlessly about with dark dull eyes. She wore a blue dress, a yellow dust-coat, a little yellow hat with a blue veil over it; everything utterly commonplace; there was no glamour or charm left, nothing of the unusual and unique which excites and torments, preoccupies and gladdens one just because it is rare and unique. Everything was a little flabby, or a little dry, the lines were a little awry, only a very little but a little meant complete disintegration. Just as her skin was faded, so there was something faded about her carriage and glance; the incomparable fragility which she had possessed at nineteen had changed into a sickly frailty; that which had been a suffering of soul had given place to the complacent ailing so prevalent in bourgeois security. The external appearance betrayed everything, and made one fear all that was to follow, making all conversation superfluous; but Maurizius wished to overlook what he perceived with a mysterious clairvoyance; he had turned around and was standing there unnerved, his arms hanging limply. Now to be able to cry, he thought, now to kneel down and cry. To say all, to ask all, to forget all and weep and weep and weep.

But Anna Duvernon was as far removed from understanding as from feeling any such impulse. Her voice was so low that it was scarcely more than a hiss as she said: "You can, of course, not stay; I have come because . . . because it must be prevented. . . . Lucky that you did not use the right name, it's risky enough. How could you . . . I am not equal to such excitement. I read of your release in the papers. . . . I could not foresee that you would even come here. Is it about anything in particular? Tell me quickly; I must go at once. I told them downstairs that you are a business friend of my husband's, with whom I have something to arrange." Maurizius took off his glasses and looked silently at the woman. She sank her eyes and her forehead folded in hard lines. "Of course, there's no point," she murmured unwillingly, somewhat oppressed. "So it would appear," he said, not averting his stern glance. "Perhaps there is no point." "I have broken with the past," she continues in the same sibilant tones, looking meantime anxiously towards the doors on the right and left. "You do not know . . . up to a few years ago. But why stir up such frightful recollections? Prayer has helped me. One must have the moral strength to free oneself from the past. And then I have children . . . life . . . duty . . . above all, duty, if one has once recognized that. You understand?" "Yes, certainly," said Maurizius. What's that, he thought in amazement, is she really saying all that, or am I merely imagining it? What manner of person is this? "I suppose I may not ask you to sit down for a few minutes?" he inquired shyly, "there are several things . . . " "Oh, God, no," she replied, frightened, although visibly relieved, by his manner and tone, of a fear which had weighed upon her and produced this hectic restlessness. Her manner became less vehemently tense, although the man's presence was still exceedingly painful to her. Evidently she had expected a stormy discussion, effusions, importunities, inquiries, demands, everything which would endanger all the settled facts of life. She had been driven here by fear; she had not planned or willed to come, but had obeyed a compulsory urge to come, to try to prevent these horrors. Now, with feminine intuition, which more quickly becomes aware of and exploits a protecting situation than it defends a menaced post, she sees that she has nothing to fear from this man and this at once makes her, in some conceited manner, feel a sense of security. She no longer feels any qualms of conscience, any disturbing memories, at most, some vague flutter of disturbing pictures, something which has been tramped upon and turned to dust, which has lost all tangible force, something devoid of blood, as bereft of memory as if it were taken from the experience of another person, preserved in the storehouse of bygone years, no longer true, no longer existing; it was something which had been calcinated, congealed, coagulated. "It is on account of Hildegard," began Maurizius. "I went to see those people in Kaiserswerth; I wanted to ask your help and advice. . . . They did not even let me in. . . . The child had been sent away."—Anna Duvernon shrugged her shoulders. "I have absolutely nothing to do with that," she interrupted him hastily. "I could do without everything else; that one demand I still cling to," he remarked gloomily. "You are addressing yourself to the wrong person. Her guardian must make the decision. I withdrew from the responsibility years ago. The responsibility was too great." During his years of imprisonment, Maurizius had formed the habit of carefully observing the person who spoke to him, and when the speaker had ceased, of continuing to look at him silently for several seconds before he began in turn to speak with a melancholy wandering glance and a certain effort, as if he had to make himself comprehensible through a wall. "Responsibilities always become too heavy when one wishes to dispose of them," he replied. This aphorism was too much for Anna Duvernon's powers of comprehension. She did not hear the bitterness in it, merely the resignation. Suddenly she interpreted everything that he said pleasantly, that is, in her favour, perhaps because the thing had been such an easy game for her up to the present, and because the man seemed as remote to her as his cause. For it was no longer in any way her "cause"; she had no longer anything that connected her with him; she even marvelled that it ever had been her "cause." He looked as if he understood her point of view, consequently she no longer felt it necessary to stay and tried to find a suitable pretext for leaving. There was no longer any risk involved. What had at first seemed a frightful blow, which had roused her from her thickly encrusted peace, was dwindling down, to her unspeakable relief, into a harmless incident. This filled her with a kind of thankfulness, a process as primitive as the greed of an old peasant woman, or the calculations of a superstitious gambler. "One must take life as it is," she said with an approach at warmth, which was, however, too slight to temper the hopeless platitude of the remark, "but one struggles, doesn't one? With self-confidence, one can overcome difficulties. Self-confidence and confidence in God. Both are necessary. We too have hard times behind us. Anyone who has not experienced this war—but frightful as it was, it helped me. It strengthened me morally. Not merely morally. It helped my nerves. A real cure. Formerly I was so subject to those seizures. A thoughtless word from anyone acted like poison upon me. Now . . . for it is true that when a whole nation, when all humanity suffers, the individual forgets his egoistic interests, one becomes humbler, less self-important, don't you think so?" "Naturally. I understand that very well." What's all that, ponders Maurizius in the greatest amazement, what is she talking about? What's going on? What does she want? What is she talking? What's the point? "Now I must go. I have stayed too long as it is. We have guests. . . . Farewell." She hesitatingly lifted her hand. Maurizius seemed not to see it. He bowed as stiffly as a Chinese god, whereupon Anna Duvernon felt that she ought to add something. "I wish you everything fine and good for the future." This was like a stab in the neck. Everything fine and good; that's splendid; where are we at, my bountiful patroness? His voice said in toneless irony: "I thank you." She was gone.

Alone, Maurizius presses his two hands, with his fingers intertwined, across his forehead. He stands thus rigidly for a while. Gracious Heaven, how stupid she is, passes through his mind, how stupid, how abysmally stupid! Beauty, soul—or what seemed to be soul—grace, charm, demoniacal obscuration, passion and the power to suffer, all of their protective hues thinly painted on the surface, which the years have washed away, leaving the bald original. Nature has exposed her own lie; no heart, no comprehension of fate, no ray of anything exalted, only *mise-en-scène* and camouflage, only stupid, stupid like those who have stood still, like those living corpses who do not realize that their hearts and minds are dead, as stupid as an apparition. And for that, for that! Almighty God, for *that*—martyrdom and crucifixion, nineteen years in a grave, for *that*. . . . He lies down flat on his stomach on the floor, pressing his face against the boards. Above his left eyebrow he feels the cool head of a nail. It is a pleasure to feel the cold iron of the nail, he would be glad if the nail would turn around in the wood and drill its point into his brain.

Time, which either covers over generously, or exposes cruelly, has a sovereign manner of finally revealing what, from lack of true measure and proportion, appears to the human eye a hopeless intricacy of mysterious depths. The original simplicity of things is only surpassed by the simplicity of fate, when the vague clouds of the fleeting moment have been dissipated. Even the word-magic of a Waremme cannot alter this. Those who imagine that they justify themselves before God or elucidate their confused meanderings by twisting the simplicity of the world into a magnificent mystery, are the real damned, for they cannot be saved from themselves. In the case of Anna Jahn-Duvernon there is, of course, one thing to be taken into account. In her the miracle of youth flowered so exquisitely that, like a great work of art, it admitted of many interpretations and took on many aspects, so that it seemed to everyone to be what he sought or projected into it. Then the years destroyed the bloom and what remained had lost all magic, was in a certain sense dust and ashes, but yet a woman, no worse than thousands of others and probably not more stupid.

7.

He leaves Echternach. At the ticket-window he takes a ticket to Mainz. He spends the night there and the next day goes to Basel. He lives in a room which has a view of the Rhine. The river seems to him merely a witness of his misery, who insistently pursues him; he packs his things quickly and takes the train to Zurich. He buys books in a bookshop, but is too uneasy to read them. He hires a motor boat and rides around the lake, but the lake is too narrow and small and presses in upon him. He talks to the door man, to the chambermaid, to the waiter, to any one of the guests, that is to say, he wastes a few words. He is interesting-looking, carries himself well, is well dressed; he is taken for a scholar, a writer; he is treated with respect, some try to start an acquaintance; but the serious, almost sinister face, with the dark glasses, presents an insuperable obstacle. He likes best to talk to the children in the public squares, where children play; sometimes he sits down on a bench and waits till one approaches him; then he speaks to the child affectionately in low tones, asks questions, passes his hand tenderly over its hair; but as a rule he perceives that the adults become distrustful, so he gets up and goes away.

Sometimes the noise of the city becomes a torment to him; sometimes again it is soothing to him to wander, half driven, among crowds of people. The grinding and pounding of machinery is easier to bear than the sound of bells, the roar of voices than the tones of a single voice. A single voice compels his attention; attention strains his nerves, until gradually the breaking point is reached. Mostly, he lies sleepless at night; but it is not dark thoughts which keep him awake; it is a condition of not feeling himself, of not being aware of himself, which places him in a condition of lethargic amazement. He has the feeling that this is already sleep and that he must not really sleep, for then he might slip even further out of hand. Then he feels parts of his body with his hand—his thighs, his arms, his hips; that helps him, he is sure of these parts at least. The beds are too soft for him, for a long time he cannot get used to sinking into feathers; often he makes up a bed on the sofa, wrapping himself up in his travelling rug, in order to feel something rough about him. Sometimes he thinks of work; but why should he work; what would it lead to? Everything is so inconsequential. There is no continuity. He does not belong. Not only does everything he undertakes and performs lead to nothing, but it is at the same time revocable in a distracting sort of way. Whether he turns off the street to the right or the left, whether he buys English or Egyptian cigarettes, whether he leaves orders to be awakened at six or at eight, whether he wears black or brown shoes, whether he draws three hundred or a thousand francs at the bank, he can at any time, and in the most irritating way, change his mind. He could always do the other, the opposite, the next thing. Nothing is important. Anything can instantly be rescinded, without regret, without consequences. Now it is a fact that the grace of life, indeed the possibility of life, lies in its revocability. He, however, in the flower of his manhood, was robbed of the feeling of revocability, for he was irrevocably condemned, he suffered his punishment irrevocably, and he is to live on irrevocably. This, however, is not possible; one cannot live under the pressure of irrevocability; and therefore his will compels him to small, common, minor, revocable deeds, as a revenging reaction of nature. Thus he becomes a detached person, free from any law, free as a bird from his own consciousness. He broods constantly on how to put an end to this; this discord within him borders on madness; at times some saving thought flashes upon him, he thinks that he sees a place where he cannot recall his acts, where the fatal irrevocability ceases to be his destiny. This would mean to find the path leading to the highest, to that which repudiates no mortal; for this he would have to be the perfect Ahasuerus.

He packs his things again and travels to the mountains. He travels over passes and through valleys, spends the night in remote inns, far away from pleasure seekers and tourists. No landscape smiles to him; no meadow smells sweetly; no woods nor snowy peak can compel him to raise his eyes. He feels neither awe nor pleasure, neither curiosity nor enticement. He gets into a train again. He travels on, and on and on. He stops at any chance hotel at night, unpacks, packs again in the morning and moves, rides on and on. A city. Again a city. Cathedrals, wells, monuments, pillared cloisters. They make no impression. It might have been a moderately interesting picture book. The halls of the Pitti Palace, Titian and Tintoretto in Venice, the Pinacotheca in Munich—nothing. Formerly he would have been overwhelmed with delight. It was the colour, the soul, the kernel of his being. The apostles of Dürer were tiresome old men. The little figure in Kassel which he had longed for seemed a bit of mildewed old bronze. Nothing stirred in him. Objects, actions and performances, the world, all murdered. Everything moved constantly further away from him. He perceives the grouping of human beings, their stratifications and the way in which they are massed together. Organization. The mysterious distance which he feels cutting him off from all this enables him to become aware of the transformations which escape the notice of him who is really a part of these things. Not only has the language changed, its modulations and the meanings of words, but the faces no longer have the same expression which they had twenty years ago; the dissatisfaction is a different dissatisfaction; the astonishment a different astonishment; and anger takes on a different form. People's eyes are wider open, more immovable, more unveiled; their gait shows more eagerness to reach a goal; the bearing of most men reminds one of a hunter with a cocked rifle; laughter sounds more convulsive. It was not thus in the other days. Everything is turning in a new direction, obeying new laws and new ties and conditions. People have a different skin, a different stature, a different tempo, a means of communication which he does not yet know, forms of love and forms of hate from which he feels as excluded as if he were a foreign substance; their dances and forms of entertainment make him feel like Gulliver in Brobdingnag. He feels sorry for the old people, and the young ones frighten him curiously; he had a similar feeling when, for the first time, as a young boy, he was obliged to strip naked in a public bath. Gulliver in Brobdingnag or, better still, a miner who has been forgotten in a mine-shaft and spent five hundred years imprisoned in the dark. When he reaches the upper world again, his state among millions of people is one of unprecedented loneliness, he does not even know the terms of sky and air and earth.

One day he travels by train from Hanover to Berlin. Opposite him in the compartment is an attractive looking woman of perhaps thirty. She is dressed in good taste, her bearing is reserved, her features curiously soft, her glance is curiously veiled; and a curiously ironical but kindly smile plays about the soft mouth. The most attractive thing about her is her hands, which she constantly moves slowly, now folding them, then passing one over the other, then again lighting a cigarette, then crossing her arms and resting them on her elbows. They seem to tell of the desire and the burden of life. They are soft white hands, with straight tapering fingers. He cannot cease studying and observing them, and the young woman smiles her ironical kindly smile. They fall into conversation. Although neither of them communicates anything of importance to the other, each of them senses from the other's words the loneliness which surrounds them both. The woman, however, seems more deeply touched; she has some inkling of a prodigious wrong; doubtless she has profound instincts She becomes more silent as they approach their destination; her manner indicates a melancholy indifference, as if her body, drugged with sleep, were half hanging over an abyss and she were indifferent or even desirous of plunging into it. Maurizius understands, more with his senses than with his brain; his heart swells and he too becomes taciturn; they gaze at one another, silent, large-eyed, shy for long, long minutes. His face is deathly pale, hers has the painful tension of a person who cannot yet guess, and does not care to know, whether she will be chastised, or caressed. They leave the train together; they walk side by side to a taxi stand; the woman gives an address in Halensee and they ride the long distance in silence. The woman notices that Maurizius trembles at times; then she looks silently straight ahead and smiles. She has a little flat in Halensee, two rooms in the fourth floor, comfortable and neat; there is even a suggestion of luxury; books and flowers are scattered about. What kind of woman is she? Divorced? Childless? Strangled by fate, driven to a last asylum? He does not learn; he is not curious about it; just as she has no desire to learn what will happen to her during the next few hours. In no case does she belong among "the dead"; that is quite certain. She stands there alive, with a kind of high-heartedness, soft, ironical and unmindful, as some women are when their hopes are at an end—and their bodies half hanging over an "abyss"—they have this sweet phlegma about them. She prepares tea, sets the table, urges her guest to help himself and, as she suddenly hesitates in addressing him, he gives his name, his correct name. She thinks, looks at him and thinks again. He says: I am such and such a person. Ten words and the content is—twenty years. She looks at him. The soft mouth begins to quiver; she is obviously struggling with the fear that he will misinterpret any emotion which she may show, any random emotion whatsoever—a wonderful and exquisite delicacy—she falls on her knees before him and, snatching his hand, presses her lips upon it almost reverently. Dear God in heaven, he thinks, and there he sits without a breath, or sound, or glance. The woman is nameless for him, how beautiful that she has no name; it raises her above all other people. Lord, release me from my name, he prays, passionately. Arms embrace him. A body lifts itself towards his. Towards him, really—towards him. If he could only do something to thank her. He has no thanks, he has no gift.

Suddenly he is alone. Where is she? Obviously she has left him. Everything is over; she will never come again. Hopeless, he gets up, looks about, listens, goes into the other room; there she lies in bed, waiting for him, her eyes shining with an overwhelming ardour. This cannot really be; it is all a dream! The light in the room goes out. They lie beside one another. Whispers and silence. Motionless. Whispers and silence. Hours pass. A hoarse, hard, desperate sobbing. It is he. The nameless woman seeks to console him. No; no consolation; no consolation. Sex has been murdered. One has therefore—here is the proof—no further share in the world. Sex too has been murdered. When day breaks at the window, Maurizius gets up and dresses quickly; the woman has fallen asleep and does not hear him departing. With his suitcase in his hand—his trunk is still at the station—he walks through the streets; the morning air refreshes him. He finds a hotel and sleeps until evening. When he wakes up, he feels extraordinarily well, takes a bath, and orders a plentiful meal. Towards nine o'clock, he goes to the station and takes a first-class ticket for Leipzig; in Leipzig he decides to take the night-train south. He has no particular destination, he mentions some city because he is obliged to. He is alone in the compartment. He reads the papers, opens a book, and lays it down again. He closes his eyes and hears his blood flowing in his veins. After a long time, he opens his eyes again, takes an apple out of his travelling bag, peels it carefully, cuts it, and eats the cool juicy fruit with great enjoyment. He feels in high spirits, something like a desire for enterprise. He leans his head against the window-pane; from the thick darkness outside lights blaze forth at times like rockets. He pulls down the window. A black landscape, a faintly illuminated sky; behind the clouds a few madly distant stars. The contours of the hills stand out clearly. The train, with its panting asthmatic engine, struggles up an incline; in the depths below, water is roaring. He throws away his cigarette, it falls obliquely into the abyss, he can follow the glowing speck for quite a distance. Whistling softly, he moves to the compartment door, presses the knob and opens the door; the cold night air rushes in. The train is rattling over a high, unfenced viaduct, close to the edge. There is a ravine directly under his feet. Holding on to the rusty iron rail, he walks down the steps of the carriage and looks penetratingly into the unknown depths with a gentle curiosity. He feels as if the world had suddenly turned upside down and the starry sky were beneath him. That he is soiling his hands on the rusty iron bar is an unpleasant thought. Ridiculously enough, he even considers going back to wash them. From the window of the forward carriage, the conductor sees him; the man is beside himself with horror and fury; he clutches at the ledge of the window, shakes his fists, screams with all his might; Maurizius does not hear him; he merely sees the wide-open mouth with its two rows of teeth like those of some beast of prey. He nods indifferently. He takes the step into the empty space outside. It is high time; a few yards farther, and the train will have passed the viaduct. He takes the step as one walks from one room into another. It is the step into the great, the real irrevocable.

THE LAST CHAPTER

I.

ETZEL'S return to his father's house caused considerable sensation among the servants and other occupants of the apartment house. Above all, of course, good Rie could not repress her exuberance and, between laughing and crying, scarcely knew what she was about. He arrived at ten o'clock in the morning; as he was extremely short of funds, he had travelled fourth class and the trip had taken almost twenty-four hours. After the first torrent of questions and interjections, and an endless wringing of hands and sighs of gratitude, Rie was horrified at his appearance; as a matter of fact he looked more like an itinerant tinker than a member of bourgeois society. His jacket was torn; his shirt was greasy; his knee-breeches looked like two potato-bags sewn together; his shoes were worn and full of holes; his hair had grown down upon his neck; his face was elongated and thin; and his eyes glowed oversized in the pale oval face. When he had gotten rid of his knapsack, which looked just as bulky as when he had left, he asked for a bath, clean clothes and food and went to his room. Rie could not decide to leave him to himself, she merely gave careful instructions in the kitchen for his breakfast; then she followed him at once. She opened closets and drawers, rushed into the bathroom to turn on the spigot, came out again and, while with trembling hands she fished out all of the things which he needed from their receptacles, she began a nervous gossiping account of events. Unimportant things at first, neighbourhood incidents, the birth of a child, a night robbery at the jeweller's, a fire in one of the rooms at the Malaperts', the floor below. Then, in between: "Ye gods, Emma, the spigot. The bathtub will overflow." The more important household affairs came next. Herr von Andergast is not at home. This of course is not unusual since he regularly goes to the office at nine-thirty. It is, however, striking that for some time he has been coming home at unusual hours, as early as eleven, or half past eleven; then he goes to his study, remaining there the rest of the day, even having his meals served there. And he has changed in everything and in every way. For example, he no longer hangs his clothes out to be brushed. Or, once he did not shave for three days. And, most remarkable of all, he does not seem to work when he sits at his desk from noon till night. Rie surprised him day before yesterday—when she was obliged to take a telegram in to him—sitting with his elbows resting on the window ledge, thoughtfully occupied in snapping his silver cigarette lighter on and off. Perhaps it is all connected with the report, which persists in spite of its untrustworthiness, that he has applied for his pension.

Etzel listened attentively, but did not say a word. He saw that Rie had something more on her heart, but first she drove him into his bath, and while he was getting ready, she took care to provide a substantial breakfast. She set the table herself and sat by in silent delight while he devoured everything that was served, and then ventured to remark: "You've grown, Etzel; you look so manly. What has actually happened to you? When I stop to consider, my brain stands still!" "Just let it stand and don't consider anything," he remarked dryly. "You'd better go on telling me things. You're weighted with news, come out with it." Rie bent over towards him and told him that his mother was in town and was living with the general's widow. Etzel jumped up. "Is that true, Rie? Your word of honour?" She nodded and added that Frau von Andergast had been at the house ten days ago and had a long conversation with his father; she had spoken to her too, not much, of course, had only expressed her thanks and said how do you do, but one could judge from that that she was completely the lady. "And what does she look like, Rie? Nice? Young? Did you get a good look at her? Tell me carefully." He put his left arm around her shoulder and stroked her cheek with his right hand. Rie, who had not been accustomed to such demonstration for a long time, became quite weak with delight and shed some tears of pleasure. "So, she's really living with grandmother, Rie?" "Yes, little Etzel, and we must telephone at once; it's unpardonable of me not to have done it before." Etzel held her tightly by the arm. "No, just wait, Rie; I don't like telephoning. That's not proper. I'll go there myself. But there must be something else before that. . . ." At that moment the door opened wide and Herr von Andergast stood on the threshold.

2.

The alteration which Rie had hinted at was unmistakable. It was expressed even in the carriage of the head, which seemed to rest more heavily on the shoulders and to thicken the neck with its weight. There were many white hairs in the beard and the fringe of hair around the bald skull was now far more white than grey. The eyelids rose and fell more slowly, the violet-blue glance seemed weaker and more fixed. Disorganization. The world of thought had come out of joint. A man could only look thus who had had a more intimate experience of certain realities than he had ever assumed or feared he might. His inviolability was gone. Immovability was being subjected to doubts. Retrograde motion. The totality blasted, and blasted again, and resolved into its raw elements. One thinks of a palace transformed back into the quarry out of which it was hewn, with the architect standing in front of it, deserted by all his workmen and no longer knowing the dimensions himself. It is not astonishing that this man should look like someone who is distractedly seeking. An expression of extreme tension in his face betrays his preoccupation with something past and done for. Examination, criticism, pros and contras, going back through courts of higher appeal within the man himself. A comfortable means of avoiding a necessity, of getting out of the way—perhaps this objection will be raised. But this has very little influence upon decisions of conscience, and these are the only things which matter for the moment. This is what I call looking at things at close range—turning back to the past—the person who keeps moving forward can keep anything which reminds him of failure and decay from touching him. But if he turns back but once, a repulsive swarm surrounds him, like bats which occupy a deserted barracks, and he ceases to be what he is, a civil servant, for example, whose professional point of view must not be clouded by any glance behind the scenes. There were evenings and nights when Herr von Andergast seemed to himself an *alter ego* of the convict Maurizius. Incarcerated in a castle full of memories, he was condemned to bear the presence and "proximity" of noxious individuals. He was surrounded by thieves and the abettors of thieves, robbers and pimps and murderers, by drunken prostitutes and mothers who maltreat their children, by bankrupts and defrauders, by swindlers, by forgers, embezzlers, counterfeiters and smugglers, by women who brewed poisons and murdered children, incendiaries, an army of the disreputable without any age limit—characters to supply the needs of ten thousand novelists—and he, as the accuser, denouncing each one as guilty. In the end it becomes a habit, like everything else, invested with dignity and supported by the credit of the nation. One becomes hardened. The legal robe isolates. One sits on a curule chair and hands over the evil-doer to the judge who, with the help of the statutes, renders him harmless. That one should handle this scum of human society with kid gloves is inconceivable; even the convict Maurizius and his sickly, romantic bosom friend Klakusch would not ask so much as this. One cannot have the stern world of facts degenerate into a puddle of irresponsibility, or reorganize the social order every Monday morning in order to admit one's incompetence and helplessness in despair every Saturday afternoon. But when the thousands and thousands of faces pass in review, one or another stands out; a sudden flash of lightning falls frighteningly upon it and in the eyes, about those bitterly compressed lips, there lies a question. Really nothing more—a question, a question without words. And that is sufficient. One or another face out of that army, and it suffices. The curious thing is this: One person always bears witness for a whole group. Just as the convict Maurizius has testified for all, for a whole world. Then, automatically, it comes to pass that the criminal who was condemned, perhaps sixteen years ago, and whose name has already been forgotten, suddenly becomes the prosecutor, because suddenly, from some obscure and overlooked crevice, circumstances come to light, or appear worthy of consideration, which, if one had regarded them formerly, would have made a human case out of a legal one, and what is one to do with a human case? The State and the law cannot cope with that. But this morbid compulsion to turn around and look back forces Herr von Andergast, with his incomparable memory for facts, to visualize the whole structure and progress of the procedure, just as he had done in the Maurizius case, at times still referring for advice to the documents, and delving and digging and delving. But since his attention is no longer upon the one case only, but half a dozen or more cases are running simultaneously through his head, everything gets mixed up at times and he feels himself transported into a Witches' Sabbath confusion, so that not infrequently—unknown to Rie—he leaves the house late at night and wanders through the deserted streets until day begins to break. And echoes of words and echoes of retorts break through the silence: The accused states that on the day in question he had lunched at his aunt's between twelve and half past one . . . but it is proved.—I propose once more to call this witness whom the defendant is vainly trying to break down. . . . "Madame, your testimony gives rise to the gravest doubts. I remind you of your oath." Shy glances, passionate protestations, timid faces filled with hate, verified hours and verified itineraries, Chance the betrayer, the betrayal of inanimate objects, personal inspections of premises, gardens and yards, on the banks of rivers and in asylums of thieves, false accusations, desperate struggles for acquittal, an unconvinced jury, arrogant lawyers, indolent judges, prejudiced judges, an unclear law, public opinion misled, and now in retrospect the whole established structure of the law placed under a macabre doubt like grain rotting in a granary. A yard of punishment for a millimetre of guilt. . . . No attention paid to the inner person and always here and there someone with that silent question upon his lips, repudiating the right to judge, and accusing the accuser. Often, when people pass him in silence, Herr von Andergast has the sensation of fear as if he were going to be called upon to give an account of himself and could not remember why and for what reason; then when the meeting has passed off uneventfully, he feels the temptation to hurry after the person in question to ask him to walk along with him for a while. He would like not to be so alone. He considers that it is not impossible that he may meet the released convict Maurizius unexpectedly at some street corner. The consideration grows into a wish, the wish into a great desire. He stands in front of the doors of hotels to watch the people coming in and out; he looks through the crevices in the curtains in front of taverns and coffee-houses; it is not impossible that Maurizius is sitting inside, alone too, certainly not less alone than Herr von Andergast. One evening he went to the house where Violet Winston had lived. He rang the door bell. A girl who opened the door of the opposite flat said that the young lady had left the week before. In spite of this information, he came again the next night as if he had entirely forgotten what he had been told, or thought that Violet might have returned between today and the day before. At the same time he had no picture of her left within him, and if she had really opened the door, it would have had no importance for him. That same night he looked at home among old letters for those which he had received from Etzel—there were only a few which he had sent from his holiday trips and from the camp in the Odenwald. These he read carefully through again and again, as if the simple words had a double meaning which it was important to ascertain without further delay.

3.

Etzel walked up to him and extended his hand saying, "Good evening, father," just as if he had seen him last on the previous evening. Herr von Andergast looked over his son's head towards Rie's apron: "So you've returned," he asked, and the way in which he opened and closed his mouth had something fish-like about it. A pause. "May I ask you to come to my room?" "Certainly, father." They crossed into the study. Rie looked after them as if she were thinking, If I see that boy safe and sound again, I'll thank God. Herr von Andergast walked ahead, let Etzel follow, closed the door and pointed to a chair: "Please be seated." Etzel stared at the hand covered with brown hair, as it indicated the chair, and sat down obediently. Herr von Andergast walked up and down the length of the room with unusual haste. Etzel had never seen him walk so rapidly before. The internal emotion thus expressed aroused a feeling of satisfaction in him. "I thought I could overcome it," began Herr von Andergast, walking more rapidly, "but I have not gotten over it. There is a kind of betrayal which one does not get over at my years. Details are not of importance. You will spare me those. The question at first runs not: What has happened, but What is to come now?" "Quite right, father, I feel the same way," replied Etzel modestly. Herr von Andergast stopped with a jerk and looked at him: "Such insight does you honour," he remarked sarcastically. He came a step closer, put his hand on the boy's forehead and pushed his head backwards. "You look astonishingly exhausted," he remarked darkly and took his hand away as if he had burned it. "I was ill, father." "Ah, ill. No wonder. Where have you been knocking about?" Suddenly he screamed, with his face convulsed, losing all self-control, screamed wildly, "Boy, where have you been knocking about?" and putting his hands over his eyes, he groaned.

Etzel had not expected this. It was the first time in his life that he had seen his father beside himself. And the touch before; it had seemed to him that his father's hand trembled and the expression about the mouth, the look of torment, all this made an impression upon him. He must think about it. And it satisfied him. While he was collecting himself in order to answer, Herr von Andergast forced himself to be calm. "When I went away, I wrote you why I had to go," said Etzel. "There was no question of knocking about." Herr von Andergast threw himself into the desk-chair, crossed his legs, and his fingers played nervously with his beard. "You certainly escaped surveillance with praiseworthy skill," he remarked into the air. "Well, if I could not even do that—" remarked Etzel raising his eyebrows. Herr von Andergast thought the tone impertinent and cleared his throat warningly. "Well, and now?" he asked with an admixture of sarcasm, intended to cloak his fear. "And now? Nothing succeeds like success, the Americans say." "I know. I have meantime learned a little English," Etzel remarked with a caustic smile, which increased his father's displeasure. "All right," he collected himself and raised his head energetically: "Maurizius is guiltless. Completely. Innocently condemned. A gross miscarriage of justice." Herr von Andergast gave a scarcely perceptible start. He looked at his finger nails. His hands "played." He replied with the frostiness which Etzel always designated as the dinner-coldness: "That is easy to state; it might be harder to produce the proof." "If I could not prove it, I should not be here." A frightened glance from the desk-chair; the glance glides to the floor as if put to flight by an unexpectedly powerful adversary. There is something about the boy's expression which it is difficult to face: the flame of certainty. "A big word," Herr von Andergast sneers stiffly. "Waremme swore a false oath," Etzel continues with decision: "I got it out of him. I found him. His name is no longer Gregor Waremme. It is Georg Warschauer. That is his original name. He lives in Berlin. I was with him almost daily for seven weeks. I shall not say that we became friends. I can't talk about that. It was . . . But that's of no consequence. The important thing is that he admitted his perjury to me. If you want to hear about it, I can tell you about it sometime. It was not easy. You may jolly well believe that. I ripped the confession from his bowels. And I have a witness too, a woman. He does not know about her, but I am sure of her. Thank God!" There is eager expectation in this brief report; Etzel looks at his father steadily; his expression is tense. Herr von Andergast gently moves his right crossed leg and stares at the point of his shoe. He finds himself in Violet Winston's boudoir, looking into the mirror. The mirror shows him a figure of David standing on the hand of Goliath, with a lantern in his own hand, throwing a gleam upon the frightful snail-like brain. The sombre astonishment of that moment is mingled with the present. He looks up again: there is the boy with the flame of certainty. He hears the peremptory question as if a steel blade were whistling through the air: "What must one do in such a case?" And he replies with icy coldness: "Nothing." Etzel bounds into the air: "What . . . nothing?" "One must not do anything. There is nothing to be done." Etzel cannot help opening his mouth like an idiot. He stammers something. Has his father lost his mind? "Any action is superfluous. The convict Maurizius has been pardoned." Etzel with eyes like windmills: "Pardoned? Par-doned?" A feeble nod across the room. "Released by pardon from further imprisonment." Etzel is obliged to laugh. He knows that he is lacking in respect, but he cannot help it, he must laugh. "Pardoned . . . but I have just told you that he is innocent!" A tired sigh from the man who is being importuned. "The proclamation of pardon takes this possibility, or probability, into account." Resounding phrases. Etzel forgets himself, forgets the respect which he has been trained to show and screams: "But if he is innocent he does not need a pardon." "His innocence is no longer a subject of discussion. Moreover, behave yourself." Etzel remembers his bringing up, which he has culpably neglected during his association with Waremme; at least for a moment discipline is stronger than indignation. "Yes . . . excuse me," he stammers, "but why is his innocence no longer open to debate, why, please?" And he makes desperate little movements with his shoulders as if to snap an invisible chain. Herr von Andergast condescends to discussion. "I will assume that he is really guiltless. I will regard it as proved. I will assume that we have incontestable proof in our hands—" "You can safely assume this." "Your subjective conviction. But nevertheless, you leave the basis of reality. Let me finish. You interrupt me constantly. Your manners are quite extraordinary. I say that you are making a fatal mistake. It is a far cry to a perfect legal unassailability. Have you the admission in writing? testified to by a notary? Well then! Confessions may be retracted. It is even the rule. There are a hundred ways of evading the consequences of a confession. The time which has elapsed since the crime makes reliable investigations and the establishment of the facts simply impossible. A first hearing would make them uncertain, the second would make them untenable. Ask yourself whether, in view of the uncertain factors which you may adduce, the result is worth the expenditure. You do not have to consider this. I *do* have to consider it." Etzel stretches his arm out. "You commenced a sentence. You supposed him to be innocent, you would regard it as proven, you said—well, what then?" "It would not alter anything." "Not alter anything? Are you serious? Not alter anything—if you yourself were convinced of his innocence?" "No, nothing. There is a barrier before which even our conviction must halt." "But something tremendous is at stake! The most important thing in the world, it is a question of justice," exclaims Etzel, who has lost all control. "A judgment can be declared invalid. Even though the punishment cannot be undone, the judgment can be reversed; one can and must restore the man's honour. And not only honour . . . for what is honour . . . what would he, what would we get out of that? Justice is like birth. Injustice is death. One must do something about it. You cannot have such things go on. That would otherwise be . . . so far as I know, there is a procedure for reopening cases!" Herr von Andergast turns his head like a wooden puppet. "The talk of a layman," he replies dully and unwillingly. "We must be careful. We who bear the responsibility may not treat law and legal administration lightly. A procedure for reopening a case! Silly boy, you have no idea what that means. One does not mobilize an army in order to raise a fallen tree, particularly when it is moreover no longer capable of life and growth. To set a tremendous apparatus in motion, to alarm the world, to reopen that old conflict which has been run into the ground—what are you thinking of? Among other things, if this perjury were not outlawed by limitation, then according to the provisions of the statute, one would have to bring action against this Waremme, carrying it through all the legal instances in order to prove that he is guilty. That would take years. I am only telling you this in order that you may see the complications of things. The superannuation needs not, of course, to be regarded as an obstacle. Moreover, there are . . . things to be considered, deserving serious consideration; existences are at stake; the treasury would be put to enormous expense; the reputation of the court in question would be injured; the institution as such would be subjected to a destructive criticism which is sufficiently undermining the structure of society as it is. . . . Drop the idea that justice and the law are one and the same and must be so. That cannot be. It is beyond human and earthly possibility. Their relation to one another is like that between the symbol of faith and the actual religious practice. You cannot live with the symbols. But when one's practice is conscientious and strict, to know that the eternal symbol is over one . . . that, how shall I put it, that brings absolution. Such absolution is, of course, necessary. That one should content oneself with it, is also necessary."

A lecture. A didactic lecture. When the voice ceases, a frightening silence pervades the apartment. Etzel stares straight ahead for a while, with compressed lips; suddenly he cries out shrilly: "No." His eyes gleam angrily. "No," he screams again, "I cannot and will not live thus." His whole intellect is kindled. The barrier of respect breaks down. "I do not recognize that," he stammers with a bitterness which expresses itself as if it were intoxication. "Symbol . . . practice . . . what not . . . rotten subterfuges. . . ." He is deaf to a second thundering: "Behave yourself!" No, he does not recognize it. The human being possesses one primary right, one which is born in his breast with him. Every single individual has a share in justice, as he has a share in the air he breathes. If he is robbed of this, his soul must stifle. "I don't recognize that other; I don't want it; I don't believe it. It's the shrewdness of caste. A plot. Priests fearing for their tribute money. Religious practice? How? What has leaving an innocent person to perish because it is the practice, and the symbol merely hangs over him like a helmet over a grinning policeman's face—what has it to do with religion?" He does not accept it. He repudiates it. Better not to live. Better that the world should be in shreds than in such disgrace. "No . . . no . . . no. . . ."

Outrageous, thinks Herr von Andergast. He is as if paralysed. He feels as if someone were holding his head over a kettle of boiling water. He gets up with difficulty. Clutching at his throat, he says with a dryness which is not easy for him: "The conversation, moreover, is pointless, for Maurizius has accepted his pardon. And accepted it without reservation." Etzel takes two bounding paces into the room. He folds his hands at the level of his eyes and presses them against his mouth. "Accepted, accepted his pardon?" he whispers shyly. "Without reservation. As I have said." "And goes on living? Leaves the injustice resting upon him? And goes on living?" Herr von Andergast shrugs his shoulders. "A human being, as you see, can do anything." A wild laugh moves Etzel's lips. "Yes, I see that a person can do anything," he replies with an impertinent double meaning, "one person can make the truth disappear and another can go to the dogs over it." "Boy," screams Herr von Andergast. "You've brought him to such a pass," continues Etzel in perfect desperation —everything that he had done was undertaken in vain, everything that he had built upon as if on a rock, crashes into nothing. "That's where you've gotten with your paragraphs and clauses, with your caution and your considerations. . . . One must hold one's tongue at all this rottenness! . . . If he lives on, he does not deserve anything better . . . perhaps he has already said thank you, that Maurizius, for the kick with which you propelled him out of the penitentiary. He thanks God for his nineteen years of penitentiary? Don't you know who fired that shot? Of course, you know! That's probably the reason for the pardon. I don't believe that I can stand looking on any longer . . . everything . . . commutation of sentence! . . . where is the judge, that I may spit his pardon in his face . . . how shall I ever show myself among people again? . . . That's Andergast's boy, they will say; the old man helped Maurizius to get a pardon, and the boy knuckles under to it, they are both in the same bag. . . . Fine . . . splendid. A beautiful world. Magnificent world. If one could only croak on the spot."

He groans as if the earth were slipping from under him, as if his soul were leaving his body, full of regret that it had been obliged to spend sixteen years and several months in such a feeble, incompetent, boastfully presumptuous, polluted dwelling. He talks on gaspingly, but the words lose their connection. He cannot overcome his deep-rooted awe of his father; it restricts him even now in his utter misery; he would like to say something far more decisive, far more fateful; but he cannot do anything against the futility, the emptiness, the platitude, the feebleness of words, he feels as if his mouth were full of dry sand. He runs like mad around the chair, his eyes bloodshot and glittering with malice; his hands snatch convulsively; he seizes the tassel of the chair and tears it off, he stuffs a handkerchief into his mouth, bites his teeth into it and grinds at it until it is a mass of shreds. His forehead is painfully convulsed and covered with curious blue spots; he emits sounds which might just as well be laughter as a howl, moving constantly the while from one foot to the other as if he had an attack of St. Vitus' dance. This is no longer the charming, controlled, sensible, thoughtful little Etzel; this is a devil. "Just wait," he rages, "you won't get away with this, you'll pay for it, your turn will come all right." Herr von Andergast stands petrified. "A pillar of stone." Suddenly he makes as if to seize the boy. He takes hold of Etzel's shoulder. The latter slips from him, his face distorted with fear, rage and repulsion. "I don't want to be your son," breaks from him wildly. "Infamous boy!" "Infamous boy!" rattles from Herr von Andergast's throat; but he looks as if he were a suppliant. Etzel runs to the dining-room door. Herr von Andergast after him. Etzel runs breathlessly through the dining-room into the living-room. Herr von Andergast after him. Etzel dashes into the hall. Herr von Andergast after him. The doors back of them remain open. Etzel throws over the chairs which are in his way. Rie stands in the hall; he pushes her aside and runs into his room. Herr von Andergast after him. His huge frame, dashing on with hands outstretched, has something decidedly gruesome about it. The whole scene has the character of a fierce hunt, senseless, ghastly. Rie, silent with horror, opens her mouth; but speech refuses to come. When he reaches his room Etzel, bangs the door and turns the key. Herr von Andergast pounds at the locked door. The cook and the maids rush out of the kitchen. From the locked room they hear the continuous jingling of breaking glass. Rie utters a piercing scream, so that everyone in the house, upstairs and down, rushes to the hallway. Herr von Andergast hurls himself with his gigantic strength against the door, succeeds in breaking it down. One leap and he is in the room. Rie follows, wringing her hands. The Andergast and Malapert servants, the caretaker and his wife, and the postman who has just brought the mail, surge over the threshold. Etzel stands by the table, covered with blood. Herr von Andergast sways towards him and takes his head in both hands. "Water, water," he mutters. Someone runs for water. Rie folds her hands in prayer.

What has really happened? Etzel has smashed the panes

of both windows, and not only that—the mirror on the closet door, the glasses on the washstand, the porcelain vases on the bureau. A mad impulse to destroy. A raging of the soul. Blood is dripping from his temples, cheeks and nose. He simply stuck his head through the panes, then he belaboured the mirror with his fists so that his hands were slashed up to his wrists and his clothes soaked through and through with blood. After that, he suddenly became quiet; he is now standing quietly at the table, looking at his wounds with a smile of wild satisfaction, and blinking his eyelids because the blood is running over his eyes. He has suddenly become strikingly silent almost as if a part of his heart-envenoming disappointment were departing from his veins with his blood. He looks like one who has had a fall and who gets up slowly and, looking helplessly about, asks the way which he has forgotten or strayed from. But from where he is standing one cannot go any further, he looks about him as if to inquire what is the next step to take. Then Etzel's glance fell on his father; something like a hesitating astonishment spread over his features, as if the familiar figure, which had once towered over him, had changed into another, of infinitely lower stature than his own, and towards which one must even bend over somewhat in order to recognize it. No longer puzzling, no longer he who knew and guarded secrets, no more the arbiter of obscure destinies, no more Trismegistus, but a broken-down, guilty man. Herr von Andergast's mouth was half open, one could see his big teeth and thus with his half-open mouth, he dropped on a chair, with his violet-blue eyes protruding like buttons from his head, absolutely devoid of expression. When, in the afternoon, accompanied by the doctor, he was taken to the sanatorium, he still looked so, his mouth half open and his eyes protruding and expressionless. Thoughtfully Etzel considered the face which was literally disintegrating before his eyes, and while Rie began washing the blood from his cheeks, forehead and hands, he said in his dry, high-pitched boyish voice, "Let someone go for my mother."

Someone did.

4.

Thus ends the Maurizius case, but not the story of Etzel Andergast.

THE END